Princess

Holly Martin

ISBN: 0692868976
ISBN 13: 9780692868973
Library of Congress Control Number: 2017904830
Holly Mullen, Waterville, ME

Prologue

The hot morning sun was beating down on Elsie Johnson's long blond curls, which were piled on top of her head. Trickles of sweat ran down between her full breasts. She should've been used to the humidity in Maine in July by now. She had come from California years ago and met the love of her life at college in Maine and consequently had decided she never ever wanted to leave. She couldn't wait to leave the pretentious "everyone and everything is perfect" city of Los Angeles behind and smell the Maine lakes and ponds in the summer and play in the snow in the winter. How she loved the fresh air by the water! She could swear that she knew what the sun smelled like as she walked through the tall grass peppered with daisies to get to the pond.

After college, she and David had married and moved to Portland so David could base his shoe-manufacturing business in the city. The couple had wanted lots of babies, so they settled down right away to begin. And begin they did; Elsie really couldn't remember when she wasn't pregnant. She had brought a baby home from the hospital every year and a half to two years. Nine gloriously healthy strapping baby boys. Just thinking about her boys brought bubbles of laughter and sparkles of joy to her eyes.

They had made a wonderful family that Elsie was grateful for every single day. David had worked night and day for the last sixteen years to build up the business. When the sports industry exploded and athletes became everyone's idols, David's athletic shoes were so sought after that he couldn't build factories fast enough. The one thing that set David's factories apart from his competitors was that all the sneakers were made right there in New England. His workers were known for their work ethic and loyalty. It had always been very important for her beloved David to give back, to be a hands-on employer and to pay it forward. He could always be found on the production floor working side by side with his people.

Elise wasn't surprised at what a great father David was. At a time when fathers didn't step foot in the labor and delivery room until after the baby was born, David was perched right beside Elsie's head holding her hand through each and every contraction. He would not leave her side, and he cut the umbilical cord with shaky hands every time. They were the perfect balance: Elsie was soft and gentle, and David was strong and strict. The boys knew better than to give their mother a hard time, but they were still boys, and they were quite a handful. She loved every single minute of her life.

Elsie and her brood of boys—plus one she had all but adopted from a neighboring house—were on their way to the pond to get some relief from the sweltering heat. She didn't feel all that well today, and the baby she was carrying was very active. This pregnancy had been so different from the rest, with lots of morning sickness and a tiredness that never went away. The doctor had pleaded with Elsie not to consider any more children. He said that this pregnancy had really taken a toll on Elsie's health. Elsie was certain this child was a girl. Finally, a little baby girl. Elsie never told anyone except her best friend Gracie how certain she was it was a girl. In fact, she had even told her youngest and sweetest boy, Caleb, that he would get his wish to name the baby after his favorite fairy-tale hero, "Jack in the Beanstalk."

Lord, it was so hot and the trek to the pond seemed so long today, Elsie thought. She was holding Caleb when her vision became blurry and vivid colors began to explode in her head. She fell to her knees and called out to the older boys. The last living thought Elsie had was that she needed to repaint the baby's room pink.

A quiet dread hung around the hospital intensive-care nursery. A small three-pound baby girl was fighting for her life. The giant man made small by grief was slumped in a rocking chair next to the incubator and silently raged at all of heaven for taking his Elsie from him but also begging for God to please not take this last little piece of her from him.

David slowly made his way to the waiting room, where nine boys with big brown eyes waited to hear news about their mother and newest sibling. He lowered himself to the coffee table, and Caleb quickly climbed into his arms. A nurse appeared seemingly out of nowhere, knelt down, and put a hand on David's arm. "Mr. Johnson, I will be taking care of your daughter tonight. Do you have a name picked out for her?" she quietly asked without losing eye contact with David.

Caleb suddenly shouted, "The baby's name is Jack!" Within seconds, it registered with the other boys that they had a sister. Laughter and high-fiving ensued.

Teddy, the third and most brilliant Johnson boy, poked Caleb and said, "You can't name a girl Jack, silly!"

Caleb got angry instantly and cried, "Mommy promised the baby's name would be Jack!"

The sudden mention of Elsie made David lose his breath. He stared at the nurse and whispered, "Jack," with tears streaming down his face. "The baby's name is Jack Elsie Johnson."

The incessant ring of the cell phone slowly pulled Jack out of the sleeping-pill haze that she often found herself in when waking up. When the dreams about another lifetime took over her consciousness, a sleeping pill helped her build a wall her dreams couldn't get through. It was still dark in her bedroom. What damn time was it anyway, and who would dare call her then? The only person who would dare call her at this hour was her friend Noah, and last she had seen him the night before, he was happily surrounded by lustful men at an exclusive gay bar in New York City.

Jack picked up her phone: ten missed calls from a number she didn't recognize. She felt a trickle of dread form in her stomach. She sat upright on the side of the bed and listened to the first message: "Jack, it's me, Caleb. It's Dad; he's gone."

The air in her lungs seized and she couldn't breathe. She fell to her knees on the floor, gasping and moaning like an injured animal. "No, no, no…"

Jack had no idea how long she had been in a fetal position on the floor when her phone started ringing again. The sun was streaming into the apartment as Jack stood and walked to the wall of windows in her penthouse overlooking the park. The sun had just started to rise and the rays should have been warm on her skin, but she had never felt more cold and alone in her life.

"I'm here," Jack whispered.

"Jesus Christ, Jack, do you know how many times I've called you?" Caleb hollered.

"Eleven," she muttered matter-of-factly. "How did he die?"

"He had a heart attack last night in his study. Marcus found him," Caleb informed her.

Marcus, the eldest of the ten children. The one most like their father and poised to take over the family athletic shoe business. Strong and serious, Marcus had always felt that Jack needed a strong hand to guide her and that their father just didn't have what it took to mold Jack into the gentle heiress she was born to be. Thank God it had been Marcus, and not one of her other eight brothers.

"It's time to come home, Jack," Caleb stated.

With a sigh, Jack muttered, "I'll text you my arrival time." Then she threw her cell phone into the mirrored wall above the bed, splintering the iPhone into a hundred pieces.

Jack had a lot to do today if she was going to catch a flight to Maine tonight. She instantly regretted destroying her phone. Regret was usually on the heels of her actions when she lost her temper, which was often. She picked up the apartment phone and dialed Noah's number. A very sleepy and slightly drunk Noah mumbled into the phone "This better be really, really important."

"I'm going home tonight, and I need you here to help me get ready and to contact my team. I really need you here with me," Jack spoke softly.

"Fuck, I'll be right there, lovely," Noah replied, suddenly sounding much more awake than he had ten seconds earlier. *Lovely,* Noah's pet name for her. The first time she'd laid eyes on Noah Cabrera, the most beautiful male next to her brother Caleb she had ever seen, he was being kicked and spit on mercilessly by the class bullies in their exclusive private hell. He was beautiful, but he was incapable of defending himself; that was very unfortunate considering his sharp tongue.

Jack had immediately pulled the blade she had strapped to her thigh and swiped at the cheek of the biggest of the boys beating Noah. The cut wasn't deep but it would leave a small scar. The boys had run off with threats of future pain thrown over their shoulders back at them.

Noah was tall and gangly with a definite Spanish heritage. "I finally get to meet the new girl and I find out that she's my guardian angel. How very appropriate that I would have a knife-wielding pissed-off girl as my angel. How very fucking appropriate," he grumbled.

"Ah, you're welcome, asshat. I should have let them beat the shit out of you, but I was afraid they would mess up that beautiful face." Jack glowered. Noah sat upright, suddenly interested.

"You think I'm beautiful," he said with a grin lighting up his eyes.

Jack couldn't help but grin back as she sheathed her blade. "You remind me of my brother Caleb. Although I think he may be a little more beautiful." The smile they exchanged was soul deep and would connect the broken souls of Jack and Noah forever.

Noah found Jack sitting on the floor with her knees pulled up to her chest, staring out the window. As he kneeled, wrapping her in his arms, she gave a little moan and lost all of her hard-won strength and indifference. The sobbing and shaking continued while wave after wave of grief rolled over her like cold ocean waves. Another time in her life that she had allowed herself to cry and lose herself to grief was five years ago when her father had sent her away. On that day, as today, the pain she felt was more than she could bear.

Noah held her as the pain slithered through her veins and threatened to shatter her frozen heart into a million pieces.

Once upon a time, Jack had adored her father and he had thought the sun rose and set in his beloved "Princess." Jack had been so much like her mother that sometimes David would catch his breath on her giggle. She was fair like her mother, soft blond curls bouncing down her back and with the most expressive blue eyes David had ever seen. Jack was so tiny and fragile that it was almost as if she would simply appear before him and put her delicate little hands on his cheeks and smile and all the world would be right again for David. There was simply no request that he could not grant his princess. Jack had learned at a very young age that no matter what trouble she got into with her brothers or her nanny, if she could just reach her father and leap into his arms, no harm or repercussions would come to her. But all of that had come to an end on that horrible August night five years ago...

Part 1

Five years previously…

"Come on, Teddy! Daddy, tell Teddy to hurry up and stop studying! We need to go!" Jack screamed. Teddy was driving one of the Suburbans that was taking half of the Johnson clan to Moose Pond where they spent every summer. Before Jack was born, Elsie Johnson had fallen in love with the small town of Harmony and more specifically with a largely neglected children's summer camp that had closed down. There was a large recreation hall that the family had renovated themselves to house their ever-growing brood. It was such a labor of love for Elsie to paint the walls and find beautiful handmade quilts for each of the beds. Everything was very basic and as far from ostentatious as you could get. Elsie had loved it. Each child made their own bed and had chores to do every day. For three months out of every year, the family lived simply and enjoyed nature and each other.

"Princess, why are you in such a rush to get out of the city?" replied Teddy. Teddy was literally a genius and hated nature in any form. On summer break from MIT, Teddy felt he was wasting his summer in Harmony instead of applying for an internship that would help him mathematically determine the exact moment of existence or some such nonsense (in Jack's opinion anyway).

Jack had tried to hurry all her brothers who were going to camp this morning but it seemed that she was the only one that couldn't wait to run down the field leading to the sandy beach and dive into the cool pond. Well, maybe she really wanted to see her brother's best friend, Jared Ross. Jared had lived in the cabin by the beach ever since he was seventeen. Jack didn't know much about Jared's home life, but she'd heard her brothers talking and heard something about an alcoholic father who liked to beat on Jared when the

1

father was drunk. When David and Elsie had purchased the old camp, there had been several small cabins that dotted the woods surrounding the beach. They had refurbished them with the thought that their children would grow up and want some privacy away from the family compound someday. Jack's twin brothers, Ty and Bobby, were the same age as Jared, and for as long as Jack could remember, Jared had been part of her summer family.

Last summer, Jack had started to notice how Jared's dark curls got a little long and wild as the summer progressed. She'd noticed other things, such as the way he wore his Boston Red Sox cap backward when he had to accomplish a task and that when he smiled at her she would temporarily lose her breath. Jared was always kind to her and never teased her like her brothers. When *he* called her Princess, it sounded like an endearment.

She remembered a time when Caleb had wrestled her to the ground last summer and wouldn't let her up because she had threatened to tell Daddy about him sneaking out at night to meet a girl. Jared had tossed Caleb aside angrily and walked with her down the field to the beach and swam with her. That had been last year when she was just sixteen and he was twenty. Jack was so shy around Jared that she couldn't form a coherent sentence. This reaction to his presence seemed strange to her—Jack had recently taken an IQ test and learned that her IQ was close to Teddy's in the genius range. Jack had never felt like this before; she had had crushes before and even boyfriends that she'd let kiss her, but never had she felt like she was going to faint just because another human being looked at her.

It was times like this when she missed her mother. She had tried to talk to Bebe, her nanny, and now all-around house mother for them all. Bebe had started out her young life so many decades ago dedicating her life to the church. She was practicing to become a nun when she and Elsie had met at a convent in France while Elsie was touring Europe just after graduating college. They became instant best friends and kept in touch with each other. Years later, when Bebe had had a crisis in faith, Elsie had opened her home and asked her to stay with her and David to help take care of Marcus.

Bebe had never left. She had been an integral part of the Johnson household ever since. But Bebe had never been in love and would never be able to understand what this malady was that came over Jack every time Jared Ross's name was mentioned.

Oh. My. God. Three very long hours later, they turned onto the gravel road that would lead to the dooryard of the family summer house. It was the middle of June, which meant that the grass was tall and in need of mowing. The green and white structure looked somewhat like a large rec hall. With ten kids, you needed a large and sprawling space. There was a huge screened-in porch with lots of rocking chairs, a couple of daybeds, and a ping-pong table. There was a chalkboard attached to the wall in the corner, where Jack used to make her brothers play school with her. Now the chalkboard listed songs that were currently being learned by a member of the family.

David and Elsie had thought it very important that all of their children learn multiple musical instruments. There was a large piano at both the estate in Portland and the summer house in Harmony. All the children played the piano, but they could choose their own second or third instruments. Most of the kids could play the guitar. A favorite afternoon or evening would be spent with David with his guitar and his children on the piano, guitars, and drums. Country music was a favorite, but as the kids got older, some of their tastes turned more toward classic rock. Jared played the drums, and David bought him his first guitar and taught him how to play. On the screened-in porch on any given day in the summer, you would most likely find a Johnson, or the adopted Johnson, writing music or having an impromptu jam session.

The house was open, with a thirty-foot cedar cathedral ceiling and a fieldstone fireplace in the center of the room. The granite bar separated the kitchen from the living room, which had a balcony above overlooking the living room and fireplace. The balcony was a large open library with books lining the walls. There were overstuffed chairs and chaise lounges for reading. Summer was a time to relax and connect with each other and nature (Teddy's objections to nature notwithstanding).

Jack ran into her bedroom, threw her backpack on her wrought iron bed, and dashed to her bureau to find her bathing suit. This was going to be a problem. Last year's navy string bikini was a little too small for Jack; she was busting out all over the place. Jack was still painfully thin. At her yearly checkup, the doctor had told her father that she was very healthy but would always find it hard to keep weight on her five-foot-ten frame. She was the tallest girl in her school and drank milkshakes every day to try to put on some weight. The popular nickname at school for her was Bones. Jack hated the nickname, but somewhere along the way this past year she had acquired breasts and some hips. Yay for her, but right now she looked like she was going to a photo shoot for a Victoria's Secret catalog.

Ugh, whatever—later I'll go online and order a couple of new swimsuits, perhaps from Victoria's Secret, she thought to herself with a smile. *But right now I can't let Daddy see me busting out of my bathing suit,* she thought as she grabbed one of her brothers' flannel shirts hanging on the porch.

Jack heard the dirt bikes revving up. There was no way she was getting left behind; she grabbed her flip-flops and flew to the front yard. Ty and Bobby zoomed by her on their dirt bikes, but Caleb stopped to pick her up.

Caleb was eighteen months older than Jack and was as dark as Jack was light. His black hair was straight and a little long, brushing his shoulders with layers framing his face. Almond-shaped brown eyes and a permanent grin on his face gave him a constant aura of mischief surrounding him.

Caleb was the most beautiful boy Jack had ever seen, and she never ever let him forget it. No boy, certainly no Johnson boy, wanted to be beautiful. That right there could get you beat up in this household and had made Caleb a pretty good little fighter.

All was quiet at the beach but for the sound of Jack, Bobby, Ty, and Caleb diving into the pond. The cold water slapped Jack's skin as she ran as fast as she could into the water. For too many years, Jack had been the proverbial rotten egg because she had taken her time getting used to the temperature of the water before taking the plunge.

Not this year. She was going to put those very long legs to good use. Her whole family was tall. All the boys except Caleb stood between six-foot-four and six-foot-six. Jack was now the same height as Caleb. At least with Caleb, Jack had a slight chance of wrestling him to the ground and pinning him. With nine boys in the house, there was never a lack of a wrestling partner, and Jack could wrestle like a cage fighter. As the smallest member of the clan, Jack had learned to use all the dirty tricks she knew to gain the upper hand. Usually after a few good pokes and scratches, the older boys would simply toss Jack over their shoulder and throw her down on the couch or chair to signal the end of the match, but with Caleb there was sometimes blood and bruises and real tempers that flared.

The Johnson children swam like fish. Jack had joined the swim team in high school, mostly to beat her older brother Garrett's swim meet records. Jack remembered going to watch Garrett's competitions and being awed as she watched his lean body slice through the water, bringing Portland High School state championships two years in a row. They had been brought up on the water and loved swimming, boating, fishing, and water-skiing.

In June, the water was still very cold in the pond. The ice sometimes didn't leave until late April, so it hadn't had much time to warm up. As Jack swam, her body got cold quickly and she started shivering. She soon had goosebumps all over her body and was starting to swim toward shore when she was suddenly pulled backward. Jack yelped and found herself underwater with Caleb on top of her. Jack flailed and kicked. The heel of Jack's right foot caught Caleb right in a male's most sensitive spot. Released instantly, Jack made her way to the surface coughing, trying to catch her breath. When she looked around, she found that Caleb had crawled to the shore and was on his hands and knees, also trying to catch his breath. As she joined her brothers on the beach, Jack realized that she had forgotten her towel in her haste to get to the pond.

"Caleb, can I use your towel?" Jack shivered.

"No way. Take the dirt bike back to the house and get one," Caleb retorted, grabbing his towel and wrapping it around him.

"Oh my God, you're such a jerk!" Jack replied angrily. Jack was shivering so violently that her teeth started to clatter.

"Perhaps, but the *jerk* is the warm and dry one," Caleb said grinning.

There was a warm chuckle from the doorway of the small outbuilding. The building housed each sibling's tackle box, rope tows, water skis, life vests, oil and gasoline for the boats, and various remnants from past water toys and games. Jack froze in place, and it had nothing to do with cold water.

Dear God! Jared Ross was gorgeous. Jared's wide shoulders took up almost the entire doorway. He was leaning casually on the frame with his arms crossed. Transfixed, Jack's eyes traveled over Jared's very large biceps and wide shoulders. He had definitely not had those last year, she thought. His old faded gray T-shirt with the Patriots logo was a little tight, emphasizing the fact that Jared had definitely filled out and bulked up this past year. Jack's eyes wandered down the V-shape of his waist to his worn-out Levi's jeans. His legs were long and muscular, with bare feet sticking out from his jeans. Lord, he must be as tall as Marcus or her father.

Jack watched Jared's legs start walking toward her as she continued her slow ascent up his body with her eyes, and as she focused on his face she realized he was speaking to her. Her eyes locked onto his and she forgot to breathe. Jared's intense brown eyes were showing concern. His dark brown curls had been brushed back with his hands and were falling back around his face. That face had been a regular image in her mind for the past year.

Jack suddenly found herself falling forward from Caleb's push when she finally heard Caleb's taunting words, "Earth to Jack, come in, Jack." Jared's large hands caught Jack by her upper arms and steadied her. As he touched her, Jared's eyes grew wide.

"Oh my God, you're freezing! Come with me; I'll get you a towel," he exclaimed, walking toward his cabin.

I believe I would follow you anywhere, thought Jack. Still fighting a brain haze that she had never before in her life felt, she followed Jared to his cabin beside the beach. *I must be coming down with the flu,* Jack thought, *or maybe scarlet fever is making a comeback.* As she climbed the steps, Jack noticed a campfire had been recently burning in the fire pit in front of the cabin.

The musty smell of a cabin that had recently been opened for the summer filled Jack's overloaded senses. Yesterday's paper sat on the white Formica kitchen table along with this morning's empty coffee cup. They walked through the small kitchen into the living room where Jack stood. Jared ducked into the little bathroom to grab a towel. He wrapped a faded pink Power Rangers beach towel around her shoulders.

"This used to be your favorite," Jared said as his hands started rubbing the tops of her arms in an attempt to warm her up.

Jack looked down at the floor. "I had this towel a long time ago, Jared. I'm not a child anymore," she murmured.

Jared stopped rubbing her arms, and Jack quickly looked up into his deep brown eyes.

"I'm very aware you're not a child, Princess," Jared said quietly. "Are you warming up?" he asked as he continued to stare at her face so intently that it was all Jack could do to nod her head.

Jack's long hair had started to dry and was curling a little at the ends, which gave her a wild bohemian look. Just then, the door burst open and Ty, Bobby, and Caleb came barging in with their tackle boxes ready to take an inventory.

Jared instantly stepped back and went to the refrigerator to grab some beers. "So you guys are going fishing?" Jack asked, taking a deep breath. Bobby took a pull off his beer and replied, "Yeah, would you tell Daddy we're staying here tonight? We're gonna take the fishing boat and check out the pond to see if there are any hot campers out tonight."

"Oh, please, like any hot girls are going to want you guys," Jack teased. It wasn't a secret that every girl on the pond or in the surrounding towns for that matter wanted to hook up with one of the Johnson boys. It wasn't the Johnson boys finding a hot camper that Jack was concerned about right now. It was their best friend.

"I'll bet Jared already knows exactly where the hot campers are staying," Ty said absently as he tried to find the perfect lure in his tackle box. Jack's eyes flew to Jared's and silently held them for several heartbeats.

"Jack, you're not coming with us," Caleb grumbled.

"Jesus, Caleb, I know. I was just trying to get warmed up. You're not supposed to be drinking either you know—you're not old enough. Maybe I should tell Daddy," Jack threw back at him, pushing his head down toward his tackle box as she walked past. With a sigh, Jack hugged the towel tighter around herself and walked down the steps toward the gravel road that led back to the house.

Jared turned to look out the window and watch Jack start walking toward the main house. *What the hell am I doing here?* he inquired silently of himself. *I should have stayed on campus and helped the coach get ready for football season like he asked me.* Coach Burns had asked him, a newly graduated Colby athlete, to spend the summer in the dorms and help him plot out drills and plays for the new football season. There would have been a small stipend available to him while he waited to hear from Boston University, where Jared had applied for the internship and masters course in the computer-science department. Jared knew he didn't stand a chance at winning the internship on his own. Just like he would never have been able to go to school with Bobby and Ty at Colby if David Johnson hadn't pulled some strings and paid his tuition. David Johnson had been Jared's *de facto* father for as long as he could remember. Jared didn't hate his own father; he was just tired of taking his abuse...

(Sixteen years earlier)

On a hot July morning, four-year-old Jared Ross woke to a silent house. He went to his parents' bedroom to find it empty again. He searched every room for a clue as to where his parents were. No luck. Every room was empty. Jared had had to take care of himself for as long as he remembered. He got a chair and climbed up on the counter to reach into the cupboard for the cereal. His little hands grabbed a box of Fruity Pebbles, his favorite.

The box was as empty as the house. He was on his stomach trying to reach the chair with his feet when the chair, which was already wobbly, fell onto its side. Jared slipped off the counter and fell to the floor, banging his head on his father's old black metal lunch box, which was sitting on the floor between the fridge and cupboards. The cut was just above his right eye and started bleeding profusely. Starting to cry, Jared grabbed the stiff, dried-out dish cloth that had soured from the kitchen table and held it to his head. Opening the front door, he started walking down the street to the little Baptist church on the corner. The nice man who always spoke to him when he rode his bike past might know where his parents were.

It just so happened that it was Sunday morning, and the worship service had not begun. Elsie Johnson was hurrying up the granite steps to the church with her eight young boys when she saw him. Elsie gasped and fell to her knees before him.

"Oh my! Are you okay, baby?"

Just hearing her soft concerned voice brought Jared's chin to a slight tremble and the tears started falling like rain down his cheeks. Shaking his head, he started bawling and crying like a girl. That's what his father would have called him if he had seen him crying like this. He would have slapped him and told him to stop being a little baby. Jared was no baby.

Elsie gathered him up and lugged him downstairs to the kitchen area in the church. It smelled like old furniture and musty cupboards. There were long tables set up with metal chairs pushed underneath. The kitchen had a long countertop with large plywood cupboards hanging above. Elsie perched Jared on the counter by the sink and started running the water to warm it up. She pulled open the top kitchen drawer to get a clean dishcloth. As she pressed the warm cloth to Jared's eye, she saw the tiny cut. Elsie asked Marcus to hold the cloth firmly in place over Jared's eye while she went to retrieve the first aid kit. When the bleeding subsided, Elsie put a small bandage above his eye.

"Look at that—all better," Elsie said as she handed him a cookie. "Are your mommy and daddy here, sweetie?"

Jared shrugged his shoulders and took a bite of the homemade chocolate chip cookie. He mumbled, "I don't know where they are."

In response, a graceful and very pregnant Elsie Johnson walked a few hundred yards down the sidewalk and ushered them all inside a white building with a sign that read Harmony Maine Police Station. The chief of police, Ronnie Keister, sat down and tried to explain to Elsie Johnson why he needed to call Human Services. Ronnie knew who Jared's parents were and knew the boy would probably be better off in a state home.

Elsie Johnson was having none of it. "Ronnie Keister, you and your wife, Katie, have seven beautiful children. How can you even consider putting this baby in the custody of the state?" she exclaimed in an exasperated tone.

"Elsie, this is not the first time a concerned citizen has brought a complaint against Billy and Tessa Ross's parenting skills. My officers have gone to their house, no one is around, the place is a dump and the fridge is empty. What else would you have me do?" the chief pleaded with open palms.

With eyes narrowed and a steely look in her eyes, Elsie Johnson took a deep breath and said, "Ronnie, think long and hard about how you respond to my request. Remember your lovely wife, Katie, is one of my closest friends, and how you respond to me will be closely related to where you find yourself sleeping for the next few weeks. I propose that no call is made to Human Services."

Ronnie sat forward. "You know I have to," he began, but up went Elsie's hand as she made some sort of clicking sound that instantly silenced Chief Keister.

"Not right now. I propose that we don't call Human Services for the time being. I will bring that beautiful boy home with me—be his foster mother, so to speak—and when his parents are found, we'll all discuss this like the mature responsible Christians that we are," she said, smiling as she held her palms out and then carefully folded her hands in her lap.

Thirty minutes later, David Johnson walked into the Harmony Police Station to collect his family. David's dark hair was flattened down by his dirty trucker's hat. He was a large man. A very large man with a big barrel chest and rugged calloused hands. Not many men would mess with David Johnson for obvious reasons, and when it came to matters regarding his family they were smart if they didn't. He had gotten up that morning and thrown on an old T-shirt and jeans to start working on repairing the rope pulley that attached to the boat so it would be ready to go when the kids got home from church. They had been after him to take them waterskiing. He had not expected a call from his friend Ronnie asking him to come to the police station and talk some sense into his wife, Elsie.

David smiled to himself. His size may have intimidated people, but anyone who knew Elsie Johnson knew that she was the real powerhouse in their relationship. David felt kind of bad for Ronnie Keister. Apparently, instead of collecting stray animals, his wife had decided to collect stray children.

A full week went by before Chief Keister came to collect Jared from David and Elsie Johnson. Elsie immediately got in the cruiser with Ronnie and Jared so she could make sure Jared was okay.

Looking pretty rough from the week-long bender, Billy Ross leaned against the open door. "Where the hell have you been, boy?" he slurred. The smell of whiskey emanating from the man was disconcerting to Elsie. Upon hearing his father's angry voice, Jared turned inward toward Elsie, who was holding his hand.

"Hi there, Mr. Ross, my name is Elsie Johnson, and Jared has been having a little sleepover with my boys this week. We have so enjoyed having him with us. What a wiz on the computer this little bugger is." Elsie brushed the curls away from Jared's eyes.

"We don't have time for no computers here; get your ass in the house. Now!" Billy hissed as he grabbed Jared by the arm.

Elsie smiled and gently touched Billy's forearm. Billy flinched and pulled his arm back. Elsie was still looking directly at Billy, and that was making him very uncomfortable. A man would probably have to be dead not to be affected by her sweet soul as well as her angelic beauty.

"Now, Mr. Ross, may I call you Billy?" Elsie asked sweetly.

"That's my name, isn't it?" Billy replied, this time with less heat.

"Excellent. Well, I was wondering if, well, it would sure help me out if Jared was able to come over to our house and keep my boys company this summer. They really enjoy playing together, and," Elsie patted her large belly, "well, it would be a great help to me," Elsie said quietly, smiling her sweetest smile.

Billy took a deep breath, picked up his soiled hat from his head, and scratched his head. "Well, I reckon I could drop him off on my way to the mill in the mornings and pick him up on my way home."

Elsie grabbed Billy's hand excitedly. "Oh, Billy, that would be wonderful, you have no idea how much this means to me!"

Billy might have stopped breathing somewhere during this exchange, because from that moment on Elsie Johnson had added another besotted man to her admirers.

Elsie Johnson had no way of knowing that Jared's mother had run off with another man, prompting the bender for Billy. As it happened, it would sure help Billy out to have some place to take the boy while he was at the mill all day and sometimes at night.

Elsie knelt down so as to be eye level with Jared and handed him his new backpack, which was filled with clean clothes and so many snacks that he could barely lift the darn thing.

"Well, okay then, little buddy, you go in and clean your backpack out and be a good boy for your Daddy, and we will see you in the morning, all right?" Jared threw his little arms around Elsie's neck for a quick hug and ran into the dilapidated old house.

Jack could feel the sun burning her skin as she floated in the pond on the unseasonably hot June day. This was going to be a very boring summer if she didn't find something to do with her time. The boys had all taken jobs along with Jared at the White Mountain Ski Resort making new ski trails. She figured it must be miserable clearing trails on a day as hot as this.

Paddling ashore with her hands, Jack decided that she also needed to try to find a job. If she wasn't mistaken, she had seen a sign in the diner by the police station asking for help. Jack got on her bike and made her way to the main house to change. Ten minutes later, wearing denim shorts, a black tank top, and black-and-white Converse sneakers with a long blond braid down her back, Jack rode her mother's old Schwinn bicycle with a basket in front to town.

The bell chimed as she entered the old diner, signaling her arrival to the four customers enjoying their afternoon lunches. It was small with tidy tables crowded into the space. The bar held several pie and cake stands with a stack of menus on the end. A small lady with a long braid of jet black hair peppered with gray and smiling eyes was standing next to the menus.

"Hi there, what can I get you today, young lady?" the woman inquired.

"Oh, hi, I came about your sign. Your help-wanted sign," Jack stammered and smiled.

"You're one of those Johnson kids, aren't you?" the woman said with eyes narrowed.

"Um, yes ma'am, I am," Jack all but whispered.

"Well, I'll be damned! You look just like your momma, child. How is your daddy? I'm Gracie." The small lady laughed and held out her hand.

"Hi, Gracie, I'm Jack. It's very nice to meet you. Did you know my mother?" Jack asked curiously.

"Know her? I helped deliver your twin brothers right here in this diner!" Gracie said with her hand held to her forehead as if lost in the past of that glorious day.

"Oh my God, I've heard that story! Daddy said Momma just had to have a slice of your blueberry pie before she went to the hospital. She thought she had plenty of time!" Jack replied excitedly.

"Plenty of time? After as many kids as Elsie Johnson had delivered, she could have just squatted and spit them out and continued on with her day! Bless her heart," Gracie said with emotion. "Well, anyway," Gracie cleared her throat. "Jack, sweetie, are you a hard worker?"

"Yes ma'am, I am, although I have never had a real job. I know I will learn fast, and I was just tested and I'm technically a genius. Oh, that actually doesn't have anything to do with getting this job, sorry," Jack stammered, slightly out of breath.

"Well, just one minute," Gracie stood up tall. "I've never had any dummies working here, unless you count Jerry, my late husband!" Gracie chuckled.

"You're hired, sweetie. If you've got the time, I'll show you around and let you take a few orders today," Gracie said as she handed Jack a white apron to put on.

Four hours later, Jack was pedaling back home, so proud to have her first job and filled with joy at all the funny stories Gracie had told her about her mother. There was hardly any talk at home about their mother because it was too painful for Daddy, but Jack wished her father knew how much Jack needed the connection that talking about Elsie Johnson brought her. Jack laughed out loud as she pedaled up the gravel driveway, thinking about how men from three towns filled the diner asking for pie just so they could watch Elsie smile and talk with each of them when she helped out at the diner in the early years.

The screen door slammed shut. "Jack!" bellowed her father as he stalked toward her. Jack ran toward him and threw her arms around his neck.

"Daddy! Guess what? I got a job!" Jack squealed as her feet hit the floor again. David narrowed his eyes and put his hands on his hips. "Where?" was all he asked.

"Downtown Diner!" Jack clapped her hands together and smiled.

"Ah, Gracie," David murmured with a slow smile forming. "That's hard work, you know," he said, putting his arm around her shoulders and leading her into the kitchen.

"I know, Daddy, really I do. Please don't give me a hard time about this. There is no way I'm going to sit around all summer while everyone is working. I need to get out of the house and maybe meet some girls who don't only talk to me because they want to date my brothers," Jack exclaimed.

"Fat chance of that, Princess," Bobby said with a snicker as he tugged on her braid.

"Oh my God, you're so stuck on yourself! But it doesn't matter because I'm going to tell them my name is Elsie Smith. Case closed," Jack retorted with determination.

"Ah, where do you think we eat every day at lunch?" Ty chimed in.

"Ugh! Whatever. I'm going for a swim before dinner," Jack stated coolly as she went to put her swimsuit on.

The cool water glided over Jack's skin as she swam back toward the beach. She lifted her goggles just in time to see Jared dive off the float and swim toward her.

"So you're a working girl now, huh?" Jared said smiling as he stopped swimming and started paddling to stay afloat.

"Wow, news certainly travels fast," Jack replied sarcastically as she splashed water at his face.

"Oh, so that's how you want to play, is it, Princess?" Jared said, splashing right back at her. Jack squealed, dove underwater, and swam toward the float. When she reached the float and grabbed the side, Jared rose out of the water so close that his shoulder was touching hers. Still not able to touch bottom, Jack balanced herself by holding onto the float.

"You're a fast swimmer," Jared said, breathing heavily as he grabbed the side of the float.

"It's all those swim practices during the winter. You know you miss us in the winter, admit it," Jack said, letting her long legs float to the top of the water and looking out toward the pine trees.

"I do miss certain Johnsons more than others," Jared said quietly.

Jack's eyes flew to Jared's and locked. It looked like Jared hadn't taken the time to shave for several days. There was dark stubble outlining his face, and his eyes were so dark and intense. His wet curls were brushed back away from his face. Jack's breathing quickened, and she was sure that he could hear her heart beating.

"I miss you too. Without you, who do I have to save me from my brothers?" Jack laughed nervously.

A quick look of anger came into Jared's eyes and he didn't laugh. "They're too rough with you sometimes," Jared muttered, looking toward shore. The moment was gone in a heartbeat, and really, had it all been Jack's imagination that he looked deep into her soul?

Probably.

With a lunge at his shoulders, she pushed him underwater and started swimming toward the beach. As she was running out of the water, Jared suddenly appeared, grabbed her from behind, and twirled her around in circles, making her dizzy. Laughing and screaming, Jack begged him to stop. Jared put her down fast, and Jack had to grab his shoulders to steady herself. A bolt of electricity traveled up her arms and spread warmly throughout her entire body, settling in her nether regions. *Oh my God, what is this?* she thought. *Think, think, think, say something, he's going to think you're an idiot.*

"Um, sorry, are you gonna have a campfire tonight?" Jack finally asked, taking a step back. She instantly felt bereft from loss of contact with him.

Jared handed Jack her towel and wrapped his around his waist. "Yeah, I was planning on having one," he said.

"Great! I'll be down with all the fixings for s'mores. Oh, wait, you don't have plans already, do you? I mean…like…a date or something?" Jack stammered.

"No, Princess, no date, just me," Jared said with an ever-so-slight grin on his face.

"Well, okay then. I'll see you later," Jack replied as she grabbed her bike and started toward the main house.

The sun had finally gone down, and Jack watched out the window as all three of her brothers got in the Suburban and headed toward town. Yes! Bebe was in bed and her father was in his office with the door closed. Jack raced to the kitchen and grabbed the graham crackers, marshmallows, and chocolate bars. It was still a little cool at night, so she threw on her red cowboy boots with her cutoff denim shorts and tank top. On her way out, she slipped on Caleb's flannel shirt. With the supplies stuffed in her backpack, Jack hopped on the four-wheeler and headed to the pond.

Jared sat on the edge of an adirondack chair with his arms resting on his knees in front of the fire holding a beer. He was cleanly shaven and his unruly black curls had been brushed back so they shined in the firelight, but uncooperative strays fell back toward his face.

"Hi," Jack said as she climbed off the four-wheeler.

"Hi yourself, I have some sticks all ready for the marshmallows," Jared replied, gesturing toward the freshly whittled sticks leaning against the chair. Jack unpacked her backpack and put the s'more makings on a large stump that they used to chop the wood for the fire.

"The first s'mores of the summer are always the best," she said as she stabbed a marshmallow with the stick and held it over the fire. Jack held out a marshmallow.

"Are you ready for one?" she asked.

"No, not right now," Jared said, not looking away from the fire. In moments, the marshmallow was a glowing ball of fire as Jack withdrew it to gently blow on it. The trick was to let it burn for a minute before blowing it out. She quickly mashed the marshmallow on the graham cracker and chocolate and smushed it together. That first bite was heaven! She closed her eyes and just savored the flavors fighting to take control in her mouth.

"Mmmmmmm, oh my God...so good...mmm." As she opened her eyes, she remembered that she had piled her hair under her ball cap after she brushed it out so she wouldn't get knots in it when she rode the four-wheeler down to the pond. She threw off her hat and her long hair spilled over her shoulders and back. When she tossed her hat on her backpack, she looked back to see Jared staring straight at her. Her eyes held his for just a moment before she started wiping at her mouth self-consciously.

"Do I have marshmallow on my face?" she asked continuing to wipe her mouth.

"What? Oh, no...no you don't," Jared replied in a husky voice, quickly standing to put wood on the fire. "So tell me the highlights of your winter."

"Well I'm sure Ty and Bobby kept you informed, but they may not have told you that I have technically graduated high school a year early. I have a signed diploma and everything. I could have gone away to college this September, but Daddy thought it would be too soon for me to go away, so he set it up at the high school for me to take all my college classes via Skype at the high school. That way I can still hang out with my misfit friends. That's what we call ourselves, the misfits. We're the self-proclaimed brainiac, school band social misfits. There are, believe it or not, a few kids who don't want to be my friend just so they can get close to my brothers. Ha! You laugh but you have no idea what it's like to be their sister. Before I caught on, I would have really pretty, popular girls talking to me and introducing me as their friend. Eventually, one of my brothers would break it off and then, without knowing why, I would begin to be bullied or snubbed. It was awful, really! In ninth grade, the six of us socially awkward nerd-nicks decided to band together to protect ourselves against the bullying. Between the six of us, we could usually outsmart and embarrass the bullies and snobby girls. My God, there are some really stupid kids in high school! There are two guys who hang out with us— they're gay, but not a couple—and when the haters start, if we can't handle the situation ourselves, I put out a phone call to one of my brothers and who- ever is closest usually handles it. On second thought, I do know that Eddie, one of the guys, is totally in love with Caleb," Jack said, finishing her s'more.

Jared was laughing and shaking his head. "I can't believe that as pretty as you are, you would ever be a considered a misfit."

"Well, believe it. It doesn't matter in the city; the girls are just plain mean. They're nothing like Harmony girls, although I guess I don't have a lot of friends here either, but I always figured that's because I'm too shy and was never allowed to go into town like the boys were. But anyway, enough about my wonderful life in the city. I'm sorry I didn't make it to your graduation from Colby. I was on a band field trip to the Boston Symphony. It was great, but I missed yours, Bobby's, and Ty's graduation," Jack explained as she pulled her knees to her chest.

"That's okay. I'm just glad it's over. Now I'm waiting to hear from Boston University's internship department. If I can get in, I can work and earn my master's in computer science at the same time. The trouble is they only accept two or three interns per semester, and although my grades were good, they aren't so good that they set me apart from the herd. I should hear by mid- August. If I don't get in, I think I'll just head to New York and try to get a job at a computer game company writing programs," Jared replied, finishing his beer and looking at her as she yawned. "You probably should get to bed if you're getting up to go to work tomorrow," he said quietly, standing up and holding his hand out for her to take.

Jack smiled and took his hand to help her out of the chair. "How right you are, Mr. Ross, thank you!"

"What time do you need to be at work, Princess?" Jared asked.

"Six a.m., but I will need to be on my bike at probably five thirty–ish," she replied, walking to the four-wheeler.

"I'll pick you up at five forty-five in the truck. I don't want you on your bike that early in the morning, and besides, I have get to the mountain early to set up for the day. Now get on back and I will bring you home, and you can pick up the four-wheeler tomorrow afternoon," Jared said, brushing Jack's hair behind her ear. He was looking at her as if he was searching for the answer to a very important question when he sighed and put his forehead against hers and said, "Move." Jack smiled and hopped on back of the four-wheeler, snuggling close to Jared. She laid her head against his back and inhaled deeply. The clean smell of soap and shampoo mixed with campfire and his worn flannel shirt was making her dizzy. All too soon, they were at her doorstep and she climbed off.

"I'll pick you up right here in the morning, okay?" Jared asked.

"Okay, I'll be ready," Jack replied, yawning. "Goodnight," she whispered as she climbed the steps to the porch.

"Goodnight, Princess," Jared whispered back as he watched her walk in the house and then gunned the four-wheeler toward his cabin. This was going to be a *very* long night.

Jared lay in bed staring at the ceiling and trying to will his body to calm down. He had been in a constant state of arousal since he had first seen Jack running out of the water with that impossibly tiny bikini on.

Jared groaned loudly and put the pillow over his head. What was wrong with him? He'd lusted after many young women and had slept with his fair share at college, but never had the feelings been so all-consuming and powerful like they were when he was around Jack. This past year, Jared had found himself holding Jack up like some impossible measure of the perfect young lady. The women he dated never seemed to quite measure up. None of them were as smart as Jack or as pretty as Jack, and his breath didn't catch when he heard them laugh like it did when Jack giggled and laughed. He had witnessed his fair share of cat fights at frat parties where girls just tore each other apart verbally. He knew for sure that Jack had the sweetest heart of anyone he knew. She was very much like her mom. Did he want Jack so much because he knew he could never have her?

Jared's thoughts drifted back to the previous summer, when David Johnson had asked Jared to help him take some old boards to the town dump with him. Once they had the truck filled and they were on their way, David asked, "You know, Jared, you have always been a part of this family, right?"

Jared had nodded. "Yeah, I know, and I am grateful for it. My dad has always blamed me for my mother running off when I was four. I think he believes if I had never come along, they would still be together. Elsie was the closest thing I ever had to a mother," Jared said quietly.

"Elsie was the best part of all of us," David said, swallowing hard. "Which brings me to what I want to talk to you about. Elsie would have done a much better job of this, but here goes anyway. I've seen the way you look at Jack. I know you have always had a soft spot for her, and I just figured that you were protective of her, you know, like a little sister. I think your feelings have started changing and that they are definitely not brotherly. That needs to stop. I'm not going to beat around the bush with this, that's my little girl, my Princess, and nobody will ever be good enough for her. Period. We've always been good to you, Jared, and I have to ask you to step away from my little girl now before anyone gets hurt. Actually, son, I'm not asking, I'm telling you to stay away from Jack, or life as you've known it will be very different. Do you hear me?" David said as he gave a sideways glance at Jared, who was sitting stiff and looking straight ahead.

"Yes, sir, I understand," Jared finally blurted out as his heart hardened just a little. The voice that he had heard his whole life chimed in his head, confirming what he had always known. Jared would never, ever be good enough for Jack Johnson, *his* Princess.

Jack was sitting on the front step with her head resting on her hands and her eyes closed when Jared pulled up. She yawned as she climbed into the truck, and Jared smiled. He knew Jack was definitely not a morning person.

Jack had on a pretty black sundress with little white flowers that fell to her midthigh and her red cowboy boots. Her hair was piled on top of her head in a messy bun, with soft tendrils falling to frame her face.

Jared frowned. "Is that what you're wearing to work?" he inquired in a disapproving tone of voice.

Jack's eyes got big. "Yes. What's wrong with what I'm wearing? Wait! Go back, I can change. What do you think I should wear?" Jack replied in a panic.

Jared instantly felt bad for being in a sour mood with her. He hadn't gotten much sleep, and now he was going to want to punch any man who looked at her today. "Too late now, Princess, that'll have to do. But maybe tomorrow you can borrow one of Bebe's housedresses and wear that. Hmmm?" he grinned.

"Oh my God! You scared me. No, I will not wear one of Bebe's housedresses, thank you very much. I happen to like this dress, and I want to make a good impression on my first day," Jack retorted, leaning her head back and closing her eyes. "I hate early mornings," she groaned.

Jared parked the truck in front of the diner and went around to open her door. Jack had already fallen back asleep. Jared touched Jack's arm lightly. "Hey, Princess, we're here; time to make the doughnuts." He laughed.

"Very funny," Jack groaned as she stepped out of the truck.

"Your first order of business can be to get me a coffee to go," Jared said as he laughed, maneuvering her through the door. A little bell chimed and Gracie stepped out of the kitchen.

"Hey there, Jared, I see you're acquainted with my new waitress," Gracie jokingly observed, handing Jack her apron.

"Yes ma'am, I am," Jared said, taking the coffee Gracie had already prepared for him. Jared never paid for his food at the diner. For as long as he could remember, Gracie had told him they had a deal: she would feed him, and he would help her around the diner when she needed it. When Jared had gotten older, he had figured that most of the townsfolk knew what an ass his father was and therefore tried to take care of him as best they could. Jared always appreciated it, and because he appreciated it, there wasn't a resident in Harmony who hadn't benefited from Jared's help as he paid it forward. He shoveled snow in the winter and helped with any repairs that were needed. On occasion, Gracie would have him deliver food to people who were house-bound or had fallen on hard times. There wasn't much that missed Gracie's notice.

Jared turned to Jack. "I'll see you at lunch, then; try not to break anything," he said grinning.

Jack narrowed her eye. "Who knew you were so funny this early in the morning?" she replied sarcastically. The bell chimed, alerting her that she had her first real customer. Jack looked at her watch. *How many hours till lunch?*

The morning flew by as Jack hustled to get the orders out as fast as she could. Who knew working was this much fun? She couldn't count how many older folks had asked her, "Are you Elsie Johnson's baby girl?" Jack loved all the stories people told her about her mother. Elsie Johnson had made quite an impression on this small town.

Suddenly, it was noontime. As Jack was filling coffee cups at the bar, the ski mountain crews started coming in. Jared, Bobby, and Ty came in and sat in the corner by the window. Jack pulled her pad and pen from the apron and headed to their table.

"What can I get you boys today?" Jack said grinning.

"Ah, I'll just have my usual, ma'am," Bobby replied, handing the menu to Jack.

"Very funny. I don't know your usual, *sir*; I'm new," Jack retorted with a sweet smile.

Jared punched Bobby's arm. "We usually always get Gracie's famous BLTs with homemade toasted white bread and fries," Jared announced.

"And Moxie—don't forget the Moxie," Ty chimed in.

"Will do, I'll be right back with the sodas," Jack said, grabbing the menus and heading to the next table to take their order.

In the morning, the crowd had been mostly older folks, but now the diner was filled with rowdy young men from the mountain. Jack could feel the little hairs on the back of her neck tingle as she instinctively knew Jared's warm brown eyes were following her as she hustled between the tables. The feeling warmed her, and she stole looks at him whenever she could. He was filthy. There was dirt and mud covering his arms and jeans. The dirt had dried and streaked down his face from sweat. His hair was smushed back as if he had been wearing a ball cap. His shirt was surprisingly clean, which meant he had been working without it on. Jack's mouth went dry remembering his broad shoulders and that V of his lean waist.

"Ah, Miss, Miss, excuse me, can I get some ketchup, please?" said a smaller man at a table. This brought her swiftly back to reality.

"Oh, sure, sorry," Jack replied as she went to the counter to grab the ketchup.

Jared swallowed hard. What was that look that Jack had just given him? He was rock hard. Wow, this could be very embarrassing. *Get a grip, Ross.* Jared wished he could throw Jack over his shoulder, put her in his old truck, and drive. But to where? There was no point thinking like this. It couldn't go anywhere.

Jared watched as Jack brought the ketchup bottle to Ned Trenholm's table. Ned was foreman of his crew just as Jared was for his. He was a big guy and would probably always work on the mountain. Ned was open about not liking anyone who didn't live in town year round. He tolerated Jared because he was a townie, but he was also jealous that Jared had gone away to college. He was a bully, plain and simple, and Jared had never liked bullies.

As Jack walked away from Ned's table, he grabbed her arm and swung her onto his lap. "Hey there, Princess, don't be in such a hurry. Let's get to know each other a little better," Ned leered. Jack struggled to her feet, but he still had a hold of her arm.

Jared saw red. Rage like nothing he had ever felt before surged through him. He bolted from his chair and grabbed Ned's arm that held Jack's.

"Let. Go," Jared said quietly...too quietly. Eyes locked, Ned and Jared stared at one another. Finally, Ned took his hand away from Jack's arm. As Jack scooted away, Jared pushed Ned back into the wall with authority. Jared's forearm was firmly planted under Ned's chin as Jared applied pressure, making it difficult for Ned to breathe.

"Stay away from her. Do you hear me? If you ever touch her again, I'll kill you, and don't ever, ever call her Princess again either," Jared spat out.

Just then Gracie came out of the kitchen. "Okay, show's over, come on, move it. Go back to work. Go on now, out." She made her way over to Jared and put her hand on his shoulder. "Jared, come on, go back to work. Enough."

Slowly Jared eased back on his arm as Ned pushed him back. They stared at each other for what seemed like forever, and then Ned threw some money on the table and walked out.

Jared turned to Gracie. "Gracie, I'm sorry I did that inside the diner. I should have hauled his ass outside," Jared mumbled.

Gracie just patted Jared on the back and told them all to go back to work. Gracie watched as Jared looked at Jack and then quickly looked away as he walked out the door.

Holy. Shit. What just happened? thought Jack. She had never seen Jared like that. Jack was used to her alpha male brothers scaring boys away from her. She never really took it seriously, but this was in a league all its own. Jared was protecting *her*. A warm feeling started blooming in her belly and spread throughout her limbs until she was sure it would shoot from her fingertips. Giddy, that's what she was. Just plain giddy. Trying to look serious and work efficiently, Jack floated through the afternoon without any mishaps.

At 3:00 p.m., Jack stepped out of the diner and started walking toward home. It was only a mile out of town, but it was hot and sticky. Jack couldn't wait to dive into the pond. She had only walked a few feet down the sidewalk when Caleb pulled up with Ty and Bobby.

"Need a lift, little lady?" Caleb said.

"Ah, yeah I do," Jack replied, starting to walk toward the truck. Caleb stepped on the gas and surged up a few yards. Jack stopped and then started walking toward the truck again. Again Caleb surged forward a few feet and stopped. Caleb was looking in his rearview mirror, smiling. Jack stopped, fuming. Again she started toward the truck and again he surged forward laughing.

"You know what, forget it! I'll walk!" Jack hollered and started walking quickly and purposefully. As she reached the truck, Ty opened the door and got out.

"Come on, Princess, Caleb is just being a dinkwad; get in," he said. Jack walked to the passenger side and climbed in the back of the Suburban.

"You're such a fucking idiot, Caleb. You shouldn't be allowed to drive," Jack snarled.

"Well, how was your first day of work, Princess?" Bobby asked over his shoulder.

"It was good, really good," Jack said looking out the window.

"Good thing Jared got to Ned before we did. That boy is an asshole," Bobby said.

"Don't say anything about that to Daddy. If he hears about it, he won't let me go back," Jack said firmly.

"Well maybe you shouldn't," Ty said, looking cross.

"Oh my God, Ty—I'm not a baby! You guys need to let me live my own life!" Jack exclaimed as they pulled into the dooryard. She yanked open the door and walked into the house. Daddy was sitting at the bar with Bebe as she made lemonade. He held out his arm and Jack went in for a big hug.

"Hi there, Princess, how was your first day of work?" David asked proudly.

"It was awesome, Daddy! I didn't break anything, and I only mixed up a few orders," Jack said, smiling.

"Good deal! Listen, after dinner I'd like to practice a few new songs I think you guys would like, and there are a few things I need to talk you all about," David announced.

Jack looked at Caleb and he shrugged his shoulders. *I guess we'll see what's up later,* Jack thought, but right now there was a pond she needed to jump into.

Jack swam to the point and back; it was a forty-minute endeavor. It felt so good gliding through the cool water. Thankfully, the new swimsuits she had ordered had come today. She got two of the same bikini, a red one and a white one. She was wearing the red bikini. She would save the white bikini for later in the summer when she wasn't quite so pale.

Jack swam to the float, climbed the ladder, and stretched out onto the painted wood. How many king of the float fights had there been over the years? Jack smiled to herself at the thought. Her only chance ever was to have Bear, Marcus, or Jared as an ally; otherwise the boys just picked her up and tossed her in. She missed the older boys. It was rare when everyone was home or at camp together anymore. She knew they were busy building their careers and living their lives, but sometimes she felt like Beth in *Little Women,* always moaning about why everyone wanted to go away and leave her.

Sighing, she sat up and hugged her knees. Looking out over the water and the mountains in the distance, she wondered why anyone would ever want to leave this perfect spot. This must be how her mother had felt about this town and its people, Jack thought.

Freshly showered, Jared leaned against the doorframe of the entrance to the cabin. He had seen Jack's towel on the beach and he figured she had swum to the point. He didn't like it when she swam alone. She was sitting with her back to him looking out over the water. Jared wondered if she was freaked out over what had happened today earlier. He had seen fear in her eyes and wished he had taken Ned outside to handle the situation. Just thinking of Ned touching Jack made Jared's hands fist up and his anger seethe.

He watched as Jack stood and executed a perfect dive. Jared walked to where she had left her towel and picked it up to wrap around her shoulders when she came in. She swam underwater until she could touch, which was quite a distance. When she came up out of the water and started walking to shore, Jared thought his legs were going to buckle. What. The. Fuck. This red bikini fit her like a glove. Although it showed less of her breasts than the old swimsuit, it formed around her breasts and lifted them perfectly. His mouth went completely dry. The red string bikini bottoms clung to the soft swell of her hips and made her legs go on forever. Breathe. Just breathe.

As she walked closer, Jack gathered her long hair to the side and started wringing the water out of it. She looked up shyly as Jared wrapped the towel around her shoulders.

"Hi," Jack said.

"Hi yourself," Jared replied quietly.

"Did you just get home from work?" Jack asked, combing her fingers through her hair to untangle it.

"I just got home, but not from work. I stopped by my dad's place to check on things," Jared said, putting his hands in the pockets of his jeans.

"Oh, how is your dad? Is he still at the mill?" Jack asked.

"Yeah, not much changes there—still drunk and still mean," Jared said, shrugging his shoulders. "Listen, Jack, I'm sorry if I embarrassed you today at the diner. Ned's a real asshole, and I lost my temper."

Jack leaned in close and went on tiptoes to put her fingers over Jared's lips. "Shhh, there's no need to be sorry, Jared. It's me that should be thanking you for putting him in his place. It made me feel special; thank you so much," Jack said, lowering her hand and starting to walk toward the four-wheeler.

Jared grabbed her hand and spun her around to look at him. "You are special, Jack. Don't you know that?" Jared asked.

Jack smiled wanly at him. "No, most of the time I feel invisible, like some beautiful china doll that they keep on the shelf. Heaven forbid if she is taken off the shelf, she might break, so instead they keep her safely tucked away on the shelf as they live their lives around her. I know they love me, but sometimes I can't breathe. I feel like you can actually see me. You've always made me feel special."

Jack squeezed Jared's hand, but suddenly felt embarrassed by her admission and got on the four-wheeler.

"Daddy has some new songs he thinks we'll like to learn, and you know we need a drummer. Will you come up later?" Jack said starting the engine.

Crossing his arms and grinning, Jared said, "Sure, I'll be up," which made Jack smile happily. *He always makes me smile,* Jack thought to herself.

Some of Jack's happiest memories had taken place on the porch in Harmony playing music with her family. Most of the time, she was parked at the piano, not because her brothers couldn't play—they had all taken lessons—but because the boys didn't like playing the piano. It was infinitely cooler to play the guitar, which Jack also knew how to play. Jack especially loved to hear her father play the guitar and sing. He had a rich baritone voice that soothed her soul. Her father would print out tabs from the Internet and sheet music for them to practice on their own. They were all gifted singers and musicians. When they were much younger, they fancied themselves a modern day *Partridge Family*. On occasion, her father hosted fancy parties, and he would let the kids play their music. Music had been very important to Elsie Johnson. She had majored in music in college with the hope of becoming a music teacher. Jack believed that continuing the kids' music education and singing together somehow made her father feel close with her mother. There was a beautiful photo on the piano of a smiling Elsie Johnson that never failed to warm Jack's heart.

With dinner over and the cleanup finished, the family made their way out to the porch to begin the jam session. Jared was already seated at the drums looking over the sheets of music. David patted Jared's shoulder.

"Hey there, son, we looked for you after graduation to come to dinner with me and the boys to celebrate. I figured you were busy with a pretty girl so we went on ahead," David said, picking up his guitar.

"No, sir, I just packed my stuff from the apartment and headed home. I actually started working at the mountain the next day," Jared replied, staring directly at Jack.

Some of the music was challenging, but the country ballads from George Jones and Randy Travis were so fun to get lost in. When they were just about ready to call it a night, Jack announced that she had been working on something this winter that she wanted to play for them. It was such a haunting piano melody that Jack knew immediately that she wanted to surprise her father with it. Jack began the Adele song "Turning Tables" and immediately became completely absorbed. She closed her eyes and just let her fingers glide over the keys as she sang with feeling. When she finished, she opened her eyes to find five sets of eyes staring at her and five mouths hanging open. She laughed out loud.

"If you could see your faces! Did you like it? Don't lie to me. Tell me the truth. I know my voice isn't strong like Adele's, but when I heard the song, I just had to try it, especially the piano solo," Jack prattled.

"Princess, that was amazing. I'm so proud of you. Your own mother couldn't have played that any better," David murmured. A higher compliment could not have been given by her father.

"Wow, that was really good, Jack," Ty said as he winked at her.

"It was okay," Caleb grumbled, which got him a pillow thrown at him by Jack.

Jared sat very still and never said a word. *He hated it,* thought Jack. Just when Jack wanted to be swallowed up by the piano, her father turned very serious.

"Now, there are a few things that I need to discuss with you kids. There is some trouble brewing in the Massachusetts plant. We're in the middle of contract negotiations, and we're hearing rumblings of a strike. The friggin' union is trying to justify its existence on my dime," David announced, running his hand absently through his hair. "What that means for you kids is I'm going to be away quite a bit this summer. I will have to stay right at the mill most days and nights. I need you all to be on your best behavior. I've told Ronnie Keister what's going on, and I don't want any phone calls from him about you guys. Do I make myself clear? I will be heading out in the morning. I have a car picking me up and taking me to the airport, so you kids can have the Suburban. I will be checking in with Bebe as often as I can. I'm counting on you to hold down the fort until I get back," David said as he looked at each of the kids and then stopped as he leveled his glance at Jared. "I'm counting on you," David said sternly.

"No problem, Daddy-O; I'm going to bed," Caleb replied as he grinned at Jack.

Oh my God, Caleb was going to sneak out and meet a girl, she just knew it. *He's such a dog,* thought Jack. He couldn't even wait until Daddy left!

Jack got up and hugged her father. "Be careful, Daddy, those strikes can be violent."

David cupped Jack's face and kissed her on the forehead. "Don't worry about me, Princess, we've been through this before," he replied softly.

Yawning, Jack walked into the kitchen to find Jared pouring a glass of juice. He lifted the glass to her; Jack nodded and he poured himself another. "That was quite a song," he said as leaned on the bar across from where she sat.

Jack's face instantly turned red and she put her hand up. "Stop, you don't have to say that. Sometimes I just get so caught up in the music, I lose myself," Jack replied smiling.

Jared leaned closer and spoke so softly she could barely hear. "It was the most beautiful sound I've ever heard. Will you sing for me again sometime soon?" he asked quietly as he stared deeply into her eyes. Completely under his spell, Jack bit her lip and nodded. Jared looked at her lips and touched her chin.

"You're killing me, Princess," he whispered. Jack heard her father's bedroom door close and Jared stiffened and downed his juice. "I'll see you tomorrow at six," he said walking toward the porch. Jack continued sitting at the bar sipping her juice, thinking about singing for Jared again soon.

By Friday afternoon, Jack was ready for a weekend off from the diner. Friday lunch was crazy busy, but she found that time really flew by when it was busy. Jack had finished all her chores and was between customers, so she was leaning on the counter reading. The door chimed, and a girl about Jack's age came in and took a seat at the bar.

"Hi, what can I get for you?" Jack asked.

The girl was lovely. She had long, wild, fire-red hair and beautiful green eyes with a smattering of freckles across her nose. She looked at Jack and then down at her book and then immediately back up at Jack.

"Is that an *Outlander* book?" she asked with big eyes.

"Um, yeah…have you read them?" Jack asked incredulously.

"Yes!" the stranger squealed. "I've read them all!"

"Me too! You're the first person I've met who knows anything about them. I mean, not many teenage girls read about the eighteenth-century Scottish rebellion," Jack said, laughing.

"I know, right? My name is Mac," the girl exclaimed as she touched her chest. Jack just stared at her. "What?" Mac asked.

"Are you shitting me?" Jack gasped, putting her hand over her mouth.

"No. Well, actually my name is MacKenzie, but everyone calls me Mac," she said.

Jack just pointed to her nametag. "Jack—it's actually just Jack, a very sad, weird story, but can you believe it? We're Mac and Jack!"

Both girls started laughing. "First let me take your order," Jack said.

Mac looked embarrassed. "Um, you're going to think I'm such a dork, but can I get an ice cream soda? I know, who orders them in our generation?" Mac stammered.

Jack looked stunned and squealed. "I love them! My dad always made them for me. Do you want to know my favorite?"

Mac nodded.

"Orange soda with chocolate ice cream."

Jack could almost visibly see the color drain from Mac's face.

"Are you shitting me? That is my all-time favorite too," Mac almost shouted out, and again they both burst out laughing.

"Two coming right up," Jack proclaimed, preparing one for Mac and one for herself. She had completely forgotten to eat lunch today. Jack learned that Mac was an army brat and accordingly had moved all over the country at a moment's notice. She seemed very smart and loved books as much as Jack. She had one more year of high school and then planned to attend culinary school in New York.

"I have a brother who went to culinary school in New York, and now he works at this really popular restaurant called Twenty Below in the city. Have you heard of it?" Jack asked.

"Are you kidding? That's like a chef's dream job! It's a very famous restaurant," Mac replied dreamily. "Do you have any other brothers and sisters?"

Jack snorted into her straw. "Um, no sisters unfortunately, but I do have nine brothers."

"Nine brothers!" Mac exclaimed.

"Yup, nine," Jack said rolling her eyes. "Want a couple?"

Jack learned that Mac was an only child and had moved sixteen times in the last ten years. "I've never been in one place long enough to make friends. You know what girls are like. So instead of going out with friends on the weekends, I would go to the grocery store and buy baking ingredients and bake very complex recipes. My parents love it, but I know they worry about me not having any girlfriends...or boyfriends for that matter. Books and baking have been my best friends," Mac said sighing. "Have I thoroughly depressed you with my sad story?" Mac asked as she finished her ice cream soda.

"No, not at all. If anything, you've held a mirror up to my own life. The facts are different, but I see a lot of similarities as well. Are you busy tonight? Do you like to go to parties?" Jack asked.

Mac leaned closer. "I would give anything to go to a party," Mac said pleadingly.

"Great, you can stay at my house tonight. Meet me here at three o'clock in front of the diner," Jack said, and Mac clapped her hands together and bolted out the door.

Already this job was proving to be a great source of information. She had heard multiple tables this week talking about a party on the pond not far from her house. She waited for her brothers to mention it to her. They had not, bastards. Well, she sure as hell wasn't sitting home while everybody else was having fun. Those days were over.

At three o'clock, Jack walked out of the diner to find Mac sitting in the cutest pale yellow Volkswagen Beetle convertible she had ever seen. "Sweet! Are you kidding me?" Jack said smiling.

"Hey, one of the perks of being an only child with no friends. My parents even feel sorry for me," Mac replied as she shrugged her shoulders.

"I think, my dear Mac, that this is going to be an epic summer indeed," Jack squealed and hopped in the convertible as AC/DC blasted from the speakers.

When Jack got home, there was a note from Bebe, who was at a knitting circle, saying there was homemade mac and cheese in the fridge and to just warm it up in the microwave. Even Bebe had more of a social life than her. Wonderful.

Jack and Mac put their suits on and headed to the pond to relax in the sun before they got ready for the party. When they got to the pond, all was quiet. Jared hadn't gotten home from work yet. Jack wondered if he would want to come with them to the party. She would ask him, she decided.

The two new friends lay on the float and swapped sad Friday-Saturday night stories. Jack felt a sweet happiness take hold of her that she had never felt before.

When the sun started to go down, Jack and Mac headed to the house to get ready. Jack fixed them both a big bowl of mac and cheese and went digging in the cupboard for a bottle of wine.

"I think this occasion calls for celebration, don't you, Mac?" Jack said as she struggled with the cork. With a loud pop, Jack poured two glasses of wine and handed one to Mac.

"Of course! I think we were pretty great alone, but together we are going to be unstoppable. Watch out, world!" Mac proclaimed as she clinked glasses with Jack.

"To a most memorable summer, indeed," Jack replied.

If only Jack had known what the summer indeed had in store for her.

Unfortunately, Jack's summer wardrobe did not leave her a lot of choices. It was camp attire, plain and simple, but she would work with what she had, and really, she wasn't trying to impress anybody—she just wanted to have fun. Simple denim shorts and a T-shirt that said Wild Thing on the front accompanied by her cowboy boots made up her outfit. She let her hair down from the bun and brushed it out and let Mac help her with some makeup. Mac was much better at applying makeup than Jack was. Mac had on a pair of denim shorts and a cute flowered top with sandals.

The two finished their glasses of wine as they felt a warm tingle begin in their bellies. Jack grabbed Caleb's flannel shirt and tossed Mac her denim jacket. Jack got a flashlight and they jumped on the four-wheeler to head to the pond. When they got to the beach, they walked onto the dock where the fishing boat was tied up.

"Do you know how to drive this thing?" Mac asked a little nervously. They got in the boat and Jack pulled the cord. The engine purred to life.

"Are you kidding? I have been on this pond since I was born. I actually think I was almost born here at the pond, literally."

Jack maneuvered the aluminum fishing boat along the shoreline of the pond in the direction that she believed the party was. Sure enough, after a few minutes, loud music and hootin' and hollerin' was within earshot. Jack pulled the little boat to the dock and cut the engine. Mac jumped out and held the boat while Jack got out. Jack tied the boat and turned to Mac.

"Okay, confession time. I haven't actually been to a party before and technically I wasn't invited to this one, but I don't think that matters as far as parties like this go. Worst-case scenario we get kicked out for no invitation and we go home and have some more wine. Best case scenario we have the time of our lives. But remember, we must stick together, okay?" Jack said, looking apprehensively at Mac.

"Oh, aye, Lassie, let's go have us some fun, shall we?" Mac said in a thick Scottish brogue.

I love this girl, thought Jack.

As they walked up the dock, Jack could make out a small red log cabin with a deck that was full of people and a lawn that was covered with people milling about. They all looked a little familiar from the diner, and probably her brothers had dated every girl there, which was why she would certainly not tell them who she was. Tonight was not a good night to be drowned in the pond by jilted past girlfriends of her brothers. It was probably best not to tell Mac of the danger of the jilted girlfriends either.

The driveway was on the side of the camp, and Jack had started walking that way when she spotted Jared's old Ford pickup. There were a couple of girls sitting on the hood, and Jared, Caleb, Bobby, and Ty were holding court with several guys and girls hanging around the truck.

Jack stopped dead in her tracks. "Oh, no he didn't," she whispered, seeing Jared.

"What, what do you see?" Mac insisted.

"Oh, my brothers and someone I'm...you could say 'interested in'...are over there," Jack whispered.

"Well, let's go over," Mac said grabbing her arm and starting to walk their way. Jack grabbed her arm and yanked her back.

"God, no! We must avoid them at all costs, or they will try to make us go home," Jack insisted. Jack turned Mac around and started for the house. "Let's go see what's going on inside, shall we?" Jack said giggling.

Bruce Springsteen was blasting, and it was hard to maneuver with so many people in the house, but Jack and Mac managed to catch the eye of the possible host of this little party. He was a little too old and a little too smarmy for them, but he was the first person to welcome them. His name was Dana, and he was happy to meet them. He immediately put beers in their hands and decided that they should all do a shot of whiskey. Dana introduced them to about a dozen guys and girls standing around the kitchen. Shots were poured and Mac and Jack clinked glasses and downed them. Coughing fits ensued, which made them start laughing hysterically.

Dana was soon followed by about a dozen young men who wanted to know all about MacKenzie and "Elsie." Well, they began, they were on break from college and vacationing here in Maine. It was so unbelievably easy to spin tall tales about their travels that Jack started to feel a little bad, but luckily they never had an empty beer bottle.

Eventually, Jack grabbed Mac and whispered to her that she needed to find a restroom. Jack thought it best to just make their way outside and go in the woods. They climbed down the stairs of the deck laughing and staggering as they made their way to the woods on the side lawn. They each squatted and did their business, and when they were coming out of the woods, Dana and a couple of his friends were right there.

"Hey, ladies, how about we go skinny dipping? It's kind of a tradition in Maine, I'm afraid," Dana said, pulling Jack's hair away from her face.

Even in the fuzzy haze her brain was slipping into, Jack knew that "skinny dipping" was not a good idea and that she needed to get Mac out of there. Jack grabbed Mac's hand and stumbled a few steps toward the dock when she ran full force into something very solid. Jack put her hands up to steady herself and found herself looking directly up into Jared's face. Jared caught her by the arms and steadied her.

"What the fuck? Jack. What are you doing here?" Jared demanded.

All of a sudden, Dana scooped Jack up and off her feet. "I believe Elsie and MacKenzie were just going to come skinny dipping with us," Dana said, starting to walk to the beach.

"The fuck she is," Jared replied, grabbing Dana's shirt. "Let her down, now!" Jared hollered. Just then Bobby, Ty, and Caleb flanked Jared's side.

"If I were you, Dana, I would put that little girl down," Ty said quietly.

"Come on, guys, go get your own sweet things. There are plenty to go around. I found this one myself. She can really hold her whiskey, I'll tell ya," Dana said laughing.

Bobby went around behind him and grabbed Dana by the throat. "That's my sister, you sick fuck," Bobby said, squeezing Dana's throat.

Jared picked Jack up out of Dana's arms. "Where's Mac?" Jack asked urgently.

"Who the fuck is Mac?" Caleb asked.

"She's the girl I came here with, asshat!" Jack yelled at Caleb. Jack wiggled out of Jared's arms as Mac yelled, "I'm over here!" She was leaning on a tree looking like she was going to be sick. Jack ran over to her and patted her back. Jared, Caleb, Bobby, and Ty all stood like a shield around Jack while she took care of Mac.

Although she was dizzy, Jack felt like she could maneuver the boat home. Jack put Mac's arm around her shoulders and tried to walk around the boys to get to the boat.

"Just where the hell do you think you're going?" Jared asked.

"Fuck off, all of you, we're going home," Jack spat out over her shoulder. Jared quickly positioned himself in front of Jack.

"Move! Now! I'm sure all the girls you were entertaining are waiting for you all to come back. Just go. We're fine!" Jack said, exasperated.

"Oh, you're fine, are you? How did you get here anyway?" Jared retorted.

"I have the boat tied to the dock," Jack said motioning toward the dock.

"Oh, for fuck's sake, are you kidding me?" Jared yelled. Jared picked up Mac and gave her to Ty. "Take my truck and get her to the house. I will take Jack and the boat and meet you there," Jared said as he picked up Jack and started toward the dock.

"Put me down, Jared, right now," Jack growled.

"I'm taking you home, so stop squirming or we will both end up in the pond, or better yet, I should just toss you in the pond to sober you up. Jesus, Jack!" Jared said angrily.

Jack stopped squirming and soon sat in the bow of the boat with her back to Jared. Jared started the engine and started down the pond. Jack grabbed the flashlight and illuminated the way home. Once the boat was tied up, Jack started walking down the dock. Was it her imagination, or had the dock just gotten much narrower, and it seemed to be swaying slowly from side to side? She walked too close to the edge and felt herself falling into the pond. Once she hit the water, she had no sense of up or down. She was just floundering in darkness. She knew in her brain that the water was only about up to her waist, but at night and under the circumstances, she was completely disoriented.

Just as suddenly, she was plucked from the water and was being carried to shore. Coughing and trying to catch her breath, she rolled out of Jared's arms onto her knees as he knelt down beside her. Jared grabbed her shoulders and tried to her calm down.

Jack threw his arms off her. "Get away from me!" she spat.

"What the fuck is your problem?" Jared asked, turning her around to face him.

"What's my problem?" Jack asked. "How about the fact that everyone was out and about again while I'm supposed to sit home and be invisible. Fuck you,

Jared Ross, I saw you with girls all around you and sitting on your truck. Next time, I'll make sure I go to a party that you and my brothers aren't at!" Jack cried out, slurring her words a little.

Jared grabbed Jack's shoulders. "You will not go to a party without me ever, do you understand me, Jack?"

Jack's clothes were soaked and clinging to her body. Water filled her cowboy boots, and the sand was digging into her knees. "I understand that you're a fucking hypocrite and I'll do what I please," Jack stammered with a sob.

Jared grabbed Jack's face with both hands and looked at her. "Jack, this can't happen," Jared said looking intently into Jack's eyes. "It can't," he murmured, almost to himself.

"Fine, then let me go and leave me alone, Jared," Jack said with tears falling down her cheeks.

Jared gripped Jack's face tighter. "I can't," he said as his lips touched hers. "I can't," he said as the kiss deepened.

Jack felt as if she was falling again. She had dreamed about this moment for so long. His lips were so soft, and they gently prodded her mouth open. The first touch of his tongue made her catch her breath, and when she used her tongue to taste him back he moaned and broke off the kiss. He gathered her close and hugged her.

"We just can't, Princess," Jared whispered firmly. Jared picked her up and set her on the four-wheeler. He got on and started up the gravel dirt road. She was tired, so tired. Jack leaned against Jared's back to rest and fell asleep.

When they reached the house, Jared carried Jack in and sat her on the bed. Mac was already asleep on the bed. Jared shook her a little and her eyes opened wide.

"Hi, could you help Jack into some dry clothes, please?" Jared asked Mac. Mac nodded and Jared eased himself away from Jack and left the room. *This is going to be another long night,* he thought to himself.

Jack slowly opened her eyes. Not horrible. She didn't feel great but she thought she could function. She peered under the covers—naked. Not sure how that happened either, but she was just going to assume Mac had undressed her and put her under the covers. Mac herself was sprawled out on top of the covers with a throw blanket tossed over her. Jack got up and dressed in old shorts and a tank top. She went into the bathroom, splashed cold water on her face, and took a couple of Ibuprofen, leaving two on the nightstand with some water for Mac when she awoke.

The boys were in the kitchen at the bar eating breakfast as Jack made her way to the toaster.

"Ah, there she is, Miss Whiskey pants herself!" Caleb said.

"Go to hell," Jack replied, putting four slices of toast in the toaster and getting the butter out.

"Well, what do you have to say for yourself?" Bobby asked, putting his bowl in the dishwasher.

"What? What are you talking about?" Jack said, turning around to face them.

"How do you feel, Princess?" Ty said quietly.

"I feel just fine. You guys better not give me a hard time about this. Do you have any idea how many secrets I've kept for you guys? You better not tell Daddy either, or I swear I will spill every single one," she warned.

"We just want you to be safe," Ty said, looking guilty. Jack went over and hugged him.

"I know, and I will, I promise," Jack murmured as she grabbed the coffees and toast and walked toward her room. "Oh, and don't give Mac a hard time either, because if you scare her away, I promise you I will tell everyone at the diner that you caught some venereal disease. See how many dates you get after that."

"Jesus," Caleb croaked as he choked on his cereal.

Mac was sitting up in bed with the glass of water in her hand. Jack handed her some toast and coffee.

"How do you feel?" Jack asked.

"Um, I'm not sure really. Kind of meh, I guess. I think we were lucky to leave when we did. The drinking damage wasn't too bad," Mac speculated.

"True that," Jack replied.

"Are you in trouble with your brothers?" Mac asked, nibbling on her toast.

"Nah, they tried to give me a hard time, but believe me I know way too much crap about them for them to tell Daddy. My father owns several sneaker factories, and right now he is in Massachusetts trying to take care of a possible strike with the union. We won't see a lot of him this summer. My brothers are here and Bebe. Bebe used to be our nanny, but now she just kind of runs the house. I don't think she really knows what to do with us kids anymore since we're all grown," said Jack. "Do you need to go home right away?"

"No, I have the day as far as I know. I'll call my mother to make sure. What do you have in mind?" Mac replied suspiciously.

"Well, it just so happens that I have loads of tips and my first paycheck that we can spend. How about mani-pedis, a little Italian food, and some shopping? How does *that* sound?" Jack inquired with a devilish grin on her face.

"Simply mahvelous, dahling," Mac said in her best British accent.

"Great, you call your mom and I will jump in the shower," Jack said, heading into the bathroom.

One hour later, the girls were walking through the porch to the driveway when Caleb and Bobby called after them.

"Whoa there, missy, where do you think you're off to?" Bobby said lazily. The boys were stretched out on the couch with their guitars.

"Mac, this is Bobby and Caleb, two of my brothers," Jack said, pointing at each one. "Ty is around somewhere. Boys, this is Mac. She has lived all over the world. She's an army brat. Her family moved here this past winter. She is also a misfit," Jack said, putting her arm around Mac's shoulder.

"Nice to meet you, Mac. You've got a sweet little ride there," Bobby said, smiling.

"Ah, you sure don't look like a misfit to me," Caleb said, flirting. Jack's hand shot immediately up in the air.

"Down boy! Remember what I said I would do this morning, Caleb?" Caleb lost all color in his face.

Mac giggled. "It's nice to meet you both," she said.

"Would you tell Bebe we have gone shopping at the Bangor Mall? I have my cell phone on me if you need to reach me. Where is Ty anyway?" Jack asked, looking around.

"He's down helping Jared with his truck. They're changing the oil and stuff," Bobby said.

Jack immediately stiffened. Jared. Her anger rose. She remembered that kiss. Just thinking about that kiss made her heart skip a beat and sent heat rushing to her girl parts. At the same time, she remembered him telling her nothing could come of their feelings. *That's bullshit,* Jack thought. I'm not playing these games. If he wanted to ignore his feelings, fine, that's what she would do as well. It's not like she didn't have plenty of experience ignoring her feelings.

"I hope the truck falls on him—Jared, not Ty," Jack mumbled as she walked out the door.

"So since we have an hour to kill in the car, would you mind telling me about Jared?" Mac asked.

Jack smiled sheepishly. "Ugh, I don't mind, but I don't understand it myself. I guess it's complicated, but I don't see why it has to be. I don't know, maybe you can shed some light on it for me. It's not like I have any experience with this shit," Jack said and proceeded to tell Mac how she had known Jared her whole life but sometime last summer she had started feeling much differently about him. Not brotherly at all. She told her how she couldn't breathe properly when he was around and how her stomach felt sick and she never knew what to say around him. Pretty much that she was a hot mess. What Jack didn't tell Mac was about the kiss the night before. She was still trying to just breathe when she thought of it. It was so private and sacred that Jack somehow knew she must keep that to herself, at least for now.

"Wow, just wow!" Mac exclaimed after Jack ended.

"I know, right? Let's forget all about that and have some fun today!" Jack said, turning up the volume for a little Bon Jovi.

The mall was a blast. They pampered themselves and stuffed themselves with Italian food. Jack purchased some much-needed summer dresses, new shorts, and tops. On the drive home, both girls started feeling tired from the excitement of the previous evening. Mac dropped Jack off and headed for home to crash. Jack wandered through the kitchen to find Bebe putting a puzzle together at the kitchen table.

"Hi," Jack said, kissing her cheek.

"Hi yourself, my child," Bebe replied, touching Jack's cheek.

"Can I help you?" Jack asked.

"Yes, I would like that," Bebe said smiling. Jack went to her bedroom, tossed her bags on her bed, and put her pajamas on, and then she proceeded to settle herself at the kitchen table to help Bebe. Caleb came into the kitchen and started packing some beer in the cooler and grabbing bags of chips.

"We're having a campfire tonight and a few people are coming in boats if you want to come down. If you're feeling up to it that is," Caleb smirked.

Jack swiped her middle finger up the bridge of her nose slyly in response.

"No, I'm good thanks," she said sweetly.

"Suit yourself, Princess," Caleb said, hauling the cooler out the door.

Bebe and Jack worked silently for a while until Jack let out a big sigh. Bebe looked at Jack and cupped her chin.

"Why are you so sad, Princess?" she said softly.

That's all it took. Tears started cascading down Jack's face, and her head fell into her hands as the sobs continued. "I don't know what's wrong with me, Bebe. I don't know what these feelings are, but I feel like I want to jump out of my skin. I need to tell you something. I have feelings for Jared."

Bebe smiled and kissed the top of Jack's head as she went to the stove to start some tea. "I may not have any experience in romantic love, but even I see how you light up when he is around," Bebe said.

"Oh, Bebe, what am I going to do?" Jack whispered.

Jared waited all day Saturday for Jack to come to the pond. He and Ty changed the oil in his truck and just basically wasted time before Ty headed across the pond in the boat. He wanted to talk to Jack and try to make her see that they couldn't be together like that, ever. He simply wasn't good enough for her. He had nothing to offer her. He fully intended to make his mark with computers, but even if he had all the money in the world, he would still always be Jared Ross, son of the town drunk. His own mother couldn't stand him and had run off, a fact that his father reminded him of every chance he could. Jack was going to go off to college—hell, she had already graduated high school a year early. Jared had always been in awe of how smart she and Teddy were. Teddy was now working for NASA, a real rocket scientist, Jared thought, shaking his head and smiling. Jack would probably earn her MBA and maybe take over the family business with Marcus one day. She had been reading the *Wall Street Journal* since she was about seven years old. She would meet some man as smart as she was from a good family and settle down and have curly-blond-haired little girls.

"Jesus!" Jared yelled and threw the wrench in the dirt. He just couldn't think about Jack with another man. It killed him. She was *his,* damn it! He thought about her tears last night; that had just about destroyed him. Her mouth was so soft and she tasted like beer and honey. That in the abstract didn't sound like an appealing combination, but Jared was instantly hard anyway.

Get a grip, he thought, running his hands through his wild curls. He wasn't feeling too well himself today. After he'd dropped Jack off at her house he had come back to the cabin and simply drowned his feelings in a bottle of Jack Daniel's. There were a few things his father had taught him, and how to not feel anything for a while was one of them. That's why as a rule he never had more than a few beers. The risk for him genetically simply wasn't worth it.

He couldn't take it anymore; he had to go check on her. What if she was sick and needed something? What if no one checked on her and she needed help? Jared jumped in his truck and bolted up the gravel dirt road to the main house. He burst through the screen door.

"Where's Jack?" he demanded, standing in front of Caleb and Bobby, who were strumming their guitars.

"Her and Mac...*ha!* Can you believe it's Mac and Jack?" Caleb said, smirking.

"They've gone to the Bangor Mall shopping," Bobby said.

"Oh," Jared said, deflated from getting himself all worked up with worry for her. Jared flopped down in the chair and picked up a guitar.

"Was she sick? How did she seem to you guys?" Jared asked as nonchalantly as he could.

"Um, she threatened to tell everyone at the diner that we had a venereal disease if we scared her new friend away," Caleb grunted. "I'd say she's just fine. Speaking of fine, her new friend, Mac, is kinda fine."

"Are you stupid? I wouldn't go there if I were you, brother. If you ever want another date, like ever, I wouldn't try to tap that one," Bobby said.

Jared smiled. Jack knew how to threaten her brothers all right. They were all just a little scared of her. The phrase "Though she may be little, she be fierce" ran through his mind. Well, he would talk to her tonight at the campfire and explain why it made perfect sense for them to remain old family friends and that the kiss had been a mistake.

It was dark, and the campfire was roaring. Girls from a couple of camps down had boated over, and everyone was just hanging around the campfire talking and drinking beer. Everyone except Jared. He sat slumped in his chair outside the circle staring at the fire. Multiple girls had tried to engage him in conversation, but they had stopped trying after his one-word grunted replies. *Where is she?* Thought Jared. *Why hasn't she come down tonight?* He knew she was home because he had asked Ty. What the fuck? He couldn't stand this anymore. Why were there so many people around? He jumped up and headed toward his cabin.

"I'm going to bed," Jared mumbled. This was going to be another long night, he thought, as he fell onto his bed and stared at the ceiling.

Jack got up a half hour early to get on her bike to ride to work. She knew she was being juvenile, but honestly she didn't think she could sit in that truck without punching Jared right in the face. There were dark circles under her eyes from lack of sleep. She was a quarter of a mile from the diner when Jared pulled up beside her in his truck. Shit. He was early. Jack kept looking straight ahead and continued pedaling.

"Why didn't you wait for me? Come on, get in. We can put your bike in the back," Jared said, driving beside her.

"No, thank you, I'm fine," Jack replied, looking over at Jared with a smile that didn't reach her eyes. He kept following her for a bit.

"Jesus! Why do you have to be so stubborn!" he exclaimed, punching the ceiling in his truck. He gunned the engine and sped toward town.

Jack took deep breaths and blew them out her mouth. As she rounded the corner into town she saw Jared leaning against his truck with his coffee. He saw her, climbed into the truck, and sped off. *Deep breaths, deep breaths,* Jack recited to herself.

Grumpy did not even begin to describe her mood. Each day began the same: Jared would drive by her on the road and wait until she got to the diner before driving off, squealing out more often than not. After work, she would ride her bike home, and some evenings Mac would come over in the afternoon to swim with her. Friday afternoon after leaving the diner, Mac pulled up beside her on the road.

"Guess what we're doing tomorrow night?" Mac said. Jack looked suspiciously at her.

"What?" asked Jack.

"We are going on a double date, thank you very much! I'll meet you at your house to tell you all about it!" Mac exclaimed as she drove off.

When Jack arrived home, she quickly hopped off her bike and walked to the front steps, where Mac was already sitting.

"Okay. Spill," said Jack.

"Well, there is this guy who works for my dad at the recruiting office this summer. He just graduated college, and he's very cute. But I digress. He asked me out to a party at some pit for tomorrow night. I told him no unless he can come up with another date so we can go out together," said Mac.

"Oh, God, I don't know, Mac. Am I really that desperate?" Jack asked.

"No, not at all. I have my whole life to date guys. I just found you, and I would rather spend time with you than any guy I know. You know what they say, Hos before bros! Besides, he said he knows your brothers, and he graduated with Jared," said Mac.

Jared. Anger.

"Well, okay then! I guess we have a double date! Let's go swimming," said Jack resolutely.

Jared was helping Gracie fix her sign out in front of the diner Friday evening when he saw Chad locking up the recruiting station. Chad walked over.

"Hey," he called out.

"Hey yourself—how's it going?" Jared said, gripping Chad's hand and man-hugging.

"Can't complain. Are you going to the pit tomorrow night?" asked Chad.

"Nah, probably not," said Jared.

"Oh, that's too bad; I'm taking Mac O'Riley, and my cousin who's in town visiting is taking Jack Johnson. Should be fun," shrugged Chad.

Jack. Oh, really. Jared's hands fisted automatically.

"Um, okay, maybe I'll see you there if you change your mind," Chad said as he walked away.

"Yeah, see ya," said Jared absently. So Jack was going out on a date. Could his guts get any more twisted?

Jack half-heartedly chose one of the new summer dresses she had purchased at the mall. The dress was slightly off the shoulder, white, with little red roses covering it and a leather belt cinching at her waist. She threw on her cowboy boots to complete the outfit. Mac wanted to play with her hair, and in the end she wore her hair pinned up with small curls spilling all over the back of her head. Jack tried to rally her spirits, because she knew Mac was excited about the party, but in her heart, Jack just wanted to curl up and stay home. She would try very hard not to disappoint her new friend.

The guys picked up Jack and Mac at about six o'clock. Chad was indeed as cute as Mac had said, with short light brown hair and a friendly smile. Chad's cousin, Tom, was also very handsome. Tom was as tall as Jack, which was a plus, because in Jack's slim dating experience she had usually been taller than most of the boys. He had blond hair and pretty blue eyes. He seemed nice enough, Jack thought, but he wasn't tall, dark, and handsome like Jared. *I wonder if I will ever stop holding Jared Ross up as the measuring stick to all other guys,* Jack thought.

The four of them went to a steakhouse on the edge of town. It was surprisingly easy to have an engaging conversation with a guy she had just met. It was only with Jared that she felt like she was tripping over her tongue. Chad and Tom both had one year left at Maine Maritime Academy and had great stories about their adventures at sea. Jack truly enjoyed hearing about the ships and the military style school.

"So your brothers will probably be at the pit tonight, Jack?" Chad asked.

"Um, probably. There will be girls there too, right?" Jack laughed.

"How many brothers do you have?" Tom asked.

"Nine," Jack answered and watched his eyes grow big. "Only three are at camp this summer, although I think a few of my other brothers will be visiting soon."

"Um, they won't have a problem with me, will they?" Tom asked.

"Only if you intend on ravishing me," Jack said, making Mac howl with laughter. Tom grew very red very quickly.

"Oh, sorry, sometimes I have the vocabulary of a ninety-five-year-old woman. No, really, I can handle my brothers," she said. It was just dusk when they left the restaurant and headed to the pit.

The "pit" was a fitting name, as it was actually a gravel pit that the town used to fill its dump trucks when repairing the roads. A big bonfire had just been lit, and a truck with speakers on the hood was blaring country music. The boys grabbed a cooler from the trunk and headed toward the bonfire. There were about fifty people already there. Many of the faces looked familiar from the diner. Tom handed Jack a beer and leaned in close to her ear.

"Is the guy across from the bonfire staring at us one of your brothers?" he whispered.

The hair on the back of Jack's neck instantly stood on end. Jack slowly turned her head to find Jared standing with his arms crossed staring at them. God, he looked like he was about to punch someone. Talk about intimidating! He hadn't shaved in a few days and his hair was wild from being pushed back. He wore faded jeans and a black T-shirt that showed the bottom of his massive shoulder tattoo. *Um, wow.* Jack's breathing became erratic and her heartbeat was thundering in her chest. Jack's eyes locked with Jared's. A very pretty petite brunette approached Jared and laid her hand on his arm, handing him a beer. He looked down at her and turned to speak to her. Jack couldn't breathe. She really couldn't breathe. Her stomach felt sick and she just wanted to bolt. No, she could do this. *This is what it must feel like to be lovesick,* thought Jack. *Oh my God, why am I analyzing this? I should just march over there and punch her in the throat,* Jack thought. Jack took a long pull off her beer before it was lifted from her hands.

"You have an ID, miss?" Bobby said as he held up the beer.

"Very funny," Jack snorted, grabbing the beer back.

"So this is your date, Princess?" Ty said looking Tom over.

"Yes. Tom, these are my brothers, Bobby, Ty, and Caleb," said Jack.

"And what are your intentions, young Tom?" Bobby said with a slight British accent.

"Um, I don't intend to ravish her," Tom replied seriously.

"What?" Caleb asked choking on his beer.

Jack shook her head. "Chill out, you guys! Tom, Caleb doesn't know what that word means so don't pay any attention to him. Just stick to one-syllable words when addressing Caleb." Jack smirked.

"Very funny, Princess. In fact, I *do* know what that means, and I fully intend to do some ravishing myself tonight. But you, my friend, had better keep your hands to yourself," Caleb said, pointing at Tom.

"Okay. Go away. All of you. Now!" Jack commanded. As they were walking away, Ty leaned close.

"You look real pretty tonight, Princess. We won't be far if you need us," he whispered. Jack mouthed, "Thank you" to Ty and pushed him away.

Mac needed to find the wilderness facilities, but Jack thought it best if they went in pairs. Jack and Mac left the guys and headed toward the woods. When they were coming out of the woods, there was a group of girls waiting for them. Jack recognized the petite brunette immediately as the girl who had touched Jared. Jack instantly disliked this girl. It would seem she felt the same about Jack, as she was staring daggers at her.

"Well, if it isn't the Princess. No, really, you laugh, but her family really does call her Princess," the brunette said with a sneer. Her friends thought it was more hilarious than it was.

Jack crossed her arms and looked at the group of girls. "So...I get it, really. How many of you have dated my brothers?" Jack asked to silent stares. "Hmm, I thought so. Well, I'm sorry things didn't work out for any of you. They try to stay away from slags, but sometimes their brains don't function properly. Oh, wait, you look confused; *slags,* that's a British term for hos, trollops, sluts...ring any bells?"

The petite brunette took a step forward. Jack took a step forward. "So, is your friend here trying to tap your brothers? That seems to be the only way you can get any friends. I hear that your own mother died rather than sticking around to raise you. You're the freak, always hanging out with your brothers. It's creepy." The brunette leered.

Red.

Jack saw red and jumped on the brunette. They toppled over, and the brunette screamed and started flailing her arms; a stray elbow managed to find its way exactly into Jack's eye socket. *My God,* thought Jack, *this girl is wriggling and slapping like, well, a girl.* Jack flipped her over and instantly had her in a choke hold.

"You are a particularly nasty bitch, aren't you? Someone should have taught you better manners when you were little," Jack whispered in the brunette's ear.

Suddenly Jack was being picked up off the brunette and Ty was holding her against his chest. Jack tried to go back after her, but Ty held her tight.

The brunette got up, dusting herself off. "Did you see that? She's like this wild animal!" the brunette screamed, dabbing the blood on her lip.

"Maybe it had something to do with you dissing her friend and talking about her dead mother," Jared said coldly. Jack looked around and found that they were indeed the show of the evening. Everyone had gathered around to watch the cat fight. Caleb, Bobby, and Jared had surrounded Jack and the brunette to make sure no one else got involved.

"Okay, move along. Nothing more to see here," Bobby called out to the crowd. The brunette stormed off, and everyone else went back to the bonfire. Mac ran over to Jack and hugged her.

"Oh. My. God. You were awesome. Like some cage fighter. You have got to teach me to wrestle like that sometime soon." Mac laughed.

Jack looked down at her dress. The sleeve was torn, which made the material hang a little too low across the shoulder. Jack touched the material and tried to dust herself off. Her hands were shaking and tears threatened her eyes. Her hair was coming out of the pins, and she supposed she did look like some wild child.

Bobby lifted her chin to inspect her eye. "That is going to be quite a shiner tomorrow, Princess," said Bobby.

Jack jerked her head away. "Don't call me that anymore," Jack hissed. Jack knew that Jared was watching her, but she refused to make eye contact with him. He was probably mad that she attacked his date. Had Jared told the brunette about her family history? Jack wondered. He probably felt sorry for her. She would not look at him.

Jack looked around and saw Tom and Chad standing off to the side of the group. Well, he must be very proud to be her date, she thought. This would probably be her last date ever, so what the fuck. She held her head high and walked over to Tom.

"Um, would you please bring me home. Now, please?" Jack said and turned to Mac. "You guys stay, really. Tom can come back. I just really want to go home," she said with a tired sigh.

"I'll bring you home, Jack," Jared said from behind her. Jack's back stiffened. Jack looked at Tom.

"Please bring me home," she whispered not looking behind her. Tom put his hand on her back and led her to his car. "Of course," he replied, leaving Jared staring after them.

They rode in silence. When they reached her house it was dark inside. Jack turned to Tom.

"I'm really sorry about this whole evening. I really do have better manners than that. I have no excuses for my behavior tonight. I'm so sorry. If you don't mind, I really would like to call it a night and be alone," she said quietly. She started to open the door.

"You know you don't have anything to apologize for. The bitch had it coming. I am actually quite proud that you were my date. I hope we can go out again," Tom said.

Jack grinned wanly. "I'd like that," she said and got out of the car.

Jack walked into the quiet house. She walked to the piano and sat down. She knew that the dam was going to break soon. Her fingers instinctively sought out the piano keys. There was just enough moonlight for her mother's picture to be illuminated.

"You would have been so ashamed of me tonight, Momma," Jack said as she started to play Adele's "Turning Tables." She closed her eyes and simply lost herself in the music.

Jared pulled up the driveway. The house was all dark, and there were no cars in the driveway. Just as he was about to continue down to the pond to check, he heard the piano. Jared shut the engine off and got out of the truck. He could hear Jack playing and singing the haunting melody. He walked to the front of the porch; he could make her out behind the piano. Her eyes were closed and she was lost in the music. Jared stood there watching her. He couldn't move. She was the most beautiful creature he had ever seen in his life. She was the sweetest, most pure-hearted human being that God had ever created. He knew he didn't deserve her, but God help him, he couldn't stay away from her any longer. It was killing him.

The song had just ended when the screen door burst open. Jack jumped and opened her eyes. Jared walked straight to her and lifted her up from the piano stool, kicking it aside. He pushed Jack back against the wall with her arms pinned on both sides of her head. His face was so close to hers their noses were touching.

"You're mine, Jack. Do you hear me? Mine. If another guy ever puts his hands on you again, I swear I'll kill him. Do you hear me? Damn it! You're mine," Jared exclaimed just before his lips found hers in a crushing kiss. This kiss wasn't soft and sweet; it was hard and punishing and desperate. Jared's tongue fought desperately with Jack's. Tasting and gliding throughout her mouth. Jack caught Jared's tongue and gently sucked. Jared groaned in need. He pressed his body against hers and let go of her arms to hold her head in his hands. Jack's hands went to the back of Jared's head and buried themselves in his curls. Closer, he needed to be closer to her. He needed to touch all of her at once.

Jared slowed down to kiss her face, her eyes, and travel down to kiss just under her ear. Jack moaned loudly. She would have fallen to the floor but for him holding her in place with his body. Jack could feel his arousal between her legs, and she was soaking wet with need. Jack pushed her hips against Jared's arousal, and he made a guttural sound in response. Jared picked Jack up by her ass and she wrapped her legs around him. She found his mouth and plunged her tongue into it as she wrapped her arms around his neck and held onto the back of his head to push his face harder against hers.

Moaning, Jared made his way outside to his truck, still carrying her. He opened the driver's side door and set her on the seat. He was sucking on her tongue when he leaned his hips into her on the seat. The way she was angled and the fact that she was still wearing the torn dress with only panties on made his bulging hard-on rub directly onto her tender opening.

"Jesus," Jared moaned. He was right on the edge. Any moment he was going to completely disgrace himself and come in his pants.

Jared grabbed Jack's face. "Sweetheart, I'm taking you down to the pond so we can have some privacy. Is that okay?" Jared asked, staring intently into her eyes.

"Yes," Jack whispered, scooting across the seat. Jared climbed in and pulled her tight against him. He was never letting her go again. As soon as they were at the pond, Jared killed the engine. Jack threw her leg over him and straddled him. She grabbed his face and found his mouth again. She tasted him and bit at his lower lip and licked him.

"Oh, fuck," Jared moaned. Jack started to grind herself against his hard-on. Jared pulled her dress down to her waist, unbuckled her bra, and tossed it aside. He desperately needed to see her breasts and touch them and suck them. His hands found her breasts, and this thumbs stroked her hard nubs. Jack threw her head back and moaned. Jared lifted her a little and put her breast in his mouth and sucked, teasing her nipple with his tongue.

"Jesus, Jared! I can't, something is…" Jack tried to speak as she rocked back and forth on the hard center of his sex. Jared sucked her nipple harder and worried the other between his fingers.

She was coming apart.

"It's okay, baby, let go, please. Come for me, baby," Jared urged. Jack exploded into a million stars. She had never experienced anything like this in her life. The sensations pulsed over and through her. She continued to ride him until she was shivering and spasming against him. She was gasping for air, and Jared was kissing her cheeks and her eyes as he whispered over and over, "So beautiful. You're mine, baby. Mine."

Jack opened her eyes and held Jared's gaze for a long moment. She touched his stubbly cheek and then his eyebrow and then his forehead, lost in awesome wonder.

"Jack, I…," Jared stammered.

"Shh." Jack touched her fingers to his lips. "I just want to look at you and feel you. No words right now. Just touching. Just feeling."

For a while they just sat there, touching each other and looking into each other's eyes as if they had each found in the other exactly what they had both been searching for their entire life.

"Sweetheart, I need to see you…all of you," Jared said as he opened the truck door and picked her up and carried her into the cabin. He laid her gently down on the bed. Jared touched her breast.

"So beautiful, so perfect," he whispered as his hands traveled down her stomach and gathered the dress and pulled it off from her as well as her boots. Jack lay before him with only her white lacy panties on. Jared could only stare. He was afraid if he spoke or touched her she would disintegrate into thin air as if she had only been a dream. A dream born of his desperate need and longing for her.

Jack started to cover her breasts with her hands. Jared gathered her hands to his lips. "Don't cover yourself from me, Princess. I will worship your body until my dying day. I have never seen anyone so beautiful. Princess, I was born to love your body," he said as he kissed her hands. "Baby, will you let me touch you and explore your body? Will you let me pleasure you and not be afraid?" Jared asked, laying down beside her on the bed and softly kissing her.

Jack nodded. "The only thing I fear is you'll change your mind about us and leave me alone again," Jack said quietly as a tear fell slowly into her hair.

Jared cupped her cheek. "No, sweetheart, I'll never leave you again, I promise," he said kissing her deeply. Jack moaned and wound her arms around his neck to bring him closer. Jared grabbed her arms and placed them above her head on the bed. "Leave your arms here," he said.

"But I want to touch you," Jack urged.

"Shhh, no, leave your arms here, do you understand?" Jared said firmly. Jack looked deeply into his eyes.

"Touch me," Jack pleaded. Jared was kneeling over her body.

"Mmm, my pleasure," he replied, taking her breast into his mouth. Jack moaned and bowed off the bed. Jared sucked and tasted one and then went to the other and worshipped it as well with his mouth. Jesus, she was beautiful! He would never get his fill of her.

Jared kissed and touched and licked down over her stomach. He made feathery light kisses over her pubic bone and gently spread her legs apart. He stroked her lips over her panties from the back to the front with his thumb.

"Jared!" Jack cried out in response, coming up off the bed. Jared eased her hips down.

"Shh, it's okay, baby, if it's too much, I'll stop," he said, kissing her inner thigh.

"Oh my God, please…please don't stop," Jack moaned. Jared smiled and with shaking fingers pulled her panties off. Jared spread her legs a little wider and knelt up to suck on her breast while he rubbed his two fingers along her lips before inserting one finger. Oh. God. She was so wet. His cock got even harder pressing against his jeans. Fuck. He stopped sucking and started kneading and pulling her nipple between his fingers while he rubbed and applied a slight pressure inside her heat as he slid his finger in and out of her. She was magnificent, her long hair was splayed across the pillow and her eyes closed as she writhed beneath his touch.

"Jared! Oh God!" Jack screamed as he took her breast back into his mouth and sucked.

"Look at me, Princess. Open your eyes," Jared commanded. Jack opened her eyes and fell into the abyss and exploded. Every nerve ending on her body screamed out in ecstasy as she rode the sensations to their pulsating end. The waves of sensations continued to roll through her for several heartbeats. When her breathing became calmer, Jared gathered her close and smoothed back her wild hair from her face.

"I need to get you back to the house before your brothers get home," Jared said softly trailing his fingers down her side.

Jack buried her face in his neck. "I don't want this to end," Jack said quietly.

"It's not going to end—not ever, Princess," Jared said seriously.

"Promise?" Jack said looking into his eyes.

"I promise," he whispered.

Jared put one of his flannel shirts on Jack and buttoned it up and she slid on her red cowboy boots. The shirt fell below her bottom. She gathered her dress and panties in a ball. *How could she get any more beautiful?* thought Jared.

"Now, I like this look on you," he said, kissing her. Jack laughed and climbed on his back. Jared picked her up, walked her to the truck, and drove up to the main house.

He carried her through the house, turning on the kitchen lights along the way. When they got to her bedroom door, he put her down and gathered her close.

"Oh, baby, I'm sorry I've been such a jerk. It's just what I feel for you is so big. It scares the shit out of me. I can't fight it anymore, Jack; I don't want to. I want to be with you more than anything I have ever wanted in my life. We'll find a way, sweetheart. But for now, it's probably best if we just keep this to ourselves. At least until we can figure it out. Does that sound crazy? I just want you all to myself for now," Jared proclaimed, pulling back slightly to look at her.

"No, it's not crazy at all. It sounds like heaven," Jack replied, snuggling under his chin. Jared kissed the top of her head.

"Will you spend the day at the river crossing with me tomorrow? I know a place that is always deserted, and we can pack a picnic lunch."

"Oh, that sounds amazing!. I'll take care of the lunch. What time do you want to leave?" Jack asked.

"How about nine o'clock? We can pick up coffee and breakfast at the diner on the way," Jared replied.

"Mmm, perfect," she said, kissing him deeply. Jared moaned and pulled away from her. He figured he'd better leave now before he couldn't. *Oh, maybe one last kiss before I leave,* he thought as he gathered her to him and tasted her lips. Smiling, but hardly satisfied, he turned and walked out the door. What had they started?

Jack had slept like a baby. She came awake slowly and stretched and moaned in complete satisfaction. She smiled as she remembered how Jared had touched her. Jack's breathing quickened and she felt a warm sensation begin to pool in her nether regions. She looked at the clock and bolted from her bed. As she made her way into the bathroom, she caught sight of her reflection in the mirror. Oh. My. God. A raccoon-like apparition was staring back at her. Jack's left eye was puffy and completely ringed in black and purple.

"Well, that certainly is attractive," she said to her reflection. Oh, well, nothing could be done about it now, and not even a shiner of epic proportions could spoil her fantastic mood.

After she showered and threw on her bathing suit and sundress, she made her way to the kitchen. Ty and Caleb were eating bacon and eggs that Bebe had prepared.

"Holy shit!" Caleb chortled. Ty just shook his head. Bebe lifted her face to look at her eye.

"I'm fine, Bebe, really," Jack assured her.

"You should see the other girl," Caleb said with a chuckle.

"You should not be fighting, ma petite," Bebe said, looking disappointed.

"All right, all right—I've had worse injuries from fighting with my brothers! No one ever seemed to be concerned then!" Jack muttered.

"Trust me, when that happens, we all take shit from Dad," Ty said. Jack smiled; she knew that was true enough.

"Bebe, what can I pack for a picnic that Mac and I are going on today?" Jack lied.

"I just made some chicken salad, and I can cut up some watermelon," Bebe offered.

"Oh, yum! That sounds great! I'll go get the basket," Jack replied as Jared walked into the kitchen. Their eyes locked, and Jared instantly looked angry as he took notice of her eye.

"Um, hi, Jared. He is taking me to Mac's," Jack announced to no one in particular and continued making the picnic.

Ty looked up. "Hey, Bub, what's up? Want some breakfast?" Ty said.

"Morning. Nah, I'm good. I'm going to check on my father today," Jared lied.

"Well okay then, all set," Jack announced a little too quickly as Jared took the picnic basket from her. "See you guys tonight."

"Oh, Jack baby, your daddy called and said he is still in negotiations but they are breaking for the holiday weekend, and he is expecting all of your brothers except Teddy to be home. That is good news, no?" Bebe said.

"That's great news! See you tonight," Jack called out, again probably too quickly. *Easy, easy,* she told herself. *Don't blow this.*

Jared put the basket and her bicycle in the back of the truck and opened the passenger door for her. She got in shyly and remained close to the door as they drove down the gravel road. Jared pulled over once the house was out of sight and turned to Jack and opened his arms.

"Come here, you," he said, finding her lips for a deep kiss.

Jack moaned. "Good morning," she murmured between kisses. He tasted like toothpaste and brown sugar. Mmm, so good. Jared broke the kiss and tilted her head in his hands looking at her eye.

"It's not as bad as it looks," Jack said with a weak smile.

"You have a shiner, Jack! That's bad. What a little bitch Jesse is," Jared said, lightly kissing her eye.

"What's her name?" Jack asked.

"Jesse French. She dated Caleb last summer," Jared replied as he pulled the truck back on the road, all along holding Jack's hand and keeping her close.

"Jesus, I remember her. Caleb is such a fucking dog and he has a big-ass mouth too," Jack said, disgusted.

"Your problem is you're too sweet. You try to see the best in people and in reality people are pretty shitty to one another. You never see it coming," Jared said, lifting her hand in his and kissing it.

Jared parked outside the diner. "I'll go grab us breakfast and coffee," said Jared.

"And I'll call Mac," Jack replied, quickly grabbing her phone. "Hey, Mac Daddy, can I ask a huge favor from you?" Jack asked.

"Ah, duh, of course. Wait, are you spending the day with Jared?" Mac squealed.

"Yes! How did you know? No, wait, can you meet me at the diner at three o'clock tomorrow when I get off work? I'll fill you in then, but if anyone asks, you and I are having a picnic today," Jack said conspiratorially.

"You bet! Bye!" Mac said and hung up. A few minutes later, Jared climbed back in the truck and handed her the breakfast bag and coffee. "All set?" he said, looking at her hopefully.

"All set," Jack said, looking over the rim of her coffee cup.

To say it was off the beaten path would definitely have been an understatement, thought Jack.

They headed up Winding Hill and out through Sandy River Road, which would eventually lead them to the river crossing. Most of the "road" they took wasn't really a road at all; it seemed more like a suggestion or a challenge. There was no way anything other than a four-wheel drive could have made it to their destination.

The rushing water slowed down and became very shallow over one section of the stream. The cold river water trickled over thousands of small rocks that made up the river crossing. Jack climbed out of the truck and onto the wet sand. The area was lush and green with ferns and moss growing everywhere. *This is exactly what the Garden of Eden must have looked like,* she thought. The air was cool from the surrounding woods, and birds could be heard in tandem with the rushing water. Jared came around the truck and drew her close.

"Hi," he said, tasting her lips.

"Mmm, hi. Um, breakfast?" Jack replied in between kisses.

"Hmm? Oh right. I'll grab it. I love to watch you eat," Jared said, grabbing the bag from the diner.

"You do? Why?" Jack said, laughing.

"Hey, would you grab those blankets? Well, you eat. You actually eat food," Jared said, shrugging his shoulders.

"You know what the dinner table is like at my house. If you're not aggressive and take your share, you go without," Jack said.

Jared shook his head. "That is so not true. I've seen your Daddy make your brothers put the last of the leftovers on your plate if you said you were still hungry, Princess," Jared said.

Jack burst out laughing. "I know! Bobby, Ty, and Caleb would get so mad at me because if I knew they wanted more, I would say I was still hungry even if I wasn't and make myself eat it."

They found a perfect spot on the bank of the stream, which was soft with thick moss. With the blankets spread, they knelt before each other and Jack cupped Jared's clean-shaven cheeks with her hands. "I'm not really hungry for food right now," Jack said shyly.

"Thank God!" Jared said, claiming her lips. She tasted like coffee and honey, and Jared felt himself harden instantly. Jack's tongue shyly explored Jared's mouth and grew bolder with each passing second. Fuck, he wanted her like he had never wanted anything before in his life. Jared gripped Jack's ass and ground it against his hardness. Jack groaned and deepened the kiss and became more aggressive with her tongue.

"Jesus, Jack," Jared moaned.

"This time I need to see you. I want to touch you," Jack said pulling Jared's T-shirt up over his head. "So beautiful," Jack said, touching his chest. She bent to kiss where she had just touched, and she continued lower to lave his nipple with her tongue.

"Jesus, Jack, do you have any idea what you do to me?" he rasped.

"Mmm," she said as she trailed kisses down his muscular stomach. Jack gently pushed Jared backward on the blanket. She let her glance travel over his hard body and land on his bulging hard-on. She gently rubbed her fingers along the length.

"Fuck!" Jared hissed and caught her fingers and brought them to his lips. "Sweetheart, I'm very close to losing all control here. Do you know how much I want to make love to you? Are you frightened by that? I don't want to do anything you're not ready for, Jack. Talk to me, baby," Jared groaned, pulling her on top of him. She let her arms frame his head and she leaned down and nibbled along his jawline and dipped down below his ear, making him close his eyes and moan with a sharp intake of breath. Jack lifted her head and looked directly into his eyes that were filled with desire.

"I want you so much, Jared. I don't really know the words to express what I want because I've never been intimate with anyone, but my body instinctively wants and craves you in a way I don't understand. I trust you and I'm not afraid. Please make love to me," Jack whispered.

With a moan Jared sat upright and straddled her legs around him. He pulled her sundress up and off her in one swoop. He unhooked her bikini top and tossed it aside. Jared splayed his fingers over her upper back, bringing her close, and lowered his head to take her breast in his mouth. Jack moaned and bowed into him and grabbed his head with her hands, urging him to take more. Jared picked up her long braid that was hanging over her shoulder and started making circles around her nipples. Jack watched transfixed as Jared licked and nipped at her nipple and ended with brushing and teasing her braid around and over her nipple ever so lightly. The slight pain and then pleasure was almost too much.

"Jared," she whispered, "more, I need more."

"I know, baby, I've got you," Jared said, lifting her and laying her on the blanket. Jared kissed her lips softly while she tried to deepen the kiss. He trailed his lips down her neck and lifted her arms above her head. Her hands were off the blanket and rested in the dark green moss. Jared continued trailing kisses down her stomach. He grasped her bikini bottoms and slowly pulled them off her. He slowly slid his hands up her long gorgeous legs. He placed his hands on her knees and spread them apart. "God, Jack, you're gorgeous," he moaned as he devoured her with his eyes. His breathing was labored and his hands were shaking. He looked into her eyes. "You're the most beautiful woman I have ever seen," Jared murmured with a tenderness in his voice that make Jack gasp.

"Jared, please," Jack said, pleading for some sort of release. Jared lowered his head and spread her lips and lapped her from bottom to top, making Jack's hips surge into the air. Jared grasped her hips and held them steady and continued to lap her. He inserted his tongue into her folds, and she cried out in pleasure, but when he began suckling on her nub, Jack completely lost control and began bucking wildly. Jared could feel her juices flood his mouth and her muscles contract violently. He continued sucking gently and licking and kissing until the spasms stopped and her breathing wasn't so labored. Jared sat up and unbuckled his jeans as his eyes locked with Jack's.

"I'm going to make love to you now, sweetheart. I'm going to love you as gently as I can, and I will try not to hurt you, baby," he announced as he stood to pull his jeans off. Jack's eyes lowered to look at his proud erection. Her eyes flew to his.

"You're so big!" she whispered and again looked at his erection. Jared pulled a condom out of his pants pocket and ripped the package with his teeth. Jack watched him slide the condom over his thick manhood and lower himself with his forearms. Jack could feel him at her entrance and she stilled. Jared kissed her deeply.

"You will stretch to accommodate me, I promise, sweetheart," Jared said, pushing into her just a bit. Jared lowered his head, took her breast into his mouth and sucked hard. Jack moaned, and he pushed inside her a little more and felt her barrier. He was losing what little control he had. My God, she was so tight and warm! His breathing quickened, and he took her mouth violently and surged forward, feeling the barrier release as she screamed into his mouth. Jared stilled and kissed her gently. Jared felt her tears on his hands as he held her head.

"Oh, baby, I'm sorry, talk to me, Princess," Jared said, shifting slightly. With the slight movement, Jack's desire spiked and on a low moan she arched her hips up and started to move.

Jared moaned. "Baby, please talk to me, I need you to be still, I can't stand much more."

"Move, please move, Jared, I need you!" Jack pleaded. The dam broke and Jared pulled out and plunged back into with her with urgency. Sweet Jesus, she was tight. He wouldn't be able to take much more of her heat without completely shattering. Jared kissed her deeply and lowered to take her breast in his mouth and began to suck while kneading her other breast and pinching her nipple between his fingers. Jack started writhing and moaning. Jared was completely filling her and pumping hard when she screamed his name.

"That's right, baby; let go. I've got you. Come for me, Princess," Jared urged, pumping harder. Jack fell over the edge in a spectacular display of emotion. Crying out and gripping Jared's ass, she totally surrendered her body to his.

Jared couldn't contain himself any longer. He had been born to love her. He was linked to her soul for eternity. With a guttural moan, Jared plunged into her harder and faster until with a loud cry he shattered into a million shards. He'd never felt the raw emotion and gut-wrenching need that he experienced at that very moment. He knew that he had always loved Jack, but now he realized that this was a love that he would never recover from. In that moment, it was a life-changing, tectonic plate-shifting experience that would change them both forever.

Jared stilled and kissed Jack gently. "Oh, baby, how are you?" he said as he settled on her side and pulled her close, kissing her forehead.

"Mmm, I'm good. So good," Jack whispered with a sigh. She snuggled very close and seconds later she was fast asleep. Jared took a deep breath as he stroked her hair. A sinking feeling of dread enveloped him. How could he protect and keep her to himself in this cruel world? he wondered. *She is mine* was his last thought before he drifted off into a satisfied languor.

The comforting sound of flowing water and birds singing brought Jack slowly awake. She was snuggled into Jared. He must have thrown a blanket over them after she had fallen asleep. She tilted her head to look at Jared and found he was sleeping. His dark eyelashes were ridiculously long, she thought, smiling.

Jared smiled and slowly opened his eyes. "Hi," he said softly.

Jack's smiled brightened. "Hi yourself," she said.

"How are you?" Jared asked.

"I'm very well, thank you," she giggled.

"Why yes, you are," Jared teased, pulling her on top of him. Jack kissed Jared lightly, nibbling on his lower lip. "You know what I'm ready for now?" Jack asked between kisses. She could feel Jared harden as he caressed her bottom and brought her closer to him.

"Mmm?" Jared grinned.

"Food, I'm ready for lots of food," Jack said laughing. Jack rolled over with the blanket and sat crossed legged. Jared sat up and did the same, covering up.

"Oh, that's what I thought you were going to say," he said looking coy. "Let's see what we have here, French toast with Gracie's famous homemade bread, bacon, scrambled eggs, and lots of syrup," Jared said, handing Jack one of the two large containers.

"Oh! How did you know that's my very favorite!" Jack exclaimed as she popped a piece of bacon in her mouth.

"I've noticed what makes you happy for a while now," Jared said quietly. Jack leaned over so close her mouth was touching his lips.

"You. You make me happy," she whispered, kissing him. Jared held the back of her head and deepened the kiss. She tasted like bacon and syrup. He could lick her. *In fact,* he thought, *I believe I will later.*

With breakfast finished, Jack looked mischievously at Jared. "Let's go skinny dipping," she said standing up. Jack looked down at the blanket and saw that it was smeared with blood. She gasped and knelt down. "Oh my God, Jared, I'm so sorry," she said, embarrassed.

Jared knelt before her and gently cradled her face in his hands. "Shh, you have nothing to apologize for. I took something beyond precious from you, Princess. I'll never be worthy of such a gift," he said, gently kissing her.

Jack touched his cheeks. "It was my gift to give, and it was meant only for you," she said. Jared picked her up in his arms and waded slowly into the cold water as she laughed and squealed at the cold temperature.

They swam a small distance away from the crossing into deeper water. Jack spied a rope swing hanging from a large tree on the bank. "Jared, is that what I think it is?" Jack asked.

Jared shook his head. "No, you are not swinging on it. Don't even think about it," he warned.

Jack's eyes narrowed. "Why? You and my brothers have used it, right? Why not me?" she asked.

"Yeah, we used to swing on it but that was years ago. It's just not safe, Jack," Jared said with finality. Jack had been edging toward the bank as he was speaking. She jumped out of the water and grabbed the rope. She climbed the bank and was poised to run and jump.

"Jack, don't do it! I mean it!" Jared hollered.

"Jared, I have to!" she said and started running while hanging onto the rope. It was just like flying. Much higher than she thought but even more exhilarating. At her highest point she let go of the rope. Everything slowed down as a scream left her body. With a giant splash she hit the water. She went deep but quickly burst out of the water. Jared was right there and grabbed her arms.

"What the fuck, Jack? Are you okay?" Jared asked.

Jack burst out laughing. "Oh. My. God! That was so much fun!"

Jared hugged her close. "Why are you so fucking fearless? Jesus, Jack!" Jared snorted, continuing to hold her.

Jack pulled back to look at him. "Hey," she said holding his face. "I'm fine. I'm not a doll that's going to break, Jared. Please don't worry about me," Jack said, kissing his face to erase the worry.

"I do worry. You've always taken too many risks, and your friggin' brothers let you. I'll never let you put yourself at risk, ever," Jared stated firmly. Grabbing her waist, he started pulling her toward shallower water. "I guess I'll have to distract you to keep you safe," he said kissing her deeply. His tongue delved deep into her mouth and she moaned. Jack was immediately flooded with white hot heat. The adrenaline was still rushing through her body and she felt an urgent need to touch him and taste him. She kissed him back and let her tongue dance with his. Jared moaned, losing himself just as she was. Jared broke off the kiss and turned her around in his arms so her back was against his stomach. He pulled her close to him and grasped each breast and rubbed and stroked her hardened nubs. Jack moaned and arched her back. She was so fucking perfect. Jared's hand traveled down her stomach and found her soft curls. He inserted two fingers, and she bucked and gasped against him.

"Shh, I've got you, baby. I want to touch you. Just relax your body into my hands."

One hand kneaded her breast and rubbed the nipple, and his other hand pushed her behind tight against his hard erection. Jared started stroking and gliding his fingers in and out of her. She was so wet. Jack started moving with his hand. He could tell she was very close.

"Do you like that, baby? Talk to me. Tell me what you want," Jared urged.

Jack was very close to coming apart. "Oh, harder, please…faster!"

Jared kissed her hard beneath her ear and she exploded, moaning and bucking wildly as she came. Jared held her to him until her breathing returned to normal and the spasms stopped. Jack turned around in his arms and touched her forehead to his, still catching her breath.

"Oh my," Jack said, pulling Jared toward the shallow sandy shore. As they were walking through the knee-deep water, Jack turned to Jared and kissed him gently. She slid her hands across his broad chest. Slowly, Jack lowered her body and let her hands slide over Jared's stomach and trace the V from his abdomen to his beautifully proud erection. Jack slowly caressed the soft skin of his erection. Jared's sharp intake of breath brought Jack's gaze to his.

"Jesus, Jack, do you know what you do to me?" Jared rasped. Jack took Jared's hard erection in her hands, brought her lips down over the crown, and sucked gently.

"Mmm, your skin is so soft," Jack whispered.

"Fuckin' A!" Jared groaned.

Jack stilled and look up. "Am I hurting you, baby?" Jack asked.

Jared gently touched her hair. "No, sweetheart, it feels so good I almost can't stand it," Jared said softly.

That was all the encouragement Jack needed. Still holding his gaze, Jack took him back into her mouth and sucked harder while letting her hand stroke his soft, tight balls. With each lowering of her head, she was able to take more and more of him into her mouth. Jared was quickly losing all control. When Jack took every inch of him, she could feel him touching the back of her throat, which made her moan low in her throat. She came up and licked the tip and around the crown and then took all of him again and sucked harder as she stroked him. Suddenly Jack was pulled up into his arms.

"Why did you stop me?" Jack whined.

"I need to be inside you, baby, now," Jared replied, lowering them onto the blanket. Jared grabbed a condom and ripped it open.

Jack covered his hand. "Allow me," she said, lowering the condom down his hard erection.

"Jack, I need to feel you," Jared muttered as he lifted her to straddle him. He kissed her deeply and pulled her hips down to enter her in one swift movement. Jack gasped and steadied herself by grasping his shoulders.

"Oh, fuck, you feel good. You're so goddamn tight," Jared said between clenched teeth. "Baby, you're in control; take what you can. I don't want to hurt you. Ride me, Princess!" Jared whispered, taking her breast into his mouth and sucking.

Jack threw her head back and moaned. She slowly started lifting and lowering herself onto his rock hard erection. Jared moved to the other breast, lowered his hand to her wet curls, and began stroking her nub, making her buck wildly.

"Jared!" she cried out and started riding him frantically.

"Baby! I can't hold back! Come for me, Jack!" Jared cried. Jack screamed and bowed her back, coming apart. Jared grabbed her hips and pumped into her harder and faster, completely out of control, and then came like he never had before.

Sweat soaked their bodies as they lay down on the blanket, entwined in each other's arms. No words were spoken as their breathing slowed and they drifted asleep, completely in awe of what just happened.

They dozed for only about twenty minutes when Jared awoke. It was late in the afternoon, and the mosquitoes would soon start coming out. Jared had a sick feeling mixed with intense awe swirling through his gut. The emotion was raw and intense. He studied her beautiful sleeping face. The ring of black and blue surrounding her eye made her look like some sort of warrior angel. So perfect. *Mine. I love her,* Jared thought again, making his guts churn with the knowledge that this sleeping angel had the power to completely destroy his world. Jared had never loved anyone or anything he couldn't walk away from. Until now.

Jared gently cupped Jack's cheek and kissed her soft lips. She smiled and kissed him back. "We need to get dressed, sweetheart, before we get eaten alive," Jared said against her mouth. Jack stretched with her full body before rising to find her scattered clothes. Jack spied the cooler that contained their lunch. "I'm hungry," Jack announced with a grin.

"Shocker, " Jared replied, laughing. "Let's pack up. There's a place I want to show you, and we'll eat when we get there, okay? Can you wait a little bit, Princess?" he said, kissing her nose.

"I'll try very hard," Jack replied, laughing and tickling his armpit. Jared yelped and whipped her around so her back molded to his body while he captured her arms.

"Still ticklish as ever, I see," Jack said, laughing.

"I think you know too much about me, little lady, and that makes you very dangerous indeed," Jared teased.

"And don't you forget it, Bub!" she said, running to the truck.

Jared drove to the height of the land that overlooked the entire town. It was his favorite spot to come and watch the sunset and think. He'd spent many nights up here in his truck when his father was drunk and on a rampage. There was something special about the quiet of the night intermingled with the stars' vast canopy above that made him feel like he could breathe and maybe dream a little.

Jared shut the engine off and turned to Jack. "Here we are," he said, kissing her lightly.

Jack gasped. "It's beautiful, Jared. I've never been here before. Let's grab the blanket and climb on the hood of the truck to watch the sunset."

It was so beautiful and quiet. This was truly a magical place, but a thought kept poking at her and wouldn't go away.

"Jared," Jack whispered as she lay beside him with his arm under her head and her hands holding his free hand.

"Yeah," he said quietly.

"Have you ever brought another girl up here?" Jack asked, quietly looking down at their entwined hands.

Jared took his hand from hers and brought her chin up to face him. "Look at me," Jared said in a firm voice. Jack lifted her eyes to his. "I have never brought anyone here, not even your brothers. I'll promise you right now, Princess, that I will not ever bring anyone here but you—ever. This is our place now."

Jared gave her a deep kiss that sent a surge of white-hot sensation through her, making her breath quicken and her nipples harden. Jack moaned and let her tongue engage his. Jared moaned and broke off the kiss and looked at her with open desire.

"Baby, you're probably going to be sore tomorrow and...I only brought two condoms," he murmured sheepishly, touching his forehead with hers. "Let me hold you for a little while longer, and then I'll bring you home."

"I'd like that," Jack whispered. They watched the sunset and the moon and stars come out to play from the hood of the old Ford pickup truck with no premonition whatsoever of the shit storm that would befall them in six short weeks.

Running to get in the shower after letting her alarm ring too many times, Jack silently acknowledged that Jared had been right. She was a little sore in her nether regions and her inner thighs. When Jared had dropped her off, her house had been quiet. Bebe had retired to her room for the night, and the boys were watching a movie in the den. Although they didn't have regular channels on their old television console, they had hooked up a DVD player to watch movies occasionally when the weather was nasty. They were watching *First Blood* with Sylvester Stallone for the zillionth time. Jack flopped down on the couch and leaned against Bobby.

"Hey, Princess, did you have a good day with Mac?" he said, putting his arm around her shoulders.

"Mmm, I did," she said yawning, feeling guilty for lying. The next thing she knew she was trying to shut off her ringing alarm. She was in bed with her bathing suit and sundress still on. Bobby must have brought her to bed, she thought. Flying into the kitchen, she spied Jared talking with Bebe.

"Good morning," Jared said, smiling at her.

"Good morning, right back at ya," Jack replied, smiling back and trying to pull her hair into a messy bun on top of her head.

Bebe looked at her black eye and shook her head. "No fighting today, ma petite, okay?" Bebe said, handing her and Jared a bagged lunch. "Breakfast?" Bebe asked Jack as she took Jared's empty breakfast plate.

"No, I don't have time this morning, Bebe, sorry, but thank you anyway. Oh, and I promise not to punch anybody today," Jack replied, walking toward the door.

It was already hot out at five o'clock in the morning. Jack instantly regretted not wearing a sundress; instead she had grabbed her jean shorts, white T-shirt, and cowboy boots. Jared pulled out of the driveway and away from the house and pulled to the side of the road. This was becoming their morning ritual. Turning, he pulled her in to kiss her.

"Good morning, sunshine," he smiled at her.

"Ditto," she said, kissing him deeply.

Jared moaned. "You're killing me, Princess," he groaned.

Jack broke off the kiss to look at her watch. "Shit, I'm going to be late," Jack exclaimed.

"We'll see about *that*," Jared replied, putting the truck in gear and speeding toward town.

"Oh. My. God," hissed Mac as she and Jack lay on the float that afternoon. Jack had just told Mac that she was officially no longer a virgin. Jack didn't convey any of the intimacy or details of her day with Jared, but she felt it was her duty as a best friend to share the basic facts with Mac, and besides, she thought she might explode if she didn't share what she was feeling with someone.

"I know! Mac, it was wonderful, but it did hurt a little. That much is true for sure, but it only hurt for a minute, and then, well, let's just say there wasn't any more pain. I totally get what all the fuss is about now," Jack said, laughing. "I've always thought my brothers were so stupid for being so obsessed with girls and dating, but now I understand a little more. Do you know how many times I have caught them, all of them really, at different times, sneaking out of the house to hook up with girls? Let me tell you, I have made a pretty penny bribing them through the years. Even now, before Daddy left, Caleb was sneaking out to meet someone. Now that Daddy is away, he just doesn't come home at night. But I get it now," Jack said with a sigh.

"Well you know you can count on me to keep your secret," Mac said dreamily.

"I know, and I appreciate it. I don't know why Jared is so freaked out by anyone finding out about us, but I actually kind of like that way, for now. My father and brothers can be so weird about that stuff. I went on a few dates last year with this really nice guy from an advanced class in economics that I took at the college. On the second date, my brother Mason—we call him Bear— he was home on leave from the military at the time. He came into the pizza parlor and sat down with us. Bear started eating our pizza and talking about hand grenades and flying body parts he had seen in Afghanistan. Well, let's just say my date suddenly lost his appetite and asked Bear to bring me home because he had to leave. I was so mad! Patrick, that was the guy, wouldn't even look at me in class anymore. My brothers are like big Neanderthals where I'm concerned. Oh, and did I tell you they're all going to be home this weekend for the Fourth of July fireworks so you will get to meet all of them? Except Teddy. The big jerks."

"I think you're so lucky to have siblings. Tell me about them. I always wished I had a brother," Mac said.

"No, you don't!" Jack snorted, diving into the pond. Mac followed her into the water. "Well first there's Marcus, he is the oldest and so bossy. He graduated college and got his MBA and now he works in the family business.

Which reminds me, I have a great idea to bounce off him and Daddy about sending sneakers to Third World countries for kids. Anyway, then there's Henry; he's a lawyer in Portland and handles all the company's legal stuff. He works for a big firm downtown. Henry is funny and so sarcastic. He's stood up for me with Marcus plenty of times when Marcus was acting like he was my father. Then, of course there's Teddy, the rocket scientist. He really is— he works for NASA. Teddy is your typical absentminded professor, but you'd never know it. He is gorgeous with tons of tattoos. He's my only brother that's blond like me, although his hair is a little darker than mine. He can't make it this weekend."

Mac looked disappointed. "I know, I wish he was coming too; I miss him. Mason is my fourth brother, and I just told you a little about him. We call him Bear because he resembles a big black bear. He's huge! All my brothers are big and tall—well, except Caleb who is my height—but Bear is really big, and he used to have this wild black hair before he went into the military and he's hairy."

Jack took a deep breath as Mac started laughing. "You laugh, but you just wait until you see him, and I guarantee at some point during the weekend, he will pick you up. He honestly can't help himself." Jack laughed and climbed up the ladder to dive in the water again. "Then there's Garrett; he's an editor and works for *Maximum* magazine in New York. He is quiet and thoughtful. Garrett would read to me all the time when I was little. He is always sending me books from authors he interviews. The twins, Ty and Bobby, you already know—Ty is a baseball player, a really, really good one. He tried out for the Boston Red Sox and is just waiting to hear. He will be playing for the Portland Sea Dogs next month. The Red Sox bring players up from the Sea Dogs, so he has a really good chance to be a real Red Sox player! Bobby will be starting medical school in September. Then there's Davey. He was named after my father, not a junior though. Davey is a lot like you, actually, he works at that big restaurant in New York. He used to love cooking in the kitchen with Bebe. I'm pretty sure he wants to have his own restaurant someday. Last but not least is Caleb, who you know and who won't stop flirting with you! See how lucky you are to have a quiet house? Why don't you stay here Saturday night after the fireworks? We'll probably have a jam session on the porch, which will be crazy with everyone here."

"I would love that!" Mac said excitedly.

The rest of the week was busy getting ready for the holiday weekend. The whole town came out to watch the fireworks and cook out in the park. Gracie was on the organizing committee, and Jack stayed after the diner closed to help her get the supplies ready. Gracie said she would give her a ride home after they finished, which was sometimes late. The Fourth of July fell on a Saturday this year, which meant the Johnson clan would arrive sometime on Friday. Jack was excited to see her brothers, but she also wanted some alone time with Jared.

Friday afternoon, Jared was waiting outside the diner for Jack when she got out of work. "Do you have a little bit of time before you have to get home?" he asked.

"Of course I do," Jack said smiling. Jared opened the truck door for her and couldn't help thinking how beautiful she was. "Thank you," she said, climbing into the old truck. Jared drove to the height of the land and shut the engine off and turned to her.

"I have missed you this week. You must be tired from working so much," Jared said, pulling her onto his lap with her back resting against the door. Jack put her arms around his neck and brought his mouth down to hers for a gentle kiss. Just that first touch of her lips and tongue had Jared moaning and deepening the kiss. Jesus, he wanted her. Her family was waiting for her, so he could wait until they had some alone time before he loved her properly, but he could give her pleasure; that meant just as much to him.

Jared held her close and with his free hand began stroking her breast through her sundress. Jack gave a low moan. He let his kisses travel down her neck and down lower to her breast. Jared stroked her hardened nipple through her dress as she bowed her back up to get closer.

"Jared," moaned Jack with wanting.

"Have you missed me, baby? Have you missed my touches?" Jared said, pulling her dress and bra down and taking her breast into his mouth. "Oh my God, yes! Don't stop! Please don't stop!" Jack begged.

"Shh, I've got you, baby. Just relax and let me touch you," Jared whispered back, letting his hand travel down to her panties. So wet, she was soaking wet with need. He slowly slid his hand inside her panties and began gently stroking her wetness. Her legs fell apart as she sighed. He inserted one finger and then two, stroking up and down and in and out. Jack's hips started gyrating in tune with his fingers, and he knew she was very close. Jared kissed her deeply and devoured her mouth with his tongue and worked his fingers a little harder and faster. Jack moaned and gripped his neck tighter while bucking her hips in the air.

The orgasm came hard and fast.

When her breathing calmed down he slipped his hand from her panties and put his fingers in his mouth. Jack watched him and gasped as a new surge of desire flooded her. It was the most erotic thing she had ever seen.

"Mmm, you taste good," Jared said smiling. He knew he had shocked her a little.

"Is there something I can do for you?" Jack asked a little shyly.

Jared smiled down at her and then laughed. "Not right now, sweetheart. When I love you, I want to take my time. I can wait." *Not comfortably though,* he thought with a grimace. "Right now I'm going to bring you almost home, and you can ride your bike to the house. I will see you at the campfire tonight, okay?" he said.

Jack nodded. "Okay, sounds good," she replied, righting herself in the seat close to him.

Jack turned the corner to find lots of cars and trucks gathered in the driveway. This was what it had always looked like in the past. God, she missed her brothers. She ran into the house to find it all quiet except for Bebe, who was in her glory cooking as she prepared for the evening meal. It had been a long time since Bebe had a full dinner table with all of her charges present.

"Are they all at the pond? " Jack asked, running to her room to change.

"Oui," Bebe called out as Jack flew by. Jack threw on her bathing suit, grabbed her towel, and thereafter proceeded to jump on her bike and head to the pond.

It looked like her brothers had just gotten to the pond. They were all standing on the beach when they spotted Jack. Jack jumped off her bike while it was still rolling and started running straight for Bear. She ran as fast as she could and launched herself at him. Bear caught her in midair by the waist, lifted her way over his head, and spun her around. She kept her body stiff with her arms outstretched. Bear started running into the water and launched her into the air so she could execute a graceful dive. Jack came up out of the water laughing and went in for a big hug.

"My Princess, how are you, baby?" Bear shouted out, holding her so he could look at her.

"I'm good, really good, Bear. I missed you so much," Jack said with tears in her eyes.

"Mmm, I missed you too, Princess, more than you know," he replied as a dark shadow crossed his face. All the boys who were in the water headed for the float. Marcus and Henry were on the float when she climbed up and hugged them both.

"Where's Daddy, Marcus?" Jack asked.

"He coming; he had some things to finish in Portland," Marcus replied, looking at her sternly. "Keeping yourself out of trouble, I hope?" he said.

"Yes, I have a job that I got on my own, thank you very much," Jack said.

"Jesus, leave her alone, Marcus, you haven't been here thirty minutes and you're already riding her ass. Give her a break; she's not a little girl anymore," Henry said, smiling at Jack.

"Um, I think we're all well aware that she is not a child anymore. As a matter of fact, do you think you could get a bathing suit that covers less than that does?" Marcus said to Jack.

Bear, Garrett, Ty, Bobby, Davey, and Caleb all climbed on the float. "I agree with Henry," Bear said, silently motioning the others to Marcus. "I also think you need to go for a swim so you can take that stick out of your ass," Bear said.

Marcus stood and looked around, suddenly realizing that he was going for a swim. The boys picked him and threw him into the pond. Then it began; every one for himself (or herself) as they pushed and shoved each other off the float.

When everyone was exhausted from playing king of the float, they swam to shore. Jack clung to Bear's back as he swam in and walked to the beach. She jumped down and grabbed her towel.

"All good in school, Princess?" Garrett asked giving her a hug.

"Yeah, as long as I steer clear of any of Bobby, Ty, or Caleb's jilted girl-friends," Jack said, giving Caleb a dirty look.

"They still call her Bones," Caleb said with a grin.

"Um, I'm not sure that applies anymore," Davey said, coming in for a hug and wrapping her beach towel around her to cover her completely.

Bear looked at Caleb like he was going thrash him. "Is this your handi-work, Caleb?" Bear said, gently rubbing his thumb around Jack's light purple eye.

"What! Fuck no!" Caleb said, shaking his head and looking a little nervous. "Not this time! Tell him, Jack. Tell Bear how you got into a catfight."

Jack narrowed her eyes and glared. "You're such an asshole, Caleb!" Jack spat at him.

"Actually she got the little witch in a nice chokehold. I had to pull her off her. You would have been proud," Bobby said, grabbing Jack and pulling her back to rest against him.

"A fucking cat fight? Really, Jack? Where did this take place?" Marcus asked.

"At the pit last weekend," Caleb offered a little too quickly. Jack started to lunge at Caleb but Bobby held her tight.

"Asshat," Jack leered at Caleb.

"Oh, nice language too. What the fuck are you doing at the pit? I can see this leading to trouble. What can anyone expect? You've been left to your own devices. Like some sort of wild child," Marcus ranted.

"Jesus, Marcus, give it a rest, will ya?" Henry exclaimed, clearly frustrated.

Bobby and Ty brought the cooler out and everyone grabbed an Adirondack chair and a beer or soda and relaxed on the beach. Even Marcus finally relaxed, and they enjoyed catching up on everyone's busy lives. As the sun started to go down, they all made their way to the main house for dinner.

Daddy was at the house when they got there. He looked tired and drained. Seeing them all together, however, brought a little spark to his eyes. Jack hugged him tight.

"How are you, Princess? Work okay?" David asked.

"Yeah, it's good. Gracie wants to talk to you about the town picnic at the end of the month," Jack said.

"Okay, I'll find her tomorrow at the park to see what she wants," David said.

They all sat down to dinner with gusto. Jack had forgotten just how rowdy the dinner table could be with all of them around it.

"Hey, where's Jared?" Bear asked.

"Um, I think he was checking on his father," Jack said trying to sound casual.

"Well he needs to be here. This is his family," Bear said.

The thought of how much her family loved Jared warmed her throughout. *He's mine,* she thought to herself.

When they arrived at the pond, the fire was roaring. Jared had already set up the chairs around the fire and was cutting up extra firewood. Bear was the first one to grab Jared and give him a big hug.

"Bubba, how the hell are you!" Bear exclaimed. Jared laughed and slapped his back.

"I'm good man, really good," Jared replied with a smile. "You?"

"Oh, can't complain. I've got a new team I'm commanding and we'll be out of contact for the next year so I intend to enjoy my weekend," Bear said.

All of her brothers were happy to see Jared, and it didn't take long before they were exchanging stories and trying to one-up each other while reveling in their shared history. Jack sat back and soaked in the love that surrounded her. As she was sitting quietly, David leaned over and said, "I want to talk to you later about this black eye," he said, quietly tracing the outline of her eye.

Jack's eyes met Jared's. "Daddy, it's nothing. You know, the usual, one of the girls Caleb dated last summer knew just enough about our family to get nasty," Jack said, shrugging her shoulders.

"She was a bitch," Bobby said. "And Jack had every right to take a swing at her. The little bitch said Momma chose to die instead of raise Jack as baby girl Johnson," Bobby said protectively. Everyone at the fire got quiet and focused on Jack and David.

"Well you know how I feel about fighting, Princess. There is always a better way to handle a situation besides fists. I'll assume that there was no other way because I trust you, so I have only one other question, and I guess it's the most important one. Did you kick her ass?" David said quietly.

Everyone burst out laughing. "Jack had her in the sweetest chokehold you've ever seen. We were all very proud," Bobby said laughing. Jack glanced at Jared, who was laughing, and he too looked proud.

"Does anybody see the craziness in this conversation besides me?" Marcus commented. "If you don't do something to reel her in, Daddy, she is going to get into trouble, mark my words. I'm going to bed. Goodnight," he said, getting on a four-wheeler and heading back to the main house.

"What a buzzkill," Caleb said sarcastically.

David stood up. "He means well. I'm beat too; I'll see you all in the morning." He kissed the top of Jack's head. "Why don't you come with me, Princess, and let the boys finish their beer."

Jack got up slowly and stole a glance at Jared. "See you tomorrow, Princess," Jared said oh so casually.

Jack was reading in bed when she heard the tapping on her window. Smiling to herself, she opened the window. Jared grasped her face and kissed her deeply.

"Fuck, I miss you so much! I wanted to touch you all night."

"Come in," Jack said, moving away from the window.

"I can't. I just had to kiss you good night," Jared whispered in a reluctant voice.

"Please, just for a little while. I'll lock the door so we won't have any surprises," Jack pleaded.

"Okay, lock the door and I will come in until you fall asleep," Jared said as he climbed in the window.

Jared sat down on the wrought iron bed and stared at Jack. She was wearing nothing but a Portland Pirates T-shirt that she must have stolen from Ty.

"Jesus, Jack, you're gorgeous," Jared whispered, eyeing her long legs.

"Thank you. You're not so bad yourself," she said, snuggling into his arms and bringing his mouth to hers.

Moaning, Jared broke off the kiss. "Sleep, Princess. Really, you're killing me here. Just let me hold you while you fall asleep. I'll see you tomorrow. How about a swim when you get up and about?" Jared said stroking her face.

"Mmm, that sounds nice," Jack said, already falling asleep.

Jack slowly woke up to someone softly brushing the hair out of her eyes and the smell of fresh coffee. Opening her eyes, she saw Marcus sitting on the side of the bed with two cups of coffee. He smiled and offered her a cup.

"Forgive me for being an ass?" he asked.

Jack sat up and took the coffee and smiled. "Forgiven," she said, taking a sip.

"You know it's just because I worry about you that I get upset. I was the first person in this family to hold you after you were born, you know," Marcus said softly. "It was the worst and best day of my life. I swore that day when I held you that I would always protect you," he said, looking Jack in the eye.

"I know, Marcus, and I love you for it, but I'm not a child anymore. You need to let me have my own life. I'm tired of being safe and tucked away. I need to breathe. Please trust me," Jack said, putting her hand in his.

"Okay, deal," Marcus said, kissing the back of her hand. "Now get up and grab some breakfast. Dad is getting the boat ready for waterskiing, and Caleb said he was going to kick your ass on the slalom course today," Marcus teased.

"Yeah, right, he is. Ass-clown," Jack mumbled.

"Classy," Marcus grinned as he left the room.

When she arrived at the pond, Daddy was towing Jared and Bobby behind the boat. It was a perfect July day. It was hot with a light breeze off the water, and the pond was like a mirror. Perfect for waterskiing. Jack grabbed her skis and vest and went down to the dock to wait her turn.

"There's our little sleeper," Bear said, splashing her. Marcus was in the boat spotting for the water skiers.

"Any pushing yet?" Jack asked.

"Not yet, but Bobby was trying to get close to Jared to push him a few minutes ago," Ty said.

Henry, Garrett, and Davey were laying on the dock lifeless.

"Are you guys hungover?" Jack asked.

"We may or may not have polished off a bottle of Jack Daniel's last night," Henry replied.

"Spoken like a true lawyer," Garrett said, chuckling.

"I think I'm going to let the sun bake the poison out of me," Davey groaned. Bear was standing in the water at the end of the dock, and Caleb was sitting on the dock beside Jack.

"So, any new tricks up your sleeve this summer, Princess?" Caleb taunted.

"Um, actually yes. I'm going to try something new. I'm going out alone before we do the course," Jack said.

"Well, are you going to tell us?" Caleb asked sarcastically.

She shook her head. "No, I'm going to show you. All in good time, grasshopper," Jack said, sliding her skis on and getting in the water. The boat did a big circle as Jared and Bobby let go of the rope and sank slowly into the water close to the dock. David saw Jack in the water and began changing the rope tow to the one Jack had asked him to buy. "Are you sure you want to try this, Princess?" David asked.

"I'm sure. Then I want to watch Caleb do it." Jack grinned.

"I will spot," Jared said, climbing in the boat.

"Yeah, me too. I want to see this from the boat," Caleb said, climbing in the boat too.

David made a few turns around the lake with Jack behind the boat so Jack could get in the groove. She dropped a ski in front of the dock on one of the turns around the pond and sliced back and forth behind the boat. When the boat was about to circle back in front of the dock, Jack lifted the foot that was not attached to her ski from behind and slowly lifted her long leg. She wobbled a little but managed to wedge her foot in the special leather loop in the handlebar. Slowly, she took her hands off the bar and lifted her arms in the air. Laughing, Jack could hear her brothers from the dock whistling and yelling as the boys in the boat gave her thumbs up. Jack managed to ski quite a distance before she noticed some waves from another boat coming at her, but by then it was too late. Jack's ski hit the wave and launched her in the air, erasing her balance. Luckily, her foot dislodged from the leather holster as she very disgracefully flew backward and hit the water with a big splash.

The boys in the boat hollered at David to kill the engine and Jared launched himself over the side of the boat and swam toward her. Jack came up coughing and looking for her ski when Jared grabbed her.

"Are you hurt?" he cried out, urgently holding her waist under water.

"No, no, I'm fine. It was those waves that got me," she said smiling. "Not bad for my first try though, right?"

"Jesus, Jack, why do you have to take so many risks?" Jared said frustrated.

"What? I'm okay, really," she said as her father pulled up with the boat.

"You okay, Princess?" David asked.

"Yeah, I'm fine," Jack replied as she climbed into the boat.

"Very impressive. You want to try that, Caleb?" David said, laughing.

"Ah, no, not today," Caleb retorted as Jack and David high-fived.

The rest of the day passed as they floated and lazed about the pond. In the late afternoon, they headed up to the main house to get changed and then walked to the park for a cookout and fireworks. Jack hadn't had a chance to talk to Jared alone and felt that he was still a little put out with her for her waterskiing trick. Jack took special care with her appearance and wished she had asked Mac to come by earlier instead of meeting at the park. She could have really used her expertise in the makeup department.

Jack let her long curls air dry and then pinned the sides back for a flower child look. This gave her a great idea. She went to the dining room table, plucked a few daisies from the vase, and wound them into her hair. With a minimal amount of makeup and a squirt of perfume, Jack observed her reflection in the mirror. The pretty white sundress was form-fitting through the bust area and a little fuller skirt skimmed her thighs. She had new red sandals that completed the outfit. She smiled at her reflection. *I hope this makes him forget he is cross with me,* Jack thought as she twirled and left her room.

David and some of the boys had already gone to the park to help Gracie set things up. Jared and Bear were in the kitchen waiting for her. When she entered the kitchen, they just stared at her. She grabbed her jacket and turned to them.

"What? Are we ready?" Jack asked. Jared and Bear cleared their throats and looked away.

"Um, yeah, let's go," Jared said, moving toward the door. "Your helmet is on the bike, Princess," Bear said.

"Bike? Bear, do you really think I'm riding on the back of your bike in this dress?" Jack said, looking down.

"You always used to like riding with me," Bear replied in a sad voice.

"I do. I love it, just not today. I'll ride with Jared," she said, kissing his cheek.

"All right. I'll see you guys there," Bear said, walking out the door.

With the sound of Bear's bike in the distance, Jared turned and gathered Jack against the porch wall and took her mouth in a desperate kiss. Jack moaned and captured his tongue and gently sucked. The kiss deepened and Jack wound her arms around his neck to bring him closer. Jared obliged and ground his erection into her soft sex.

"Jack, I want you," Jared moaned.

"Mmm, I can't wait to be alone with you again," Jack whispered between kisses.

Jared cupped her cheeks and looked at her. "You look beautiful, Jack. Thank God your brothers are here because I would have to punch any guy that looked at you tonight," he said, kissing her again. "No guy dares to look at you with your brothers around," Jared said, taking her hand and walking her to the truck.

Jack stopped him at the truck so she could look at him. Yum. Jared had on old worn Levi's that hung off his hips nicely and a black T-shirt that skimmed his muscles perfectly. His Celtic shoulder tattoo peeked from under the sleeve of his shirt, and he was wearing worn leather flip-flops. His hair was a little wild, and he had a couple of days' growth of beard started.

Jack gently pushed him against the truck and leaned into him. "Um, just for the record, you look delicious and I want to lick you," she said nibbling on his lip. "And, if no one wants to see another catfight tonight, the women better stay way away from you. You're mine, sweetheart. All mine," Jack said possessively.

Jared gathered her face in his hands and looked deeply into her eyes. "I've always been yours, Princess," he said, kissing her gently.

Jack and Jared were walking into the park when Mac ran to greet them.

"Hi," Jack said hugging her.

"Hi," Mac said to them both.

"Let's find out about tables and you can stash your backpack there. I need to go help Gracie and you can help, okay?" Jack asked Mac.

"Sure, I'd love to," Mac replied.

When they found their table, her brothers were already there on their first beer.

"Some of you guys haven't met Mac yet," Jack said, immediately lifting her hand to Caleb. "Don't even say it, moron."

Marcus, Henry, Garrett, and Davey got up and hugged Mac. Bear got up and hugged her, lifting her off the ground and twirling her around. "Hey there, Red, can I call you Red?" Bear asked.

Laughing, Mac said "Um, sure! Jack, you were right."

"See! He can't help himself," Jack said, laughing.

The girls went off to find Jack's father and Gracie to help set up for the picnic. Jack could feel Jared's eyes following her. She turned around and shot a quick smile in his direction.

After the cookout, Jack and Mac took a blanket and spread it out a few feet from the tables to lie down and watch the fireworks. A few minutes before the fireworks were to begin, Chad and Tom came over and sat down with the girls. Jared glared at the foursome.

Caleb noticed the boys sitting with Jack and Mac. He nudged Bear to look over at the girls. Bear started to get up.

"Sit down, Bear, let her be," Marcus said firmly. Bear looked at Marcus for a moment and then slowly sat down, never taking his eyes off the foursome on the blanket.

"We need to trust her. It can't be much fun for her to have us constantly smothering her," Marcus said.

"Well he better keep his fucking hands to himself," Bear said gruffly.

Great. Just fucking great, thought Jared. *Let's get these damn fireworks over with already.*

The show was spectacular as usual, but Jared didn't see any of the lights in the sky. He was too focused on the foursome on the blanket. When the fireworks were over, Chad and Tom walked Jack and Mac back to the table. David came forward and put his arm around Jack. "You two are the bravest boys here tonight," David said, holding out his hand.

"Why is that, Mr. Johnson?" Tom asked.

David motioned toward the table. "These are Jack's brothers, and I have never seen a boy brave enough to talk to her when they are around," he replied, grinning.

Needless to say, the boys suddenly remembered they needed to be somewhere and quickly left the park. Jack and Mac rode home with Jared. Jack sat next to Jared and held his hand. It felt nice not to have to hide from anyone even if it was only for a minute.

As soon as they were all home, David told them to grab their instruments. Jack made herself comfortable at the piano and gave Mac the tambourine. The boys grabbed their guitars, and Jared took a seat at the drums. They played music and laughed well into the night. When they had played their last song, David said it was time to call it a night. Jack looked at Jared and said good night to everyone. Jack and Mac went to her room and talked until they each fell asleep midconversation.

By the time Jack and Mac made their way out to the kitchen Sunday morning, it wasn't morning any longer but noonish, and there wasn't a soul around. Jack went hunting and found Bebe in the den knitting.

"Is everyone gone, Bebe?" Jack asked, bending to give her a kiss on the forehead.

"I'm afraid so, Princess. They had planes to catch and places to be. Your Daddy said he will call you later this week," she said. Jack wandered back to the kitchen to find Mac pulling out ingredients from the cupboards.

"I'm dying to make some cinnamon buns—do you mind?" Mac asked.

"Please do," Jack replied enthusiastically.

After a delicious breakfast, the two walked down to the pond for a swim and found Jared, Bobby, Ty, and Caleb all jumping in Jared's truck.

"Where are you guys going?" Jack asked.

"We're going to the river crossing; would you like to come?" Jared asked, looking at Jack.

"Ah, hell yeah!" Jack exclaimed.

Jared looked at the boys. "Out. You guys get in the back."

"You heard the man. Out!" Jack laughed.

Bobby, Ty, and Caleb got out of the truck and Caleb caught Mac's hand. "You can ride in the back with us, Red," Caleb said flirting.

Jack smacked his hand away. "Down boy," she commanded and climbed in the truck with Mac right behind her. Jared looked longingly at Jack and put the truck in gear.

They swam at the river crossing and jumped off the rope swing, each trying to outdo the others' heights and splashes. Mac could not be convinced to try the rope no matter how hard she was coaxed. When they were all tired, but more importantly when the boys were hungry, they headed home. Jared dropped Mac off at her house and stopped at the main house to see what Bebe had prepared for dinner.

Nothing, that's what Bebe had made for dinner. A note was propped up on the counter telling them that she was at a knitters' circle and there were leftovers in the fridge. Bobby, Ty, and Caleb decided to go into town and grab a pizza and see what was going on. Jared said he was just going home.

The boys headed down the driveway, and Jared came back in the house and walked straight to Jack, picking her up and putting her on the counter. He kissed her desperately, his tongue making love with hers and leaning into her to be as close as possible. Jack moaned and tried to deepen the kiss.

Jared embraced her face and looked into her eyes. "I need you, Jack. Will you come the cottage with me for a while? Please," he said, kissing her eyes and nose and mouth lightly.

"Yes," Jack replied breathlessly.

Jared helped her down and took her hand to lead her to the truck. Once inside the cabin, Jared locked the door, led her to the bedroom, closed the door.

"Let me help you out of that wet bathing suit," he said, smiling as he lifted her T-shirt over her head, quickly followed by her bikini top. As Jared stared at Jack's hard nipples, his pulse quickened and his hands went to touch her breasts. Jared let his thumbs stroke the hard nubs, and Jack let her head fall back as she groaned with desire. Jared leaned down, captured a breast in his mouth, and suckled. Jack grabbed his head in her hands and moaned again, this time longer.

"Jared," was the only word she could form. She was on fire, and she needed to touch him. Jack pulled at his shirt; he came up and helped her pull it over his head as he maneuvered her toward the bed. They both climbed on the bed, kneeling and embracing each other, touching as much skin as they could.

Jared grabbed Jack's ass and ground it against his hard-on. "I can't take my time, baby," he said, grinding his hips into hers. "Jesus, I need to be inside you," Jared said, pushing her onto her back and sliding her bikini bottoms off and unbuckling his jeans and pulling them off. Jared leaned over and got a condom from the bedside drawer.

Jack could hear the package ripping and watched him slide it on. God, he was big; she would never get used to the fact that she stretched to accommodate him. Jared leaned over her and took her breast in his mouth as he reached to spread her legs. He slowly rubbed along her opening, making Jack gasp as she let her legs fall wide apart. When Jared inserted two fingers, he felt her wetness. Jesus, the white hot response to that made his hands shake. Jared rolled on top of Jack and in one swift pump completely filled her.

"Oh God, you're so tight," he said, starting to pump in and out of her. "Baby, talk to me, I'm so close I can't stand it. So tight, Jesus," Jared muttered. He was clearly in stream of consciousness mode as he pumped into her relentlessly.

Jack was right there with him. She had never felt such a fevered need to find a release. "Jared! Harder, faster, please!" Jack screamed.

Jared couldn't stop himself. He pumped into her like a man driven beyond desire, and Jack's cries of release sent him over the edge, crying out and kissing her passionately as he came violently.

Several long minutes later, they both floated back down to Earth. *Jesus, will it always be this intense?* he wondered.

After several moments of trying to catch their breath, Jared rolled to her side and brought her in close, kissing her temple. "Wow," he said against her temple.

"I second that emotion," Jack whispered back.

They were each content to lie quietly in each other's arms and just enjoy their alone time until Jack broke the silence. "I've been thinking," Jack said, starting to trace her fingers lightly over his chest. Jared picked up her fingers and brought them to his mouth and started sucking on her finger.

"Mmm, tell me what you're thinking and I'll tell you what I'm thinking," Jared replied grinning.

Jack gasped as sudden heat warmed her nether regions. She pulled her hand away and turned to lay her body on his chest looking at him. "I'm being serious. I was thinking that if you go to Boston in September, I will tell Daddy that I'm ready to go away to school. I already have early acceptance to Harvard, which will be close to you. Just a train ride away. I could at least start a semester early, in January. I think that's reasonable. We could see each other on weekends. What?" Jack said as Jared frowned and shook his head. "You don't want me to be close?" Jack asked, holding her breath.

"No, Princess, that's not it. Of course I want you close by, but there are a lot of *ifs* in there," Jared said, taking a deep breath. "First, I don't think your father is going to be very happy about 'us,' and second, I haven't got the internship yet," he said, tucking her hair behind her ear.

"Well, my father is just going to have to get used to 'us,' because that's not going to change, and of course you're going to get the internship. You're brilliant with computer software," Jack said, kissing his chest.

"Jack, sweetheart, your father doesn't think I'm good enough for you— and he's right," Jared said as Jack bolted to her knees. "At least not yet," he continued as he sat up and took her face in his hands, looking deeply into her eyes.

Jack shook her head. "Stop. Please stop, Jared. Why would you say that or even think that?" Jack said in a frustrated tone.

"Shh, Jack, he told me that last summer when he saw that things were changing between us," Jared replied, tracing his thumb across her lower lip.

"What? Jared, you're one of us. You always have been. How could he say such a thing?" Jack cried out, shaking her head as tears started to fall. Jared stilled her head with his hands and brushed the tears away with his thumbs.

"Because you're his Princess and he loves you fiercely, baby. I wouldn't want it any other way. I am going to be worthy of you one day, I promise," Jared said, kissing her.

A moment later, Jack's cell phone pinged with a text message. Jared broke off the kiss. "You should get that," he whispered, grabbing her cell phone off the nightstand.

It was Ty. "Where r u?" the message read.

"The boys must be home," Jack said sighing. "At the pond, b home soon," she texted back as Jared watched. Sighing again, Jack tossed her phone onto the bed and touched Jared's cheek.

"We need to talk about this some more," she proclaimed firmly. Jared took her hand and brought her palm to his lips.

"No, we don't, baby. The only thing worth mentioning is that I did try to stay away from you and not think about you, but I couldn't. I couldn't because I love you, Princess. I love you so much," he whispered.

Jack couldn't breathe. She stared and swallowed hard. "I love you too, Jared, so much," Jack said breathlessly and kissed Jared as the emotions surged through her.

"I need to get you home," Jared said, breaking the kiss and smiling. They both dressed and Jared walked her up the gravel road leading to the main house. The loons were calling to each other in the distance as they made their way hand-in-hand in the moonlight.

The weeks passed in a beautiful summer haze. The diner was busy, and Gracie was gearing up for the town's summer celebration, which would take place at the pond this year. Gracie had talked David into hosting this year's celebration with the one condition that she did all the planning, which meant Jack was part of the planning as well. Jack was excited to be helping out and recruited Mac to help as well. The party consisted of a cookout and swimming on Saturday afternoon and into the evening, with different local bands playing on the platform stage that Jared, Ty, and Bobby had built on the beach. The town's people could come by car or truck and park in the field or they could come by boat and tie up at the dock. Jack had the boys carrying chairs to the beach and making space for multiple grills to be set up.

Saturday morning brought a gorgeous late July day, perfect for the planned festivities. David called to say he would be there shortly and that he was bringing an old friend. Bebe and her friends were busy in the kitchen preparing salads and sweets. With the whole house bustling, Mac and Jack went to her room to get dressed. They each threw on their bathing suits and cover-ups that looked like summer dresses.

As Mac curled Jack's long hair, she seemed preoccupied. "Um, can I ask you a question?" Mac asked.

"Of course, Mac Daddy, anything," Jack replied, applying lipstick.

"Can you tell me about your brother, Davey?" Mac said shyly.

"Whoa, stop the train!" Jack said looking at Mac in the mirror. "Are you crushing on Davey?" Jack said, smiling.

Mac fidgeted uncomfortably. "Maybe? Would that bother you?" Mac asked, looking concerned.

"No! I'm just playing with you, really!" Jack laughed. "Davey is a sweetheart. You already know that he's a gifted chef. He's sweet and always takes my side when I fight with Caleb. I'm pretty sure eventually he will own a famous restaurant. He had a steady girlfriend all through high school and then she dumped him when they were at college and broke his heart, the bitch," Jack said, shrugging her shoulders. "He's a great guy, really. Now I think we should make our way to the pond to see what needs to be done."

"So you're okay with me fantasizing about your brother for the next year until I go to New York and marry him?" Mac said, grinning.

"Sweetheart, you were born to be part of this family," Jack said, smiling back.

People were starting to arrive at the pond, and Mac and Jack found her brothers and Jared hanging out with Jared's mountain crew. Soon the young women were flocking to their little corner of the beach vying for the guys' attention. This was going to be a long day, thought Jack, watching the girls flirting. Jack knew that her father expected her to act like a lady, but seriously, if one of those girls touched Jared, she was going to punch someone. To distract herself, she grabbed Mac and walked to the water, where some kids were playing.

"I had to get away from there," Jack said, taking off her cover-up and tossing it on the beach.

"Seriously, does that happen all the time around your brothers? It's embarrassing to our sex the way they drool all over them. I mean, really, have some dignity already," Mac said, tossing her cover-up on the beach with Jack's. Together they waded out in the water toward the float.

Every guy who was not a Johnson was looking directly at Jack and Mac as they stripped down to their bikinis. Jared's hands fisted. Did she even have any idea what her body in that white bikini was doing to every guy who was not related to her? Jesus, this was going to be a long-assed day, he thought, as he went to change into his swim trunks. Time to ward off the sharks, he thought to himself, with a scowl.

It was a good turnout, with plenty of beach volleyball and king of the float for the young people. The older folks just relaxed and caught up on current events and talked about how brutal the past winter had been. Lying on the dock with Mac, Jack spotted her father walking toward her with two people she didn't know.

"Princess, I'd like to introduce you to an old college friend of mine and his son. This is Jim Green and his son, Trevor. Jim, Trevor, this is my daughter, Jack, and her friend, Mac," David said beaming.

"It's nice to meet you, ladies. It looks like you will see Trevor next year at Harvard. He's leaving in September," Jim said, patting his son's back. Trevor looked embarrassed. He was very easy on the eyes. If there was a stereotypical preppy Harvard student, Trevor would be the poster boy, thought Jack. He stood about five-foot-nine—short, in Jack's opinion. He had short blond hair, perfect teeth, and an easy smile.

"It's nice to meet you both. Feel free to have a seat on the dock if you like. It looks like we will be eating shortly," Jack said, gesturing toward the dock. Trevor was easy to talk to, and Mac seemed to really enjoy his company. David and Jim walked over to Jared's cabin, where the boys were sitting around the fire pit. Jack could see David gesturing toward the dock, and suddenly she felt Jared's cold stare. *Shit*. What was she supposed to do? Lord, she was sick of the men in her life dictating who she could talk to and who she spent time with. It was perfectly okay for gaggles of lustful women to hang around Jared. He just sloughed it off as "they weren't really there for him" but for her brothers. *Yeah, right.*

As if on cue, Jack spied a petite brunette sashaying over to the fire pit. Jack returned the cold stare as she saw Jared grab a beer for bitch brunette. A rolling anger bubbled in Jack's stomach. Two could play at that game.

"Trevor, how would you like to take a tour of the pond?" Jack asked flirtatiously.

"Sure, I'd love a tour, but won't that get me beat up?" he asked.

"Excuse me?" Jack said, standing up.

"Um, I'm sure you're aware that there's a dark-haired guy over there that would like to see me dead…at least that's the vibe I'm getting. Is he yours or yours?" Trevor said, pointing to her and Mac.

Mac whipped her head around and looked. "Not me!" Mac said a little too quickly. Jack glared at her. "What?" Mac said looking innocent.

"Whatever," Jack said, shrugging and smirking.

"It's fine, really; boat ride?" Jack said, untying the small fishing boat. The three of them piled in and Jack maneuvered the small boat across the pond toward the point, all the while feeling cold eyes drilling into her back.

Jack showed Trevor all the camps along the shore of the pond. He seemed a little bored, which gave Jack a very bad idea. "How would you guys like to jump off the train trestle?" Jack asked, slowing the motor down.

"What! Are you serious?" Mac asked.

"Yes! It's actually a tradition that you have to jump at least once every summer. My brothers have been doing it forever, but I just jumped with Caleb last year, and I haven't jumped yet this year. Come on, you'll love it!" Jack exclaimed, gunning the engine toward the trestle.

As they sat in the boat looking up at the trestle, Mac shook her head. "You're crazy. She's crazy, you know. You don't have to do it," she said to Trevor.

"Actually, I'm on the diving team and high dive is my specialty," Trevor said, taking his shirt off.

"No way, me too!" Jack snorted as she dived out of the boat.

The worst part of the jump was the climb up. It was up about thirty feet, with rocks and broken glass scattered about. Once up on the trestle, Jack turned to Trevor.

"Are you okay?" she asked. He nodded and suddenly dove in. Jack was very impressed and she quickly followed.

When they got back to the beach, food was being served and the three walked to grab their plates. Jared and Jack's brothers, along with most of the mountain crew, were standing by the utensil table.

"Hey, there you guys are. Where'd you go?" Bobby said, tugging on Jack's wet hair.

"Oh. My. God. These two just jumped off the trestle. They're crazy!" Mac said, laughing until she saw Jack's face. Oh shit. Jack had forgotten to tell them not to mention the trestle. Her brothers had been forbidden by their father to ever take Jack there or they would suffer the consequences.

Jared grabbed Jack's arm tightly. "You jumped off the trestle?" Jared said in a low voice. Jack could smell hard liquor on his breath. She yanked her arm away.

"What is the problem? Jesus, you guys do it all the time. Besides, I haven't done it yet this year…" Jack retorted as her voice trailed off.

"This year?" Bobby asked, looking at Caleb.

"What? She was always tagging along last year, and I didn't think she would actually jump," Caleb admitted while glaring at Jack.

"Enough. I don't have to answer to any of you," she said, glaring back at all of them with her eyes eventually landing on Jared. Jared lifted his hand and stepped back and crossed his arms. Jack was sick of this game between her and Jared. She stepped over to him.

"Can I talk to you for a minute?" Jack said quietly. Jared looked at her coldly.

"You should get your friends something to eat, Princess," he said as bitch brunette brought him another beer and slyly handed him a small flask. Jack just stared at him. She was sure everyone could hear her heartbeat thundering in her chest. With shaking hands, Jack picked up plates for the three of them and turned away.

Jack brought them back to the dock to eat their dinner. She suddenly had zero appetite. *What the fuck?* Jack thought to herself as she sat crossed-legged on the dock. "I'm sorry about this," Jack said to Trevor as she started to cry a little. She sat with her back to the beach so no one would be able to see her fall apart. "I don't know why he's acting like this," she said.

Trevor nodded. "I do. He's jealous. I get it. I don't blame him a bit. I have a girlfriend, and if this situation happened to me, I would be rip-shit too. Do you want me to talk to him?" Trevor asked, rubbing her arm.

"No! I mean, no. Thanks anyway, but I think I will wait until tomorrow to discuss this with him. He has to be able to talk to me and to trust me, you know?" Jack replied, wiping her eyes and smiling weakly. "Tell me about your girlfriend," she said, and the three of them talked until the band started to play on the beach.

Jack needed a break from the tension, so she suggested that they head up to the main house so they could change out of their bathing suits and maybe, considering who was in the house, have a shot or two. All was quiet at the house. *Thank God,* thought Jack. She turned on the stereo and she and Mac headed to her room to change. Putting on a summer dress and brushing her snarled hair made her feel a little better.

Jack went through the liquor cabinet and grabbed the Jim Beam and three shot glasses. Trevor showed them a hilarious drinking game that they played for about an hour (or three shots later). Jack grabbed her cowboy boots and they headed back to the pond with a warm tingle in Jack's belly.

The music was playing and everyone looked as though they were having a great time. At least it looked like Jared was having a great time. He was at the fire pit with the members of his mountain crew. To his credit, and their safety, there weren't any women hanging off him as he joked and laughed at something the guys were talking about. Jack, Mac, and Trevor joined her brothers and others dancing in front of the band on the beach. Out of the corner of her eye, Jack saw Jared go into the woods along a path leading to an old bathroom and shower building that was still in use since the property had been a camp for youths. No one knew about this path except the family. Jack told Mac that she would be back and headed up the path to talk to Jared. Jack could run this path blindfolded if she had to. She knew every knot and stump in the old path.

When she got to the bathrooms, everything was quiet and dark. "Jared," Jack hissed as she walked around the building.

"Go back to your friends, Princess," Jared hissed back as he leaned against the building.

"No, I'm not going anywhere. What the fuck is your problem anyway?" Jack exclaimed, putting her hands on her hips.

Jared banged his head twice against the building before throwing his empty beer bottle into the woods, smashing it against a tree. "No, that would be too much to fucking ask, wouldn't it, to actually do something you're asked to do? Why the fuck don't you just go back to your Harvard friend, because that's where you belong. Just go. Get the fuck away from me," Jared said, starting to walk away.

Jack grabbed his arm. "Jared, please——" she began. Jared grabbed her by both arms and pushed her roughly against the building.

"Jared, please what? Jared, please fuck me? Jared, please visit me at Harvard? Jared, please wait for me? What, Jack? What the fuck do you want from me?" Jared growled at her.

Tears stung Jack's eyes. "Jared, you're hurting me. Stop. Why are you acting like this?" she said as the tears fell.

Jared inhaled sharply. "Stop crying right now! You're acting like a child who can't get her way. What is it you want, Princess? Do you want me to fuck you? Is that what you're after, and then you can go back to your new friend?" Jared growled roughly in her ear. He brought his mouth down on hers in a punishing kiss. Jared cruelly held her head as he deepened the kiss. Despite the roughness, Jack felt electric shocks pulsate through her body, ending with a desperate heat between her legs. Jack moaned into the kiss as their breathing came in gasps.

Jared suddenly grabbed her shoulders, turned her around against the building, and kicked her legs apart. He pulled her dress up around her waist and ripped her panties in two, yanking them off. His hand was between her legs in an instant as he sunk two fingers into her soaking wet core. "See how fucking wet you are, baby?" he muttered, bringing his fingers to his mouth beside her ear and sucking on them. "Well, let me give you what you want," he muttered again darkly, unbuckling his jeans, and in one swift movement he pulled her hips out and drove himself into her all the way.

Jack gasped and would have fallen, but Jared pushed her back against the building and started pumping into her. Hard.

There was pain. Jack didn't know if it was from his size and the angle or from him being so rough, but despite the pain, Jack could feel the stirring deep in her belly of something roaring for release.

"Jared!" Jack cried out with her face flush against the building.

Jared grabbed her hair and roughly pulled her head back. "Come for me, baby! This is what you want from me isn't it, Princess? Come now!"

As if on cue, she couldn't help herself. Jack erupted as the strongest orgasm of her life bloomed inside her. Jared could feel her muscles contract around him like a vise as he completely shattered and came long and hard with her.

Still leaning against the building trying to catch his breath, Jared pulled out of her. Jack's back went pin straight and she turned and walked a few feet away.

"Jack, I..." Jared said sorrowfully. Jack stopped walking and stood ramrod straight with her back to him. She dabbed her tongue to the inside of her lip, tasting blood. "I'm going into the bathroom to wash up and get myself together, and when I come out, I want you to be fucking gone," she said coldly. With an eerie calmness about her, Jack walked into the bathroom, where she fell completely apart.

When Jack came out of the bathroom, Jared was gone. She was tired... so very tired. Jack went to find Mac and go home. The party was definitely over for her.

Jared groaned as he became conscious. Where the fuck was he? It seemed familiar but surreal at the same time. Garbage——he smelled garbage and piss. Ah, now he knew where he was, his father's house. Jared felt in his jeans pocket, hoping like hell they weren't there. *Please, please, please don't be there.*

He slowly pulled out Jack's ripped panties.

Jesus. What had he done? He knew goddamn well what had taken place at the pond. He hadn't been that drunk, but the combination of drunk and jealous beyond reason had provided him with enough stupidity to lash out and hurt the only good thing in his pathetic life. Did he feel so goddamn worthless that he needed to sabotage the one sliver of love that had managed to find him?

Yes, apparently he did. The image of Jack standing with her back to him, telling him to be the fuck gone came to the forefront of his brain, making him bolt to the bathroom and vomit his guts out. On and on he heaved, replaying each hurtful word and each rough act that he had inflicted on Jack. The words echoed in his brain like an old worn VHS tape. She would never forgive him. Hell, he would never forgive himself for treating her like that. He knew he didn't deserve her, and hurting her was totally unacceptable. If there had been a sword available he would have gladly fallen on it to stop the constant replay of her crying and him fucking her from behind like she was a fucking whore.

More heaving. His guts were turning inside out. He passed out on the filthy, pissy bathroom floor, thankful that at least the dirty linoleum was cool under his cheek.

Some time later, Jared was pulled out of his coma-like state by someone tapping his shoulder with their boot.

"Hey, boy, get the hell up, you pussy. I gotta take a piss," his father yelled at him. Jared slowly rolled over and hoisted himself up. Fuck, he hurt all over.

"What time is it?" Jared said hoarsely.

"It's suppertime, you piece of shit. You've been lazing about here all god-damn day. Don't be such a pussy; just go pour yourself a goddamn drink, and you'll feel better," Billy snorted as he started taking his piss.

Jared staggered outside to his truck and squealed out of his father's drive-way. He had driven there last night in hopes to drown the demon that had him tightly in its clutches. As he downed the fifth of Jim Beam he had been treated to a steady stream of invectives by his father about how worthless he was and that his own mother couldn't stand him. It had been the perfect ending to a perfect shithole of a day. The fact that it was of his own making twisted his guts to the point of heaving again, only there was nothing left to heave.

Jared managed to make it to the diner and staggered into the back kitchen, where Gracie was preparing food for the next day. Gracie took one look at him and ran to get him a chair.

"Jesus, baby, what happened to you?" Gracie asked, wetting a cloth to put on his head.

"I fucked up, Gracie. I fucked up big time," Jared moaned. Gracie pulled a chair up beside his and simply held him. It was too much kindness for Jared to handle, so he cried until the tears ran dry. He couldn't remember the last time he had let himself cry like that. He was pretty sure the last time had been when his real life angel, Elsie Johnson, had come into his life, but like everyone else, she had deemed him unworthy and left him.

"You think I don't know, mister man? I know. I have eyes in my head. I see the way you two look at each other. Actually, you know what it reminds me of? David and Elsie Johnson. Jesus, those two were like dynamite and a match. It was a powerful love, no doubt about it. David doesn't know, does he?" Gracie said as she got up to rummage through the fridge.

"No," Jared replied in a drained voice.

Gracie started making Jared a ham and egg breakfast sandwich and poured him some orange juice.

"This is certainly a pickle you two have gotten yourselves in," she said, handing him the juice. "David is not going to accept anyone for his Princess. It's like she is the last best piece of Elsie he has left, and he is not going to give her up easily."

"It doesn't matter anyway, Gracie, Jack is never going speak to me again after last night," Jared replied sadly.

Gracie laughed. "Oh, she'll speak to you, baby, mark my words. A love that big doesn't just disappear in a puff of smoke," she said, shaking her head. "Oh, if I could just sit down and have a glass of wine with my best friend Elsie and tell her all the goings on. Oh, she knows, she knows," she said to herself, laughing some more and shaking her head. "Look what you put into motion, my friend," Gracie ended, staring at the ghost of Elsie with a sad faraway look on her face.

Gracie put Jared's sandwich in a bag and proceeded to order him to go home, take a shower, eat, and then go directly to bed. Jared finally made a good decision and followed orders.

After Jack and Mac woke up Sunday morning, Jack suggested that they go to the mall in Portland and stay at the house in Portland for the night. Jack needed to get away from everything for a while so she could breathe. Her heart was breaking in two.

Jack waited at Mac's house while Mac packed a bag, and then away to Portland they went. They proceeded to spend all of Jack's accumulated paychecks on food and mani-pedis and some killer shoes, all of which Jack couldn't have cared less about.

However, it was so nice to have Mac there with her to take her mind off the awful, sick feeling she was carrying around inside her. Daddy was still in Massachusetts, so they had the giant house the family lived in during the winter all to themselves. Mac just wandered around in awe of how big and beautiful the house was.

"I don't think my mother really liked the ostentatiousness of this mansion," Jack said. "I think her heart was really in Harmony always, but my Dad had a growing business—not to mention they had nine kids—so they needed lots of room. But somehow, I don't know how I know this, but my mother really just wanted her family and the simple things in life," Jack said dreamily. "I always fantasize about how we're so much alike, but I feel it in my bones that I really don't need all of this," Jack declared as she lifted her arms to show the house and material luxuries. "I feel like she left me one great gift in lieu of raising me—the gift of truly appreciating the love and people who surround me. Crazy, huh?" Jack said, shrugging her shoulders.

"No, I don't think you're crazy at all," Mac said, hugging Jack. "I think you're the best friend I've ever had or ever will have."

Jack put her arm around her best friend's shoulder. "Oh, Mac Daddy, how about we go into the den and watch the biggest goddamn TV you have ever seen? There must be a horror movie of some sort on," Jack replied, laughing.

Jack called Gracie and told her she was stuck in Portland but would be in to work on Tuesday morning if that was okay. Jack and Mac lounged around the pool on Monday, and in the late afternoon they headed back to Harmony. Mac dropped Jack off after dinner on Monday night and went home herself, tired from staying up most of the night talking about what the hell Jack was going to do about her present situation. Jack figured doing nothing worked as well as anything. She was sorry for her behavior, as childish as it was, but it in no way negated Jared's horrible treatment of her. He obviously didn't trust her or feel she had a brain to make responsible life choices. She wasn't going to feel bad about Trevor. He had been a perfect gentleman. She had done nothing wrong. What was this stupid shit Jared kept bringing up about how he didn't deserve her, and why did he keep making reference to her and Trevor going to Harvard? So what? He was going to Boston to be some big-time computer programmer. Jack really wished she had a mother to talk to about this bullshit, because her brain was ready to explode.

Jack walked in the house, and Bebe asked her if she would like dinner. "No, thank you, Bebe, I'm not hungry," Jack said, kissing Bebe on the cheek.

Bebe caught her face in her hands and looked deeply into her eyes. "What is it, ma petite? You look so thin and fragile," Bebe whispered.

Jack covered Bebe's hands with her own. "I'm going to be fine, really," Jack said, and Bebe nodded and kissed her forehead.

Jack threw her stuff in her room and went searching for her brothers. Jack found Ty lying on his bed watching the Red Sox on TV. Jack crawled on the bed and snuggled up to him.

"Hey, Princess, how was Portland?" he said, bringing her in close.

"Oh, the same," she replied in a monotone voice.

"Guess what?" Ty said. Jack shrugged her shoulders. "I got the call today. The Red Sox called me up. I might have a chance to get some meaningful playing time later this year," Ty said quietly.

Jack jerked up on the bed. "Oh my God! Ty, that's fantastic!" she exclaimed and hugged him.

"Thanks, I'm pretty psyched," he said as they hunkered down to watch the game.

Jack fell fast asleep on Ty's bed, so he put a blanket over her. It had never been unusual for Jack to wake up on any of her brothers' beds growing up. When she needed comfort, her brothers were willing to move heaven and earth to let her know that she was loved and cared for.

Tuesday morning, she woke up right on time and went to her room to shower and get ready for work. Ugh. Rain. Pouring down rain. *Well, that's just fantastic,* she thought to herself. With rain like this the boys probably wouldn't be making trails on the mountain today, so she was going to take the Suburban to work today. Screw them. They could bike into town to get the truck if need be.

She dressed in jean shorts rolled up and a white T-shirt and braided her hair down her back. She threw her cowboy boots on and grabbed her denim jacket and off she went.

Work was slow with no mountain workers and the rain. At three o'clock, Jack got off work and headed over to Mac's house to watch movies. She didn't see the point in rushing home to do nothing, but she wondered where Jared was. She kept her phone with her at all times so she wouldn't miss a call from him. She wondered if this was it as her heart broke. How could love be so fickle that with one fight, albeit a really bad one, he was giving up on them? She had moved past sad and hurt and was living in angry now.

Jack yawned. It was really late, and she needed to get home to bed. She said good-bye to Mac and her parents and headed home. It was a driving rain that made for a scary drive home. Once she parked the Suburban, she made a beeline for the porch. Just before she reached the door, she thought she heard something and turned around.

"I fucked up," Jared muttered as he stood in the pouring rain, his jeans and flannel shirt soaked. Jack just stared at him. Her heart was thudding against her ribcage. Jack just stared. Her breath leaked out of her in shallow gasps.

"Say something, Princess, please. I'm sorry. That's not enough, I know, but I am. I'm so fucking sorry," Jared whispered, walking closer to her. Jack just stared. She couldn't breathe. The hurt and anger was just choking her. She let out a small cry and brought her hand to her mouth to stifle it, staring at him.

"Jack, for fuck's sake, say something please! Scream, shout, cry, Jesus— just do something! I can't take this," Jared moaned, motioning toward her just standing there.

She couldn't move, and Jared started moving ever closer to her. Jack saw red. All of a sudden, the bottled up hurt and anger bubbled up and sent Jack over the edge. She lunged at Jared, catching him off guard and off balance. He caught her and they both fell to the ground, rolling around in the driveway. Jack beat her fist into Jared's chest, and he rolled over and on top of her, pinning her arms over her head.

"Stop, Jack, just stop. Talk to me. I can't stand this, it's killing me!" Jared cried in despair.

"You hurt me," Jack spat out at him, turning her head away and starting to sob. The fight completely left her, and her body started to shake.

"Oh, Jesus, baby, I know! I'm so sorry!" he cried out. He let go of her arms and completely covered her body with his to protect her from the rain as he held her tight.

"I can't do this. I can't make you trust me. I don't know what I'm doing here. I have no one to tell me it's going to be okay, because it's not okay. I'm not okay. I'm heartsick and I'm scared. I'm scared because I've lost you, and I don't even know why. Why can't you love and trust me?" Jack sobbed. Jared gathered her up and got in the back seat of the Suburban with her on his lap. Water was dripping everywhere. Jared was desperately trying to get her wet hair off her face. He couldn't stop touching her face.

"Fuck, Jack, I have no right to be here, but I can't stay away from you. I fucking love you more than I've ever loved anything ever. I'm broken, baby. I mean really seriously broken. That's no fucking excuse for what I did to you, but this is new to me too. I'm just trying to learn as I go, and I have fucked it up *big time,* I know that. I'm so sorry for hurting you, and I promise, I will never—"

Jack put her fingers over Jared's mouth. "No, no promises. I forgive you, and I'm sorry for being childish and making you jealous. I love you, Jared. You big fucking idiot. This love is so big. It scares the shit out of me. From now on if you're angry or jealous, please talk to me, please," Jack pleaded, touching his face and resting her forehead against his. Jared brought her mouth to his in a kiss so gentle it melted her heart.

"I love you so much, Princess," Jared said on a sob. Jack held his head with both arms as he cried and her tears mingled with his. They sat in the Suburban

102

for a while in silence. Jared eventually opened the door and lifted her out of the vehicle.

"Go in the house, get ready for bed, and unlock your window. I'm going to get a change of clothes, and I will come back and hold you until you fall asleep. I really need to hold you, baby," he said, walking her to the door. Jack nodded and went into the house.

About ten minutes later, Jared came through her window. They settled in the bed and Jack snuggled close to him, breathing him in.

"Kiss me," Jack commanded. Jared kissed and touched her softly and just drank her in.

"You're mine, Jack. I'll never be able to share you with anyone. I know that with every fiber of my being. It's not logical, I know; you have a family and brothers who will want to beat the shit out of me, but I don't care. You don't belong to them anymore. You belong to me. You're mine," he said into her silky, just-brushed hair. "I promise nothing will ever hurt you again, most of all me," Jared said quietly as she drifted off to sleep.

But even as she heard the words, an uneasy dread settled inside her heart. She refused to let the feeling enter into her thoughts. "Jared loves me and nothing else can hurt me ever again. There's nothing Jared and I can't handle together," she thought, smiling as she drifted away.

Jared lay there holding Jack for a long time after she went to sleep. It was wrong. He knew it. He knew in his bones it was wrong to keep their love a secret. Maybe her plan of him in Boston and her in college would work out. If they could lay low for the next year, she would be eighteen and they might stand a chance against her father. He would be established in the internship and be able to afford an apartment somewhere in between Connecticut and Boston for them. An apartment with Jack. Now that made him smile. What would life be like to wake up to her in his arms every morning and have their morning coffee in bed? I'll have to learn to cook better, thought Jared, because she can't cook at all. Even as the warm glow of excitement started to spread through him, he could feel icy fingers begin to squeeze his heart. He laid his head back and looked at the ceiling. He knew. He knew—like he knew his father was a shit bag—that as soon as David Johnson found out about them, he would take her away from him.

August came in even hotter than July, which was why most days after work Jack, Jared, Mac and her brothers just floated around the pond, too tired to do anything else. For the last two weeks, Jared had been waiting to hear about Boston. Jack had e-mailed her advisor at Harvard about starting school this September. Her advisor didn't think that would be a problem, but she would have to have her father sign off on it because she wasn't eighteen and he was paying the tuition. This was fair enough, but now they would just have to convince David Johnson to let his little girl go.

"Are you going to the pit tonight?" Bobby asked Jared as he paddled by on his inner tube.

"Nah, I've got some things to do," Jared said, stealing a glance at Jack.

"Ah, and just for the record, you girls are not coming," Caleb said, splashing Jack.

"Like I would go anywhere with you, fuck nut," Jack said splashing him back.

"Ah, a classic. They're going to love a good old-fashioned Maine girl like you at Harvard," Ty said chuckling. Jack splashed him.

"I can't go tonight anyway. I have to go to some boring military ball with my parents," Mac said with a tired sigh.

"Lots of men in uniforms," Jack said, wiggling her eyebrows.

"Um, when your father is the general, no one, and I mean no one, dares to talk to you," Mac retorted as she started to swim toward shore.

"I'll be your date, Red," Caleb said, wiggling his eyebrows. Mac could touch bottom now; she turned to face Caleb and smiled.

"One look at you, Caleb, and my father would shoot you dead and lock me away for the rest of my life," Mac replied coolly, waving good-bye and then walking up the beach.

"Jesus, she's hot. It just might be worth getting shot," Caleb muttered as he watched her walk to her car.

"You're such a whore dog," Jack said, rolling over yawning. This heat just sucked all her energy. She couldn't remember a time she felt so drained.

Her brothers decided to go see if Bebe had made anything to eat before they headed out to the pit. Left alone, Jared and Jack climbed on the float to lie down.

"Um, am I one of the things you need to 'do' tonight?" Jack asked, smiling with her eyes closed.

"Nice talk, potty mouth," Jared replied, smiling with his eyes closed.

Jack laughed. "You can't expect me to grow up with nine brothers and not have a dirty mouth," Jack said, poking him in the ribs. Jared caught her hand, brought it to his mouth, and started sucking on her fingers.

"I love your dirty mouth," he said, sucking. Jack gasped and instantly she was wet. "Let's get out of here," she whispered.

"My thoughts exactly," Jared whispered back, standing and helping her up. "Let's go get something to eat at the house and go to the height of the land to watch the sunset," Jared said.

"Oh, that sounds nice. Race ya!" Jack shouted out, already diving in. Jared smiled and dove in after her. She would win. She always did.

The boys had just left and Bebe was walking to her car as they drove up.

"Hi, kids, I'm going to evening services. There is some mac and cheese in the fridge for you," Bebe offered.

"Thanks, Bebe, that sounds great," Jared replied, opening her car door for her. Yum. Bebe made the best mac and cheese.

Jack and Jared finished up the leftovers and Jack went into her room to change. Jack had just taken her suit off and was standing in front of her dresser naked when Jared came in and pulled her back against him. His hands covered her breasts, and his thumbs stroked her hard nipples. Jack sucked in her breath and stared at him in the mirror hanging above her dresser. Jared was looking at her as he touched her breasts. His eyes were dilated and heavy with desire.

"So beautiful," he said, kissing her neck. One hand traveled down her stomach and cupped her sex. Jack's head fell back against Jared's shoulder. Jared stilled his hands.

"Look at me," he said firmly. Jack's head jerked back up, staring at him in the mirror.

"I want you to watch yourself come apart, Princess," Jared said as he began stroking and kneading her breast and inserted two fingers into her. Jack's back bowed and she moaned—she continued to watch herself in the mirror as her cheeks became flushed and her eyes took on a faraway look. Jack moved her arms back to grasp the belt loops of Jared's jeans to pull his arousal closer to rub on her backside. Jared slowly stroked her sex from back to front, rolling her clit around. Jack gasped. She needed more.

"Jared! Please!" Jack cried.

Still stroking slowly, Jared asked, "Please what, baby? What do you want? Tell me."

Jack moaned loudly. Jesus, she was coming apart just after a few touches. "I need more! Please I'm going to come," Jack said breathlessly.

Jared inserted a third finger into her. She was so close as she watched her body gyrate beneath his hands. Her ass grinding against his hard-on was sending him dangerously close to coming in his pants as well. Jack screamed and her head went back as her body spasmed. Jared could feel her core muscles contract around his fingers. Jesus, that was hot, he thought, as he struggled to get his ragged breathing under control.

"Fuck," Jared said, kissing her neck. Jack looked into the mirror and smiled. She rubbed her ass against his hard-on and he groaned.

"Let's get out of here," she whispered.

"Jesus, fuck yes," he choked out, not even knowing what he was saying. "I'll wait for you in the truck," he said, walking out of her room.

Jack threw on a sundress with no bra and no panties. She felt particularly naughty tonight, she thought, smiling. Jesus, watching herself being touched and shattering was the most erotic thing she had ever done. She had an idea forming in her mind about the ride to the height of the land that was already making her belly tingle and warmth blossom in her sex.

Jack bounced down the steps and Jared got out of the truck to let her in. He noticed instantly that she wasn't wearing a bra. The bodice of the dress hung low, and when she got in the truck he saw her beautiful full breasts straining against the material. Jesus, she was going to kill him. She had braided her hair, which coiled over her shoulder and rested on her breast. She scooted over in the seat and sat on her knees facing him.

"Ready?" Jared said, starting the engine and pulling out.

"Yup," Jack replied with a dirty grin as she reached over and unbuckled his jeans.

Jared stepped on the brakes. "Whoa, what are you doing?" he said, looking down at her as she continued unzipping his jeans. Hard. He was as hard as a steel pipe.

"Um, I'm pretty sure you have a clue," she whispered as she lowered his underwear, revealing his hard sex. She licked her lips. "Drive," she ordered, as she lapped at the crown.

"Jesus!" Jared gasped.

Jack stilled her tongue and looked up at him. "Drive, I said."

Jared put the truck in gear and stepped on the gas. Jack took all of him into her mouth and gripped his base with her fist and started stroking up and down as she did the same with her mouth. She could hear him moaning and saying incoherent random swear words. Jack smiled and hoped he could keep the truck on the road. She sucked and licked down the backside of his manhood, which seemed to be the most sensitive part. Jared jerked and she took him back into her mouth, sucking hard, and set a rapid rhythm. Jared swore and pulled the truck over to the side of the dirt road and threw it in park. He brought his hand to the back of Jack's head and applied pressure for her to take him deeper. He lifted his hips to fuck her mouth. "Jesus, Jack, I'm gonna come! You need to stop before——"

Jack sucked harder and worked her fisted hand. Jared hollered and she felt the hot come in the back of her throat. She swallowed quickly and felt some dribble down her chin. *Wow, that was hot,* Jack thought, knowing she was soaking wet. She was going to need him inside her soon. Jack wiped her chin on the hem of her dress and sat up. "Hi," she said simply.

Jared lifted his head from the seat. "Hi, yourself" he said, smiling as he took her face in his hands and kissed her deeply. "Jesus, I love you, Jack," he said against her lips.

"Mmm, I love you too," Jack replied as she snuggled beside him on the seat and he put the truck in gear. Luckily they had made it out of town and were sitting beside a cornfield at the base of Winding Hill. Windows down, the hot breeze felt good on their sweaty skin. They continued on until they were parked at their spot at the height of the land at the very top of Winding Hill.

The sky was blazing orange, and they watched the sun set behind a range of pine trees. The music was playing softly on the radio. Jack was snuggled up beside him with her head resting on his shoulder and her hands on his thigh.

Jack looked up. "Jared, promise me we'll always have this," she said, touching his cheek.

Jared looked down into her eyes. "I promise, Princess. Nothing can ever take this away from us," he replied, taking her mouth in an urgent kiss.

That fire took hold of Jack again she sat up in the seat and swung her leg over him, straddling him. Jack took over the kiss and sucked on his tongue. Moaning, Jared reached for the top of her dress and pulled it down, exposing her breasts. Jared broke the kiss to take her breast into his mouth. Jack moaned and arched her back. She could feel Jared growing hard and she started rocking back and forth on him. Jared brought his mouth up and licked around the nipple. He then took her hard nub between his teeth gently and pulled. Jack jerked back and gasped. The licking and slight pain brought her to a fevered pitch. Jared moved to the other breast and did the same. Jack was rocking and held his head in her hands to make sure he didn't move from her breasts.

"Jared," she moaned, rocking slowly.

Jared opened the truck door and got out, still holding her. She wrapped her long legs around his body. He walked to the front of the truck and sat her on the hood. He lifted her dress over her head. Jesus, she was naked. He heaved himself up to stand on the winch attached to the front bumper. He lay her back on the hood. Holy shit, he would remember this sexy-as-fuck image in his mind for the rest of his life.

Jack let her arms lay out on both sides of the hood as Jared slowly spread her legs wide apart. She had never felt so exposed or so turned on. Jared dipped his head to her light brown curls and spread her lips and licked so slowly from bottom to top, stopping at the top to suck on her clitoris. He swirled his tongue around it and gently pulled it.

Jack's hips thrust in the air on a gasp. Jared grasped the back of her thighs near her butt and pulled her wider apart, holding her in place. Jack moaned and moved her head from side to side. Jared inserted his tongue and began to fuck her sex with his tongue. He took one hand and began strumming her clitoris with his thumb, and she completely came apart. Bucking wildly, she rode his face until the spasms subsided.

Jack threw an arm over her eyes and laughed. Jared kissed her curls and kissed his way up her long glorious body until he was kneeling over her face. "What's so funny, Princess?" he said, licking her lips.

Jack brought her tongue out to taste his lips. They tasted a little sweet and a little salty. "I was just thinking about the birds in the trees. What must they be thinking?" she said, looking at him.

"I'll tell you what they're thinking, baby, they're thinking I'm the luckiest bastard on the planet!" Jared exclaimed, kissing her and suddenly deepening the kiss and thrusting his tongue deep into her mouth. A sudden jolt of heat spread through Jack. God, so soon after her orgasms, Jack thought. She couldn't get enough of him.

"Come on, I have a blanket in the truck bed we can spread out. I really need to be inside you, baby," he said, crawling down the hood. She scooted down and he picked her up and walked to the back of the truck. Jack grabbed the blanket and spread it out. She sat on the blanket and watched him take his clothes off. He was spectacular. He was so big. He had massive biceps from working the mountain this summer, and then there were his broad shoulders and tanned chest, ending with his ripped abs and that special V that Jack loved so much. His manhood was rock hard and standing proudly. He was so magnificent, she knew now exactly why the Romans created so many statues of naked males. They all paled in contrast to the naked male before her.

"You're so beautiful, Jared," she said as he joined her on the blanket. He had a condom wrapper between his teeth. She pulled it from his teeth.

"Let me put it on you," she whispered, ripping the package and pulling it out. She rolled it down his hard length, and he gathered her close against him and kissed her softly. They were both on their knees with their thighs touching with Jared's hard erection grinding against Jack's stomach.

"Get on your hands and knees, baby," Jared said softly. Jack looked a little confused but turned around. Jared reached around and stroked her core. "Ah, baby, you're so wet," he murmured, continuing to stroke. Jared could see the rigid line of her back as he put his other hand on her upper shoulders and rubbed.

"Relax, baby, if you don't like this position, just tell me. Relax," he said as he sat up and took hold of himself and rubbed his sex along her entrance, and in one swift stroke he entered her from behind, filling her completely.

Jack gasped. He was so big that there was a bit of pain, and the angle put him inside her farther than any time before. "Okay?" he said, pulling out slowly.

Jack moaned at the absence of him. "Oh, Jared, you're so deep," she said. He pushed in again, and this time there was no pain, just mind-blowing pleasure.

"Fuck, you're so tight, baby," Jared said, starting to pump harder. Jack pushed back onto him with each pump, and before long they were both moaning and all they could hear was their bodies slapping together.

"Jesus, Jack!" Jared swore as he pulled out of her and flipped her over. Jared covered her body with his, entering her by lifting her thighs high and wide. He held her thigh and watched as he drilled into her. He lifted his eyes to hers and saw that she was watching as well.

Fuck. That was hot.

He was so close. He let go of her leg and kissed her passionately. "Wrap those sexy long legs around me, baby, and come," Jared commanded, starting to pump furiously.

Jack wrapped her legs around him tight and felt with each thrust of his manhood his pubic bone grinding against hers and hitting what must have been her G spot. Suddenly all she saw were stars. Her legs tightened and she gasped.

"Jared, I'm coming! Faster! Harder!" she pleaded.

Jared was losing his fucking mind. He was pumping into her as her legs held him like a vise. Shit. He was losing it. With an unintelligible cry Jared came long and hard, with spasms shooting throughout his body one after another. Eventually their bodies melted into each other. While he was still inside her, they both drifted off to sleep to the sound of each other's breathing.

Jared was wet. He jerked away to find it raining. Both of them were soaking wet. *Shit, shit, shit, shit.*

"Baby, baby, wake up," Jared whispered, gently shaking Jack awake.

Jack opened her eyes, smiling. "Oh, it's raining!" she said, stretching.

"Get up. Quick. I don't know what time it is, but I think it's really late," Jared said, getting up and grabbing his jeans from the ground. Jack just lifted herself and was resting on her elbows smiling.

"Jack, for fuck's sake, get dressed. I need to take you home!" Jared barked, pulling on his wet shirt and tossing his boots in the truck bed. Jack jumped down from the truck and met Jared as he was trying to turn her dress right side out with jerky movements.

Jack took the dress and grabbed his hands. "Relax, Jared; it's okay. The boys probably still aren't home, and besides they would just think I was in bed and go to bed themselves," Jack replied, sliding the wet dress over her head. She threw her cowboy boots on the passenger floor and snuggled up to him as he revved the engine and sped off down the road.

"Maybe, maybe. Did we close your bedroom door before we left the house?" Jared asked in a slightly panicky voice.

"Um, dunno, I kinda just had a mind-blowing orgasm before we left the house, remember?" Jack said, trying to be serious.

Jared looked at her, smiled, and brought the hand he was holding to his lips. "Yeah, I remember. I'll never forget it," he said kissing her hand. "Okay, let's just get you home," he said, relaxing a little.

The lights were on all over the house. It was lit up like a fucking Christmas tree. Jared's guts turned inside out. They drove up the driveway slowly. David Johnson was leaning against the rented SUV, soaking wet with his arms crossed as they drove up.

Jared cut the engine. "Jack, I think——"

"Shhh. It's fine, really…it's best if we just tell him and then we can move forward with our plans for next year," Jack said, sliding over to get out of the truck.

"Wait, Jack, listen——" Jared tried to catch her arm but she opened the door and jumped out. As she walked up to David, the sopping wet dress clung to her breasts, making her nipples jut out and leaving no question that she was not wearing a bra.

Shit. Shit. Shit. Shit, thought Jared as he climbed out of the truck. David motioned for them to go into the house, and Bebe met them with towels and hugged Jack.

David motioned Jared toward his office and he turned to Jack. "You sit your ass right there, and I will deal with you in a minute. Sit!"

Jack jumped. "Daddy, please listen, please! It's not what you think. It's all my fault. I just needed a ride home from Mac's," she lied.

"Sit and shut the fuck up! I should have listened to Marcus! He's been telling me for years to be stricter with you. Jesus! No more. I'm going to rectify that tonight, mark my words!" David snarled back as he hurried into his office, slamming the door behind him.

Jared was sitting in a wooden chair across from the desk, leaning on his thighs with his head in his hands. David picked up his cell phone and dialed. "She's home. You boys can come home now. I'll tell you when you get home. Yeah, she's fine," he said, ending the call.

Jared looked up and met David's eyes. David's face was red and flushed with a rage that Jared had never seen before.

"It wasn't her fault, David. We just nodded——" Jared began.

"Shut the fuck up. Do not say another word. Not one fucking word. Do you understand me?" David hollered. "Do you understand?" he hollered again louder and smashed his fist on his desk.

Jared physically winced. "Yes, yes, I understand," he replied quietly.

"Good. Do you have any fucking idea what you have done? You have defiled my little girl. You just couldn't stay away from her, could you? You couldn't keep your fucking little pecker away from her. That was the only thing I have ever asked you to do. Stay the fuck away from my daughter. All these years I have taken you in and treated you like a son. I paid for your college education and let you live in the cabin when your father wouldn't stop hitting you. Well, let me fill you in on some things you probably don't know. The day I walked into the sheriff's office and saw Elsie holding you close and arguing with the chief of police, I knew the moment she looked at me that she was on a mission and you were as much hers at that moment as if she had given birth to you. There you were on her lap, with her holding a towel on your bleeding head, surrounded by her sons she had brought to church that day. No one was going to take you out of her arms, and no one ever did. She loved you completely, and did you know that she tried to get your father to let her take you back to Portland with us in the fall? She actually offered your father money for him to sign the papers for us to adopt you. Your piece of shit father took the money but refused to let you be adopted. I never wanted to beat the shit out of anybody the way I wanted to whup his ass. Elsie did manage to get him to agree to let a nanny or babysitter be there with you when you weren't in school, but that still didn't protect you from him, and Elsie knew that. She cried that whole winter worrying about you. Finally, Gracie told Elsie that when Elsie wasn't in Harmony she would watch out for you and make sure you had food and your backpack was stocked," David said, looking away as if he was back there all those years ago.

Tears streaming down Jared's face, he remembered Elsie and that fucking backpack that she always kept filled with snacks and juice. Jared sobbed harder, remembering the only person he had ever loved as much as Jack.

"It was the same every September. She would cry and go into a depression. It was like she lost one of her own flesh and blood. Oh, and Jesus, I remember when the hitting started. Gracie called one day to say she thought your father had hit you because you had a black eye. Jesus! Elsie tore out of that house and drove to Harmony. I was in Massachusetts and she didn't call me until after it was over. She walked right into the mill where your father was working and started hitting and punching him. Someone pulled her off him and they went outside to talk. She threatened that if she ever heard of him hitting you again, she was going to find him and gut him like a fish! I believe she would have done it. I had never seen her that upset, and I never did again. I believe your father was smitten with Elsie, like everyone else, and I think it did bother him that he had upset her. He didn't want her to think badly of him, as fucked up as that was, and he promised her he wouldn't hit you again. I suspected that what he really meant was he wouldn't let anyone see visible signs of your beatings," David said, sighing.

Jared wiped his tears on his sleeve, realizing David knew the truth. He wanted to melt into the floor.

"She always looked after you, and you were there the day she dropped in the field..." David stammered as a single tear dropped from one eye. "They had to cut my daughter, my Princess, out of my dead wife in order to save her. She was too little to be born, but she was a fighter and she survived. And you were still right here in this family and watched her grow up. You were supposed to protect her, not fucking rape her!" David hissed between clenched teeth.

"David, it's not like that—I love her more than anything!" Jared said with a sob.

David put his hand up. "I told you not to fucking say a word. You will not ever go near her again, do you understand? *Ever!* I want you to pack your shit and leave. You are not welcome at this house *ever again!* Oh, and you know that internship you were waiting on? Well, it's not fucking going to happen. I have made some calls tonight, and it's over. Just get the fuck out. Now!"

Jared stood up but stood his ground. "What are you going to do to Jack? It's not her fault. Don't you fucking lay a hand on her," Jared warned as his hands formed into fists.

David's face got redder as he walked around the desk and got dangerously close to Jared's face. "Do not ever tell me what to do or not to do with my daughter. That little girl out there is my life, and I would never lay a hand on her, but I am having a damn hard time not tearing your fucking head off your shoulders. Now get the fuck out of my house, and I want you gone for good in the morning," he said, pointing to the door.

Jared stumbled out the door in a trance, knowing that he had lost forever the only man who had loved him and had treated him like a son.

Jack ran up to him. "Jared, it will be okay, really, let me talk to him. I promise it will be okay," she whispered.

David came to the door. "Jack Elsie Johnson, get your ass in here right now," he hollered, pointing inside his office. Jack looked into Jared's eyes with a silent plea.

Jack walked into the office and sat down, her head down. "I'm sorry, Daddy. I didn't mean to make you worry. I love him," Jack said quietly.

David put his arms on the desk and clasped his hands together. "There is going to be a car coming to pick you up in the morning," David said, too calmly, as he checked his watch. "At five o'clock—in three hours actually—and they will be taking you to the airport, where a flight attendant will be escorting you to the plane and making sure that you get off the plane with a man who will be waiting for you at the airport. Then you will be driven to a halfway house, so to speak, for at least the next few months to let things get sorted out here and get your schooling in order. You will not have any contact with me or your brothers while you're there. This is what the director of the place says is best. She handles a lot of teenagers and told me I need to hand control of you over to her for a while and well, fuck, I sure as shit haven't done a very good job with you. So I'm going to listen for once when it comes to you. You don't need to pack anything. She said you will be provided everything you need," David said.

Jack jumped up and her chair went backward with a thud. "No!" Jack screamed. "You can't make me go away! I won't go! I won't!" she screamed.

As Jared stood outside the office, still stunned by what he had just been told, Bobby, Ty, and Caleb came through the door just in time to hear a loud thud in the office and Jack screaming no. Jared jerked and shook his head to clear it.

"What the fuck did you do to her?" Caleb shouted, landing a punch to Jared's mouth. Caleb pushed Jared to the floor and started whaling on him. Jared tried to grab Caleb's arm to stop him, but he couldn't fight him. He had done enough damage tonight.

Bobby and Ty pulled Caleb off Jared. "I think you better leave," Ty said quietly to Jared. Jared got up and looked at the office door. He could hear yelling and crying from Jack. Jared's guts twisted, and he barely made it outside before everything in his stomach hurled onto the ground. Heaving and sweating, he climbed into his truck and drove to the cabin to pack his stuff.

All of Jack's pleas and promises landed on deaf ears. David was determined to rectify his wrongs of not being strict enough with her. He had been on the phone all evening with his attorney, who had found this place called Beckett's House—a sort of home for wayward teenagers, but only the ones who come from very wealthy families. This house gave teenagers who had messed up a clean slate and brought order and structure to their lives. It sounded exactly like what his Princess needed. He would get it right for both of them this time.

"Daddy, please don't do this," Jack sobbed.

"You go to your room and try to get some rest, Princess. The car is going to be here shortly," he said, kissing her forehead and walking her to her room.

The boys were in bed and the house was quiet. Jack walked to her room, brushed her hair and braided it, and changed into a pretty dress with sandals. She sat by her window. She was certain that Jared would be there any second to take her away. He had promised, right? Yes. *He will be here any second,* she thought, as she looked out her window at her own reflection.

The car's tires crunched in the gravel driveway. David opened Jack's bedroom door and saw that she had fallen asleep leaning against the window. He picked her up and walked outside, grabbing her jean jacket from the hook on the porch. Jack woke up as David was putting her in the backseat. She bolted upright and grabbed his hands with her own shaking hand as tears instantly streamed down her cheeks in a torrent.

"Please, Daddy, please don't do this," she whispered brokenly. With tears in his own eyes, David shook his head.

"I have to, Princess. I love you," he muttered back as he closed the door and tapped the roof of the car to take off.

Jack never looked back. She sat ramrod straight in the backseat as the car turned the corner to the dirt road. David put his hand in his pockets, tears streaming down his cheeks as he walked into the house. Jesus, he was tired.

Jared waited until 9:00 a.m. to make his way to the main house. His stuff was packed and in his truck. He would stop at the main house and ask to say good-bye to Jack. He would whisper to her that he was heading to New York to find a job and that he would come find her when she started college next month. They would lay low until she turned eighteen. Then they could say "fuck you very much" to everyone. He would take care of her. She was his, and no one would take that away from him.

Jared gunned the engine and headed to the house. When he got there, the rental SUV was gone. He killed the engine and got out of the truck. Caleb came bounding out of the house and pushed him.

"What the fuck do you want? Haven't you done enough already?" Caleb snarled. Bobby and Ty came out of the house to where Jared and Caleb were standing.

"I just wanted to say good-bye to Jack," Jared replied quietly.

"Yeah, well join the fucking club, asshole. She's gone, and Daddy won't tell us where she is. She doesn't have her phone, and she didn't pack anything. She's just fucking gone," Caleb said, throwing his arms in the air. Jared looked at Bobby and Ty.

"He's right. Daddy took off a little while ago. Said a car picked her up and took her to the airport and that we wouldn't have any contact with her for a few months. He's mad as hell. He started kicking Caleb's ass when Caleb got up in his face about his refusing to tell us where she was," Bobby said.

Jared glanced at Caleb and saw that he had a fat lip. Jared leaned over and grabbed his knees. Jesus, he was going to be sick again, but this time there was nothing left in him to come up. After a few dry heaves, Jared staggered over to his truck and got in. He turned the engine on and started down the driveway when he noticed Jack's red cowboy boots on the passenger floor. Jesus, here come the heaves again.

Part 2

The flight was short, about an hour. Jack was escorted by a flight attendant into the terminal. New York. So this was where her purgatory was located. Who knew? She could last here for a couple of months if she had to, but she was certain that Jared was going to come get her. He loved her and had promised her that he would never leave her, right?

The tall African American flight attendant guided Jack through the terminal. She must have thought Jack was a little simple, because she seemed to speak in short sentences and end all of them with "okay?" Jack felt like she was living a nightmare that she couldn't wake up from. How could she have gone from the happiest day of her life to the worst day of her life within a six-hour period?

Up ahead there was an overweight balding man with pock marks holding a sign that read "J. Johnson."

"Oh, here we are," the flight attendant announced in a sickly-sweet voice. "I hope you enjoy your time in New York, and be safe, okay?" she said, never meeting Jack's eyes as she walked off.

"Come with me," the man said, walking toward the exit. Jack started to follow him, but for one split second considered running. *Just run,* she thought with a wave of panic setting in.

The man must have sensed her thoughts, because he turned and grabbed her arm to propel her through the exit. "Don't even fucking think about it," he hissed at her, propelling her toward a parked black sedan. He opened the door, pushed her in, and slammed the door. He climbed in the driver's side and sped off.

What just happened? Why would he throw me into the car? Jack felt lightheaded as she wondered when she had last eaten. More than hungry, though, she was tired...bone tired. She laid her head back and closed her eyes.

It was dark when someone poked her in the shoulder. "Hey, wake up, kid. It's time to move your ass," the man said coldly. The smell of sweat and body odor assaulted her senses. Jack sat up and climbed out of the car. It was some kind of secluded 1970s mansion set among the trees. There was lots of stone and brick with large windows and a roof that had many angles. As Jack made her way to the front door, she could hear the crickets calling to one another. There was a large lady with her arms crossed waiting in the entry for them. Jack was pushed forward violently and landed in a heap at the lady's feet.

"Jesus, you can't make these teenagers move," smelly man said behind her. Jack was speechless as she slowly got to her feet.

"George, don't be so impatient," the lady smirked, shaking her head. "Well, you must be Jack Johnson. Apparently, your parents wanted a boy. Just the first of many disappointments, I suppose. Anyway, I'm Mary Beth, the Director of Beckett's House, and this is George the caretaker. Follow me," she said, walking into a huge living area with a cathedral ceiling.

There were floor to ceiling windows surrounding the back wall of the living area. They walked through the living room and turned a corner to a large, spacious office with lots of windows. Mary Beth took a seat behind the big desk and pointed to the cushioned wingback chair in front of the desk.

Jack sat and stared at Mary Beth. She hated Jack! Jack could see the hatred staring back at her. Mary Beth narrowed her eyes and looked Jack up and down.

"You think you're pretty special, don't you, Missy? I can tell already that you have a definite problem with authority, which we will address, and you're used to getting your way. Well, your father has given us the task of teaching you how to follow orders. Every kid under this roof is a disappointment and a problem to their parents—their very rich parents—and they have asked us to assist them," Mary Beth said sneering. "You will have no contact with anyone outside of this house, and you will certainly not have any contact with your family. You will be given a job, and you will spend ten hours a day doing that job, longer if you don't do it right. This is a coed facility, so I suggest you keep those long skinny legs of yours closed up tight. If you disobey in any way, you will be punished. This will be your only warning, so I suggest that you don't fuck up. You will be given a bunk, and there is a trunk at the end that contains the clothes you will be wearing for the duration that you are here. I guarantee there aren't any pretty little sundresses in that trunk," Mary Beth mocked. "After dinner, you will have two free hours in the rec room and then bed. I will show you to your room now, and I suggest you keep to yourself. They're not exactly a welcoming bunch," Mary Beth ended, getting up and chuckling.

Jack stood up and towered over her. Mary Beth grabbed her braid and pulled her head down so they were eye to eye.

"You're a real beauty, aren't you, Princess?" Mary Beth said, leering.

"Don't call me that," Jack said in a whisper but never letting eye contact go. Mary Beth gripped Jack's braid tighter and her eyes narrowed in anger.

"What did you say to me, Princess?" Mary Beth hissed, so close to Jack's face that her nasty bad breath was making Jack nauseous.

"Nothing," Jack gulped, wincing from the pain on her scalp.

"I didn't think so, but I think we should start teaching you some respect right now," she said, dragging Jack around the desk. Jack could hear her rummaging in her desk. Then a snip, and Jack's head suddenly jerked free. Mary Beth held up Jack's long blond braid and sneered at her, tossing the braid on her desk. "Now follow me," she commanded, walking out of the room.

Jack felt the back of her head. There was nothing left at the base of her head but wisps of hair. She had no memory of not having masses of hair falling everywhere. Her head felt too light. What was happening? What kind of place had her father sent her to? *Jared will come for me. Jared will come for me. Jared will come for me.* Jack repeated the sentence over and over as she followed Mary Beth up the back stairs to a long corridor with two doors on each side. One side was the girls and the other the boys.

Mary Beth opened the door and walked in as the room suddenly became quiet. There were about twelve girls lounging on their bunks. Mary Beth pushed Jack forward.

"Ladies, this is Princess. I'm sure you will treat her with the respect she deserves," Mary Beth announced, fluffing Jack's hair and walking toward the door. "Lights out in one hour," she barked, slamming the door and locking it. Jack looked around as all the girls came to surround her.

"Well, look at you—little miss Princess, in your pretty sundress," said a short punk-rocker girl with nose and eyebrow piercings. The other girls chuckled at the punk girl. *She must be Fearless Leader,* thought Jack. She had always hated punk rock. Jack walked over to one of the only two empty bunks and sat down. Punk girl stalked over and grabbed the back of Jack's hair, pulling her off the bunk. *Jesus, what's up with my hair?* Jack thought.

"That bunk belongs to me," punk girl said. Jack started to walk to the other bunk and was pushed from behind and fell on her face. "That bunk also belongs to me," punk girl sneered. "You will fucking sleep on the floor like a dog," she said, throwing a wool blanket at Jack. "Now get the fuck over in the corner where you belong," she said, kicking Jack's thigh.

Jack got up and walked to the corner; she slid down the wall and pulled her knees close to her chest. Then she closed her eyes as the tears started to fall. She tried to will herself to stop crying, but the tears just wouldn't stop. She needed her brothers. Why was her father doing this to her? The feeling of something very dark and slimy started to bubble in Jack's chest at the thought of her father. She pushed it down. No, her father loved her and he would come to get her soon, she was certain. Well, maybe she wasn't certain, but she was pretty sure. Right? Jack slumped over into a fetal position and fell asleep.

The overhead light coming on woke Jack up. She stretched, making herself wince from lying on the hard floor all night. She slowly got up and made her way to the trunk at the end of the bunk. Inside she found the standard blue coveralls that the other girls were wearing and two black sports bras, one size fits most, and five pair of underwear briefs that looked an awful lot like diapers. The coveralls were way too short for Jack and came up to just under her knee. Great. There were white slip-on shoes to complete the outfit. The outfit reminded Jack of an astronaut in a low budget science fiction movie.

Just as Jack finished dressing, a wave of nausea hit her and she looked around desperately for the bathroom. One of the girls from the posse saw that she was in distress and pushed her toward the bathroom.

"I'm not cleaning up your fucking puke, bitch," the girl sneered. Jack barely made it to the toilet, but nothing came up. There was nothing in her stomach to bring up. She just heaved and heaved until she collapsed on the floor in sweat and exhaustion.

Jesus, I'm dying, she thought.

A young African American girl came in and knelt down beside her. "If you don't come to breakfast, you won't get any food for the rest of the day, so you better get up. You'll need your strength," she whispered.

Jack found the dining hall by following the smell of cooked eggs. When she walked in, all eyes were on her. There were a few whistles from the boys' table. The smell of eggs was making Jack nauseous again. Grabbing a tray, she leaned against the counter to let the sickness pass. Jack was shoved ahead violently.

"Come on bitch, we haven't got all day!" punk girl yelled. Jack took some toast and juice and looked around for a seat. There was a half-empty table with the girl who had talked to her in the bathroom. Jack went over and sat down at the end and ate her dry toast. She was halfway finished with her toast when a group of boys came and sat down beside Jack. A tall blond boy, probably the same age as Jack, put his arm around her.

"Hey there, sweet thing, you must be new here. I'm Justin, Justin Time to make all your dreams come true," he leered. Jack tried to pull away, but he held her tighter and tried to unbutton her coveralls with his other hand. Jack jerked away and struggled to stand up. Justin held her tight, so Jack swung her elbow back and caught him in the eye. Boom. He let her go and held up his hands.

"Fuck! Oh you little bitch, you're going to regret that little move, Princess," he hissed, holding his eye. The other guys at the table laughed as a buzzer sounded and everyone emptied their tray. As Jack was dumping the rest of her toast in the garbage, the girl stood beside her.

"That was stupid. You might as well have a target on your back now. That motherfucker is crazy, but more than that he's mean. Watch your back, girl," she advised, walking away.

"Wait, what's your name?" Jack asked.

"Norma, but don't fucking talk to me because I don't feel like getting the shit beat out of me. Do you hear? Jessie took a real dislike to you last night, and she's another mean one. Just stay away from me," the girl replied, walking away quickly.

Jack saw a tall skinny boy watching her from across the room. He was sitting by himself. He quickly looked away from her. *Well, aren't we popular?* she thought. *Please, please, hurry, Jared.*

As she came out of the dining hall, George was standing there leering at her with his arms crossed. "Making friends, I see," he sneered. "You're mopping the floors today. Follow me," he said, walking down the hall to a maintenance room with a mop and bucket on wheels.

"Take that to the kitchen and fill it up. Start with the dining hall and come find me when you're done," he said, coming to stand way too close to her but at Jack's height he had to look up at her. "You've probably never mopped a floor in your life have you, Princess?" he said, pulling at the top button of her coveralls. Jack batted his hand away and he grabbed her wrist and squeezed hard. It felt like her wrist bone was going to snap.

"You watch yourself, you little bitch. I think you and I are going to have lots of fun while you're here," he leered, touching the end of her nose. Jack jerked away, grabbed the mop bucket, and took off down the hall.

Jack spent the morning mopping the dining room and listening to the kitchen staff regale each other about the ridiculous amount of money they spent on cocaine and heroin the previous weekend. Justin walked into the dining room without a glance at Jack and went straight into the kitchen to speak to the guys in there. The kitchen guys walked past and leered and laughed at Jack as they walked out of the dining room. Moments later Jack, was grabbed from behind and dragged backward by her hair into the kitchen. Jack started flailing her arms trying to grab onto something but couldn't quite manage to grasp anything. Justin slammed the back of her head onto the floor. Jack could tell she was barely conscious but tried hard to stay focused.

"There's my little Princess. I think you should apologize for embarrassing me in front of everyone this morning, don't you?" he whispered, inches away from her ear.

"I'm sorry, I won't do it again," Jack gasped with tears running down the side of her head.

"Aww, shhh, don't cry, Princess, yes, you're right, it won't happen again, because I have to teach you a lesson now," Justin snarled as he lifted her to a standing position and drove his fist into her stomach. Jack doubled over in pain and couldn't breathe.

"All you cunts are the same, just worthless whores," he said grabbing her hair and punching her in the face. The force of the punch was so fierce that Jack lost consciousness before she hit the floor, so she was not aware of the brutal kicks to the stomach and ribs or when he sat on her chest and pummeled her face until she was unrecognizable.

"She needs to be in a hospital. I don't know the extent of her injuries, but I'm pretty sure that she has extensive internal damage. The miscarriage was brutal and…"

"That's enough, Sherry. You know she can't go to the hospital. Her father would drag her out of here and sue us until we were all penniless. Not to mention there may be prison time involved. Need I remind you that you have withheld hospital treatment for years on kids that should have had it. Maybe you have forgotten Dylan, hmmm? He might not have died if you had sent him to the hospital," Mary Beth replied, looking around.

The lady named Sherry gasped. "You wouldn't let me send him or the others to the hospital," she said defensively.

"Oh really, so you were just following orders and you let a child die and others get maimed because you were afraid for your job. That will be a great defense, I'm sure," Mary Beth taunted.

Sherry took a deep breath. "Look, this girl has severe internal injuries. So severe that she will probably never conceive a child again once the scar tissue forms over all her organs if this isn't taken care of properly. It's a miracle that she didn't hemorrhage to death. I've never seen anything so brutal in my life,"

Sherry whispered. Jack tried but wasn't able to stay conscious and floated away.

The smell of antiseptic and bleach wafted through Jack's nostrils, bringing her slowly awake. Pain. So much pain. She hurt all over. What had happened to her? Jack tried to think back, but her head was throbbing...not just her head, but her face as well. Jack groaned and got the attention of a person she assumed was a nurse.

"Hey there, how are you feeling?" the woman asked.

"Are you a nurse? Am I in the hospital?" Jack asked in a whisper.

"Oh yes, I'm the nurse at Beckett's House; my name's Sherry. You're still at the house. You suffered quite a beating, my dear. You've been out, or sedated really, for four days to let the swelling go down. You have extensive injuries, so you will feel like you have been hit by a Mack truck for a while," she said.

"Was it Justin?" Jack asked.

"I believe so; he was the one they pulled off you. He's a mean one," Sherry said.

"But why? Why would he hurt me so bad?" Jack cried as tears started to fall.

"Oh, sweetie, don't cry. He really hates women. He scares me to death. You just stay away from him, okay?" Sherry said.

Jack could feel the blackness oozing into her soul slowly. "I woke up at some point and thought I heard you tell someone that I had a miscarriage. Did I dream that? Was I pregnant?" Jack asked, holding her breath.

"Yes, I'm so sorry, baby. It appears that he kicked you repeatedly in the stomach and ribs. You have several broken ribs as well," Sherry replied softly.

Jack couldn't breathe. She tried to sit up so she could catch her breath but the pain that shot through her chest made her cry out.

"Oh, honey, you need to calm down, lie down, breathe, you need to breathe," Sherry said as she inserted the needle, letting Jack instantly drift away.

Daddy will be here soon was Jack's last thought.

Jack could tell someone was in the room with her. She slowly opened her eyes and saw the tall skinny boy from the dining hall standing at the end of her bed watching her.

"Hi," Jack said hoarsely. The boy jumped and turned and walked out the door, almost running into Sherry. Sherry walked over to Jack's bed and sat down.

"Hi there, are you feeling any better?" she asked.

"Who was that boy?" Jack asked Sherry.

"The boy who just left? I think his name is Noah; he's been in here several times because of Justin as well. He's actually come in a few times to check on you. It's very sweet really," Sherry said.

Out of nowhere, Mary Beth walked in with narrowed eyes. "You will not be having any more visitors," she said harshly. "You will be moved to solitary tomorrow. I'm not sure you understand, but this is not a game. We are not here to dote on you, Princess. You seem to have made enemies rather quickly," she snarled.

"When is my father coming?" Jack grimaced.

Mary Beth clenched her teeth in anger. Sparks seemed to shoot from her eyes as she leaned down very close to Jack's face. "Your father is not coming. No one is coming to save you, Princess. You are mine for at least six months and for your insubordination just now, you will spend the next two weeks instead of one in solitary confinement," she growled before she stood up and stalked out the door with Sherry following behind.

Jack gasped. Jesus, six months. A hopelessness like Jack had never felt before enveloped her. Six months? Could she survive another six minutes in this hell?

Survive.

Some spark of self-preservation went off somewhere inside her. When she got out of solitary confinement, she would need to be able to protect herself better. What a fucking nightmare. It was like something that she and Mac would see at the movies, only it was her real fucked-up life.

Jack started looking around the room for some kind of weapon she could use. She got up slowly and edged out of bed. The pain shot through her and buckled her legs. Crawling over to the chest of drawers, Jack pulled herself up and opened the first drawer. Nothing but gauze and bandages. Jack opened the second drawer and spied a leather pouch. When she opened it she found a small scalpel.

Perfect.

Jack took a roll of gauze and wound it around her pathetically skinny leg and inserted the scalpel. If anyone noticed the gauze, they would just think it was another wound.

Jack crawled back to the bed and collapsed against the pillow, sweating and in so much pain the tears fell unchecked down her face. She put her hands across her hollow stomach. Hers and Jared's baby, she thought. Oh to have a piece of him with her right now. She was certain she could go through any kind of hell if she thought she had Jared's baby to protect and love. She had nothing now. Nothing at all to keep her going. The tears wouldn't stop, and this blackness surging through her just consumed her. Hell. That's exactly where she was.

In the morning, George came in with a wheelchair and Sherry helped her get into it.

"Come on, Princess, you're moving to a more private room," he said, laughing.

"She should not be moved," Sherry whined in frustration.

"Oh, stop your bellyaching. You've got to stop babying these little bastards," George retorted as he wheeled Jack out. As he wheeled her by the dining hall, Jack heard the gasps. She hadn't seen her reflection, and judging by their reactions she was glad of that.

George wheeled her to a doorway and then stopped the wheelchair and came around to pick her up. Jack instantly flinched. Would he feel the scalpel she had secured to her leg?

"Jesus, you don't weigh anything, Princess. You need to get some meat on those bones. Boys like a girl with a little meat on them, you know?" he said, leering at her. Jack's stomach flipped. Between his body odor and nasty breath so close to her face she thought she was going to vomit.

There was a cluster of small rooms with heavy doors in the basement. There was a room at the end with its door open. George walked in and deposited her on the bed—if you could call it a bed. It was a metal bunk secured to the wall with a thin foam mattress on top. There was a stainless steel toilet and sink. That was it. No window, no chair, no books or anything that remotely addressed basic human needs.

George turned and walked out, stopping only to threaten her. "Maybe I will come and visit with you while you're down here. Would you like that, Princess?" He smirked as he slammed the door.

Shock.

Jack just lay back on the mattress and stared at the ceiling. What the fuck did she do to deserve this? she wondered. No answer was forthcoming.

The grief was suffocating her. Grief for everything and everyone she had ever loved, but mostly for the life that had been inside her growing. The loss of something so very precious made her physically sick. Jack replayed every scene in her head over and over. The days all ran into each other. She only knew it must be night because the overhead light went out, leaving her in total darkness. What had her father said to Jared to make him walk away from her without a backward glance?

Her father.

A black bitterness clawed at her insides, threatening to completely take possession of her heart.

The voice started as a whisper that she couldn't quite understand. Slowly, as the days wore on, the voice became clearer and sharper.

"No one is coming to get you. You need to save yourself. Are you really going to just let them win? I thought you were much tougher than that."

I'm going insane, thought Jack, but she answered out loud anyway. "What am I supposed to do? How can I fight back?" she asked as she started to cry.

"*I know you have a blade tucked away. That will surely come in handy, but you need to start eating or you are just going to wither away. You cannot let them win. Look how much they have taken away from you. You need to make them pay.*"

Jack stopped crying, her interest piqued. "How, how can I make them pay?" Jack whispered.

"*You need to build your strength up and stop feeling sorry for yourself. No one is going to swoop in and save you, Princess.*"

Jack bolted up in the bed, still seeing total darkness. "Fuck you! I will make them pay with or without your help," Jack said to the blackness.

"*Ah that's my girl! You need to get mad and get focused. Now find the tray on the floor and eat.*"

Jack got down on her knees and felt around the floor in front of the door. "I will make them pay. Don't you ever fucking call me Princess again. Do you hear me?" Jack said to the darkness.

Utter silence.

Jack found her tray and with her fingers shoveled whatever was on her plate into her mouth, and even after eating, she had no idea what she had consumed. With her belly full, Jack climbed back on her bunk and fell into a dreamless sleep.

For two more days, Jack ate all her meals and paced back and forth in the cell, plotting how she was going to teach Justin a lesson and get him to protect her. The others all seemed to be scared to death of Justin—rightly so, as he seemed to be a psychopath in training. A plan started to take shape in which she was going to try to get him alone and then she would make him pay.

Hopefully they would let her shower before she got put back with the others. Even Jack couldn't stand the smell of herself in this small cell much longer. When the lights went out, the grief would start to creep up on her, but her Dark Twin would speak to her. Jack had started referring to the voice that spoke to her in that way. Dark Twin would occupy her mind until she fell asleep.

The door opened, and George walked in and covered his mouth. "Jesus you stink! Come on, you need a shower, and then you will go to the dining hall for breakfast. You will be working with the kitchen staff today, so report to them when breakfast is done," he said, grabbing her arm and propelling her out the door.

Jack was still wearing a hospital gown, so she tried to hold the back closed as she was pulled along to the sleeping quarters. Jack grabbed a towel and entered the bathroom. There was a small room that had one large overhead shower nozzle, and all the girls were to stand under it and shower together. Jesse and her posse were already showering as Jack removed her gown and stood under the water and closed her eyes. No one said a word, although Jack thought she heard a few gasps. Jack's whole body was covered in deep black bruises that had started to turn yellow. There wasn't much skin that wasn't discolored and swollen.

"These bitches couldn't have taken the beating you just survived, but you know they think you're weak and pathetic. You need to show them you're not scared anymore and you won't be taking their shit. You must get them before they get you."

Jack shook the water out of her eyes and toweled off. She walked to the bunk that she had been initially assigned to and found the scalpel. Still naked, she suddenly lunged at Jesse and pinned her to her bunk. The other girls all backed away as soon as they saw the blade Jack was holding against Jesse's cheek.

"What the fuck!" Jesse spat.

"No, *you* shut your fucking mouth! I'm going to make a few things fucking crystal clear to you brainless bitches right now. Number one, I will be taking that bunk right over there, and no one had better bother me in it, ever! Number two, you and your little gang had better not ever speak to me or even look in my direction. I don't want to be your friend or lover or in your fucking pathetic little gang. If you or your little minions aren't able to follow these two simple rules, I will start by cutting off your nose and throwing it in the toilet and flushing it. Now, I'm not sure how that works, but if they have nothing to sew back on you, I'm pretty sure you go through life with a fucking hole in your face. If you still don't learn, I will then cut off your ears, and so forth and so on until, well, you get the fucking picture *n'est-ce pas?*" Jack said, getting off Jesse and walking to her bunk.

"Oh, and if any of you has the crazy idea to tell lady fucking Mary Beth about this blade, well, I have more hidden, and you will most assuredly go through this life without a nose," Jack ended, making a motion that she was cutting off her nose.

"You went completely bat-shit crazy in solitary confinement," Jesse croaked, standing and edging her way around Jack who was still standing there naked.

"Maybe so, bitch, but you just remember what I've said because I *will* cut you," Jack hissed, never dropping eye contact.

Jesse threw her hands up. "What the fuck? Fine!" she retorted as she walked out the door with all her little groupies quickly following. Jack smiled and carefully wrapped the gauze around her leg that held the blade.

Jack made her way to the dining hall without any fear. Everyone must have sensed a difference in Jack, because although they all avoided eye contact, they couldn't take their eyes off her. She felt a sense of freedom about her that was born of not having anything left to lose. Her hair was wild, with soft blond waves framing her face, making her eyes stand out with a blue that held the depths of the ocean.

Jack picked up her breakfast, went over to Justin's table, and sat down next to him. He was surprised by this and apprehensively stared at her.

"Hi," she said as shyly as she could.

"Hey, beautiful," Justin replied with a smirk.

What a fucking psycho, Jack thought to herself. He had absolutely no remorse or guilt for what he had done to her.

Jack nibbled on her toast. "Um, I thought we might talk in private," she murmured while looking down at her tray. Apparently he liked her subservient demeanor, because he puffed up and gave the other guys at the table the signal to scram.

"What did you want to talk about, Princess?" he leered. "My throbbing member?"

Jack's anger rose and her breathing altered. She reached for the last button on her coveralls to access her blade so she could just slice his throat right then and there. However, suddenly a wave of peace spread over her as she felt the presence of an unseen other.

"*Hey now, calm down. You need to charm him, sweetheart. We will make him pay dearly for what he has done to us,*" her Dark Twin cooed.

Jack looked Justin in the eye and tried a pouty, seductive look. "Um, well, you know that you didn't have to hurt me so bad. If you wanted to spend time with me and be my boyfriend, all you had to do was tell me. I'd like to spend some time alone with you if we can manage it," she whispered and literally tried to bat her eyelashes. Jack could see Justin instantly was aroused and almost salivating as he leaned over close to her ear.

"Now we're talking, Princess. I can make that happen. I'll get us on raking leaves duty today, and we can have some fun," he said, slipping his hand along her thigh very close to the blade. "Wait here and finish your breakfast. Let me take care of this," he commanded, getting up and practically running out of the dining hall.

Justin came back a couple of minutes later and leaned on the table beside her. "You have kitchen duty this morning, and after lunch we will rake leaves with a bunch of others, but we can manage to sneak off for a while," he whispered.

Jack smiled back coyly and walked slowly to the kitchen, all the while knowing he was watching her ass sway the whole way.

The morning dragged by, but it gave Jack an opportunity to relive the pain that Justin had caused her and ultimately what he took from her. By the time lunch rolled around, Jack was vibrating with anticipation to avenge herself.

Jesse and her friends were in line to get lunch when Jack entered the dining room from the kitchen. Jack sashayed over and stood in front of them as she grabbed a tray. Jesse bristled but didn't say a word.

With her back to them, Jack couldn't hold back a small smile. The others already in the dining room didn't miss this interaction, especially Justin, who felt very proud to have this alpha female as his "girlfriend."

Jack waltzed over to Justin's table. Justin elbowed the guy sitting next him and told him to get lost. Jack sat down.

"Hey, Princess," he leered, making her fingers tingle.

"Hey yourself," she replied and instantly wanted to retch as she remembered how Jared would greet her like that. Icy anger flowed through her veins. Soon.

There were six of them raking leaves with George watching them. They had raked for about an hour when Justin walked over to George and muttered something to him. Justin next proceeded to take Jack's hand and lead her into the woods.

"What did you tell him?" Jack asked as she was pulled along deeper into the woods.

"George and I have an understanding. He knows that I would puncture his skull if he fucks with me. I probably will anyway before I leave this hellhole," Justin replied, looking back at her with his ever-present leer. "I turn eighteen in a month, and then I'm outta here."

Jack unbuttoned the last button on her coverall and fished inside for the scalpel. She had just palmed the blade when Justin thrust her onto the side of a tree, banging her head. He took her mouth in a violent kiss. His teeth banged against hers as his tongue filled her mouth, making her want to gag. Instead, she moaned erotically.

Her reaction seemed to incite something inside him, and he grabbed her breast roughly and squeezed. The pain was sharp, and Jack gasped. Justin grabbed Jack by the back of the head and pulled her head back.

"You like this, don't you, Princess? What a sweet little mouth you have on you. I think it's time you showed me what a good little girlfriend you are. Get on your fucking knees," he rasped, so close to her face their noses were touching.

A spike of excitement surged through Jack. She knew right away that her Dark Twin was with her.

"*Now we're talking. We are going to make him pay so good. Give him pain and take the most important thing to him, just like he did to us.*"

Jack smiled and nipped Justin's lower lip. "Oh, baby, I'm going to be the best girlfriend you've ever had," Jack moaned, continuing to nip and lick at his mouth while she unbuttoned his coverall and slid it off his shoulders. Jack kissed his chest as she lowered herself.

Justin's eyes were glazed over with teenage passion and his breathing was ragged. He turned her so he was leaning against the tree. Jack knelt down and was eye level with his hard needle dick. Bile rose in her throat as she wrapped her free hand around the shaft and moved up and down.

Justin flinched and moaned. Jack leaned closer so she was breathing on his dick. Justin was staring down at her, and she stuck her tongue out like she was going to lick him. Then she brought the scalpel to the base of his dick. The shiny metal glittered in the sun.

Justin's eyes immediately focused on the blade and he gasped.

"Ah, look at this," Jack said, looking at Justin's instantly limp dick. "What's the matter, Justin? Don't you want me? We're going to have so much fun, right?" Jack sneered. She moved the blade ever so lightly over the top of his dick and immediately a thin line of blood formed and started to drip.

"Wow, this is really sharp," she smirked. Jack could feel Justin shaking and could feel his thundering heartbeat through his dick.

"Now that I have your attention, I just want you to know that you hurt me very badly and took things from me that I will never, ever get back. That was not very nice of you, was it Justin?" Jack whispered as she grabbed his balls. God, the skin was so soft and tender under there. How easy it would be to just slice the whole package right off. But if she did that, she would have to run. She didn't have a plan yet. She would be caught and thrown back in solitary confinement, or probably worse, probably much worse. Jesus, she needed a plan.

Jack's Dark Twin surged up. "*Just cut him. A little pressure and it will be done. Just fucking do it already!*" she was screaming in Jack's head.

Jack looked up at Justin. He was hardly breathing. Tears and snot were running down his face. When she made eye contact with Justin, he could see there was no bluff in her. She was going to cut his dick off. Justin started shaking his head slowly.

"Please, please don't do it. I won't touch you again, I promise. I'm so sorry I hurt you. Please don't cut me," Justin whimpered between cries and shakes.

"Well, Justin, here's my problem," Jack replied, very casually looking from this limp dick to his eyes very purposely. "This," squeezing his penis and pointing with the blade, "is going to be cut from your body violently. Jesus, you may even bleed out. You know, like if you hit a vein in your thigh and blood just starts squirting everywhere. I bet that is what will happen to you. I actually hope it doesn't, because I don't want you to die. I just want you live the rest of your life without what is most precious to you. I don't think that's too much to want, do you? I mean really, you probably don't even know what you took from me, but I'm going to tell you. I was pregnant when you decided I needed to be taught a lesson and beat me almost to death. The baby died and the beating was so severe that I can't ever have children," Jack said, feeling her Dark Twin beginning to surge. Jack tightened her grip on Justin's balls and dick. Could she control her? Did she want to control her?

Justin winced. Was she really going to steal his manhood, right now, this way? He was well on his way to passing out.

"I'd say that was a very high price for me to have to pay, don't you, Justin?" Jack stared at his dick with her fingers tingling, the blade already smeared with blood from the slice. Jack couldn't take her eyes off the shiny blade. It glinted back and forth.

"Please, don't do this. I'll do anything, give you anything. Please!" he moaned, sobbing as he shut his eyes tightly.

"Do anything."

Justin's plea registered deep in Jack's brain. Maybe she could work with this, Jack thought absently as her Dark Twin raged.

"*Fucking do it! Do not let him get away with this!*"

Jack started to sweat and her hands started to shake. She couldn't concentrate with her Dark Twin shouting at her.

"Shut the fuck up!" Jack screamed.

Justin tried to stifle his sobs. Silence. Ah, that was better.

Jack smiled. "This is what I'm not going to do, Justin. I'm not going to cut your dick off today."

Jack watched Justin slump into the tree. "But I am going to cut it off one day. It may be in a month, or it may be on your fortieth birthday. You will never know when or where. I am going to make it my mission in life to keep track of you at all times. I don't care where you are on this planet, I will find you when it's time, and I will take your most precious possession," Jack said, squeezing and waving his limp dick back and forth like a rag doll.

"For now, though, you are going to make sure no one bothers me. I don't want them talking to me or touching me. That includes fuck-face George. You do whatever you need to do to insure that I am not fucked with. Do you hear me?" Jack asked firmly.

Justin wiped the snot from his nose and nodded quickly. "Yes, yes, I promise. No one will bother you," he whimpered.

"A few more things," Jack said, looking him squarely in the eye. "I *am* going to cut your dick off, and when I do, I will be destroying it like flushing it down the toilet or maybe a garbage disposal. However it is done...well, it won't ever be in any shape to get reattached. And, lastly, if you ever call me Princess again or let anybody else call me that, I will slit your throat— period, end of story," she hissed as she took the scalpel and made a deep two inch slice on the patch of skin just above his pubic bone and crossed it with another incision. Justin cried out in equal parts pain and fear.

"Now, this little *X* is a reminder of my promise to you. It will make a scar, and you will never forget me or what I'm going to do to you. Now get the fuck to the house for some stitches before you bleed out, and remember, not a fucking word about me," Jack muttered as she stood up. "Oh, and if you start to think why should you do anything for me if I'm going to cut off your li'l lizard anyway, the answer is you will just move up your 'operation' date."

Justin grabbed his abdomen and started running for the house. Jack turned and leaned against the tree; she watched him with a slow smile forming. It was dusk now, and it was probably time for dinner. Good, she was starving and she needed to wash this blood off her hands, she thought, as she slowly made her way toward the house.

One month. That's how much time Jack had to come up with a plan of escape. Her interactions with Justin and Jesse seemed to have the desired effect. No one talked to her or bothered her in any way. It would seem that bullies needed a target like an addict needed heroin. They seemed to be concentrating their hatred toward Noah Cabrera, the boy who Jack had found in her room after she'd been beaten nearly to death. Jack had noticed Noah the first morning in the dining hall. He was beautiful, and he reminded her of Caleb. God, she missed her brothers! She had seen Noah show up for breakfast with black eyes and fresh bruises. Jesus, she hated bullies! On many occasions, Jack had seen her brothers defend people who weren't able to defend themselves. She had always been proud of her brothers, and now she would try to make her brothers proud (assuming she would ever see them again to tell her story).

Jack waited until after dinner when they were all in the rec room. Jack was reading one of her favorite books, *Great Expectations*. Funny how she felt she could relate to how alone in the world the character Pip felt in the book. Jack looked around and didn't see a lot of the boys, although Justin was watching TV in the corner. Noah wasn't there.

Jack got up and went to the staircase. She heard some muffled voices and then a loud thud. Jack bolted up the stairs, and as she did, she reached into her coveralls to grab her blade. She walked quickly into the boys' room through the open door and found one of the larger boys on top of Noah. Noah was on his stomach and the bigger boy was trying to take Noah's pants off.

"You like it up the ass, don't you, faggot! Well, you're going to love this steel pipe I have for you then," the bigger boy said as he pulled Noah's pants down just past his bottom. Jack could feel the surge of her Dark Twin coming to full attention. With the blade ready in her hand, Jack kicked the boy off Noah with her foot. The bully momentarily lost his balance and fell back, only to quickly jump up and lunge at Jack.

All Jack had time to do was flail her blade at him. The tip of the blade caught his cheek and sliced it wide open. The boy grabbed his cheek and then realized who it was that had cut him. The blood drained from his face as he shouted to the other boys to get the fuck out. They all ran out of the room, but not before promising Noah his time was coming.

Noah jerked his pants up and sat with his head between his legs trying to calm his nerves. After a few minutes, he looked up at Jack. "I finally get to meet the new girl and I find out she's my guardian angel. How very appropriate that I would have a pissed-off, knife-wielding girl as my angel. How very fucking appropriate," he grumbled.

Jack raised her eyebrow. "Ah, you're welcome, asshat. I should have let them beat the shit out of you, but I was afraid they would mess up that beautiful face," Jack retorted.

Noah's interest immediately was piqued. "You think I'm beautiful?"

Jack couldn't hold back her grin. Jesus, he was full of himself, just like Caleb was, she thought.

"You remind me of my brother Caleb. Although, I think he's maybe a little more beautiful," Jack smirked.

Noah decided to stay on his bunk and chill while Jack went downstairs to get some sodas to bring up. When she went into the dining hall, she grabbed the sodas and walked over to Justin watching TV. Justin saw Jack and flinched. Jack smiled and sat down next to him leaning very close to his ear.

"Tell your boys to leave Noah Cabrera alone. He is off limits. Got it?" Jack whispered, looking Justin straight in the eyes. Justin swallowed hard and gave a nod. Jack smiled and went to bring the sodas upstairs.

Noah told her about his very Catholic upbringing. Noah had known that he was gay from a very early age, and so had his parents. They had tried to force him to "be like the other kids." He was forced to go to church every day and visit psychologists to erase his "homosexual tendencies."

By the time he was five years old, his family knew they wouldn't be able to suppress Noah's "tendencies," so they had sent him away to boarding school for the next twelve years. They, in essence, threw him away. They wanted nothing to do with him and told him quite plainly that when he turned eighteen he was on his own and to not ever come home. They felt their obligations to him were fulfilled. He had been nothing but a disappointment and embarrassment to them. The last straw had been when at his last expensive boarding school he had been caught having sex on the altar in the church.

"That's when I was sent to this hellhole," he lamented.

"Well, I'm leaving this place, but I need to come up with a plan, and I have to do so within a month," Jack replied.

"Do you mind if I come with you? Otherwise, I'm guessing a steel pipe up my ass is in my future," Noah said grimly.

"I don't think you have to worry about that anymore, but you're welcome to come with me if you want to," Jack said.

"Speaking of beatings, how did you go from being tormented to people giving you a wide berth? It's amazing really, I have been watching you since you got here, and the transformation is a little scary if you want to know the truth. What happened to you when you got beat so bad, and why the hell are you cozying up to Justin now?" Noah asked.

Jack instantly felt her Dark Twin surge to attention.

"*Don't tell him anything. Never tell anyone ever about me or we will be locked away forever!*" Dark Twin whispered.

Jack turned cold. "That's none of your fucking business. If you want to come with me, fine, but don't ever ask me any personal questions again," Jack replied flatly.

"Um, or what, you'll slit my throat?" Noah asked sarcastically.

Jack leaned in close. "That's an option, although I wouldn't want to."

Noah blanched. "Jesus, how come I think you mean that? Okay, all right. I won't ask any questions. Just tell me what the plan is when you come up with it," he said.

Jack got up and headed to the door. It was five minutes to lights out.

"Hey, lovely, thanks for saving my ass, literally," Noah smiled.

"You're welcome," Jack said not able to hide her smile. "Good night."

Jack lay in bed listening to the train in the distance. That was how they were going to disappear. She needed to figure out how far the train was from them and pay attention to the times of day it went by. She knew it traveled at night. If she and Noah could take off after dinner, they might be able to hop on it. She would take a little sightseeing trip tomorrow to find the train.

At breakfast, Jack sat down next to Justin. He seemed to immediately lose his appetite.

"I need to get put on outside detail today," Jack said.

"I can manage that," Justin gulped.

"Good. I also need to disappear for about an hour, but I will be back. You need to cover for me," Jack barked, glaring at him. Justin looked very uncomfortable.

"I'm not going into the woods with you again," he whimpered.

"No, just me, but I need you to cover for me. Say I got sick or something. You're a smart, resourceful guy, think of something," Jack said as Justin got up from the table and left the dining hall.

Jack was assigned to rake leaves again today with Justin. As soon as they were outside, Jack took off in the direction she thought the train was. She was only about fifteen minutes away from the house when she came across the train tracks. As she was walking along the tracks, she heard the train whistle. Great! She was in luck, she could just hop on now and get the hell out of here.

Jack crouched on the side of the tracks and waited. The cars were going by slowly and there were several open cars that she could climb in. Jack was poised and ready to jump but she waited as car after car crawled by.

"*Come on, jump already!*" whispered her Dark Twin.

Soon the last car slowly passed by her. Too late.

"*Why didn't you jump?*" Dark Twin yelled.

"I told Noah he could come with us," Jack yelled back.

"*He is going to slow us down; you know that, don't you?*" said Dark Twin.

"Yeah, I know, but I'll take care of him," Jack replied softly.

"*If he becomes a threat, I will hurt him,*" Dark Twin warned.

"I know," Jack whispered to herself as she ran back to the house.

Three nights passed. At dinner on the fourth night, Mary Beth strolled in and stood before the tables.

"Starting this weekend, the house will be on lockdown until further notice. We have guests coming, so there will be no going outside or household duties. You will be confined to your bunks unless it's meal time or rec time," Mary Beth announced, and then she walked directly out of the dining hall with a look of disgust.

Noah quickly looked at Jack. "How are we…" he began.

"Tomorrow. We need to leave tomorrow after dinner," Jack replied firmly.

Jack filled her backpack with fruit from breakfast and granola bars and Pop-Tarts. Jack had timed the trains, and the night train would be going by at nine o'clock, which meant they had to make an appearance in the dining hall and then run into the woods to hide until the train came. She was going to have to rely on Justin to cover for her so they wouldn't be missed.

At the start of dinner Jack took Justin aside. "Hey, big boy," Jack snarled loud enough for others to see them talking privately. "Listen, you're going to cover for me and Noah tonight. Right after we're done speaking Noah and I are taking off. While you're eating, you need to make sure people know that I'm waiting for you and we're going to have some fun and no one should bother looking for us," Jack said as Justin started shaking his head until he felt her hand grab his balls under the table. He had no idea whether the blade was in her hand or not. Justin inhaled sharply.

"That's a good boy. Now you better not let me down, Justin, because how much mercy I show you someday depends on how you play this out," Jack said softly.

Justin nodded and closed his eyes. "You're insane," he muttered. Jack tapped his cheek.

"Hello pot," she replied sarcastically and headed out of the dining hall with a nod to Noah, who followed unnoticed.

Jack dashed upstairs to grab the backpack and they silently made their way out the back door. It was dusk and getting darker by the minute. Jack and

Noah sprinted to the woods. Noah stopped and bent over, trying to catch his breath. "I need to stop. I can't breathe," he huffed.

"Come on, Noah, we can't stop now. We need to make it to the tracks before it's pitch black out here," Jack replied urgently, grabbing his arm and running. They made it to the tracks just as it became really dark out and sat down beside a tree to wait for the train.

"So what's the plan once we're on the train?" Noah asked, tipping his head back to rest against the tree.

"Well, I think we should try to get some sleep and then try to get off as close to New York City as possible. I have fifty dollars that I made Justin give me. We need to find a Goodwill store to get some clothes and toss these coveralls."

"I'm scared, Jack," Noah said quietly.

Jack shook her head. "Don't be. We only have ourselves to rely on, Noah. We will trust no one. Do you hear me? I will always have your back and you will have mine, or I will cut your balls off," Jack said, smiling.

Noah laughed, easing the fear that was building. "Yeah, okay, Lara Croft Tomb Raider."

Jack smiled. "Exactly."

They sat in silence for some time before they heard the train approaching. Jack put the backpack on and they crouched behind the tree. The steady thud, thud, thud of the train came slowly upon them. The train was about halfway past them when Jack spotted an open car. She pointed to the car and they started jogging alongside the train until the open car was upon them. Jack jumped up and grabbed the metal ladder beside the open door. She vaulted herself into the car and immediately threw her arm out to grab Noah. He was already falling behind when she grabbed him by the forearm.

Noah tried to run faster, but Jack started to feel him slip until she was almost dragging him.

"*Let go of him. He's only going to slow us down*" Dark Twin whispered.

Jack jumped from the train and pulled Noah with her to get him away from the tracks. They landed in a heap and just lay there as the train labored out of sight.

"Jack, I'm so sorry," Noah gasped, out of breath. He glanced over at Jack as she lay with her arm over her eyes, appearing utterly defeated. Dark Twin was raging inside her, and Jack could feel her anxiety rising to dangerous levels. Dark Twin simply wanted to hurt somebody. Somebody, anybody really, but shockingly not Noah. She felt no anger whatsoever at Noah. She had no idea why, but she knew she would protect her friend no matter what.

"We get the hell up and walk the tracks. We will eventually come to a town and we'll go from there. But Noah, you are going to haul ass right now so we don't get caught, or I'm going to kick your ass. Got it?" Jack said firmly.

Noah jumped up immediately. "Yeah, I got it. You wait, someday you're going to want me to teach you some dance routine and I'm going to kick *your* ass," Noah said.

Jack smiled as she too got to her feet and started walking. "Yeah, right," she retorted.

It was lockdown at Beckett's House because a parent was flying in to retrieve their child, and Mary Beth didn't want anyone to know about the slave-like conditions at her "house of recovery." Mary Beth was pacing back and forth, wringing her hands, not looking forward to hearing from the parents after they learned their child had run away.

The door flew open and David Johnson and all nine Johnson boys burst into Mary Beth's office.

"Where is she?" David said in a murderously low voice.

"Now, Mr. Johnson, calm down! I had no idea she planned to run off!" Mary Beth implored.

"When did she leave?" David asked, leaning on her desk.

"Two days ago," Mary Beth said, looking down at her desk. David slowly lowered himself into the fake leather wingback chair and pinched the bridge of his nose, sighing. "Tell me what you have done to find her," David said quietly, sounding already defeated.

Bear, Ty, Bobby, Davey, and Caleb made their way into the rec hall, where all the kids were hanging out. Bear immediately took over with some military commander in-your-face shit. To say he was just a little intimidating was a vast understatement.

Caleb noticed one of the girls whisper something to another girl and he thought, *Oh, I've so got this,* and walked over and stood between the two girls with his arm around each and smiled.

"Hi there," Caleb said, trying his best to cozy up to the two.

"Hi," Jessie said apprehensively.

"What can you ladies tell me about my sister, Jack Johnson?"

"Well I can tell you that you better not call her Princess," Jessie chortled. "That girl is batshit crazy, I tell ya."

This exchange got the attention of the other brothers and they surrounded Jessie, which made her understandably very nervous.

"I mean she was fine until she got out of the infirmary, and then she went crazy," she said rapidly.

Bear stepped closer. "Whoa, whoa, what do you mean 'got out of the infirmary'?" Bear said, leaning in and looking particularly dangerous.

"Um, well, she was beat up pretty bad. I heard she almost died. She was in the infirmary for about two weeks, and when she got out, she wasn't the same girl who went in," Jessie replied quietly.

"Who. Beat. Her?" Bear growled. Jessie knew immediately that she had said too much, and if she disclosed any more information she too would end up in the infirmary, because Justin was scowling at her.

"I have no idea. She didn't make many friends before she went peace out," Jessie said, walking away from the group.

Bear stood up to his full height and glowered at the room. "Someone is going to tell me who put their hands on my sister!" he bellowed, walking over to a table and flipping it over, spilling all the games and soda bottles everywhere.

Silence.

Bear walked over to a group of boys and punched a giant hole in the wall above their heads, making a smaller boy wet his pants. Bear completely destroyed the room, every lamp, every table, and punched multiple holes in the walls, but still no one said a word.

David walked in and put a hand on Bear's shoulder. He was the only person in the world who would have dared to touch Bear in the state he was in. David's voice penetrated Bear's rage.

"Come with me, son," he said softly.

All ten very large and very pissed-off men walked outside to the vehicles. David pulled out his cell phone.

"Ronnie. It's me, Dave Johnson. I need you to call all the authorities in upstate New York. Jack is missing from a group home, and I need the entire area and surrounding towns searched. I need your help now. Jesus, my baby girl is g-gone," David stammered, his voice breaking. A single tear dripped onto his flannel shirt.

They walked and walked for hours. When the sun was starting to rise, they rounded a corner and found a railway yard with abandoned cars. A short distance away Jack could make out a main street and neighborhoods. Finally, they could hunker down in one of the abandoned railroad cars, get some rest, and figure out their next move. Jack spotted an empty car away from the others with an open door and pointed at it. They started walking toward it.

"Let's get some sleep in there and later today we'll figure out what we're going to do," Jack said, climbing into the car.

"Sounds like a good plan. I don't think I could walk another step," Noah said as they climbed in the empty car. Noah sighed as he pulled out some Pop-Tarts. He opened one package and handed Jack one, and he ate the other. They both ate in silence and when finished, stretched out and slept fitfully.

Jack awoke disoriented and cold. It seemed unusually cold even for a late October afternoon. Jack got up and looked out from the railroad car. She could see a busy main street with a gas station and several small businesses peppering the main street. Behind the gas station, Jack could see a small neighborhood connected by side streets.

Noah rolled over and grunted. "Jesus, this is hard," he said, standing and rubbing his face as he walked over to stand beside Jack. "So this is what a one-horse town looks like. We need to get to the city," Noah muttered, looking at Jack.

"I know we do. We are certain to get caught in a small town. People notice things like two young people wearing coveralls wandering aimlessly around town. And you can bet your ass that Mary Beth is looking for us hard considering we're a good chunk of change for her. I have a plan, sort of. The first thing we have to do is get some different clothes so we don't stand out so much. If we take a walk in the neighborhoods we might be able to see a family that is just getting home from school and work. Once we know who lives where then we can go back there tomorrow when they leave in the morning and get some clothes and supplies," Jack said, narrowing her eyes in thought.

"Wow, you've put some thought into this. I'm impressed," Noah exclaimed, putting his arm around her. "How about we finish up the Pop-Tarts and take a little walk?"

They finished off the Pop-Tarts and water and took off toward the neighborhood. "I think we should act like boyfriend and girlfriend," Noah proposed. "It will attract less attention if we appear to be into each other instead of scouting out a place to rob," he said, putting his arm around Jack's waist and pulling her close.

"True enough, I guess," Jack replied.

As they were walking along their second neighborhood, a car pulled into the driveway of the last house. A mother and two young kids along with a very tall teenage boy got out of a minivan. Jack stopped, turned to Noah, and embraced him so she could watch the family get out of the minivan and walk into the house. Perfect. The house was situated at the very end of a dead end street, which meant that they could enter from the woods and not be seen from the street. They could sit in the woods and wait for them to leave in the morning. Jack didn't see any signs of a dog, and the house wasn't nice enough to be protected by much of a security system.

"Okay. This is the one. We will stay the night in the railroad car, and in the early morning before the sun comes up, we will make our way to the woods to watch until they leave," Jack said, taking Noah's hand and walking down the street.

"That's some real James Bond shit right there," Noah chuckled, pulling her close and smiling.

Jack grabbed his face in one hand and gently squeezed. "That's called surviving, my friend, and I think we're going to have to learn to do it for a while. At least until we're eighteen and then...well, fuck 'em. Unfortunately, I think we need to make our way back to the railroad car and not let anyone see us," Jack sighed.

"Fine by me, lovely. Just chillin' with you and not getting the shit beat out of me sounds like heaven," Noah gushed.

"Amen, brother," Jack said smiling.

The branch swung back and slapped Jack in the face. *Smack.* "Jesus, Noah! Watch where you're going!" Jack hissed.

Noah slowed and crouched down. "Sorry, I can't see where I'm going. It's still too dark," he said defensively.

"Maybe we should stay here until it gets lighter. It was important that we get into the woods before anyone spotted us, but we need to see where we're going to find the house," Jack said, sitting down on the leaf-covered ground. They had spent the afternoon and evening sleeping and talking. By the time four a.m. rolled around, they were both ready to leave the railroad car.

The sun was starting to rise as they made their way to the edge of the woods overlooking the house and driveway. They waited. An hour or so later the tall teenage boy and his siblings, along with their mother, marched out of the house and piled into the minivan.

Jack and Noah waited about twenty minutes and then made their way to the back of the house. The back door was locked; that would have been too easy. The window above the kitchen sink was unlocked, so Noah lifted Jack up and she gently cut a small hole in the screen so she could grasp it and pull it out. Jack slid the window open and climbed in head first toward the kitchen sink. Noah gave her a slight push and she dove head first to the kitchen floor, completely bypassing the counter. Jack landed in a heap on the floor. Dazed she lay there for a minute, making sure nothing was broken or twisted. God, Noah reminded her of Caleb.

"Jack! Hey! What the hell! Where are you?" Noah shouted.

"Quiet down! Jesus! Go to the back door," Jack instructed. Jack unlocked the back door and let Noah in. They made their way into the kitchen. The kitchen was a mess with breakfast dishes and school papers everywhere.

Jack grabbed some bowls and some sugary cereal from the counter. They ate in silence until the edge was taken off their hunger. Jack washed their dishes and they made their way upstairs to find some clothes.

Jack immediately went to the older boy's room to find some pants that would fit her long legs. After several attempts, she found two pairs of jeans that fit her adequately. The waist was a little big, but she found a belt in the mother's room that helped. Jack found two long-sleeved T-shirts and a hooded sweatshirt from the boy's room and a warm-looking down parka from the mother's room. She grabbed several pairs of underwear and socks from the mother's drawer. She found a hat and mittens in a bin beside the front door along with a pair of insulated Bean boots.

When she was finished packing her backpack with the clothes, she found some snack food in the cupboards and then went in search of Noah. He had a full backpack hanging off one shoulder and a stack of money in his hand that he held up when Jack walked in the mother's room.

"No," Jack said firmly. "Put it back, Noah."

"What? Are you kidding? We need this money. There's four hundred dollars here, and we need every cent," he said, pocketing the money. "I don't like it either, but Jack, you need to be sensible here, we're going to need it."

Sighing, Jack swung her backpack onto her back. He was right. They did need it.

"Okay, let's get out of here."

On the way out of the house, Jack spotted a magazine with the mother's name and address on the corner. Jack tore the address off and slipped it into her back pocket. Someday she would send this mother every cent they stole from her and more, Jack vowed.

Jack knew that taking the train was way too risky. There would be cameras that would record them getting on and off the train, but if they took a low-budget bus, their chances of getting caught were slimmer.

They stopped at the gas station closest to the railroad and asked where to find the bus station. There happened to be a cab driver in the gas station, and he offered to take them to the station. The overweight, bearded, white cab driver pulled out of the gas station peering in the rearview mirror.

"So where you two lovebirds going?" he sneered, staring at Jack intently.

"We're going to the city," Noah said, squeezing Jack's cheek. "Isn't that right, lovely?"

Jack slapped his hand away, looking directly into the rearview mirror. "We're not lovebirds, we're friends, and it's none of your fucking business where we're going," Jack said bluntly.

The cab driver held up his hands. "Hey, no problem, girly, I was just trying to make conversation. Relax."

Jack could feel her anger rising as she put her hand over the blade that was in the front pocket of her jeans. She sat ramrod straight, not moving a muscle until they made it to the bus station. Jack jumped out of the cab as Noah paid the driver and apologized for Jack, saying she was tired or some such shit.

Jack was waiting at the side of the building when Noah walked over to her. Jack pushed him against the building and got in his face. "Don't ever fucking apologize for me again. Do you hear me? If you don't like how I act, then we can just divide up the money and go our separate ways," Jack spat out.

"God, would you just calm down? I'm sorry, I just felt it would be better if we didn't attract any attention while we're traveling. Okay? I thought you were ready to slit his throat back there. I don't want to separate, really. Jack, you can count on me, and besides, you need me to give you fashion advice because that outfit is pathetic. You look like a fifteen-year-old boy," Noah retorted.

Jack couldn't help herself and grinned. "You wish I was a boy," she said, squeezing his cheek and walking toward the entrance to the bus station.

They were in luck; there were two seats available on the next bus, which was due in about thirty minutes. Jack had never been in a bus station before, and the smell was making her nauseous. There was every color and size imaginable of customer getting on this bus. Instinctively, Jack felt for her blade in her pocket. Out of paranoia, Jack palmed her blade just to make sure she could act quickly. It felt like everybody was watching them and knew they were on the run.

Jack was pacing and sweating, and just when she was ready to bail and run from the bus station, the bus pulled in, emptying the night travelers onto the sidewalk.

Jack and Noah made their way to the back of the bus and hunkered down for the two-hour drive into the city. A tall, lanky African American teenager with his shorter but stockier friend sat beside them.

Trouble. Jack instinctively knew they were trouble. Dark Twin reared her head and decided to stay fully alert for the ride into the city, just in case she was needed. Excitement flowed through Jack's veins. She was ready for these two, she thought.

"*Oh we're ready, sista,*" Dark Twin whispered.

Jack sat by the window and just stared out into the night as the miles swept them toward the human garbage heap called the New York City streets.

Noah slept peacefully from what Jack could discern from his snoring and leaning on her. As they pulled into the deserted bus station, Jack nudged Noah to wake him. Jack still had her blade in her palm and looked over at the two teens. They sat with their hoods up covering most of their faces. Dark Twin was on full alert. She was aching for a fight tonight.

Noah picked up his backpack and set it on his lap. When it was their turn to get off the bus, the two teens held back and motioned for Jack and Noah to go ahead of them. It made Jack very uneasy to have them behind them, but there was little they could do but get off the bus.

Once they were off the bus, they started walking up the street; that turned out to be the worst thing they could have done. They were walking away from the crowd, and as soon as they turned the corner, Jack realized they were in a very deserted part of the city. It was also about two o'clock in the morning, so there wasn't a soul around.

Jack had taken the lead and walked until she heard Noah grunt. Jack looked back; the two guys from the bus had Noah around the throat with a gun pointed at his chest.

Shit.

"Okay, now this is how this is going down. You're gonna to give me all your cash or your boyfriend is gonna die. You hear me, bitch?" the tall, lanky one hissed.

Jack put up one hand to try to keep the boy calm. "Okay, okay, I hear you. Just don't hurt him!" Jack cried out, looking into his eyes. Somehow, Jack knew that they would kill Noah without hesitation if they didn't get what they wanted.

"Noah has the money. Give them the money, Noah," Jack said, nodding. Jack could tell Noah was scared out of his mind. He fished in his pockets and pulled out the remaining bills left over from the bus tickets—about $350.

Shit, shit, shit.

The stocky thug grabbed the money, and the tall one pointed to Jack with the gun. "Okay. Now you, Princess—hand over your money," he demanded, waving the gun back and forth between Jack and Noah. Jack could feel control slipping from her.

"*Relax; I got this,*" Dark Twin whispered to Jack.

"I don't have any money. He was holding all the money!" Jack hollered. Even as Jack spoke, Dark Twin was getting the blade ready, and Jack knew if either of them came close to her, they would get their throats slit.

A noise from the alley they were standing in front of spooked the thugs. They shoved Noah to the dirty street and ran into the night. Jack caught Noah as he was falling forward and broke his fall. They both landed softly on the ground.

Noah was shaking and a little in shock. Jack just held him for a while. She nudged him. "Hey, come on, get up—we need to get off the street. Let's go back to the bus terminal and stay there tonight; we'll take off in the morning."

Noah got up without saying a word and they walked back into the smelly terminal and found a bench against the wall to hunker down for the night. Jack could tell her Dark Twin was still on edge and wouldn't let her get any rest tonight.

Jack was just dozing off when Noah shook her awake. "Hey, lovely, come on, it's time to get out of here. I've seen a few characters walk by a couple of times looking at our backpacks."

Jack rubbed her face and pushed her slouch hat up away from her eyes. "Okay, where to? We still have a few granola bars left and a little money. Do you want to share a coffee?" she replied, pulling her backpack up on her back.

"Yeah that sounds good. If we can find a McDonald's, they have any size coffee for a buck," Noah said, falling in line with Jack.

It was early, but the streets were full of people hustling to their destinations. There were a lot of homeless people propped up against buildings sleeping and cardboard dwellings littered the alleys.

Jack spotted a McDonald's on the Lower East Side and slapped Noah as she started to run. They raced to the doors laughing as Jack grabbed Noah's backpack and pulled him back so she could reach the doors first.

Grimacing, Noah tried to catch his breath. "You're a dirty fighter, my Lovely," he said, pushing the doors open.

"Um, did I mention I have nine older brothers?" Jack smirked.

They ordered a large coffee and found a booth to eat what they had left for food. A cup of coffee had never ever tasted so good.

"Okay, we need to have some kind of plan, don't you think?" Jack asked.

"Well, we should probably find a shelter for tonight. After we find a place to sleep for the night, I think we should explore the city. Have some fun!" Noah exclaimed mischievously.

Jack was immediately uncomfortable and anxious. Dark Twin was on full alert. "We're not on vacation, Noah; we need to figure out how to survive. We can't get jobs until we're eighteen, and we need to not get caught by Beckett's House."

"Oh my God, lighten up! We're free! Let's just explore the city and pretend we're on a holiday and this evening we will be retiring to the Ritz-Carlton. Please, Jack, let's just forget for today, okay?" Noah pleaded.

Jack sat back and closed her eyes. Dark Twin was cautious but felt no anger toward Noah.

Weird.

"Okay, two things though," Jack relented, holding up two fingers. "One—we first find a shelter for the night. Two—we visit the New York City Library."

"Whoa—you're a crazy party girl, aren't you? Deal!" Noah shouted out, putting out his hand to shake on it.

Jack thrust her hand into his and shook firmly. "Deal."

Jack and Noah spent the morning watching street performers and finally found a soup kitchen that was closed but would open at five o'clock. They decided to make their way back there later for dinner and ask about the area shelters.

When Jack saw the giant lions outside the library, she sighed in relief. It was almost a religious experience walking through those doors into the mammoth stone building. The smell of old books and old building hit Jack and made her heart melt a little. At least some things never changed; books had always been her friends, and now more than ever, she needed to feel as though her world hadn't spun off its axis. She needed to feel some semblance of normal, whatever that turned out to be.

Noah parked himself in a deep chair and told her to wander around and come find him later.

Jack slowly walked through the aisles and gently touched the books reverently. As Jack walked through the classic literature section, her eyes focused on *Wuthering Heights.* Her heart skipped a beat, and with a quick intake of breath she picked up the book and just stared at it. Jared was her Heathcliff, and their love was seemingly just as tragic. She was as stubborn as Catherine and as mad as Heathcliff. She put the book down quickly and continued down the aisle.

Next Jack spied *Great Expectations* and smiled. Now *here* was a book she could get her head around. Jack wondered about Dickens's life and how painful it must have been to be able to write about life's heartbreaks like he did. This book had it all: fear, convicts, tortured childhood, madness, tragic love, and above all, the desperate need to just fit in somewhere in this fucked-up world. Jack found a soft chair and sank into it with Pip, quickly becoming blissfully lost.

Jack was being pulled so slowly back to the surface of reality that she found herself starting to whine and curl up tighter into a ball. The shaking became more forceful.

"Jack, come on, you need to wake up. They are closing the library and we need to go to the soup kitchen. Come on," Noah said softly. Sad to leave the unconscious plane, Jack nodded and got up and put the book back.

As they made their way down the granite steps Jack touched the lion and uttered a silent oath to visit often.

It was already dark, but the lights of the city made it seem like some strange dream reality. They walked in silence, and when they rounded the corner to the soup kitchen Jack could see a long line that stretched down the street. Suddenly her hard-fought-for freedom didn't seem so wonderful after all.

The tall skinny girl moved like a wary fawn, barely looking up and hugging herself tightly. Moving to the end of the line, Sam could see that she was way too thin, making her big blue eyes appear almost ghostly.

Goddamn kids, thought Sam, as he watched them try to be invisible in the line. He could tell they hadn't been on the streets long. But still Sam could tell that she wasn't a stranger to trauma. Sam sighed and walked away from the window to unlock the doors for the evening meal. The line never ended, and it seemed as though the people standing there got younger and younger. At least he could make sure some of them filled their bellies tonight, he thought, frowning.

Sam had run this soup kitchen ever since he'd met Joe and gotten back on his feet after his release from captivity in Syria. He had been so cocky and full of himself, a tough-as-nails special-forces serviceman. He had fully intended to retire from the military. That is, until he was captured on a mission in Afghanistan and moved to a Syrian torture camp. For two years, Sam endured daily torture sessions for which death would have been a blessing. But even worse than the torture sessions was the unending hunger and near death from starvation. It was the slowest and most painful death imaginable, as the body feasted on itself and slowly withered away.

Sam had been hospitalized for two months prior to being shipped home to the states. When he landed in New York, there had been no one to meet him, much less anyone who cared about his mental health. He was alone in the world in every sense of the word. He had been orphaned as a small boy and shuffled around from foster home to foster home until he turned eighteen and joined the military. His military team had been the only family he had ever had or would have. Sam was always ready to lay down his life for any of them. When they had walked into that ambush, most of the team had been killed, but those who survived were taken captive. Sam had watched as each member of his team was decapitated in front of him and a camera. The Sam that walked out of the airport that day back on American soil was a hollow husk of a human being. He had been completely broken and was unable to adapt to life outside the military or captivity.

The military had put a very large chunk of money in an account to try to compensate him for the two years in captivity. Even with money in the bank, he was not able to function enough to take care of himself. Each day passed with Sam in a drunken haze. If it wasn't alcohol, it was any drug that promised to make him forget for a little while that he was still breathing. With each needle, bottle, pill, or pipe he prayed that his heart would simply stop.

It never did. Instead, he would wake somewhere on the street or in an alley and find that he had shit or pissed himself, or both, and never ever did he know where he was, or particularly care for that matter.

One day, Sam woke up in a soft bed with Christmas music playing softly in the background. Sam was certain he had finally died, and the relief that flooded him was profound.

The relief was only momentary.

A small thin man whistling off-key to the Christmas music came shuffling into the room. When his eyes met Sam's, they brightened and the man smiled.

"Well, hello there, young fella! I'm glad you decided to stay in this world. I had a hunch your work here wasn't quite done, my friend," the man said, touching Sam's arm.

Sam jerked his arm away, instantly pissed off that he in fact was still in this shitty world.

"Where am I?" Sam muttered, sitting up and holding his head in his hands.

"You're at my home in the Bronx. My name is Joseph Foss. It's a pleasure to finally meet you," Joe said, holding out his hand for Sam to shake.

Sam ignored Joseph's hand and lifted the covers to find himself naked. "Where are my clothes?" Sam asked gruffly.

Joseph stepped back and walked to the chair to pick up a pile of new clothes. "Oh, Good Lord, I had to throw those away. Don't worry, anything that was in the pockets I saved and put on the table over there. These are new, and I hope they meet with your approval. May I ask you your name, young man?" Joseph inquired, handing Sam the pile of new clothes.

Sam grabbed the clothes and started to dress. He almost immediately started weaving and staggering, suddenly very lightheaded and sick.

"Whoa, take it easy, son. Your body has been through a lot. You need to give yourself time to get better and get your strength back."

"Listen, Joseph——"

"Please call me Joe," Joe interrupted.

"Joe, I really don't mean to be a dick, but I need to get out of here," Sam spit out as he pulled the thermal long john shirt on.

"Why? Where do you have to be? You and I both know that as soon as you leave here you're going straight to the liquor store to buy some booze. I know really deep down that you just want to die. I know this to be true," Joe said, seemingly looking straight into Sam's soul. "Please tell me your name, son," Joe implored.

For some unexplainable reason, Sam felt like his feet were glued to the floor. He crossed his arms over his chest. "Sam. My name is Sam. Tell me, why did you bring me home and do all this?" Sam asked, holding his arms out to ask about the new clothes and comfortable bed. "Aren't you afraid that I'm going to rob you or worse, kill you? I could, you know, kill you," Sam said, recrossing his arms.

Joe chuckled and touched his fingers to his chin. His eyes were twinkling. "Sam. I like it. A good solid name. Oh yes, I'm certain you could rob me and kill me. No question about it, but you won't. Now let us talk over breakfast, and I will answer any questions you may have," Joe said, shuffling out of the room. "Come on now, son, you need to eat. You probably won't be able to keep much food down for a while but you still need to eat."

Sam sighed. The old man was right. He did need to eat, and he had no place to go. He would leave as soon as he ate. He was intrigued, so figured he would get a few answers before he hit the streets. The thought of a bottle of vodka and the cold pavement somehow didn't appeal to him at all, so maybe just a little while longer here in this cozy little house wouldn't hurt.

Sam found the small kitchen and sat down at the bar. Joe put a cup of coffee in front of him and proceeded to finish making breakfast. The smell of the breakfast turned Sam's stomach inside out, and his hands were shaking as he tasted the coffee. Sam groaned, and Joe turned quickly from the stove to see what the matter was.

"Everything okay?" Joe asked.

Sam took another sip of coffee. "Yeah, fine. It's just been a while since I had a real cup of coffee. It's good, real good," Sam replied, finishing his coffee in one gulp.

Joe put a large plate of eggs, bacon, home fries, and toast in front of him and refilled his cup. Sam eyed the plate, and without looking up or touching the utensils he said softly, "Why are you doing this? What do you want from me?"

"You eat, and I will talk. Okay?" Joe replied. Sam nodded and began eating slowly.

"Well, first of all, I know you are a special forces vet by the tattoos on your arm. I've seen you every day as I pass you somewhere between Grand Central Station and the Lower East Side soup kitchen. I've also seen you at the soup kitchen from time to time. I too am a veteran. I was in World War II in the navy. I was on the USS *Maine*. Believe it or not, I was a cobbler," Joe said chuckling. "The ship was bombed and sunk. The rescue ship circled the sinking ship three times to recover as many bodies as they could. I was knocked out, and on the third swipe they saw me and hauled me aboard with a grappling hook to the jaw," Joe said, pointing to a scar under his jawline. "They thought I was dead. Anyway, the war ended shortly after that, and I was shipped home. I have a tattoo as well," he said, unbuttoning his shirt and lifting his undershirt. There was an outline of half a ship across his chest.

"I only got half a ship because I sobered up real quick after that and high-tailed it outta there!" Joe said grinning. Sam couldn't help but grin himself as he sipped his coffee.

"Well, I came home and tried to settle into normal life. I went to this dance one night, and that's when I saw her," Joe's eyes looked as if he was a million miles away. "She was the most beautiful girl I had ever seen. She had the most vibrant red hair and blue, blue eyes. Well, a fella could just get lost in those blue eyes," he said as his eyes misted over just a bit. "I walked up to her and her friends, and when she finally looked at me and smiled, I do believe I stopped breathing." Joe cleared his throat and sipped his coffee.

"Well, anyway, you get the idea. Katey and I got married, and after many years of trying we had a boy, Joe Jr. I opened up a shoe store that became very successful. I would wager that I might have been the happiest man in all of New York City," Joe exclaimed, beaming with pride. "Then one day Katey started coughing, and the cough just wouldn't go away, and she started to feel sick and so tired. Turned out she had lung cancer. Never smoked a day in her life, don't ya know. She was gone so fast. It was just little Joe and me. I did the best I could, but I was lost. I just wasn't me without my Katey. I drank a lot, a real lot. The years just went by with me in a perpetual stupor."

Suddenly, all the food Sam had just eaten was on a return trip. Sam flew into the bathroom and retched uncontrollably. He had lost the entire contents of his stomach. When his body was done retching, Joe appeared. He held a cold wet cloth on Sam's forehead and led him back to the bed.

"It's okay, son, you need to rest some more and we'll eat again later. Please, just lie down and sleep. We'll talk some more when you wake up."

Sam was so weak that he couldn't have done anything else even if he wanted. He fell onto the bed. Joe covered him up as Sam slipped away into blissful unconsciousness.

Pain and uncontrollable shivering jerked Sam awake. There truly was no God, thought Sam. He had never really asked God for anything, not a family, love, or even to keep him alive while in captivity, but for the past year he had prayed every day for God to end his suffering and stop his heart. All he got for that request was a big fat *fuck you* from God.

Joe must have sensed he was awake, because he entered the bedroom and sat on the side of the bed holding a glass of water for Sam. Sam sat up slowly and tried to hold the glass, but his hands were shaking too violently.

"Easy now, I'll hold it. You just drink as much as you can," Joe said, holding the glass to his lips. Sam was so thirsty that he gulped and gulped until he tasted the foul liquid. He started coughing and fell back against the bed.

"What the fuck is that shit?" Sam gasped between coughs. The taste was bitter and coppery.

"You drank a lot, that's good. It's a Chinese medicine to help those recovering from substance abuse. It will help you get through the next two days. Can you be strong for the next forty-eight hours? I promise this will all be worth it if you just break through to the other side," Joe replied as he gently laid a warm cloth on Sam's forehead.

"Is that what helped you get over your alcohol addiction?" Sam asked.

Joe smiled and his eyes crinkled at the corners. "Oh, no, no, I did it cold turkey. I only wish someone had cared enough to help me get through it, but truthfully, I wanted to die. I welcomed death, but my work was not finished here, and so I fought my way to the other side."

Sam's eyes narrowed. "Where was your boy? He didn't help you?"

Tears instantly sprang to Joe's eyes that were not smiling any longer. "No, that would have been a great ending to the story, but it's not what happened," Joe murmured as he pulled up an old tattered wingback chair beside the bed.

"Tell me," Sam said hoarsely.

"I drank myself into a stupor every day as my son grew up, and I totally missed it. I was never at his ball games and never even looked at his report card. He raised himself and took care of me as well," Joe said, stopping to collect himself before he continued. "He was a good son and smart. Smart as a whip he was. He used to ask me about my time in the service and always wanted to see my dog tags and tattoo," Joe said smiling again. "Well, it shouldn't have been a surprise to me when he came home the day after graduation and told me he had enlisted in the army. I didn't know whether to be proud or mad at him. I guess I was both. He left two weeks later and never came home to stay again. He went into the special forces, so I didn't know much about what he was doing. When he called, he couldn't talk about his missions, but sometimes he would tell me little snippets of things that had happened when he had a particularly traumatic day. You know, like if someone on his team didn't make it. That's how I knew you were special forces, by your arm tattoos," he said pointing to Sam's arms. "Little Joe had some of the same. He was so damn proud of his team—his brothers, he called them—and it was so hard on him when they lost one. Well, I was sinking lower and drinking myself to death. One day, a soldier showed up on my doorstep." Joe stopped talking and simply sat there with his eyes closed, trying to collect himself. "Well, you know what that means. He was in the mountain range in Afghanistan looking for Bin Laden when he stepped on a landmine. They shipped him home, and in his personal belongings were these dog tags." Joe pulled four tags out of his shirt and tossed them on the bed. Two were Joe's from the navy, and two were from Little Joe.

"Damn kid was wearing both mine and his tags when he died," Joe's voice trailed off.

Sam shifted in the bed to ease the pain in his legs. Joe got up abruptly, looking concerned. "How are you doing? I'm going to make us some lunch and you another Chinese drink. Can you make it to the bathroom and come out to the table?" Joe asked, standing beside the bed with his hand outstretched to help Sam out of bed.

"I don't need your help," Sam retorted as he tried to stand on his own only to fall back onto the bed. His legs just wouldn't hold him up.

Joe again put his hand out there. "I know you don't, son, but I sure do need to give it. Will you help an old man out and let me help you? It's kind of healing for me to talk about my Katey and Little Joe," Joe said with a misty twinkle in his eye.

Sam grabbed Joe's hand and lifted himself from the bed.

Jack's stomach growled loudly. Noah laughed and hugged her from behind. "We're almost inside, lovely," he pointed out as he squeezed her. Finally a large group came out at once and Jack and Noah entered the large room and went to the buffet line. There was a tall thin man with gray hair that kind of feathered back away from his weathered face. Deep lines of sorrow etched themselves into his brown eyes. He wore a thick silver-and-gray mustache. He looked like some kind of grumpy mountain man. He held out a paper plate loaded with mashed potatoes, turkey, green beans and a large yeast roll. A plate of food had never, ever looked so good to Jack.

Jack looked at the large plate of food and up at the mountain man. "Thank you," Jack whispered, looking away as she took her plate and turned to find a couple of empty seats.

Jack hunched over her plate and devoured her food. Noah did the same, not stopping until every bite was gone. As Jack and Noah got up to throw their plates away, someone grabbed Jack by the arms from behind.

"Excuse me, Princess," the old man said, trying to maneuver around Jack in between the tables. The touch and reference to Princess made Jack see red. Dark Twin's arms instantly went to a battle stance and she grabbed the blade from her back pocket. The blade whipped around, swiping the air. The child in the seat across from Jack saw the blade and started screaming. Chairs were pushed back and people backed up to give Jack a wide berth.

"Whoa! Jack, no, sweetie, he didn't mean any harm, he was just trying to move past you. That's all. Really. Put the blade away, Jack." Noah was trying to calm Jack down, but he could see her eyes darting wildly and she was very close to losing all control.

"Jack!" Noah hollered. As Jack's eyes met Noah's, she froze.

"Put the blade away, Jack. It's okay. Please," Noah pleaded softly.

Jack looked around at all the scared faces and the crying children and turned and ran out the door and down the street as fast as her legs would carry her. Noah followed, trying to keep up and hollering for her to stop.

When she came to a crosswalk full of people waiting to cross, she stopped and turned to see Noah rushing toward her. Jack ran into his arms sobbing. "I'm sorry, I'm sorry!"

"Shhh, it's okay, we're fine, and nobody got hurt," Noah said stroking her hair. "Come on, we need to find a place to stay tonight."

They walked until they found the shelter that they'd seen a flyer for in the window of the soup kitchen. There were groups of people standing around outside smoking and drinking from paper bags. Jack and Noah started to approach the front door of the dilapidated old brick building when someone hollered out, "It's full up for the night."

Jack and Noah stopped and looked around. The group was looking at them, but they looked sympathetic and not threatening at all. The old African American man who had touched Jack stepped away from the group.

"Are you okay, Missy?" he asked softly. "My name is Leo, and I meant you no harm, little one," he said smiling sadly.

Jack forced herself to lift her head and look into Leo's eyes. Her heart dropped. What she saw in the depths of his kind eyes was anything but threatening. She saw pain and suffering and love. Tears threatened to spill and she said softly, "I'm sorry."

Leo shook his head. "No need to apologize, little one. I've been out here long enough to recognize someone with a dark passenger. I know someone who can help you when you're ready, but in the meantime, you kids need to find a place to settle down for the night. It's not safe out here after dark."

We just got into town, and we don't know where to go. Do you have any suggestions?" Noah asked with his arm firmly around Jack.

"Well, I can tell you that the shelters are probably the most dangerous. The folks in there will fight you for anything of value you have or just outright take it while you sleep, the thieving rats. A few blocks down is an abandoned church. If you go around back, you can see there is a boarded-up window that someone pried apart, and you can climb in. Others may be in there, but you can probably find a place to rest for the night," Leo advised, stuffing his hands into the thin coat he wore.

"Thank you. We appreciate it, and again I'm really sorry," Jack said, turning and walking away, pulling Noah behind her.

They found the church and Jack was able to shimmy through the plywood and window and open the door for Noah. Inside it was dark, but Jack could make out at least two families at the far end that were hunkered down for the night. Jack walked up behind the altar and sat with her back to the pews inside the choir loft. Noah joined her and she leaned her head on his shoulder.

"I'm scared," she whispered.

"I know, lovely—me too. Listen, you get some sleep and I'll keep the first watch, okay?" Noah replied, pulling her hood close around her face.

"Okay," Jack said, already feeling herself drifting off.

Jack awoke to a baby crying and the mother trying desperately to quiet it. Jack glanced at Noah and saw he was fast asleep. *Great watch you are,* she thought, taking a deep breath. *What did Leo mean about helping me with my dark passenger? How could he have possibly known about that?*

Jack was getting more frightened about these episodes. She couldn't really remember much about them except that when she finally came around, people were scared and fearful of her. Maybe she would ask Leo about it if she ever saw him again.

Jack shook Noah awake. It was barely dawn, but Jack had to use the bathroom and wanted to wash her face and brush her teeth. It was important for her to feel some sort of normalcy in her life, and the basic routine of washing her face and brushing her teeth would be a good place to start...even if the act took place in the bathroom at MacDonald's.

Noah stretched and yawned as he slowly woke up. "Yeah, I feel very safe with you standing guard," Jack said sarcastically.

"Sorry, I just couldn't keep my eyes open," Noah replied, smiling sheepishly.

"Whatever. Let's head over to MacDonald's so I can use the restroom," Jack snorted as she grabbed her backpack.

Jack felt better. She had washed herself as best she could with soap and a paper towel, so at least she didn't smell too bad, but her hair, God, it was gross! She took her hat off, and the greasy curls were matted to her head. Jack quickly shoved the hat back on her head and made a face in the mirror. "Whatever," she whispered to herself in the mirror and left the bathroom to find Noah waiting in the hall between the men's and ladies' bathrooms.

The next few weeks settled into a surreal, foreboding routine of sleeping in the church, walking the streets, reading in the library, and using what was left of the money Justin had given Jack to feed themselves. One day when Jack was reading in the library, Noah left the library and investigated a club that they had walked by dozens of times. The club was a gay bar called The Wildflower, a little dive on the lower east side.

Noah entered the club and looked around. It was mostly empty except for a couple of men at the end of the bar making out. It was the middle of the day, so it was probably normal for it to be empty, but Noah had never been in such a place, and his heart was beating fast.

The young, good-looking bartender looked him over and smiled sweetly. "What can I get you?" he inquired.

Noah was breathless: the bartender was the most handsome man he had ever seen. "Um, sorry, I have passed this place a lot and just wanted to check it out. I don't have any money," he mumbled, embarrassed. Noah turned to flee, totally humiliated.

"Wait! First drink is on the house. That's the rule," the good-looking bartender said, spreading his arms out as if having no choice but to serve Noah a drink on the house. "My name is Pete. What are you drinking?" he asked, leaning on the bar with both arms.

Yum, thought Noah, starting to sweat. His breath came in short bursts. "Noah, I'm Noah. How about a vodka tonic with lemon?" This was the only drink he could think of. It was what had seemed to always be in his mother's hand on the rare occasion he had spent any time with her.

Noah sipped his drink and found Pete to be very easy to talk to. By the time his drink was empty, Noah had spilled all about his and Jack's miserable adventure and how desperate they were. Pete told Noah that he was a model and tended bar to pay the bills. He invited Noah to accompany him to a modeling gig the next day. Pete said he could help set Noah up with people to put together a portfolio for him. Pete asked him to meet him at the Wildflower at closing time and he and Jack could stay at his place for the night.

Noah was so excited about the thought of actually having a safe place to sleep for once that he practically flew back to tell Jack. However, Jack was having none of it.

"Absolutely not!" Jack exclaimed, shaking her head. "What were you thinking? We don't even know him!"

"Um, okay, I'm sure he isn't trying to take advantage of us. We have nothing and haven't even showered since I can't remember! We're going, and I'm going with him tomorrow to his modeling gig," Noah said firmly. "We're flat broke and hungry and he has offered us a roof over our heads and the use of a shower. *We are going!*" he exclaimed with his arms crossed, staring her down.

The crosswalk light changed and people were rushing past and bumping into them, but they remained cemented in place locked in their showdown. After several long minutes, Jack threw up her arms in defeat. "Fine, but if we get our throats slit tonight, it's your fault," she said, turning to cross the street.

Noah smiled and hurried to catch up, putting his arm around her. "OMG, he is so gorgeous, Jack, you are going to die!" he exclaimed with a smile lighting up his face.

Jack was sound asleep when Noah shook her awake. It was the first sound sleep she had managed since the family with the baby had gotten into the shelter. Jack waved off Noah and curled herself into a tighter ball on the floor.

"Come on, Jack, we need to get over to the Wildflower before it closes," Noah pleaded as he grabbed her arms and pulled her to her feet. Jack started to protest but then got a whiff of herself and thought a shower did sound like a great idea.

It might as well had been two o'clock in the afternoon instead of two o'clock in the morning out on the streets. The night was turned into day with the giant billboards illuminating the city and people coming and going with seemingly important places to be. *Not a lot of upstanding citizens milling about,* thought Jack. She immediately felt on edge. There was something off about this place.

Noah led the way inside and headed straight for the bar. The bar was about half full, with most of the patrons already paired off in anticipation of the after-closing activities. Jack tried to look anywhere but at the openly public displays of lust playing out before her.

Pete came to the end of the bar where Noah and Jack were seated and held out his hand to Jack. "Hi, I'm Pete. You must be Jack," he said, smiling. "You're right, she's gorgeous."

Jack ignored Pete's hand and looked at him suspiciously. "I don't trust you. I don't trust anybody. I'm only here for Noah. If you hurt him, I will hurt you," Jack said matter-of-factly.

Noah shifted uncomfortably. "Jesus, Jack, lighten up, will you?" Noah said, locking glares with Jack.

"I'll be outside waiting," Jack replied without looking away for several seconds until she finally turned and headed out the door.

Jack leaned against the dirty brick building and watched and waited. It was cold, really cold. Her mind drifted back to happy winter evenings being curled up by the big fireplace with a good book and not a care in the world. Now all the cares of the world were on her shoulders, she thought, or so it seemed. She felt empty, as if someone had scooped out all the good in her and left a crusty shell to continue to exist.

Jack's eyes were closed. She had slipped into a dream-like state when she felt hot breath close to her cheek. "Well, what do we have here?" said a deep voice. Jack's eyes flew open to see three really big guys dressed in leather jackets and headbands surrounding her. Her head was suddenly slammed back against the brick building and a knife was wedged under her chin. *Shit, shit, shit.*

The hot sticky breath on her face made Jack gag. The dude's lips were almost touching Jack's closed lips.

"What are you doing here, sweetheart? There's not one guy here who can give you what you really want," he leered, grabbing her crotch. "Or is it pussy that you prefer? Is that it, Princess? Well we are going to have some fun with you tonight. Aren't we, boys?" the brute snarled.

The change was almost instant. Jack's breathing slowed and her eyes became dark and cloudy, almost demonic. A slow smile lit her face as the eyes of her dark passenger focused on the biker dude pressing the blade to her throat.

"Do you really think that you have anything that I would even consider letting touch my body, you dirty cretin? I wouldn't let you lick my dog's balls, you pathetic loser," Jack hissed, smiling as she brought her thin blade to his cheek and sliced deeply.

The creep jumped back and grasped his face. Blood was pouring through his fingers and dripping on the dirty sidewalk.

"You bitch! I'm going to gut you!" he snarled, taking a step toward her with his hunting blade pointed toward her stomach. All of a sudden Jack saw the thug fall to the ground, convulsing, and then she too felt electrical shocks pulsating through her entire body. She was powerless and felt herself being heaved over someone's shoulder. Someone tall; it looked like it was a long way to the ground. She heard voices. Noah was arguing with the dude she was hanging from. Then blackness.

Jack sucked in a roomful of air as she tried to sit up and get her bearings. She sat halfway up and was jerked back because her hands were tied above her head to the metal bedpost. Jack's eyes flew to her hands and then to survey the room. It was a fairly large room with high ceilings and white walls. There were no windows and very few furnishings. A metal framed twin bed sat in the corner with a ratty wingback chair against the wall in front of a small stand with a nineteen-inch television. The television was old. It could play DVDs and VHS tapes from the bottom of the set. A small paint- chipped dresser with an attached mirror was against the wall at the foot of the bed. Sparse and lonely was etched into every furnishing of the drab room. Standing beside the door with his arms crossed was her weathered and worn captor. He was tall and thin with worn blue jeans and even older boots. A thin green tee shirt and old flannel shirt with the cuffs rolled up completed his wardrobe. His hair was mostly gray with some black weaved throughout and salt and pepper sideburns. He had an out-of-date mustache and the kindest green eyes Jack had ever seen, and they were just staring at her.

"Who are you and what do you want from me? And why the fuck am I tied up?" Jack said, glaring at the man, all the while trying to wrench her arms free. The man just stood there and stared at her. Jack threw herself back against the pillow and stared at the ceiling. The man finally rubbed his face violently, put his hands in his pockets, and started to pace.

"My name is Sam, and I don't rightly know what the hell I'm doing, to be truthful. You're at the soup kitchen that you came to a while back, you know, where you threatened Leo with your blade?"

Jack vaguely remembered. "Listen, I'm sorry about that. I've already apologized to Leo…"

Sam nodded his head. "I know, I know. This has nothing to do with that incident. Well, I guess it does in a way." Sam stopped pacing and stood beside the bed and crossed his arms. "Leo and I have been looking for you everywhere. You're not an easy girl to find."

Jack instantly paled. "Has someone been here looking for me?" Jack said quietly.

Sam nodded again. "As a matter of fact there have been people asking about you," Sam replied, looking at her intently.

"What did you tell them?" Jack whispered.

Sam continued to stare at her, arms still crossed. "I didn't tell them anything. That's not why Leo and I were looking for you. First off, what is your name?"

Jack took a deep breath. She was so tired. "If I tell you the truth, are you going to call those people?" she asked.

Sam shook his head. "No, you're safe here always," he said.

"Jack, my name is Jack Johnson."

Sam raised his eyebrow as he tried to hide a small grin.

Jack sighed. "I know, but if you knew my brother Caleb you would understand," she observed with a small grin of her own.

"Okay, well…"

"Um, Sam, would you mind untying me and letting me use the restroom?"

Sam looked startled. "Oh, Jesus! I forgot! Do you promise me you won't run away?" he asked, starting to untie her hands.

"I promise," Jack replied, rubbing her wrists to get the blood flowing. "It's not like I have anywhere to go," she mumbled, following Sam to the restroom. It was a small bathroom off his bedroom with a sink, toilet, and shower all crammed together. When Jack finished, she washed her face and hands. She felt a little better as she entered the bedroom again to find it empty. Jack walked out of the bedroom and into the large soup kitchen. Jack made her way out back to the kitchen to find that Sam had set up a stool at the counter and was scrambling some eggs for her. Jack sat down on the stool and soon she had eggs, bacon, and toast sitting in front of her. Sam poured them both a cup of coffee. Jack ate like she was starving. In fact, she was starving. This was pure manna to her. Sweet Jesus, this breakfast rivaled Bebe's any day of the week. When Jack finally put her fork down and looked up, Sam was leaning against the counter staring at her, smiling.

"Sorry," Jack said meekly.

"Balderdash! That's why I run this place. There's nothing quite like a full belly," Sam proclaimed as he put her plate in the sink. "Now I want you to just listen to what I have to say before you get mad or scared and run away. Deal? Just listen to me."

"Okay, deal."

"I was in the service, and I saw some pretty bad stuff over there. When I came home, I started hearing voices. Well, to be truthful I heard the voices long before I came home." Jack's head jerked up and her eyes widened.

Sam's arms came out and he spoke very softly. "I know, Jack, I know you hear them too. They're not your friends. I know you probably think they protect you, but you're wrong; eventually, they will kill you. Like I said, I heard them too, and to drown them out I drank. I drank a lot. I drank so much that I never knew where I was. I almost hurt innocent people. There was a man who helped me. I guess he is what most would consider a guardian angel to me. I loved him like a father. I had many years with him, and when he died I took over running his soup kitchen. I went back to school to learn more about my voices and became a counselor.

"Dark Twin," Jack whispered.

"What's that?" Sam asked.

"It's one voice, and I call her my Dark Twin," Jack replied softly.

"Oh, I see. That's very appropriate, isn't it? That's kind of what she is. You have a condition called PTSD—Posttraumatic Stress Disorder. It occurs when a person has suffered severe physical or mental trauma or both. It's your brain's way of trying to protect you. It occurs when you begin to feel fear or anger."

Jack's eyes grew wide. "How did you know I had it?" she asked.

"Well, like I said, I'm a counselor, and I also suffered from it. So did Leo. He has been looking everywhere for you."

"Can you make my Dark Twin go away?" Jack asked, holding her breath.

"Short answer? Yes, I can help you, but you will have to be willing to have counseling and group sessions with me, and there are some other things you're going to have to do as well."

Jack jumped off the stool and looked like she was going to bolt. "I'm not going to let you turn me in!" Jack cried out, turning toward the door.

"Now wait, Jack, just wait. Please. I'm not going to turn you in. I promise. Just hear me out and then you can make a decision, okay?"

Jack looked into those kind green eyes and instantly calmed and sat back on the stool.

"First of all, you need to get off the streets. It's too dangerous, and it's too cold. I have a friend at the shelter near here, and they need someone to help out around the place and help with the kids staying there. There isn't a paycheck, but you will have a room to yourself every night. Three evenings a week, you come to the soup kitchen for counseling and group sessions. The group consists of others who suffer from PTSD. You will eat here at least once a day, every day. You will need to keep your strength up for the last of my conditions. Two mornings a week, after you've helped at the shelter, you come here for Krav Maga instruction," Sam said, crossing his arms and smiling, making his eyes twinkle.

"What the hell is that?" Jack said, eyes narrowing.

"It's a form of self-defense and hand-to-hand combat. I taught it in the military. The object is to avoid harm and neutralize attackers by any means necessary. You need to be able to protect yourself, little one," Sam explained.

Jack immediately teared up. "Why are you doing this for me, Sam?"

There was a long silence as Sam closed his eyes. He sighed and opened them and looked directly at Jack. "I don't rightly know, little one. Maybe

I see what someone saw in me a long time ago. What I do know is that I am compelled to help you and maybe, just maybe, chase the darkness from your eyes. And with that, I am going to take you to the shelter for you to shower and get settled in. I sent Leo and Jasmine to buy you some clothes. They should be in your room at the shelter," he said, motioning for her to come with him.

Jack started shaking her head. "Wait a second, Sam. I really appreciate all the trouble you have gone to, but I haven't agreed to anything. First off, I've heard really bad things about shelters, from Leo actually, and second, if Noah can't stay with me, then it's a deal-breaker. I won't abandon him. As a matter of fact, I need to go find him. He probably thinks you've killed me the way you threw me over your shoulder and took me!" Jack replied, getting off the stool.

Sam held up his hands in protest. "Okay, now, wait a minute. I'm not finished. You're right, shelters are generally shitty places to be, but I know a woman who tries really hard to help the people who stay there retain some dignity. Her name is Jasmine, and she truly is an angel here on earth, and trust me, I don't give that label out freely. She works tirelessly trying to find jobs for the homeless and counseling. You name it, Jasmine is the most connected person in New York City and the most determined woman I have ever met. You will like her, trust me. I just have this hunch that you can help her and contribute. I learned many years ago to trust my hunches. They kept me alive in more situations than I care to remember. And second, Noah knows where you are and he's going to meet us at the shelter tonight. He can stay with you, but only if he helps out and doesn't cause any trouble. I'm not sure why you have hooked your wagon to him, little one, but I suspect he is going pull you down into the rabbit hole if you let him."

Jack looked Sam straight in the eye. "Well, I don't throw people away. He's my friend, and I'll take care of him. With that said, I will accept your offer of help, and I will not let you and your Jasmine down. Do you really think you can make my Dark Twin leave?" Jack whispered, tearing up again.

"Nope," Sam said, ushering Jack out of the kitchen to go to the shelter. "I know I can make the bitch leave."

Jack followed, trying to hide a smile and letting a little grain of hope settle into the pit of her stomach.

Jared sat staring out the window of the cafe. He had arrived early for the meeting to make sure they got a booth by the window. He always sat by the window so he could watch every face that passed by.

Jack.

He was always searching the sea of faces for his precious Princess. Today he was meeting with a private investigator he had hired to try and find her. He had been in New York for about five months now, and he finally saved enough money to hire a PI. He had arrived in New York the night Jack's father took her away. He had driven straight until he reached the city. It had taken a few weeks, but he'd found a job as a video game programmer at a small startup company. He shared an office as well as a very small loft apartment with two other computer nerds. Chase and Adam were hardworking Midwesterners. A wild and crazy night for those two was going to the local pub and watching all the attractive women but never having the nerve to actually talk to one. They suited Jared just fine.

Jared spent all his time writing programs. When he was at work, he wrote programs for his employer, but at home he worked well into every night for himself. He had so many crazy innovative ideas for new programs. What he worked on was so cutting edge that he talked to no one about it, not even his roommates. He didn't know how, but he knew he was going start his own video-game company and change the gaming world.

Working night and day was the only thing that kept Jared from going completely insane. The guilt and emptiness almost consumed him daily. If he didn't work all the time, he knew the alternative was booze. It was as if his very DNA was crying out for some sort of relief from the pain. On a very basic level, he was beginning to understand why his father was the way he was. It certainly didn't give his no-good son-of-a-bitch father a pass, but he now understood the reasons why he was the way he was a little more.

The door swung open and a large man with a buzz cut and aviator sunglasses walked in. This man screamed law enforcement, Jared thought.

"Mr. Morelli?" Jared asked. The man turned and removed his sunglasses.

"Jim, please," the man replied, holding his hand out. Jared shook his hand and waved him over to the booth. "Thanks for meeting with me, Jim. I assume you have a series of questions for me?"

Jim sat ramrod straight and clasped his hands together on the table. "Actually, based on the information you've given me already, I've made some inquiries. I have to tell you that you're not the only person to employ a private investigator to try to find Miss Johnson."

Jared looked deep in thought for a minute. "Her father, David Johnson?"

Jim nodded. "Yes, he has at least one PI working for him. I spoke with the head investigator, and we have agreed to exchange information whenever we have something to report. I hope you don't mind, but I assumed that the ultimate goal here was to get her back home safely as soon as possible."

Jared nodded. "Absolutely. All information can be shared. Did the other PI have anything to report?"

"Yes, quite a lot, actually." Jim proceeded to tell Jared about Jack's extended stay in the infirmary at Beckett's House along with the very few details of her beating that the spokesperson for Beckett's House was willing to give out.

Jared's eyes exploded with rage. "How badly was she hurt and why?" Jared asked calmly.

Too calmly.

"I couldn't get any details about that. I'm assuming they are concerned about getting their asses sued off," Jim replied.

Jared felt his pulse quicken.

Jim told Jared about the possible escape on the train. "She wasn't alone when she escaped," Jim said quietly.

Jared's head jerked up. He hadn't quite caught up to the conversation after Jim said Jack had been severely beaten. "She's with someone?"

"Yes, another student from Beckett's House. Noah Cabrera. He's a few months older than Jack, and from what the investigator told me, he also had a hard time adjusting in the home because he was gay and the other residents bullied him."

Jared physically relaxed and started to breathe again. A small smile formed on his face as he shook his head. "That doesn't surprise me. Jack would've protected him. She's just like her mother—very protective. If you're lucky enough to have Jack love you, well let's just say you're pretty lucky," Jared muttered quietly as he stared out the window.

Jim cleared his throat. "There have been ground searches by private parties as well as all the local authorities, and they've turned up nothing. They could be anywhere, and if they are here in the city, well, it really would be like looking for a needle in a haystack. However, with that said, I will begin searching here in the city and put out feelers across the country, concentrating on the East Coast. I do have to say that in my experience, if someone doesn't want to be found, they usually don't turn up. I just don't want you to get your hopes up too high. I don't have to tell you how very dangerous this city is on its best day. If you put homeless, broke, and desperate into the mix…" Jim trailed off as he stared at Jared and saw what little color Jared had drain from his face.

"Um, sorry, don't get me wrong, I'm very good at what I do, and I will do my best to find her. Believe me. I just wanted to give you all the information there was. I will be in touch." Jim finished up by shaking hands with Jared, sliding out of the booth, and strolling out the door.

Jared walked slowly back to work, deep in thought. He turned the corner and almost ran straight into a solid barrel chest. David Johnson was standing at the entrance to the video game company where he worked. His hands were in his pockets to keep them warm, and a look of utter defeat was tattooed on his face. Jared stopped suddenly and felt sick.

"David what are you doing here? Did Jack come home? Is she all right? *David, tell me what's happened!*" Jared hollered.

David held out his hands. "No, son, I haven't heard from Jack. I'm sorry to scare you like this. I came to see you. Is there a place we can talk?" David asked quietly.

Jared just stared at him. David appeared so old and broken that Jared was taken aback. "Um, sure, my apartment isn't far from here. I just need to make a call and tell them I'm going to be working from home today," Jared replied, pulling out his phone and punching the number to Chase. "Hey, buddy, I'm going to work from home this afternoon, okay? I'll see you later tonight." Jared tossed the phone back in his pocket and started walking toward his apartment.

"You live with the guys you work with?" David asked. Jared looked at David, surprised. David looked a little sheepish. "I did some checking on you also."

They made their way up the three flights of stairs to the small loft apartment. David looked huge and out of place in the tiny space. Jared got them both a beer and brought one to David, who was standing at the window looking down at the busy street.

"I was wrong," David said quietly, taking a pull off the beer.

"Sorry?" Jared asked.

"I was completely wrong. I acted like a complete ass. I always have when it came to Jack. When I lost my Elsie, well, I lost my whole world, son. When people use that phrase—*the sun rose and set with her*—well, the sun really did rise and set for me with Elsie. I loved her with every fiber of my being. Don't get me wrong, I love my boys as much as a father can love his children, but if it hadn't been for that little Princess, well I probably would have swallowed a bullet a long time ago. When I looked into my little girl's eyes, I could literally see my Elsie staring back at me, and she has all her mother's sweetness. I've never seen a more loving child in all my life. She never gave me a moment's worry. She wasn't like most daughters I hear my friends complain about. She didn't give a hoot about material things. She just loved her brothers and loved school and, my God, she loved music. My kids filled our home with so much music and love that on some days I could almost believe Elsie was right there with us. But I knew she wasn't really with us, and any pain you are feeling right now worrying and missing Jack, well, multiply that by a million and that's what I felt, feel, every goddamn day of my existence. It doesn't get better, it gets worse and harder to breathe and harder to put one foot in front of the other every friggin' day. But my boys and Jack were worth the pain. Look, I know there is no excuse for my behavior, and what I'm trying to say is, I'm sorry. So very sorry for how I treated you and my baby girl. Hell, even my boys. I've had to beg my boys to forgive me and to help me make it right. They blame me and are so angry for not letting them say good-bye to her. I fucked up royally, and I will spend the rest of my life trying to make this right. Which brings me to why I'm here. I know you were hoping for that internship, and I fucked that up too. Well, I'm here to make it right. I know how bright you are, son, and I also know that you have always wanted to start your own company. I've drawn up the papers for you to do that. I will be a silent investor and will put up the starting costs with no interest for the first year until you get on your feet. You will be the CEO and build the company from the ground up. What do you say—will you forgive me and let me help you?" David said, putting his big hand on Jared's shoulder.

Jared was speechless. "David, I don't know what to say," he stammered. "Of course I forgive you. You were angry and hurt. Jesus, if that was my daughter, I probably would be in jail 'cause I would have killed the son-of-a-bitch. David, you were more of a father to me than the piece of shit that I share DNA with. I can never repay what you and Elsie did for me, but I have to be straight with you: I love Jack more than anything and if I ever—I mean *ever*—get the chance to tell her that again, well, I won't be staying away from her. I will never, ever stop searching for her, and I will never stop loving her."

Jared stepped away from the big man as his throat began to close up. David smiled wanly and pulled Jared in for a big hug. "That's the boy I raised. You were always the toughest little shit," David said with tears threatening his own eyes.

As David pulled away and made his way to the door, he stopped and turned toward Jared. He pulled a card out of his pocket and laid it on the end table. "This is my attorney here in the city; he has all the account information along with the paperwork that needs to be signed. I have signed everything I need to. Please let me try to make this right. All I'm doing is putting up startup money. You're doing all the hard work, and you can start paying it back in a year, but my guess is your company is going to be wicked success-ful and you will have this loan paid off within the first year. And keep in mind, son, you're going to have to take care of my little girl someday, and she deserves the very best."

David gave Jared a wink and walked out the door. Jared sank into the chair and stared at the door until the sun went down and shadows crossed the floor.

Jasmine was busy with paperwork when Sam and Jack arrived at the Hope Shelter. The moment Jasmine saw Sam, a big smile lit her face and she jumped up and hugged Sam.

"Jasmine, this is Jack, the young lady I was telling you about," Sam said with his arm outstretched but careful not to touch Jack. Jasmine smiled and held out her hand. She was much shorter than Jack and had tons of gorgeous braids gathered into a ponytail at the back of her head. Her eyes were soft and caring, but there was a slight set to her chin that made Jack think that if someone pushed Jasmine or threatened something she was passionate about, they would have a spitfire on their hands. Jack liked that, and she instantly liked Jasmine.

Jack offered her hand and smiled. "Hi, it's very nice to meet you," Jack said politely.

Jasmine raised her eyebrows at Sam. "Well, let me show you to your room and go over the ground rules," Jasmine said, leading the way to the staircase.

They climbed the stairs to the third floor, which was just a small room with a twin bed, a cot, and a dirty overstuffed chair in the corner.

"It's not much, but it's yours for as long as you need it and as long as you agree to help out here at the shelter. I understand that you have a friend who will be using the cot. That's fine as long as he doesn't cause any trouble, and he must be inside the building by ten o'clock at night, which is lights out. Our purpose here is to give people a safe place at night from the streets and weather. I'll need you to help with the children—you know, reading to them or maybe helping with schoolwork. I may need help checking people in and just generally helping out. How does this sound to you, Jack?" Jasmine asked.

Jack looked around before meeting Jasmine's direct gaze. "It looks perfect; thank you, Jasmine. I promise I will be as much help as I can possibly be. Um, there are a few nights that Sam wants me to attend group counseling sessions and some sort of self-defense classes," Jack said, looking at Sam.

Jasmine laughed. "Of course, that is no problem. In fact, I fully encourage both of those endeavors for you."

Jack put the bag of clothes that Sam and Leo had gotten for her on the bed, and Jasmine showed Jack around the rest of the shelter. Jack was particularly interested in the children's corner in the living room. It was sparse, and the small number of books the children had to choose from was pathetic.

When the tour was done, Sam looked at his watch. "Well, we need to get back to the kitchen to help Angel prepare the evening meal." Sam looked at Jack. "Noah is going to meet us there."

Jack nodded. "Thank you again, Jasmine, for your trust in me. I will be back tonight after I help clean up after the meal."

Jasmine nodded and smiled. "It's good to have you here, Jack. I'll see you this evening."

Noah was waiting on the steps of the soup kitchen when Jack and Sam arrived. He jumped up and embraced Jack.

"Oh Jesus, there you are! Are you okay? What the fuck happened?"

Jack put her hands on his upper arms and held him at arm's length. "Whoa, hold on! I'm fine, Noah. This is Sam, and he is helping me—er, us. He found us a room at Hope Shelter, and we will help out here for our meals here each day."

Noah's eyes narrowed, and Jack could tell he was trying to decipher whether Jack really was okay. Jack shook him and smiled.

"Really, I'm fine. Doesn't everybody get attacked by a group of biker dudes and then tased and kidnapped on a regular weeknight? Come on!" Jack exclaimed, laughing.

Noah backed up and looked at Sam. "Wow, something has changed. I've never heard her laugh before. Thank you," he said and clapped his hands together. "What would you like us to do?" Noah asked Sam.

Sam nodded and entered the building. "Well, for starters you can go ask Angel if he needs help with the cooking," Sam said, pointing toward the kitchen.

Before they even entered the kitchen, the soulful and moving sounds of Aretha Franklin singing "Respect" filled the air. At the giant industrial cooking stove stood a very large Mexican man wearing a do-rag with a diamond earring shimmering from his left earlobe. He had a big barrel chest that reminded Jack of her dad, which made her sober up. She could feel her Dark Twin take notice as anger and hurt bubbled to the surface.

Angel was swaying and bopping to the music from the old clock radio on the counter when he suddenly exploded into a twist and turn that ended when he spotted Jack and Noah standing there watching him. There was an awkward silence before the big man cleared his throat, wiped his hands on his apron, and extended his hand.

"You kids must be Jack and Noah. I'm Angel, nice to finally meet you," he said with smiling eyes.

Jack averted her eyes and shook his hand, quickly mumbling a quiet hello. Noah looked at Jack, a little confused, but quickly looked back at Angel and shook his hand.

"Nice to meet you too. What would you like us to do?" Noah asked.

Angel gestured toward the counter, which was covered with vegetables for salad. "You can cut up those vegetables and make a big salad in that bowl. The shepherd's pie is already in the oven. After you make the salad, you can start bringing the bread and plates to the dining room," Angel replied, walking to the back door. "I'm going to be just outside here having a smoke if you need anything."

Jack suddenly smelled the shepherd's pie in the oven, and her stomach growled audibly. Noah looked at her and tilted his forehead against hers.

"Tell me what's going on, lovely," he said softly. Jack closed her eyes for a moment and sighed.

"I'm broken, Noah. That's what's wrong with me. I'm irrevocably and spectacularly broken," she muttered with a sigh.

Noah gently held her face in his hands and looked her in the eye. "Talk to me," he commanded, walking her over to the counter and grabbing a knife to chop vegetables. Jack grabbed a knife to help and proceeded to tell him about what happened after Sam spirited her off over his shoulder.

Noah shook his head. "Wow. I think this may be the break we're looking for, lovely. I think you should take Sam up on his offer to help counsel you and for the self-defense. He seems like a good guy," Noah replied as he threw a piece of green pepper at her.

Jack caught the pepper in her mouth, which made Noah laugh. "Impressed, are we?" Jack laughed. "My brother Caleb and I used to have contests to see who could catch the most with their mouths. Dumb, huh?"

"Not dumb at all. An impressive skill that might come in handy someday," Noah replied, trying to look serious but ending up bursting out in laughter.

"Okay, Mr. High and Mighty, now it's your turn to tell me about your night with Pete," Jack said, wiggling her eyebrows.

Noah leaned in close to her and was about to spill when Angel came in whistling. "I'll tell you later tonight," Noah whispered conspiratorially.

Jack and Noah ate before the doors were opened and thereafter helped pass out food and drinks. Jack kept an eye out for the children, and when the first wave had finished eating, she asked their parents if it would be okay for them to go over on the rug in the corner with her so that she could read to them. The look of pure relief on each parent's face touched Jack. These parents were so consumed with trying to keep the family together and surviving that having someone give them just a small break was such a gift.

Jack sat down and began reading one of the tattered Dr. Seuss books that was on the floor. Jack noticed that several of the children had blank looks on their faces. All at once Jack understood, and she read the title out loud in Spanish. The children's eyes grew big as they smiled and nodded their heads. Jack began the story again, and this time she read each page first in English and then Spanish. Before she knew it, she had at least a dozen children laughing as she made faces and strange voices in both languages.

Sam was leaning against the wall watching Jack interact with the children. He'd bet just about anything that these kids hadn't laughed in a very long time, and when he looked around he could see the parents as well as other diners grinning at the joyful sound of the kids' laughter. *This one's special,* thought Sam. There was a small flicker of something he couldn't quite name starting to bloom in his heart.

Sam looked away and walked into the kitchen. *Don't get involved,* he told himself. He'd seen too many kids through the years get fucked up by drugs or instead watch the street chew them up and spit them out. It was better to just not get involved. He would counsel her and try to get her to go back home—that's it. He thought about the private dick who had been sniffing around a few weeks ago. Something told him that he shouldn't tell the investigator anything. He would try and help her and let *her* make the decision to go home or not. It was none of his business otherwise, he told himself.

Sam stretched his arms out and leaned against the counter with his head bowed down as the sound of laughter and giggles tried to fight their way into his heart.

Later that evening, when Jack and Noah made it back to the shelter and helped everyone settle into their spaces, Jack showed Noah their room and was surprised herself when she realized that they had a very small bathroom off their room. It only had a toilet, sink, and a shower that would hold someone small, but to Jack, it was the world. Jasmine had even put soap and shampoo in the shower and toothbrushes and toothpaste on the counter. Jack just stared, speechless. She would never in her life take such a small luxury like bathing for granted again.

Jack turned to Noah. "I'm going to take a shower, and then you're going to tell me about Pete," she said firmly.

Noah smiled. "Yes, ma'am," he replied, giving her a mock salute.

The hot water drizzled from the top of her head down her back, enveloping her in a warm cocoon of steam. Jack sighed and soaped her hair up for the second time. She had worn her hat so long that she wasn't sure if her hair would ever come clean again.

After she applied conditioner to her clean hair, it felt just like silk as she ran her fingers through it. With a last sigh, Jack turned off the shower and stepped out, rubbing herself dry with the thin towel. She wrapped the towel around herself and combed her hair with the large-tooth plastic comb sitting beside the toothbrushes. As she finished brushing her teeth, she lifted her head from the sink and peered into the mirror at a girl she didn't recognize. She just stared.

Who is that? she thought. The girl was much too thin and her eyes looked too large for her face. Her hair was a mass of loose blond curls framing her thin face.

Then she saw her—her Dark Twin staring back from the mirror at her. Jack jumped back and gasped.

Jack quickly left the bathroom to get some clothes. When she came into the bedroom, Noah was lying on the cot with his arm over his eyes.

"Stay like that while I get dressed," Jack warned, grabbing the bag that Sam had given her. She found a pink flannel nightgown. It was like something Laura Ingalls from *Little House on the Prairie* would wear, thought Jack, smiling to herself. Leo had meant well and at least it was clean and warm, she thought.

"Okay, you can look now," Jack said.

Noah opened his eyes, looked Jack over, and burst out laughing. He laughed and laughed until Jack started to get angry.

"Stop it, Noah! Stop laughing!" she shouted, poking him.

"Oh. My. God! Jack, you look like my grandmother!" Noah exclaimed, doubling over again. "Okay, okay, I'll stop. You do smell much better," he said, sniffing the air.

"All right, enough about me, tell me about Pete. Are you guys an item or what?" Jack asked.

Noah sobered and turned over on his stomach with his arms under his chin. "No, he's just helping me. I think he sees himself in me when he first moved to the city. Don't get me wrong, I think he is superhot, but I don't think he likes me like that. He is going to help me get a modeling portfolio together and bring me to jobs with him. His apartment is super small, just a room really, and he even has to share a bathroom with other tenants. I don't really remember much because after Sam took you, Pete brought me into the bar and told me to drink some booze to calm me down. It did help," he said defensively, looking at Jack.

"Noah, you don't even know him! He could have put something in your drink! Please don't do that again," Jack pleaded.

Noah looked angry. "Jesus, Jack, I'm not your brother or your boyfriend! You can't tell me what I can or can't do! I trust him, and I'm going to be spending a lot of time with him, so get used to it. I'm tired, so let's go to sleep," he muttered.

Jack nodded in agreement. "Sure. I'm sorry, I didn't mean to be a bitch, Noah," Jack said, getting into the bed.

"No problem. 'Night," Noah said as he turned over on his side facing the wall.

"'Night," Jack said, flipping off the lamp. Jack suddenly felt very lonely, and as she lay staring at the ceiling, tears flowed from her eyes onto the pillow as she remembered each one of her brothers and how badly she missed them.

The first few weeks of settling in at the shelter and soup kitchen, not to mention starting the group sessions and Krav Maga lessons, had worn Jack out mentally and physically. But it also felt good to have some sort of purpose in life. The kids at both the shelter and the soup kitchen brought Jack so much joy. She had been able to help with homework, and the kids and parents were asking Jack for her help even during closed hours at the shelter and soup kitchen. One day as Sam was walking to the soup kitchen, he spotted Jack huddled on a park bench with a young Spanish boy with a book open. The tyke was trying to write with gloves on because it was so cold. Sam walked over. "What are you guys doing?" he asked, recognizing the boy from the kitchen.

"Oh, hi, Sam," Jack said, looking up. "Emilio is pretty behind in class because of the language barrier, and he has moved around a lot, so I have been tutoring him. He's very smart. I don't think it will be long before he is caught up," she said, beaming at Emilio.

Sam's heart swelled. Jesus, he was not going to let her get to him. There wasn't a complaint anywhere in her tone.

"Well, come into the soup kitchen and set up at the table. At least you'll be warmer. Where are his parents?" Sam asked.

"They are going to meet me at the shelter tonight. They were hoping to apply for jobs today in one of the new hotels," Jack answered, gathering up the books and papers.

After about an hour of working on reading and writing, Sam came out of the kitchen with hot chocolate and cookies.

"Oh, Sam! I love cookies and hot chocolate!" Jack squealed. Emilio laughed as Jack held a cookie up and slowly pronounced it. Emilio echoed back "cookie" perfectly.

"Oh, I thought so! How come you know how to understand *cookie* but not *multiply* and *divide*? Hmmm." Jack grinned.

Sam laughed at them both and caught himself. Turning serious, he looked at Jack. "Are you ready for group tonight, little one? I think you need to start sharing instead of just listening," he said, taking a sip of hot chocolate.

"I know, I will," Jack said, looking away.

Dinner was uneventful, and while Jack waited for the kids to finish their meals, she took the time to talk to Sam about something that was on her mind. As Jack scooped the mashed potatoes onto plates, she knew this might be a good opportunity to bring up breakfast for the kids to Sam.

"Sam, I've been thinking about something that I would like to run past you."

Sam looked up. "Oh yeah? What's that?" he replied gruffly, putting meat-loaf onto the plates.

"Well, at the shelter, the families are made to leave at seven o'clock in the morning. I understand that it is just a housing facility, but the kids are pushed out the door with no breakfast. How are they supposed to concentrate in school all day without breakfast, having to wait until lunch? And that's the kids who get to go to school and have lunch. There are some that, well, I don't really know what they do all day, but they probably don't eat until they come here at night. It's not right," Jack said tentatively, looking to see Sam's reaction.

Sam stopped serving for a minute and just looked at Jack, his eyes narrowing. "Couple of things you need to learn, little one. First, there ain't no such thing as 'right' out here on the streets. Second, you're absolutely right. They should have a full belly at the start of their day, but refer back to comment number one. And third, you can't care too much or it will consume you. Just mind your own business and do what you can," Sam said with finality.

"That's not an answer but a sad commentary of the mentality out here on the streets. It has to change! If we just keep doing the same old thing, then the cycle perpetuates and nothing ever changes! I believe that if even one person decides to make a difference, then more people will pitch in and the problem will get smaller. How do we know that the next Edison, or Mozart, or Jane Austen isn't sitting right here in this soup kitchen, and if just one person believes in him or her and helps, well, who knows what he or she can accomplish? And if helping that one child results in that child going on to help another child and so on until there are no more hungry bellies or foggy brains out there, what's wrong with that?" Jack proclaimed, plopping a giant helping of mashed potatoes onto a plate of a little Asian woman.

Sam continued to stare at Jack even as the woman smiled and bowed her head in thanks for the large portion of food.

"Well I see you're all fired up tonight, aren't you, little one? That's good, because I expect to hear all about what got you here in this soup kitchen and shelter in the first place later tonight in group." Sam turned away so Jack wouldn't see the grin he was trying to hide.

"Jesus, this girl has spunk," he thought as Jack made her way to the carpeted corner where she had set up as many books as she could find. She had read all the books there multiple times, but it didn't matter. The kids felt safe with her, and they felt like they mattered—even if it was only for an hour a day.

Sam heard her tell the children that tonight was going to be different. She was going to tell them a story from Greek mythology about a woman named Diana. As she told the story, he saw her making gestures of shooting a bow and arrow. Her hands would fly into the air as she increased the drama of the story. The children's eyes were as big as saucers. As Sam looked around the room, everyone was silent as a mouse, completely enthralled with the story. Sam had never seen anything like it. Even the strung-out junkies were completely caught up in Jack's storytelling. "I'll be damned," thought Sam, shaking his head.

Jack sat fidgeting with the buttons of her flannel shirt. The group members had assembled in the back room off of the kitchen. The room was empty except for six gray metal folding chairs and a black gym mat folded in the corner along with the members.

The group had just sat down in a circle with their paper coffee cups. The group consisted of four older men and Jack.

Sam sat across from Jack and began the meeting. Sam cleared his throat and then bowed his head as did everyone. "Dear Lord, please bless this meeting and help us to find peace that can only come from you. Amen. Now, I believe this evening we will hear from the newest member of our group. This is Jack. I believe some of you have met her or had the pleasure of watching her with the children. Jack, I want you to know that you're safe here in this group, and you are free to tell us anything without fear of judgment. Whatever is said here, stays here," Sam announced, nodding to Jack.

Each man in the group got up and held out his hand for Jack to shake. First Leo got up, held out his hand, and smiled with the very few teeth he had left. "Good evening, little one."

Then Jay, an older gentleman with a trench coat and a prosthetic leg, went next. "Hello, little one."

Big Mike was next. He was a gentle giant of a man with Mexican heritage. One side of his face had been badly burned in a gang fight as a teenager. "Hola, little one."

And last was Stanley, who was rocking back and forth in his chair. He was a small stout man with blond curls and Coke-bottle glasses. He jumped up and thrust out his hand. "Give me some skin, little one," he said with a lisp.

Jack smiled shyly and clasped his hand, which he shook vigorously for several seconds. Jack laughed as he broke off the handshake and whipped around to take his seat, aggressively pushing his chair outside the group. He grabbed his seat and scooted inch by inch back into the circle.

Jack wrung her hands together and looked up at a water stain on the ceiling. "I don't really know where to begin," she said quietly. "Sam says that talking about my Dark Twin will make her go away. She scares me. She tries to hurt people, and sometimes she tells me to hurt myself. What scares me the most is that whenever I get scared or really angry, she just takes over. I don't remember the things she does. What if she kills someone and I don't even remember it? Well, anyway, Sam says that if I talk about it I can release some of her anger and power, and I can learn some coping strategies.

I come from a very large family. I'm the only girl and the youngest. I have nine brothers. My mother died the day I was born. My brother Caleb named me which is why I have such a fuck—er, messed-up name. He's a pinhead."

Chuckles were heard around the room. Stanley laughed loudly. "I know, right! Who the hell names a baby girl Jack?" he replied, slapping his thigh. The other men glared at him. "Um, sorry. Please continue, little one," Stanley gulped, looking embarrassed.

Jack smiled at Stanley. "Exactly. I had a very privileged childhood. My father worked a lot, but I know that he loved me and my brothers…" Jack's voice broke and she had to stop. "Well, they're the best brothers any girl could ever want." Jack let out a big sigh. "School was very easy for me. My brother Teddy and I were blessed with really high IQs. He's a rocket scientist—literally," she said, smiling. "I guess it all began when I started having feelings for my twin brothers' best friend sometime last year."

Leo shifted in his seat and made a loud "Mm-hmm" as he took a sip of coffee.

Jack continued. "Well, it was wonderful, really. I've never felt a love so big, and I'm certain I never will again. I still don't understand why he didn't come after me…" she said as her voice trailed off. There was a moment of silence.

"Um, so, in August my father found out about us and sent me to this group home until he could figure out what to do with me. It was awful. The people who ran the home loved to torture and abuse kids, which made the kids themselves like little monsters."

Jack went on to tell the group about Justin and the beating she endured, but when she started telling them about being pregnant and losing the baby, she started getting agitated and her whole demeanor changed. She was having trouble breathing, and tears were falling down her cheeks. She was trying to fight the sobs. Sam could actually see her Dark Twin starting to emerge, so he shouted at Jack.

"Look at me, little one! Jack! Look at me!"

Jack glared at Sam.

Sam came slowly over until he was crouching before Jack, and he put out his hands for her to hold. "You're safe here, little one. I promise. Take my hands, Jack, and let go. Let it out. Let all the grief and suffering out. It will be okay."

Jack looked at his outstretched hands and then into his own pain-filled eyes, laying her hands in his. As soon as her hands connected with Sam's, it was like a dam broke inside her, and she sobbed as she never had before. So much pain and hurt spilled out of her.

After what seemed like forever, Jack blew her nose and wiped her face with the paper towel that Big Mike gently put in her hands. She continued telling them how they had escaped and found their way to the city, and now here she was helping out at the shelter and soup kitchen.

"I guess my plan is to wait until I turn eighteen this summer so I can get a job and take college classes," she said with a wan smile. There were audible sighs from the group, and Stanley blew his nose loudly. Jack's smile grew bigger.

Sam cleared his throat. "Thank you for sharing, little one. I think we made some progress tonight. A very important part of the process is talking about it and letting go of some of the pain, and I think you made a good start tonight."

Sam then bowed his head. "Lord, thank you for being here in our midst. Please watch over all who are here tonight. Amen."

Thereafter the group quietly folded their chairs, leaned them against the wall, and filed out of the room. Sam touched Jack's arm. "I will walk you to the shelter," he said, grabbing their coats.

"Okay," Jack replied, exhausted. They said good-bye to the others, and then Sam and Jack walked in silence. When they were standing outside the back door, Jack got her key out.

"Can I ask you something, little one?" Sam asked.

"Sure," Jack said.

"What do you think would happen if you called your father?" he asked quietly.

Jack bristled. "He would send me back to Beckett's House. I'm not going back there, ever, Sam," she replied with finality.

Sam took his hands out of his pockets and held them up in resignation. "Okay, okay, I just wanted to know what you thought would happen. Nothing, I mean nothing, is going to happen without your say-so. Okay? Now get in there and get some rest. Maybe you can tell the children about King Neptune tomorrow?" he suggested.

Jack's eyes lit up. "Why, Sam, you know Roman mythology?" she laughed.

Sam leaned down to her and waggled his bushy gray eyebrows. "I'm not just another pretty face in the crowd, ya know!"

Jack laughed and climbed the stairs to the brick shelter. All of a sudden, she felt almost completely exhausted. "Good night," she called out, closing the door behind her.

Weeks turned into months as frigid winter turned into spring, and the city came alive with activity and tourists. Jack enjoyed the mundane routine she had created at the shelter and the soup kitchen. Sam was right: there were too many homeless kids and families that flowed through their doors.

Word had spread about Jack's multilingual tutoring. One particular day, Jack had taken a few hours for herself and had escaped to the library, and when she showed up at the soup kitchen, Sam met her at the door.

"Where have you been? I've been waiting for you to show up and tutor today. Jesus, don't scare me like that again," he grunted, roughly running his hands through his gray hair.

"I didn't have anybody to help today, so I went to the library to read. What's up?" Jack asked, not rattled at all by Sam's gruff manner.

Sam crossed his arms and smiled. "Well look who's all calm and shit— nice job. Sorry to come on so strong; it just made me worry. There was a guy here asking for you," Sam said, looking at Jack. Jack immediately stiffened and looked scared.

"No, no, I know the guy. It's the principal at the school a few blocks down," Sam said in a reassuring tone.

"Oh, I know that school. I pick up some kids there and tutor them here on Tuesdays and Thursdays. I wonder what he wanted with me," Jack said.

"He's coming back tonight at six o'clock to talk to you. I can join you if you don't mind," Sam offered.

"I'd like that, thank you. Um, do you suppose Angel has frosted that cake yet?" she asked with big eyes.

Sam laughed. "I do believe he has, and I know for a fact that he is on a smoke break," Sam replied conspiratorially. Jack squealed and ran toward the kitchen.

Dinner was a full house, and more than the usual number of kids was waiting for her on the carpet for story time. Jack had formed a great relation-ship with the librarian at the local branch of the New York Public Library, and as a result, she was now able to check books out even though her residence was the shelter. Jack felt that the librarian must have recognized a kindred spirit and could see that books were as essential to Jack as breathing. The book she had gotten for the kids today was a fun, interactive book for the little ones. The title of the book, *We're Going on a Bear Hunt,* made her think of her home state of Maine. The children loved it. By reading in English, Spanish, and tonight French, coupled with the sounds Jack had the characters make as they hunted through the mud and tall grass, the children were rolling around on the floor giggling and laughing.

After all the good-bye hugs were given, Jack stood and was met by Sam as he escorted a short, thin, balding man with round wire glasses into the reading area. "Jack, this is Zachary Smith, the principal at East End Elementary. He would like to have a word with you," Sam said as the man held out his hand.

"Mr. Smith, it's nice to meet you," Jack said shaking his hand.

"Call me Zack, please, and it's a pleasure to finally meet you. My parents and students all rave about Jack the angel," he said, laughing. "I can see why they love you. You have a natural way with children, and your foreign languages are superb. Can we talk?" Zack asked, gesturing toward the table.

"Sure," Jack said, taking a seat beside Sam.

"The children you have been tutoring have tested higher and have more confidence in the classroom since they met you. I know it is a huge problem for teachers who are not able to relay the lessons in their native language. The school budget just cannot afford to hire teachers who are bilingual or trilingual. This is what I would like to talk to you about. Would you be willing to come to the school for an hour each afternoon to help explain the lessons to the children in their native language? I would not be able to 'hire' you, but I could pay you fifty dollars per week. This money will come from a petty cash fund we set up out of our own pockets to make sure these kids at least have a fighting chance at making it at school and hopefully breaking the cycle of poverty and homelessness. Most of these kids are very bright, but they just can't read or understand English, so they are lost. You must already see how bright they are," he said, smiling. "It would mean a lot to me and all the teachers, but mostly it would mean the world to the children if you would come join us."

Jack looked down at the table and sighed. Zack held up his hands. "Look, I know this is a lot to ask, and now that I see you are so young yourself, I understand if you don't have the time to invest in this. Really, I get it. At your age, the last thing I would want to commit to would be a bunch of hyperactive kids. Hell, I was more concerned about where the next party was," he said, starting to get up. "Thank you for all you do with the kids, Jack."

Jack held up her hands to stop him from leaving the table. "I have no problem coming to the school each afternoon; actually, I will be able to help more kids that way. But I do have a problem taking your money—especially money from your own pockets. However, it would be nice to be able to have a little money in my pocket, so here is my offer. I will come to the school each afternoon to help the children with their lessons for an hour, and for the next hour I will teach the children and their parents English. I will also be available Saturday mornings for extra help and English lessons. That's my offer, Mr. Smith—take it or leave it."

Zack Smith just stared at Jack and then at Sam. Sam never said a word but looked from Zack to Jack with a smirk on his face.

"Sam?" Zack said.

"Don't look at me, Zack, Jack is her own young lady. I know she is very trustworthy, and if I were you, I'd take the offer on the table and count my blessings," Sam said quietly.

Jack turned quickly to Sam, surprised by the depth of pride in his voice. Zack grabbed Jack's hands quickly, but she immediately pulled back and gasped.

"Oh God, I'm so sorry to scare you, Jack. I didn't mean to. I just got excited. Yes, I will take your gracious offer. Can you come to the school tomorrow at three o'clock?" he asked.

Jack sat back down. "It's okay. Sometimes I get a little jumpy. Yes. I will be there tomorrow at three," she said.

"Great, I'll see you then, and thanks to you as well, Sam, for helping me make the connection," Zack said, nodding as he walked out the door.

Jack looked over at Sam, shifting uncomfortably. "I think I need some cake," she said.

"I think you have a hollow leg there, 'Jack the angel,'" he teased.

Jack laughed. "Yeah that's me all right—more like fallen angel," she murmured, walking to the kitchen to plead with Angel for some more cake.

Sam sighed and shook his head. He didn't know quite how it had happened, but she had burrowed deep into his heart, and he would make sure that no one ever hurt that little one ever again—at least not while he was still breathing. Cake, that wasn't such a bad idea, he thought as he ambled toward the kitchen.

Jack slammed into the mat, the breath knocked out of her. Sam was relentless this morning with their Krav Maga lesson. Jack lay on the mat trying to catch her breath.

"Jesus, Sam, what's up this morning! You haven't been this tough on me since we started these lessons in the early winter. Why now? I thought I was doing really well," she said, finally standing up. Sam was trying to catch his own breath, bending over with his hands on his knees. "You've done very well, little one, but I need to teach you as much as I can before you're grown and gone. I need to know that you will always be able to take care of yourself, so we're stepping up the pace," he said, lunging for her again. This time, Jack was ready; she quickly flipped him on his back and stepped on his neck with her boot.

"Nicely done," Sam choked out.

Not quite finished, Jack grabbed his arm, flipped him over, and pulled his arm high up his back, making him holler.

"Okay! Okay, fuck, I think we're done for the day!" he announced breathlessly. Jack held his arm for a few moments longer and then released him. Sam stood up, rubbing his arm.

"Where's Noah? I thought he was going to take these lessons with you," Sam asked.

Jack rolled her eyes. "He's too busy with Pete and getting his modeling portfolio together. Whatever the hell that is," Jack snorted. "He stays about half the time at the shelter with me and half the time with Pete. All he wants to do is talk about Pete anyway, but it's all good; I'm glad he's found someone," she said, shrugging her shoulders.

She was glad that Noah was happy. She didn't have to tell Sam about the hole in her heart, because she knew that he too had the same hole that would never heal. They were both broken human beings, and Jack felt blessed to have Sam in her life.

"What's on the agenda for today, little one?" Sam asked.

"Well, Laura from the library has asked me to lead a story time with the kids on Saturday afternoons after I finish at the school and maybe one morning during the week in the summer. She said I was famous for my 'stories,'" Jack replied with air quotes, laughing.

"Well that's good. I like to see you busy. It keeps you out of trouble," he said, ruffling her curls.

Jack rushed into the school, almost running into a man coming out of the building. The man grabbed Jack by the upper arms to steady her, but she physically recoiled fearfully.

"Whoa!" he said, letting go of her immediately upon seeing her fear. "I'm so sorry, are you okay? Can I help you find someone? Do you have a child here?" he asked, motioning toward the front doors.

Jack looked up to see kind eyes and a very handsome face. His hair was really short and he had a few days' worth of stubble grown in. She wasn't sure if the stubble was because he thought it was cool or just because he didn't bother to shave. From the look of him, she would have guessed because he didn't want to take the time. He looked like a skater boy with a black T-shirt and black skinny jeans and a flannel shirt tied around his waist.

"Um, no, no, I'm here to see Mr. Smith about tutoring some students," she said, starting to wring her hands.

The man pointed at her. "You're the angel with curls," he said, looking at her slouch hat.

"Um, yeah, I guess that's what some of the kids call me. I'm Jack," she replied nervously.

"Jack?" the man said, surprised.

Jack smiled. "Yes."

All at once he realized he was staring. "Jesus, I...sorry! I'm usually not so rude. I'm also Jack, but it's short for Jackson. I teach fifth and sixth grade," he said, holding out his hand.

Jack gave it the minimum one shake and dropped his hand quickly. "Nice to meet you, Jackson. I'm sorry, but I'm running a little late and I don't want to keep Mr. Smith or the students waiting," she said, reaching for the door. She smiled and waved as she entered the school. As she was walking into the school, she looked back through the window in the door to find he was still watching her.

The class of students was small, but after she had tutored the children, each and every parent of the students she had just tutored showed up to be taught to read and write English. She was able to converse with every person in the room except the Chinese mother and father of a young boy. Jack immediately made a mental note to go to the library and check out some books on speaking Chinese. The class lasted longer than expected, but when they finished up, each parent brought her a dish from their ethnic origin. Jack was genuinely touched and thanked them profusely. She offered Mr. Smith some of the treats to take home to his wife to enjoy.

"No, the students bring me goodies all the time. These are yours to enjoy," he said as they walked out of the school. "Can I give you a ride somewhere, Jack? I hate to have you walking by yourself," Mr. Smith offered.

Jack smiled. "No, thank you. I can take care of myself, trust me. See you tomorrow, Mr. Smith," she said waving.

"It's Zack!" he hollered after her.

Jack was feeling lighter than she had in a long time, and she decided that she was going to buy herself a treat. There was a new coffee shop in the theater district that she had noticed when she was looking at all the posters for the new shows. Jack loved imagining herself going to the newest show, and sometimes she would come to stare as the men and women, all decked out in their finest, arrived at the theater. She was earning a little bit of money, so she could treat herself to a coffee once in a while.

The coffee shop was busy, but it didn't make Jack anxious like most closed-in crowded places. A pretty little redhead smiled at the counter.

Mac.

And just like that, Jack felt sick to her stomach. God, how she missed Mac! She would have given just about anything to sit and talk to her best friend, but Jack knew that Mac would just worry about her, and it wasn't fair to burden her with that. Jack was broken and wouldn't let her Dark Twin anywhere near Mac. She couldn't chance it.

"Hi, I'll have a medium vanilla soy latte please."

The redhead barista nodded. "What's the name?" she asked.

"Jack."

The barista looked puzzled. "Just Jack?" she asked.

Immediately Jack's hackles rose. "Yes, why?" she asked.

"Um, well...there is this gorgeous guy who comes in all the time, and he always asks if we have served a girl with long blond hair named Jack—said she is missing or something."

Jack pulled her hat off and smiled nervously. "Short hair, and Jack is short for Jacquelyn," she replied, handing her money to the girl.

The barista shrugged and rang up the coffee. "Your loss, sweetie. He's seriously gorgeous."

Jack moved to the opposite counter. Someone was asking questions about her. She felt as if someone had just walked over her grave. Jack could hear her name being called as if she were under water. She could feel her heartbeat increase and her breathing quicken. Then she heard the voice.

I will not let them take us back there—not ever.

Instinctively, Jack felt for her blade that she wore clipped inside the back of her jeans. She knew her Dark Twin was here now, and she needed to use every available coping strategy available to her. The first would be to leave this environment at once and get to a safe place.

Jack grabbed her coffee and hurried out the door. She made a beeline for the crosswalk whose light had turned to DO NOT WALK, but she kept running even as the cars started to honk. Just as she reached the other side of the street, she felt compelled to look back at the coffee shop. Jack stopped dead in her tracks and dropped her latte to the sidewalk with a splat.

Jared.

Jack watched the back of him open the coffee shop door and walk in. She couldn't breathe. Jack doubled over and tried to catch her breath. She had to go back.

Run! Now—go back!

No! This was what her Dark Twin wanted her to see. It wasn't real, and if she waited any longer she ran the risk of her Dark Twin taking over and hurting someone. She must get to the soup kitchen to see Sam…and fast.

Jack started running and never stopped until she reached the back door of the soup kitchen. She burst through the door to find Sam bringing a cup of coffee to his lips. He took one look at her and threw the cup in the sink and ran to her. Jack couldn't breathe as she sensed the blackness closing in. She cried out as she collapsed into Sam's arms.

Jack jerked awake. Sam was right there beside the bed.

"Easy, little one. Relax; you're safe. Deep breaths in and out," he coaxed, breathing with her. "Okay, good. You're fine, relax. Let go—keep breathing. Can you tell me what happened to trigger the episode?" he asked quietly.

Feeling calmer, Jack sat up and crossed her legs on the bed. "After tutoring, I decided I wanted to try that new coffee shop in the theater district."

Sam nodded. "I know the one," he said.

"Well, when I was ordering they asked for a name, and when I told the girl, she looked at me funny and asked if that was my real name. I thought that was weird, so I asked her why and she said some guy has been asking about a girl with long blond hair named Jack. I kinda freaked a little and pulled my hat off and said nope I have short hair and my full name is Jacquelyn. I could feel myself getting agitated, and 'you know who' told me we were never going back. It's been a while since she came out. Well I bolted across the street, but when I turned back to look at the coffee shop, I thought I saw Jared walking in, and I just lost it completely. I wanted to run back over there, but I knew I needed to get somewhere safe so I couldn't hurt anybody."

Tears were streaming down Jack's cheeks. "It couldn't have been Jared, could it, Sam?" she whispered.

Sam gathered her close as Jack began to sob violently. "Shhh. It's okay, little one. You're safe now. You did exactly what you were supposed to do. You got yourself out of the situation. I'm so damn proud of you, Jack. No, I don't think you saw Jared, little one. You know you can't trust anything when she rears her ugly head. You stood strong. So damn proud of you…" he whispered, squeezing her tighter.

Later on, before the soup kitchen opened its doors, Noah arrived to see Jack. He hugged her and looked at her intently.

"You okay, lovely?" he asked.

Jack laughed. Honestly, did anyone else on the planet have as many nicknames as she did?

She nodded. "Yeah, I had a bad day, but I'm fine now," she said with a small smile.

Noah put his arm around her and walked her toward the door. "Well, why don't we go to the movies, and I will buy you popcorn and candy, and then we can go back to the shelter and talk until all hours of the morning. I have so much to tell you!" he said with a giant grin on his face.

Jack grinned. "You're such a girl! Let me tell Sam I'm skipping out and we'll go," Jack replied, seeing Sam in the crowd and pointing to the door. Sam nodded and waved as she and Noah left hand in hand.

If felt good to just relax with Noah for the evening. Jack chose not to tell him about her incident today. It would just make him worry unnecessarily. Jack just kept it light and let Noah gush about Pete. Noah was totally infatuated with the young bartender/model. Jack hadn't seen much of Noah because he was either helping out at the bar or hanging with Pete at his place. Jack was a little concerned about Noah's drinking and experimenting with drugs, but he just waved her off as being a goody two-shoes. Jack had met most of the crowd that hung out at the bar, and most of them were great people, albeit a little manic concerning their passions. Many were model wannabes and therefore very catty regarding those whom they saw as competition. But they made Jack laugh and they had accepted Noah into their group, so they would always get a pass from her. As her eyelids began to close, Jack yawned. Noah held open the blankets on her bed and she climbed in. Noah stayed on top of the blankets but held out his arms for Jack to snuggle in close to him. He was warm, and his arms held her tight. It felt so good to have some human contact. Jack sighed as Noah stroked her curls. "Sleep now, lovely," he said quietly, as Jack drifted off to sleep feeling warm and safe.

The days and weeks became a beautiful rhythm of routine for Jack. Zack had asked her to continue tutoring the children and parents through the summer, and Jack was happy to do so. The PTSD group was going well, and Jack had not had a single incident with her Dark Twin since that day at the coffee shop. They had lost Stanley, a member of the PTSD group, to suicide; that tragic episode emphasized how important it was to talk about things and engage coping strategies whenever possible.

Jack woke up early, before anyone was stirring in the shelter. She walked to her favorite coffee shop. She had a pretty sundress on that she had gotten from the free clothes closet at the shelter. Her hair had grown, and she was able to wear it in a short braid down her back. Today was a monumental day for Jack. It was her birthday. She was officially eighteen today. She could get an official job or enroll in school—anything—without the fear that she would be sent back to Beckett's House or anywhere she didn't want to go. It was as if a huge weight had been lifted off her shoulders, one that she wasn't even aware she was carrying. Jack decided not to tell anybody about her birthday. She knew and that was sufficient.

She made her way back to the shelter and helped get people on their way. Jasmine was in the kitchen making some coffee when Jack came in.

"Mmm, you read my mind," Jack said, motioning toward the coffee maker.

Jasmine smiled and patted the chair next to her. "Great. Sit down and visit with me. You're always so busy helping everyone. We never get a chance to talk. How are you doing?" she asked, handing Jack her coffee.

"Good. Really good. I like to keep busy. I think I'm going to look into getting a job and taking some classes at the community college," Jack replied as she took a sip of coffee.

Jasmine's eyes got big and she smiled. "Oh that is so great, Jack! What are you interested in studying?"

"Business. I've always been fascinated by starting something from scratch and watching it grow. As a child, I would read the *Wall Street Journal* and pick, pretty accurately, the businesses that were going to succeed," Jack replied, shrugging her shoulders. Jack instantly thought of her father and what a good businessman he was. He had started from nothing and built an athletic shoe empire. Her guts twisted thinking about him. How can you be so angry and hurt with someone but still miss them so much? Jack sighed deeply. She wasn't going there today—not today.

"Well I better be heading out to the school," Jack said, washing out her cup.

"Okay, I'll see you tonight," Jasmine replied. Jasmine instantly looked guilty of something.

"Tonight?" Jack asked. Jasmine was usually gone home by the time the night crew got people settled in for the night.

"Oh, I just mean I might still be here doing paperwork this evening," she mumbled. Jack grinned and waved as she walked out the back door. *Guilty of what?* Jack thought idly and then let it pass.

It was hot. People were lounging on their stoops and sitting in their windows trying to catch any breeze that might come through. When she entered the cafeteria, it was so hot it felt like a sauna. The students and their parents were all sitting in the same seats they always sat in.

"Okay, everyone, follow me. It's way too hot in here to hold class. You won't be needing your books anyway. Follow me," she said, waving her arm at the group for them to follow her.

There was a large elm tree on the playground that would give nice shade. When they had all taken a seat on the grass, Jack handed out flash cards that she had made up with everyday phrases for them to practice their English. They would read the phrase and ask the question phrase out loud. The phrases ranged from ordering a cup of coffee to simple things like "I need help." They all struggled with their cards at first, but they felt so comfortable with each other and with Jack that after each question or phrase, they all ended up giggling and laughing at themselves. Time quickly got away from them, and pretty soon some were scrambling to get back to work. Jack walked to the library and sunk into a large cracked leather chair with *Pride and Prejudice* and lost herself for a couple of blissful hours.

Jack leaned against the front entrance to the soup kitchen, staring at the large brick building across the street. Angel came out to have a smoke.

"Hey there, little one. How you doin'?" he asked, smiling.

Jack smiled back. "Hi. Angel, can you tell me what that building used to be?" Jack said, pointing to the empty brick building across the street.

Angel nodded his head enthusiastically. "I sure can, little one. That there building was the recording studio for some of the greats: Billie Holiday, Ray Charles, Gladys Knight, The Temptations, and Elvis. This was the heart of Motown back in the day," he said, taking her in his arms and twirling her around as she laughed.

Sam ambled out. "What are you two up to out here?" he said, crossing his arms with a mock stern countenance.

"I was just telling Jack here about when this was the heart of Motown and all the greats walked in and out of that building."

Sam looked at the building. "I bet it was a hopping place," Sam murmured.

Angel looked a bit sad. "It surely was. It was another time. A better time," Angel replied, crushing out his cigarette and walking back into the soup kitchen.

Jack walked into the soup kitchen and her eyes immediately zeroed in on the baby grand piano sitting on the reading carpet. She stopped dead in her tracks. Sam stood beside her.

"It's here on loan. Do you play?" he asked.

Jack kept staring at the piano. "I used to," she whispered.

Sam chuckled. "Why doesn't that surprise me, little one?" he said, gesturing toward the piano. "By all means, play as long as you like. I think the kids will really like to listen to you tonight."

Jack walked slowly toward the piano and sat down, reverently touching her fingertips to the white ivory keys. Jack was a hot mess of overwhelming emotions. As she played the first note, her whole being rose to a different plane of consciousness. Adele's haunting melody soon permeated the soup kitchen, down the street and perhaps throughout the entire city as Jack closed her eyes and let the magic seep into her very soul.

As people started to stream through the doors for dinner, Jack played soft notes to relax and soothe their tired souls. Jack smiled as diners raised their paper cups in thanks for her playing for them.

When the children had finished their meals, some came over and sat with her on the bench, and others sat on the floor around the piano. Jack began to play and sing "Amazing Grace," and the entire room became still. Her eyes closed, she sang of redemption and grace in such a way that Sam was sure the heavenly angels themselves had stopped to listen. Jack's thoughts drifted to the piano on the porch in Harmony, and she was surrounded by her father and brothers. She could feel the breeze on her face and love pierced her heart.

As the song ended, she jerked her fingers off the keys as though they were burning embers. She opened her eyes to find everyone out of their seats and standing all around the piano. Some were smiling and most were crying as they burst into applause. Jack jumped and laughed as she realized her face was wet with tears.

Jack began to notice people who were not there for a meal. Mr. Smith, Jasmine, and all the parents and students that she tutored were standing by the doors. Then she spotted Noah and Pete.

Suddenly, Angel parted the crowd carrying a huge sheet cake with white frosting and "Happy birthday, little one" in big letters across the middle.

Jack smiled and tried to wipe her eyes, but the tears wouldn't stop flowing. She felt so blessed to be surrounded by people who cared about her. On the day that she was missing her family so much, she was reminded that she did have a family who cared for her.

Jack hugged Sam and Angel. "Thank you, everybody, this means so much to me...you have no idea. Well, maybe if anybody does, it would be you guys," she said, laughing and crying at the same time.

"Okay, it's time to blow out the candles!" Angel proclaimed, backing away from the cake. "Hurry before the fire department gets called!" someone hollered.

As they all sang "Happy Birthday," Jack blew out all the candles. When she stood up, she locked eyes with Jackson from the grade school. He smiled at her, and she looked away shyly and began helping to serve the cake. When everyone had cake, Jack made her way around the room, thanking everyone who had come and many of the parents who had made her special ethnic treats. The children had painted pictures that Jack assured them she would hang around the soup kitchen and the shelter. Sam and Angel had bought her a little iPod shuffle with ear buds and loaded it with all kinds of music. Jasmine had bought her a velvety soft blanket for her bed. Leo came to her and gently laid a wreath of tiny wildflowers on top of her head. "There, you are officially a princess now," Leo announced, smiling at her.

A dark shadow passed over Jack, and for a minute she couldn't breathe. Jack closed her eyes and willed herself to take a one deep breath after another until she felt centered again. She opened her eyes to find Sam staring at her with concern. Jack looked away and smiled a big smile at Leo. "Thank you, Leo, I feel like a princess tonight!" Jasmine came around with a camera and snapped a photo of Jack's appreciative smile and her beautiful wreath of flowers.

Jackson offered Jack some apple juice in a paper cup. "Can I buy you a drink?" he inquired.

Jack laughed. "Why, yes, I would love one! How did you know this was my favorite wine? So subtle with just a hint of apple!"

"So you help out here and at the shelter?" Jackson asked.

Jack nodded. "I do help out here, and I sorta work at the shelter for a room there. I'm going to try and find a job now that I'm eighteen and take some classes at the community college," she replied.

They talked about the different courses offered at the college. "How did you get interested in being a teacher?" Jack asked. "I would never have pegged you as an educator. Maybe a graffiti artist, but never a teacher." She laughed.

Jackson acted insulted. "What! How did you know! I do have my fair share of tags across the city. My parents were both teachers, and I guess I just naturally gravitated toward education. I'm a big kid and I really think I can make a difference here in the city," he said, shrugging his shoulders. "You might want to rethink this business program yourself. You would make an awesome teacher. You're a natural with kids," he said, touching her shoulder.

Jack flinched and was instantly embarrassed. "Sorry," she whispered.

Jackson pulled his hand away. "No, I'm sorry. Please forgive me," he said, embarrassed.

Just then Noah came up behind Jack and picked up her and twirled her around. "Hey there, lovely! Happy Birthday!" he exclaimed, putting her down and handing her a small gift box. Jack looked sternly at Noah as she opened the box. It was a beautiful silver necklace with a thin silver plate with "Lovely" engraved on the front.

Jack's eyes filled with tears. She hugged him tight. "Thank you," she whispered in his ear. Noah hugged her tight. "You're welcome."

Jack hugged Pete and thanked him for coming. Noah looked Jackson over and offered him his hand. "I'm Noah, the BFF," he said, tilting his head toward Jack.

"Hey, I'm Jackson. A new friend…hopefully," he said, looking at Jack.

"Okay! Well I'm going to help clean up, excuse me," Jack said, withdrawing to head toward the kitchen.

"Wait," Jackson said, touching her arm tentatively. "Would you like to have dinner with me tomorrow night?" he asked faintly. Jack looked down at her old sundress and back up to his eyes.

"Oh, just at my place, nothing special," he hurried to add. Jack tilted her head in mock offense.

"Oh, I didn't mean it like that! Just casual at my apartment, and we can watch a movie. I'm a poor school teacher you know," he stammered.

Jack nodded. "Um, yeah, I'd like that," she replied, already anxious about accepting.

Jackson smiled and turned to walk away. "Great! I'll meet you at the school tomorrow," he ended, disappearing into the crowd before she could back out. Jack sighed. *What am I doing?*

The good thing about having very few clothes was that you didn't waste time worrying about what you were going to wear. She threw on a pair of tan chino shorts and a white T-shirt with her flip-flops. *There, done,* she thought smugly.

Unfortunately, her weight had not climbed since she had resumed a regular diet, but at least the gauntness had disappeared and her color was normal. Her hair was long enough to pull up in a messy bun that saved lots of time.

Jack had butterflies in her stomach as she neared the school. She was just having dinner with a new friend, she kept repeating to herself. There was a little voice in her head telling her that he deserved a better friend than her. One that perhaps didn't have the capacity to turn into a raging lunatic and slit his throat at the slightest provocation. *That's it, I will cancel. It's the only thing to do really. There is no future in this and he will be infinitely better off because of this decision.*

"Jesus, Jack, I'm not asking you to marry me or tattoo my name on your body! I just want to have dinner with you," Jackson retorted, smiling as he leaned up against the lockers in front of her classroom.

Jack halted abruptly and stared. Apparently she had been pacing in front of his door! Had she really said all those things about him being better off out loud?

Oh, Jesus.

"Um, I wasn't aware I was talking out loud. See, I'm crazy. You really would be better off just walking away," she said, covering her face.

Jackson walked over to her to stand directly in front of her and gently pulled her hands down away from her face. He was standing eye to eye with her.

"Stop. Dinner. Okay?"

Jack looked into his kind eyes. "Okay," she whispered. Jackson turned her around and gave her a little push toward the door. "Now, let's go eat."

Dinner was delicious. Hamburgers were cooked on the little gas grill that sat on his very tiny balcony attached to his very tiny apartment. It was basically one average size room with an attached bathroom that was a step up from Pete's apartment, where he had to share a bathroom with other renters. The joys of living on an island with a zillion people. Any way you looked at it, it was better than her setup, a homeless shelter.

Jack looked around approvingly. He had an old, really worn, brown leather sofa that doubled as a bed and a folding canvas chair like the kind they had around the campfire in Harmony. A small lobster trap with glass on top as a coffee table completed the furnishings.

"Is that a lobster trap?" Jack asked, laughing.

"Why yes it is!" Jackson grinned. "I visited Maine a few years ago and saw this in an old junk shop. I liked it and put some glass on top to make it functional."

Jack laughed. "You could be on HGTV! I love those shows!" Jack exclaimed.

"I know, right? You're the only one I will admit that to. I like to watch them with my mother. Corny, huh?" Jackson replied, shrugging.

Jack turned to him. "No, I don't think it's corny at all. I think it's sweet."

There were pictures hanging on the wall of his graduation from college with his mom and dad and a pretty young girl. "Is this your girlfriend?" Jack asked.

"No, Jack, if I had a girlfriend I wouldn't have asked you out to dinner. That is my younger sister, Nina."

"Oh," Jack said quietly. "She's pretty."

"Yeah, well she's also a pain in the ass—but I still love her," he said with a smile. "Do you have brothers and sisters?" Jackson asked.

Jack looked startled. "Oh, I'm sorry. I didn't mean to pry," Jackson said.

Jack took a deep breath. "I do, brothers. A lot of them, but I really don't want to talk about my life. I would really like you to tell me about yours," she said sincerely.

Jackson made a face. "There's nothing to tell. We're incredibly boring," he said, bringing the salad and burgers to the coffee table.

"Trust me, I would love to hear about boring and normal." Jack laughed, filling her plate with salad.

Jackson proceeded to tell her about growing up in a household that was a constant learning experience with teachers for parents. He talked about how every day at lunch he took out his brown bag and the sandwich was always cut sideways, never down the middle, and there were homemade cookies and carrot sticks.

"Just once I would have loved to open the bag to a Twinkie or Ring Ding!" he said in a longing voice. They both laughed.

"I know! Bebe always made perfect french pastries and desserts. There certainly was never a Hostess cupcake around. But at least when we went to camp in the summer, we always got Pop-Tarts. YUM!" Jack laughed.

"Who's Bebe?" Jackson asked.

Jack sobered up. "Um, she is, was, my nanny and general house manager for all of us," she said, looking for a clock. "This has been great, Jackson. But I really need to get going and help settle people at the shelter. "

Jackson popped up off the couch. "Hey, I'm sorry. I didn't mean to make you uncomfortable. I'll walk you home," he said, tossing the dishes in the sink.

"No, you don't have to, really," Jack replied.

Jackson looked serious. "I know I don't have to, but I'm going to," he said firmly as he opened his apartment door.

Jack wouldn't make eye contact as she descended the stairs from his apartment. They walked silently back to the shelter. When they were at the back door, Jack looked awkwardly around.

"Well, thank you for walking me home. I had a nice time," she said, turning toward the stairs.

"Wait, I have an idea. Do you want to come to the skate park with me tomorrow? I can teach you some moves," Jackson urged, making hand gestures like he was on a skateboard.

Jack laughed. "I don't have a skateboard," she said.

"Please! I have a closet full. My sister used to collect clothes and makeup, I collected skateboards. I'll meet you at my favorite coffee shop. It's by the theater district."

"The Coffee Shop?" Jack said. Jackson nodded. "That's my favorite!" she said.

"Well, there you go." he said, holding his hands out. "Ten o'clock?"

Jack smiled. "Sure."

What are you doing, again? Jack thought to herself.

Thank God for the knee and elbow pads Jackson had brought with him. Skateboarding was much harder than she'd thought it would be. She was going to have some serious black and blues tomorrow, she thought. Despite the pain and humiliation of trying the new sport, it was so much fun and exactly what she needed. Jack had almost forgotten how much she enjoyed the adrenaline rush she got from pushing herself to try new, and at times crazy, things. She had been so consumed with *not* having an adrenaline rush that might awaken her Dark Twin she had forgotten how to have fun. She had come to learn from Sam that the two were not the same. When her Dark Twin made an appearance, she always felt in danger or out of control.

Jack and Jackson ended up going to the skate park at least three times a week. It was the middle of August, and Jackson had to start thinking about school starting. One night after they left the skate park, Jack was telling him about her idea to provide backpacks at the shelter for the kids so they would have something for breakfast and snacks throughout the day. The backpack would be theirs and refillable. They could keep their school stuff and their personal belongings in it.

"It's really important for the kids to have something for themselves. When you're homeless, you have very little to call your own and even less if you're a child. I believe it would give them a small amount of power. The fact that they know if they get hungry, they have food. If they have little keepsakes, they would be able to take them out and hold them when they needed to. It's really the little stuff that makes a big difference. Of course, each backpack would have a book in it as well," she said as they sat on a park bench.

"Wow. Jack, that is a fantastic idea. The school could really use them as well," he said, looking deeply into her eyes.

Jack couldn't look away. Slowly he lowered his head and touched his lips to hers softly. It lasted for just a moment, and he lifted his head to look at her. Jack kept her eyes closed.

"Look at me, Jack," Jackson said quietly.

Jack shook her head slowly. "I can't." Tears started to fall down her cheeks. Jackson sucked in a breath and lifted his hand to cup her cheek and wipe the tears away. "Don't. Jack, please don't cry. Talk to me, please," he begged.

Jack sniffed and opened her eyes and grasped his hands. "Jackson, I'm broken. This can never happen for me," she said, motioning toward them both. "There was a guy, there is a guy that I am still in love with. I don't want to be in love with him, trust me. He broke my heart in so many pieces that I know it can never be mended. It wasn't just him that broke my heart. Well, let's just say that the things that have happened to me since I first loved him are such that I will never let anyone get that close to me again. To be perfectly honest with you, it's just not safe for someone to get that close to me, and I would never in a million years knowingly put you in any kind of danger. I do have feelings for you, but mostly they are deep feelings of friendship. I don't trust many people, and I let fewer in, but I feel safe with you and I cherish our time together," she said, squeezing his hands.

"So you're not going to tell me what hurt you so bad?" he asked, not bothering to mask his hurt.

Jack shook her head. "No. That is locked away in such a deep place that I just can't dig it up. Please don't ask me to do so. "

"This doesn't change how I feel for you. I—"

Jack put her fingers over his lips. "Shhh, no, please." Jack put her arms around his shoulders and hugged him tight. "I'll see you in a few days," she whispered and left the bench quickly, walking toward the shelter with tears streaming down her cheeks unchecked.

The next day, Jack sat brooding on the barstool beside Noah. "Wow, you're in a really bad mood. Are the streets safe today?" he said, nudging her.

"That is so not funny," Jack replied, glaring at him. She hadn't felt like even getting out of bed today, but she needed to help get people out of the shelter and on their way this morning. She didn't need to teach, so she was at odds with what to do with herself today. She already had an appointment with the college to discuss the enrollment process later this week. She figured maybe she would work on her résumé at the library. Lord knew it would be short and sweet. High school and waitressing.

Brilliant.

Jack scowled at Noah. "I know—you can come with me to my modeling audition!" he exclaimed, clapping his hands together.

"What? No way!" she growled, shaking her head.

Noah jumped off his stool and pulled her with him. "Yes. That's exactly what you need to get you out of this funk. We can make fun of all the beautiful people," he said, laughing. "And besides, you have nothing else to do. Although we probably should do something with your hair and maybe some makeup," he said, looking at her beanie with curls sticking out from under it.

"Fine, you win, and you're buying me a cheeseburger. Let's go," Jack replied in a resigned voice, pulling him out the door.

The room was so full of bony bodies that it could easily have been an acting audition for some postapocalyptic genocide movie. At least they were tall, and Jack didn't feel like some freak of nature as she took a seat in the corner of the room while Noah went to sign in.

Jack was starved. She had skipped dinner last night and cried herself to sleep. Jack was thoroughly enjoying the double cheeseburger when a gasp beside her made her look up. Every eye was on her, including the staff that was checking people in behind a giant glass window. Jack stopped eating to look around. Noah started laughing while trying to be quiet. "Jesus, Jack, you're going to make them all commit hara-kiri," he whispered.

Jack grunted. "Do you even know what hara-kiri is?" she replied as she took another big bite of her burger.

Noah and Jack shared a laugh and Jack snorted, making them laugh harder. Someone came out and called for Noah. He jumped up.

"Wish me luck," he said.

"Luck!" Jack hollered after him as she glared back at everyone glaring at her. The window with staff checking in people caught Jack's eye. There was a large group looking out the window at what appeared to be her. Jack looked around, popping the last bite of cheeseburger into her mouth. The door opened and a geeky-dressed guy with horn-rimmed glasses and white skinny jeans walked up to her.

"You. What's your name?" Geeky Guy asked, tapping his foot rapidly. Jack pointed toward her mouth and continued to chew. Her mouth was way too full to answer. The geek grabbed her hand and pulled her up. She towered over him.

"Doesn't matter. You're next. Come with me," Geeky Guy ordered, pulling her behind the closed door. Jack tried to stop him, but all at once there were all these hands pulling her to a large room with white wedding dresses everywhere. One lady was unbuttoning her blouse and another was pulling her shorts off.

"Wait a minute! Hold it, just wait! I'm not even here for this. You've made a mistake!" Jack protested, holding her hands out in front of her to make them stop. Geeky Guy yanked her shorts down.

"No mistake, Princess, Mr. Worthington himself wants to see you in this dress, like, yesterday."

The dress was pulled down over her body, and she was escorted out the door. She would have resisted had her breathing not escalated and were she not feeling all tingly.

Princess.

Breathe.

In. Out. In. Out.

She could see them all talking, but she was having a hard time focusing on what they were saying. Finally, she turned and saw Noah walk in the room. He was wearing a tuxedo and shiny black shoes. He took one look at Jack and rushed to her side. He grabbed her face in his hands.

"What is it? Tell me—are you okay? Talk to me, lovely," Noah whispered urgently.

A small man from across the room hollered. "There they are!" and the room suddenly went black.

Jack woke up to a very strong smell being waved under her nose. She batted it away.

"Oh, there you are, darling," a voice said from the chair across from the couch she was lying on. Geeky Guy with a jar of smelly stuff scampered out of the way. Jack sat up to find her head had been in Noah's lap. She looked at Noah.

"Okay?" he asked. Jack nodded.

"Do you know who I am?" the man asked Jack. He was wearing what looked like a burgundy smoking jacket with black slacks and short black boots. His hair was dyed jet black and he looked as though he had had a few facelifts in his time. There was kind of a cat-like quality about him.

"Um, no. Should I?" she asked.

"My name is Brock Worthington, and I run a global empire of clothing design. Really that is where I began. My empire is much more diverse now. It involves housewares and interior design. But I digress. Do you even know what you were auditioning for today?" he asked, incredulously.

Jack didn't look impressed in the least. "Actually, I was just here supporting my friend Noah," she said pointing to Noah. "Who, by the way, is a brilliant model."

Brock Worthington inhaled sharply and steepled his fingers together, all the while staring intently at her. Jack stared back. All at once, he blew out his breath and patted his thighs.

"What is your name?" he asked.

"Jack," she replied, continuing the stare down.

Brock tilted his head in suspicion and narrowed his eyes. "Very well. Jack, I am looking for a new face for my wedding collection. This is the most ambitious collection I have put together. It will start in my Europe houses and stay there for quite some time before coming to America, possibly in a few years. I want you to be that face. Every bride will want to be you. What do you say?" he said, positive she was going to kiss his black booties any time now for this chance of a lifetime he was offering her.

"No thanks."

Jack got up and started looking for her shorts. All eyes in the room were staring at her, dumbfounded.

"No? Whatever do you mean? There isn't a woman alive who wouldn't jump at this chance, I assure you," Brock sniffed, standing up.

"Well, apparently you found one," she replied holding up one finger, "who isn't in the least bit interested. Thank you again for the offer; now where are my clothes?" She felt her head and whipped around, looking for her beanie.

Brock Worthington stood up suddenly. "No, no, this won't do. You must be my face. What can I do to change your mind?" Brock stammered, suddenly looking at Noah who, like everyone else in the room not named Jack, was in shock.

"Miss...Jack, you will be compensated with more money than you could possibly spend, but more importantly, I believe, your friend here will not be working for my company or any others if you do not agree to work with me," he threatened, pulling his arms behind his back.

Jack jerked up. "What! That's blackmail! You can't do that!" she shouted, stomping her foot.

"Oh, I can and I will, I assure you. It's shocking, really, what you can get away with when you own a billion-dollar company. Now what do you say, do we have a deal?" Brock Worthington replied smugly.

Jack looked at Noah and closed her eyes. "Whatever," she whispered.

Part 3

*J*ack leaned her head back and looked out the window at the white puffy clouds. She thought of Sam as he had leaned against the counter at the soup kitchen, looking anything but impressed when she had informed him of her new adventure.

"Sam, Mr. Worthington says he's going to make me a household name in Europe, and every girl will want to look just like me on their wedding day!" Jack had exclaimed, trying to sound enthusiastic.

Silence.

Sam continued to look at the worn linoleum flooring. He looked up and sighed. "Why does it seem like you're trying to convince yourself as well as me how great this 'adventure' is? Why don't you tell me the real reason you agreed to do this? You're the very last girl in the world who would give two shits about being a household name in Europe. I have zero experience with young ladies, but I know this isn't you. The truth. I want the truth," he said firmly.

Jack jumped off the stool and paced around the kitchen wringing her hands. Sam just waited patiently until she stopped and turned to him.

"It's Noah; Mr. Worthington won't hire Noah, and as a matter of fact, he said he would make it so Noah never, ever gets a modeling gig if I don't accept his offer," she said breathlessly.

"Jesus!" Sam grunted, turning around to start cutting up vegetables. He picked up the knife and turned toward her, pointing it at her. "Noah is trouble, little one. He's not good for you."

Jack went to stand next to the counter. "Sam, I have to help him. I know you don't understand, but I have to help him, and besides it will get me away from the city and whoever is searching for me. Sam, you will not believe what they are paying me for—what, letting them take my picture and walking—*walking*—down some runway! I will be able to help fund the soup kitchen and the shelter. I have already gone to L.L.Bean and arranged to buy backpacks for the shelter, the school and some to be kept here at the soup kitchen for the children. For that reason alone, it's worth it. They are flying me to Paris to live, at least for the next eighteen months—that's how long the contract is for."

Jack touched Sam's arm. "Please, Sam, be happy for me. I couldn't stand it if we parted on bad terms," she murmured, her eyes glistening with tears.

Sam stopped cutting vegetables and turned to grasp Jack by the shoulders. "That will never happen, little one. I only want what's best for you—you know that. I know this isn't what you want and that pisses me off. I could knock that boy's block off, but I know you love him and you protect him fiercely. I admire that. I do have some concerns though. What about your Dark Twin? You have been doing so well in group. I would hate for you to have a setback."

Jack nodded her head and went to sit back down on the stool. "Mmm, I've thought of that. I know I will be outside my comfort zone, way outside, but you have given me a lot of tools to use when I start to lose control. I also have a genius plan if you will agree to it," she said, smiling slyly.

Sam raised his eyebrows. "I'm listening," he replied cautiously.

Jack went to her backpack and retrieved two cell phones. "Well, I bought us both very basic cell phones and programed each of our numbers in them. We can carry on counseling sessions weekly by phone, and anytime I feel like I'm in danger, I can pick up the phone and you can talk me off the ledge, so to speak," she explained, holding a phone out to him.

Sam looked at the phone and slowly reached for it. "Little one, I—"

Jack held up her hand. "I will teach you how to use it, okay?" she said quietly with tears threatening to spill.

Sam smiled, tearing up himself. "Well, do I have to wait until there is a crisis to talk to you, or can I call just to chitchat?"

Jack laughed out loud. "You have never chitchatted a day in your life, Sam, but yes you may call me anytime you wish, and I promise to do the same."

Sam wrapped his arms around Jack in a big bear hug. "You take care of yourself and remember all the self-defense moves I taught you, little one. I don't need to tell you how big and scary the world out there is, and by God if that boy gets you hurt in any way, I'm going to kick his ass all over Europe," he said, squeezing her roughly.

Jack yelped and laughed. "So noted."

Noah placed a cup of coffee on the table and sat down in the leather recliner opposite her. "I've flown first class before, but this shit is unbelievable," he muttered quietly, leaning toward Jack.

Jack turned from the window and picked up the coffee. "Mmm, thank you. Yeah, not bad at all," she replied, looking around the private jet. Mr. Worthington was stretched out in a matching white leather recliner a few feet away. The two assistants/bodyguards who traveled constantly with him were flanked on either side of him with their heads tilted and their eyes closed. Jack opened the worn copy of *Pride and Prejudice* that the librarian had given her after Jack had informed her she was leaving the city. She had seen Jack read the book on the leather chair countless times as she waited for the reading group to assemble. This was a gift that Jack would treasure: the classic piece would always have a place on her book-shelf…if she ever had a bookshelf, she thought wryly.

Jack woke suddenly to the jet's tires touching down roughly on the tarmac. She slowly sat up, scrubbed her face with her hands, and looked out the win-dow. Mr. Worthington was sitting up and drinking a mimosa; he smiled and held up his glass.

"Good morning, my dear! How did you sleep?" he asked.

"Um, pretty good actually. Where's Noah?" Jack replied.

"He is sitting in the cockpit with the pilot. He seems to have a slight crush on Andre," Mr. Worthington chuckled.

Jack sighed deeply. "Right. So where are we going to stay while we're here? The contract said that you would put us up in apartments and transportation would be provided to work assignments."

Mr. Worthington nodded appreciatively. "My, my, you did read your contract well, didn't you? Yes, I will go over all that with you both in the car. Come now, let's get off this jet and into the beautiful sunshine!" he exclaimed gaily, standing and smoothing out his cream suit.

The door opened and the pilot appeared with Noah not far behind him. They descended the stairs and immediately got in the black stretch limo that was waiting. Apparently, the very rich weren't subjected to the security checks that lesser mortals had to endure, thought Jack.

The sheer beauty of the lush greenery and blossoming flowers blew her negative thoughts away. It was gorgeous as they drove through Paris and passed what must have been the Louvre and then the Eiffel Tower. Jack and Noah had their faces pressed against the windows as they shouted and pointed out the sites.

They had traveled about fifteen minutes out of the city to what must have been the suburbs with pretty stone walls and lots of greenery. They parked in front of a large old brick building with ivy hugging it, giving it a majestic air.

"Is this our apartment?" Jack asked as they got out of the limo.

"Yes. Actually it's a series of duplex apartments. I own the building. You and Noah will have attached but separate apartments that occupy the fifth and sixth floors of the building. The top floors. They are completely furnished, and all you will have to supply are your own clothes and food," Mr. Worthington informed his two newest models, looking at the single backpack that Jack had traveled with. "You will have most of your evenings and weekends to yourselves, unless there is a fashion show or other obligations assigned to you. A car will come for you each morning at nine o'clock to bring you to my home, where you will be told what the day holds."

There was a code required to enter the building. "The code is one nine three three, the year that this building was erected," Mr. Worthington said, punching in the code. The door buzzed open, and he led the way through a large room that looked a little bit like an old-fashioned French salon. There were velvet chairs and an ornate couch. Wallpaper printed with large flowers adorned the walls. There were boxes in the walls that people's mail was slipped into.

Jack looked closer as she read "Mademoiselle Jack" and "Monsieur Noah" in side-by-side mail slots. Mr. Worthington came in and stood before Jack.

"As you can see, this is where you will retrieve your mail." He handed Jack and Noah each a large key. "This is your elevator key."

He next pointed to the elevators on the extreme right and extreme left of the room. "This key will open directly into your apartment. Jack, you are on the left. Noah, you are on the right. Your apartments are connected by a locked door. Let's go to Jack's apartment first."

They entered the elevator, and Jack inserted the key, which immediately brought them to the fifth floor. The doors opened to a bright and airy entryway. The walls were off-white and the floors were marble with shades of off-white, gray, and black. There was a black bench beside the elevator where you could put your shoes on or drop your purse as you entered the apartment. There were beautiful dried flowers arranged everywhere that gave a pop of color to an otherwise plain color scheme. They did a quick walk-through that ended in the largest closet Jack had ever seen. It was a room, really, with lots of drawers and shelves, a small crystal chandelier hanging in the middle, and mirrors everywhere. Surprisingly, there were clothes already hanging in the closet. Jack touched a black velvet evening gown.

"The other tenant still has clothes here," she said absently.

Mr. Worthington smiled. "No, my dear, these are your clothes. My assistant has gone shopping and gotten you started with the things you will need right away and hopefully some fun clothes you will like. I instructed him as to your sizes and told him a little about you—only a little, because alas that is all I know of your likes and dislikes—and told him to go shopping for you. Noah has already gone shopping with me and picked out lots of lovely outfits. Don't forget, dear girl, that you will be representing me and my company for the next eighteen months, and I want you to look the part as well as conduct yourself as a proper lady."

Jack snorted. "Proper lady, my ass," she mumbled.

Noah coughed to cover up her sarcasm. "Um, let's go look at my apartment now, shall we?" he said loudly.

Mr. Worthington waved his hand in a dismissive gesture. "No, I will leave you both to it. I must be getting on to the estate. I will send a car around tomorrow morning at nine o'clock. Do not be late," he warned as he walked out of the closet.

Jack and Noah looked at each other. "Do not be late," Noah mimicked in his most nasally aristocratic voice as they both burst out laughing.

Jack sprawled on Noah's bed as he unpacked his suitcases. How could one guy have so many clothes? It looked like a clothing hurricane had touched down.

"I can't believe you're leaving me on our first night in Paris," Jack whined.

"Lovely, did you see that pilot? Mmm? Enough said. Besides, I already know how your evening will go. You will flop down on your bed with a book. Period. The end. Come on, Jack! We're young, we need to have adventures!" Noah exclaimed, whipping a cashmere scarf round his neck.

Jack snorted. "I think I've had enough 'adventures' to last a lifetime, but I do agree with you to a certain extent. I fully intend to have some fun—just not tonight. I did see a full bookcase of books in my apartment," she said, trying on one of Noah's fedoras.

"Well there you go! I do believe those books are all in French—oh, wait," he said stopping to admire himself in the mirror, and then turned to look at her. "Jesus, you can read them all, can't you?" he said, throwing the scarf at her.

Jack watched it slowly float through the air and caught it midair. "Yup!" she said, laughing.

The car was waiting downstairs when Jack banged on Noah's adjoining door. She had made him a coffee to go along with her own. The cupboards held scads of food already, including coffee. She'd spent most of the morning figuring out the elaborate coffee maker on her counter. Turns out it did it all, everything from espresso to tea. Nice! Jack had found some jeans in her closet that fit her like a glove, right down to the length, which she had always had a problem with because her legs were so long. Each drawer held some secret treasure. Her underwear was in a drawer all by itself. The price tags were still attached.

OMG!

One pair of these undergarments cost more than Jack had ever spent on an entire outfit—one pair.

Jesus!

It felt like silk, and she opened another drawer to find matching bras in the same silk. Jack sighed and grabbed a matching black pair. Perfect fit. How is this possible? She found a plain white T-shirt, slipped her own dirty flip-flops on, and headed out the door.

As she approached the limo, the driver got out and opened the door. He was large and looked very stern.

"Umm, my friend is coming also," she mumbled, motioning toward the building.

"Monsieur Cabrera will meet you at the office, Mademoiselle," the driver replied, motioning toward the open door with his right hand.

"Okay, thank you," she said quietly and got in the car. *Noah is such a slut,* thought Jack, smirking and looking out the window.

The "office" was Brock Worthington's estate, which was very large and sprawling. Jack was let off around back as a young man pranced down the steps to greet her. The young man was very beautiful, with short blond curly hair and sort of pixie-like features. He spoke very broken English.

"Hello, Mademoiselle Jack! My name is Phillip, and I will be yours and Monsieur Cabrera's assistant. Did you find your apartment to your liking? Oh! I see you have found the clothes. You look *tres* chic!" he said, kissing his fingers. That is until his eyes landed on her flip-flops.

"Did you not find the sandals to your liking?" he whined, looking hurt.

Jack looked at her old flip-flops and back up at him. "Um, actually I didn't even look at the shoes. Sorry. I will look at them tonight. Did you pick out my clothes?"

Phillip nodded enthusiastically. "Oui, yes—yes, I did. I will be taking care of all your needs, mademoiselle. Please don't hesitate to tell me of your needs. Okay?" he said as he grabbed her hand and held it to his chest as he walked them into the estate. "We are going to be fast friends you and me, ma petite Jack," he exclaimed, smiling.

Jack stood a full head taller than Phillip. He seemed a bit touchy-feely to Jack; nevertheless, she liked him immediately.

They entered the large sitting room with a giant ornamental desk in the middle. Overstuffed couches and chairs were scattered throughout the room as well as mannequins with clothes pinned to them. Mr. Worthington sat at the desk furiously sketching something. Noah sat on a purple corduroy-stuffed chair with his legs swinging off the arm. Noah looked up when she and Phillip entered the room and smiled.

"I see you have met Boy Wonder," he said, looking at Phillip.

Jack narrowed her eyes, silently telling him to play nice, and then she clapped her hands together. "So, what's on the agenda for today, boss?" she inquired, plopping down in the matching chair beside Noah.

Mr. Worthington looked up for a brief second and then right back at his sketch. "You both are going to the spa today. You will gladly accept all the treatments that are ordered for you. No arguments. That will take the entire day. I will see you here tomorrow, and we will go over the rest of the week." As an afterthought, he looked up quickly and then down again to his sketch. "I trust you are all settled in?" he asked absently.

"Um, no, actually someone broke in and blackened both my eyes," Jack replied sarcastically.

"Yes, well, you're welcome, now move along, don't keep the spa waiting," he muttered without looking up. Jack and Noah smiled at each other.

As they started to leave the room, Phillip jumped in front of Jack with a horrified look on his face. He stared at Jack's face.

"It was a joke, Phillip. My face is fine," Jack assured him as she looped her arms through his and Noah's. Phillip laughed, relieved.

"Oh, thank God, ma petite! Look! We are the three musketeers!" Noah rolled his eyes.

The word *spa* elicited feelings of well-being and relaxation to Jack, but instead it turned out to be a special level of hell. The first room brought more pain that any person should have to endure.

Body waxing.

It had been a good long time since she had really shaved her legs, but Jesus! Every square inch of her legs and underarms were waxed. It took a long time because she had to keep telling them she needed breaks because her legs were on fire. The little Asian women began speaking quickly and tried to spread her legs apart when she jumped off the table.

"Whoa, no way! You are not going to wax me down there! Are you crazy? If you come near me with that wax I'm going to snap your tiny little necks!" Jack hollered.

One of the ladies grabbed the phone and thrust it toward her. Jack glared at her and grabbed the phone.

"No! I will not wax there! You can't make me!" Jack exclaimed, her voice shaking.

Mr. Worthington's calm voice came across the telephone. "Now Jack, we have a deal, my dear. I told you this morning that you must willingly accept all spa services that were ordered," he replied patronizingly.

"You are one sick fuck! There is no possible reason for this. It's not like I'm going to be posing nude—which I am not!"

He sighed. "Of course you're not, but you will be modeling swimsuits and sheer clothing. This really is the way it is done, dear girl. Please, unless you want Noah on the first plane back to the ghetto, I suggest this be the last fight we have about such things. Just go along to get along, my dear. Understand?" he said with sickening calm.

Jack took many deep breaths before uttering "fine" and handing the phone back to the ladies. One of the ladies stood in front of Jack with a glass of water and a little pink pill. She held it out and said something soothing that Jack didn't understand, but she got her meaning. Jack looked at the pill for a minute before picking it up and tossing it back with the water. She lay back down on the table and the lady put a warm towel around her face. Jack started to relax *a lot.* She could feel all her troubles just float away. This was nice, very nice, Jack thought, as she drifted off to a land of milk and honey.

Jack slowly heard someone calling her name. It sounded like they were underwater or she was…she couldn't tell. She opened her eyes and saw Noah leaning over her and smiling.

"Have you been in la-la land, lovely?" he said, smiling. He looked gorgeous. His skin glowed and his hair had been cut into a very metrosexual French style.

Jack sat up to find herself in a big white fluffy bathrobe. Every inch of her had been scrubbed and polished and painted. Her hair had been washed and deep conditioned and trimmed and was coiffed into a bun on top of her head. Her face felt like silk. She looked in the mirror and didn't recognize the girl who stared back at her. Jack stood up and walked to the mirror. She touched her face.

She looked at Noah. "That doesn't even look like me," she muttered quietly.

Noah laughed. "Sure it does, lovely. You are just so used to not really looking at yourself that you don't see what the rest of the world sees. Jesus, Jack, that face is the reason we are here in fantasy land."

Noah came and stood behind Jack in the mirror. "You are the most beautiful woman I've ever seen, Jack. It doesn't matter if you're standing in the line at the soup kitchen slopping mashed potatoes onto plates with your hair in a fucking net. You are still the most beautiful woman most people will ever lay their eyes on, and you don't see a goddamn thing. Pitiful."

He turned her and held her chin between his fingers. "The face that launched a thousand ships, or some such shit," he said, kissing her forehead. "I do know that I'd like some of whatever pills they gave you though!" he laughed.

"Are we done here? Because I'm starving," Jack grumbled, grabbing her clothes and starting to dress.

"Yeah, it's actually four o'clock, let's go out to dinner and then watch a movie at my place," Noah replied, leading her out of the spa to the waiting limo.

Wow, four o'clock—she had been out the entire day! Maybe those pills would come in handy during this willing imprisonment.

Jack stayed the night in Noah's room, and accordingly had to listen to him go on and on about Jim the pilot. She missed Mac. How many nights had they talked and laughed about boys. Well, to be truthful, she had only ever talked about one boy.

Jared.

Just the thought of him made her lose her breath.

Not good.

Breathe. In. Out. In. Out.

At some point, she fell asleep and woke to Noah shaking her and shouting for her to get up. Jack flew over to her apartment and showered and threw on the first summer dress she came across. She grabbed some sandals and flew out the door.

The driver's name was George. Jack had asked his name when he opened the door for her and Noah. When they got out of the car, Jack turned and offered her hand.

"Nice to meet you, George, I'm Jack."

George looked surprised and smiled. "So nice to make your acquaintance, mademoiselle."

As they neared the steps, Phillip bounded down to them. "Oh, good morning! I am so happy you are here!"

"Good morning, Phillip. What's on the agenda for today?" Jack inquired.

"Come in, please. We have much to discuss with Monsieur Worthington," Phillip said, ushering Jack into the office.

Mr. Worthington sat sketching at his desk. They all sat down and silently waited until he addressed them. After long moments, he looked around the room as if just discovering that they were there.

"I trust you are recovered from your spa experience yesterday," he said, looking directly at Jack.

Jack took a deep breath. *Do not punch him in the face,* she repeated to herself.

"Indubitably," she replied flatly.

"Wonderful, wonderful. Today we will be starting the photo shoots for the party on Friday night. Phillip will take you to the dressing rooms and escort you to the gardens where the first of the shoots will take place."

"Whoa, what party?" Jack said, crossing her arms across her chest.

"It is the red carpet launch of this year's wedding line. Everyone who is anyone will be attending the gala. The press will be in a frenzy. This is a much-anticipated event. I will expect you both to be on your best behavior and not to speak with the press. We have an entire team of spokespeople to handle that. Actually, don't speak at all. You will be introduced but that is all. You are to remain a mystery at all times. I will do the speaking for you. Do you understand?" Mr. Worthington said in what for him was a warning tone.

Do not punch him. Do not punch him.

Jack smiled. "Well, I wasn't aware in the contract that we signed that I was obligated to shut my mouth at parties. Noah, did you see that in the contract? I know that it said we must attend all functions pertaining to the Worthington line, but I don't believe it said I couldn't speak or burp, much less pass gas," she said, smiling.

Brock Worthington sighed. "You catch on very quickly, my dear. What, pray tell, will it take for you to have control of all your bodily functions as well as your mouth?" the billionaire asked dryly.

"Well, now that you ask, I would very much like a piano in my apartment and a bicycle. Oh, and a basket—I want a bicycle with a basket," she replied, continuing to smile.

Noah looked from one to the other confused. "Well, I would like a—"

Mr. Worthington stood and held up his hand to silence Noah without taking his eyes off Jack. "Done. Phillip, take Jack and Noah to the dressing room. I will see you Friday night. Adieu," he grumbled, walking purposefully out of the room.

Adieu my ass, thought Jack as she jumped up and linked her arm with Phillip. "God, let's get this party started, Phillip."

It was every bit as tedious and tiresome as she suspected. What seemed like hundreds of changes of clothes into seemingly the same frilly white dress only to stand and pose in front of multiple photographers was perhaps the dullest way she had ever spent her time. Her brain actually shut down in humiliation and protest.

They were told not to smile. Jack was pretty sure that most brides smiled on their wedding day, but instead apparently forlorn and lethargic was all the rage.

At the end of the day, when they were told they were done, Jack bolted onto Noah's back and he swung her around madly until they were both laughing and they landed on the grass in a heap with Jack lying across Noah. Jack lay still with her head on his chest until the ground stopped spinning. Finally the handlers came to get them off the grass, worrying Jack had gotten grass stains on the priceless gown.

After putting their street clothes back on, Noah and Jack met Phillip beside the limo. "Let's go into the city tonight," Jack proclaimed to both Noah and Phillip.

"Can't tonight, lovely—I have plans."

"Ugh, don't tell me: the pilot." Jack rolled her eyes.

"Yup!" Noah smugly replied, looking at himself in the rolled-up tinted car window.

"Mademoiselle Jack, why don't you come over to my place for dinner? My boyfriend is cooking his specialty, beef stew and bread fresh from the bakery," Phillip burst out excitedly, then looked horrified. "You do not have to eat, mademoiselle, if you do not wish. I forget models rarely eat."

"Um, I'm really not your typical model type, Phillip. I do eat—like a trucker, I'm told—and I would love to spend the evening with you and your boyfriend!"

Jack knew it was impolite to stare, but *oh my God!* Phillip's boyfriend was a bad-assed biker dude named Dirk. He was tall and thin wearing black leather pants with a thin chain hanging from his belt loop attached to his wallet. On top was a white T-shirt with the sleeves rolled up and tattoos covering both arms. His hair was greased back, and he had a cigarette hanging from his mouth as he stirred the crockpot. She felt like Sandy from *Grease* meeting Danny Zuko. Jack smiled and held out her hand.

Dirk scrambled to find the ashtray and shook her hand. Phillip looked apologetic. "I'm sorry, Dirk doesn't speak any English, mademoiselle."

Jack, without missing a beat, said hello and thanked him for inviting her to dinner in perfect French. Dirk laughed and hugged her and then gave Phillip a big hug and kiss. Jack would never in a million years have put these two together. It warmed her heart and made her, curiously, a bit envious.

The meal was lovely, and their apartment was small and homey thanks to Phillip's talent for decorating. Jack learned that Phillip and Dirk had met at a party given by a mutual friend a few years back. It was easy to see that they adored each other. When Jack didn't offer any insights to her life, Phillip and Dirk were kind enough not to ask. They spent the evening talking about Paris and all the sights Jack needed to see. At the end of the evening, Dirk led Jack to his motorcycle parked on the street. They put their helmets on, and Jack held on tight as Dirk perfectly maneuvered the dark streets of Paris to bring her home. *What a nice evening,* thought Jack before she drifted off to sleep.

Friday found Jack and Noah back at the spa to get scrubbed, polished, and poofed for the red carpet gala designed to introduce Jack and Noah to Europe's fashion scene. How ironic that they would be the face of bride and groom fashion given the fact that they were the two least likely people on the planet to ever get married!

This time it was much easier to endure the procedures, as they only involved massages and lotions and lots of makeup. Jack was still wearing her sundress and flip-flops when they turned her around to look in the mirror at her transformation. She stared, transfixed at her reflection. Who was that looking back at her? Her curls had been emphasized and teased to reveal a huge mane of wild hair. She couldn't look away from the stranger in the mirror. The makeup was so flawless that she didn't even look real to herself. It was as if she was wearing a mask. Jack felt a glimmer of hope that she would actually be able to pull this off for the next eighteen months. When she was made up, she would be Jack the model. She would separate herself from this image. In her mind, she would actually become a different person. She could definitely do this.

Noah swaggered in slowly, very much in love with himself—even more than usual. He did look spectacular, and he didn't even have his tuxedo on yet. He let out a low whistle.

"Ooh la la! Look at you, lovely! Wow!" He too just couldn't look away from her reflection. "What do you think?" he murmured.

Jack shrugged her shoulders. "This isn't me, Noah," she said, pointing at the stranger in the mirror. "This is who I will be tonight and every day we are working, but she's a stranger to me. To me, this will always be just a soulless stranger."

Getting up from the chair, she walked to the car, and before she got in, she made eye contact with George and leaned in to whisper in his ear.

"George, can we go through the drive thru and get a milkshake?" she begged, making a praying motion with her hands. "Please?"

George tried not to smile, but he couldn't help himself. "Of course, mademoiselle." Jack squealed and dove into the car.

She was never going to be able to walk in these heels. They were crystal strappy open toes with a red bottom. Wow. Even a girl who would rather wear cowboy boots and flip-flops would be hard pressed not to truly appreciate these shoes. The black velvet dress that had been hanging in her closet had ultimately been chosen for her to wear. It reminded Jack of an old-fashioned movie starlet. It was form fitting and came off her shoulders with a crystal between her breasts. She had long white gloves that came up to her upper arms. She wore a diamond choker and diamond teardrop earrings. She stared at the apparition in the wall of mirrors in her closet.

Phillip rested his hands on his hips and shook his head. "My sweet Jack, I have never seen such a beauty as yourself. But even with all your beauty, I still see such sadness in you. Why is that, ma petite? Are you not happy being the most beautiful woman in all of Paris?" he asked, letting his head rest against hers.

Just a hint of a tear sprang to Jack's eyes as she clicked the stereo on to fill the room with Journey blaring "Midnight Train." They sang and danced, and soon Noah came in with a drink in his hand and started playing the air guitar. As the song finished, Phillip glanced at his watch.

"Jesus! We must get you to the car now! George must be waiting downstairs. Chop, chop my beauties!" Phillip grabbed a white fur stole and rested it over Jack's shoulders.

Downstairs, he helped her into the car. "Good-bye, my pet. Call or text me if you need me," he called out, waving as the limo drove away.

Mr. Worthington sat ramrod straight in his seat as Noah and Jack flew into the car. The pair were laughing loudly until they viewed his face and tension-racked body. Her smile quickly disappearing, Jack muttered a terse hello. Mr. Worthington nodded solemnly.

"Let's go over some important points regarding tonight's behavior, shall we? First, you are both supposed to give the impression that you are deeply in love and preparing for the wedding of your dreams. Second, you are to smile and be gracious and polite. You do not give your opinion or answer any questions. You will defer all questions to me, and you will have handlers with you at all times. There will be no drinking or smoking. Do you understand the ground rules for tonight and for every event you are obligated to attend?"

Jack bristled. "Okay, so let me get this straight. Noah, who is obviously very gay, is supposed to be totally in love with me? Don't get me wrong, we have a lot of chemistry together as *brother and sister,* but that's it! Who's going to believe that he would choose me over, oh, I don't know, how about a man with a *penis?* And then to top everything off, we are supposed to act like mindless robots. What kind of message is that sending to this generation?"

Mr. Worthington suddenly leaned forward until his face was almost touching Jack's, making Jack gasp and sit back. His face was beet red with blue veins crawling up the sides of his head.

"*You* are not sending any kind of message, my dear! You are a face and a body—that's it. Do you hear me?" he growled, but then he caught himself and took a deep breath. "If you misspeak one more time, one of you will be on the next plane back to the streets. Do I make myself clear *this time,* Miss Johnson?"

All color drained from Jack's face. "Crystal," she replied between gritted teeth.

The car came to a halt and the doors opened. A hand appeared and Brock Worthington grasped it, gracefully emerging from the black stretch limo.

Noah turned to Jack. "Who is going to be on that plane home?" he whispered.

Jack looked at him and smiled. "Ah, me? Duh," she said as nonchalantly as possible.

Noah looked relieved. "Well I won't let that happen," he whispered, kissing her forehead.

Another hand appeared and Jack first pretended to bite it but grasped it instead. Noah laughed. The lights and flashes were absolutely blinding. Jack simply smiled and held Noah's hand. When her eyes started to adjust, she could make out giant billboards and posters everywhere with pictures of their first photo shoot. Jack stood transfixed, staring up at the billboards. They had chosen the photo of Jack lying on Noah's chest, and you could actually see real love in both their eyes.

Jack teared up as Noah gently put his hands on the sides of her face and looked her in the eyes.

"Breathe, lovely."

Jack smiled and took a deep breath as she leaned her forehead against his. The crowd went wild. The paparazzi were screaming questions at them and the flashbulbs were blinding. The handlers gently began escorting them into the glitzy party.

Opulence and affluence were literally dripping inside the large ballroom with hanging chandeliers and ice sculptures flowing with champagne. Jack and Noah did their due diligence by smiling and laughing at all the witty quips the millionaires and billionaires fired at them. When Jack and Noah just couldn't stand not making some smartass comment in response, instead they would lean into each other and whisper in the other's ear, at which point the other would laugh coyly. People thought they were the most adorable American lovers they had ever seen. It was killing Jack that these people truly did think they were just stupid, shallow American pinheads. Jack could hear the conversations going on around her and was shocked at the rude sentiments about how unsophisticated and stupid these Americans were. If there was one ace Jack felt she had up her sleeve, it was that they would never imagine that she understood and spoke their language fluently. This brought a slow smirk to her lips. Snobbish pricks.

After four hours that seemed like eight of absolute torture, they were finally ushered back to the car and brought mercifully home. Noah was restless in the car; that meant he wasn't going to stay home for long. Sure enough, as soon as the car dropped them off at their apartments, Jack spied a little red sports car parked out front. Noah took off his bowtie and jacket and handed them to Jack.

"Come with?" he asked.

Jack smiled a tired smile. "No, thank you. There is a giant bathtub calling my name. But, Noah," she said as he was walking toward the car. He stopped and turned to her. "Thank you. I wouldn't be able to get through this shit without you."

He ran over to her and grasped her face with both hands. "Oh, lovely, we're a team, you and I, mon amie!" He kissed each of her cheeks and ran toward the car.

Jack lay back and closed her eyes and let the hot water envelop her. She had added lavender incense to her water, which soothed and relaxed her. She couldn't help but be in awe of the total turnaround her life had taken in the last two years. Suddenly Jack began to have flashbacks of Moose Pond and swimming with

Jared, her walking down the road angry with her red cowboy boots on and Jared in his truck following her and pleading with her to get into the truck, her spread out on the hood of Jared's truck as he licked and tasted her...

Jack's eyes flew open and she gasped. The water in the giant white porcelain claw-foot tub splashed over the edge. Jack began to sweat and her heartbeat grew faster. She tentatively touched herself and her breath quickened. Jack lay her head back against the tub and began to touch herself, this time with a purpose. With her other hand, she began worrying her nipple as she inserted two fingers inside her sex. Jack bit down on her bottom lip and increased the pressure and rhythm. Flashes of Jared driving into her and crying out with his head rearing back sent Jack spiraling out of control and she cried out with the force of the inevitable orgasm. Slowly her breathing returned to normal and she realized that the water had grown cold. She took her time getting out of the tub, more relaxed than she had been in a very long time.

Wrapped in her white silk robe, Jack made her way to the beautiful new baby grand piano that was sitting in her living room. She traced her fingers lightly over the black lacquered wood and sat down. She gently ran her fingers over the white ivory keys, barely touching them. Jack pulled out some new music that she had printed off the computer at the Worthington Estate. It was the song from the movie *Frozen*. Jack and Noah had watched it on the plane, and Jack had fallen in love with the song. Perhaps she identified with Elsa. Perhaps she, too, was destined to be alone in life. To never let anybody get too close lest they become hurt by her damaged soul. Her fingers flew over the keys and she read the words as she sang them for the first time. Her soul felt absolutely free as she allowed herself to get lost in the music. She wished she had the beautiful picture of her mother on her piano. She hadn't realized how much comfort the picture had provided her as she played as a child. It was as if she had been channeling Elsie Johnson through the music, Jack mused. After playing for God knows how long, Jack was completely spent, so she padded silently to bed and was asleep before her head hit the pillow. It was a fitful sleep full of faces and disappointments, leaving tears soaking her pillow but not quite waking her to allow her soul respite.

It didn't take long for Jack to fall into a regular routine of bicycling to town for fresh vegetables at the farmer's market; she knew the farmers by name as well as the local coffee shop workers. She fell in love with Paris, and Paris fell in love with her. Jack was able to send very substantial sums of money to Sam and Jasmine to sustain the soup kitchen and shelter. She talked with Sam several times each week, making sure to tell him about her dreams. Jack felt good and grew stronger as the days stretched into weeks and then months.

Each day on her way to Worthington Estate, they passed a large children's hospital. Jack didn't know why, but she felt a great need to stop and visit with the children. One Friday afternoon, she had been told that there were no parties and Mr. Worthington was going back to the states for an indefinite period of time; nevertheless, they were to keep the same work schedule. Jack was elated with the news, and as they passed the hospital she asked George to please stop and accompany her inside. As they walked inside, Jack felt a negative energy permeating through her. She shivered as they approached the nurse's station. Speaking in French, Jack asked the nurse if they had a recreation room for the children.

The nurse looked confused. "Um, yes, yes we do. Do you have a child here in this hospital?" she asked.

"No, I actually pass by here almost every day and I just wanted to visit with the children if that's acceptable." Jack replied and watched George's head turn quickly to look at her.

The nurse's eyes narrowed. "Yes, yes, I will show you. Do I know you, mademoiselle?" she asked suspiciously.

Jack smiled as she followed her. "I don't think so. Are you planning a wedding?"

The nurse whirled around. "No! I'm never getting married!" the pretty nurse declared.

Jack clapped her hands together as they entered a deathly quiet room with bald, sickly looking children quietly playing with toys on the floor. "Then no, we have never met, mademoiselle," Jack said absently. The nurse shrugged her shoulders and sauntered away.

George took a seat in the far corner as Jack knelt down on the floor. "Hello, little ones," she said quietly. Jack proceeded to engage the children and the parents with questions about their lives and their lovely country. Finally Jack asked the children if they would like her to read to them, and they all clapped and pleaded for her to do so. Jack looked through the stack of books and proceeded to pick out several. She then sat on the floor leaning on the couch as the children gathered around her. She read them story after story until the nurse finally came in to tell them that supper would be served in their rooms shortly. As the children groaned about her leaving, Jack laughed and looked at them.

"How about if I come back each afternoon that I am able to and we can spend time together. Would you like that?"

The children all cheered, which broke Jack's heart. These children had seen more pain in their young lives than most, and yet they got excited that someone would take the time to visit with them.

Jesus, how humbling.

Each day thereafter when she was able, Jack visited the children's hospital and brought sweet treats and new books. She got to know the parents and fell totally in love with the children. One day in particular, after the children asked Jack to read the book *Frozen* for the hundredth time, Jack asked the children if they would like her to sing Elsa's song and play it on the old broken-down piano in the corner. The children looked suspiciously at her as if she was pulling their legs. Jack chuckled again.

"No, really! I can play the song. Would you like that?" she laughed as she picked them up and sat them on top of the piano, hugging several on the stool with her.

As her fingers warmed up on the keys, Jack quickly realized that the piano was old and out of tune, but it would do and they would have a good time singing. She started playing the beginning verses of "Let It Go," and the children looked shocked.

Jack laughed. "Now I know you all know this song, so I may need your help. Would you sing with me?" she asked, continuing the introduction.

The children all had a reverent visage and nodded their heads in the affirmative. "Okay, here we go!"

Jack started out slowly, but before too long she and the children were belting out the Disney tune without reservation. When the song was finished and Jack sat back and laughed, she could see the nurses and doctors and parents all gathered in the recreation room clapping and wiping the tears from their eyes. Jack covered her mouth with her fingers as she spied George in the corner also wiping his eyes with his handkerchief. The kids laughed and squealed and begged for more. She played that song at least four more times, and each time the children gave the same roaring round of giggles in response.

The head nurse eventually came in and clapped her hands twice, signaling the children it was time for dinner and to say good-bye to Mademoiselle Jack.

Many hugs later, Jack found herself with several parents, who thanked her for bringing smiles to the faces of their sick children. "I think they help me more than I could ever possibly help them," she told the grateful parents.

As Jack and George made their way to the outside doors, the head nurse bustled toward them. "Mademoiselle, a word please," she whispered softly. Jack turned and gave the nurse her full attention.

"Do you remember Rene?" the nurse asked.

Jack thought for a minute. "The very little boy with big blue eyes?"

"Yes, yes, he is the one. Well I just wanted to tell you that sadly he passed away last night, but this morning we found this in his room and I think he would want us to give it to you," the nurse said as she handed a drawing to Jack.

Jack stood immobile, staring at the drawing. It was a stick figure girl with lots of blond curls reading a book, but the book had come alive with King Neptune and his trident and Samson crushing some huge building. Jack's legs gave way, and George had to gather her up and walk her to the car with her head resting against his chest and tears streaming down her cheeks.

The car drove up to the apartment, and George opened the door. By then Jack had composed herself and got out of the car. George looked worried.

"I'm okay, George. I'm sad but I will be okay. How about you? Are you going to be okay?" Jack asked.

George teared up and nodded his head. "Yes, mademoiselle, but I must confess I cannot wait to get home and hug my children tonight," he sniffed.

Jack nodded. "I understand. I will see you on Monday. Have a good weekend, George," she said, walking to the stairs.

"Until then," George replied, climbing back into the car and driving away.

Jack got in Noah's elevator and let herself into his apartment. It was quiet at first, but as she walked into his bedroom she was met with sounds of moans and naked flesh.

"Oh Jesus!" Jack hollered and turned abruptly to leave.

Once inside her own apartment she shook her head to get the images out of her brain. She fixed some tea and sat down at the kitchen bar. Seconds later Noah sauntered in with only jeans and a white T-shirt and bare feet. He grabbed an apple and took a bite.

"Way to knock, lovely. Did you get an eyeful?" Noah smirked.

Jack looked annoyed. "Um, I want to stab my eyeballs out with a toothpick, thank you very much! And since when do we properly knock?" she retorted as she sipped her tea. She looked around. "Where is the flavor of the hour?" Jack said snidely.

Noah feigned outrage. "I'm hurt, mon amie!" he said, but he couldn't help but laugh at himself. Turning serious for just a moment, Noah suddenly blurted out, "Come out with me tonight. Just the two of us. We will dance the night away."

Jack looked at him, pondering the request. Noah was surprised that she was actually thinking about it and accordingly ramped up his charm.

"Please, lovely. We are meant to be married soon, and you never make time for me! Come on! It will be fun, please!" he pleaded.

"No cameras or paparazzi?" Jack asked cautiously.

Noah shook his head. "No, none. It's a gay nightclub, and trust me, they protect their own. No cameras or paparazzi allowed. We will have a blast! You have to let me dress you though," he replied briskly, pulling her toward her closet.

Noah was absolutely right—she had a blast. He dressed her in a black silk one piece pantsuit that tied at the neck like a halter top, black Jimmy Choo heels, and a black faux fur jacket. They danced all night and not a soul bothered her except to dance with her and make her laugh. It was exactly what Jack needed that particular night.

At about three in the morning, Jack fell into her bed with Noah beside her, and she didn't wake up until she felt Noah violently shaking her.

"Jack! Wake up! Worthington is on the telephone and he doesn't sound happy."

Jack scrubbed her hands up and down her face and took the cell phone that Noah was handing her.

"Um, hello?" she said tentatively.

"Have you seen the newspaper or been on the Internet yet?" Mr. Worthington asked.

Jack tried to think about last night. She hadn't done anything that would have caused her to get into trouble. Had she? "Um, no. I haven't quite woken up yet. What's the problem?" she asked, starting to get annoyed. She needed coffee before she dealt with this prima donna, dammit.

"I suggest you go online and buy a paper. I will be in Paris later tonight and will see you tomorrow at the estate. We will see what sort of damage control is needed then."

Click.

Shit.

Noah walked in and handed her a hot cup of coffee. "Thank Christ," Jack grunted, taking the cup and taking a big swig. "Go get your fucking computer. Apparently I'm the feature story. For fuck's sake!" she muttered, rubbing her temple and taking a big swallow of coffee.

Noah sat in bed with her as they logged onto the Paris headlines. "Our Very Own American Ice Princess!"

What. The. Fuck.

The article said that "Jack, the American supermodel" regularly visited the children's hospital and sang to the sick children, and it linked to a tear-jerking performance on YouTube of the "Ice Princess" in action. Noah clicked through to YouTube and it appeared that someone had recorded her and the kids singing "Let It Go." The children, their tiny hands swaying in the air, were singing at the top of their lungs.

A big lump formed in Jack's throat. *Fucking paparazzi, intruding on such a special moment with her kids. Her kids.* Jack smiled.

"That's it? Jesus, I thought it was something bad." Jack looked at Noah, who had tears streaming down his cheeks. He was staring at her.

"I fucking love you, Jack Johnson," he said emotionally.

Jack grinned. "Well I fucking love you too, Noah Cabrera!"

Jack showered and got on her bike to go to town and get some fresh vegetables. Fuck 'em all. She ended up spending the day preparing and cooking a large chicken stew and invited Noah, Phillip, and Dirk over for dinner. There was something she had been trying to get the nerve to ask Dirk, and tonight she was ready. She didn't know how much time she would have left here in Paris after Mr. Worthington fired her. She wasn't afraid of being fired. She welcomed it, actually—even though she hadn't saved as much money as she would have liked, at least she wouldn't be treated like a highly paid slave any longer. Not long after meeting Dirk, Jack had learned that he was a tattoo artist by trade. She had been secretly thinking about getting a tattoo of remembrance. Jack finally felt strong enough both mentally and physically, but she never wanted to forget the pain that she had slogged through to get to where she was today.

Noah, of course, had a date, so it was just the three of them sitting down to dinner. Phillip was gushing about all the press the YouTube clip was creating. Jack hadn't bothered to buy a newspaper after she had seen the YouTube clip, and quite frankly she couldn't see what the big deal was. If anything, she wished it would all just die down so the children would be left alone. They certainly had enough on their plates without the paparazzi bothering them.

"Have you heard anything from Mr. Worthington since this all broke?" Jack asked Phillip.

Phillip shook his head. "No, only that he will be here tomorrow evening and he wants to meet with you and me."

Jack looked at Dirk and then back at Phillip. "Well, whether I get fired or not, I still have a request for you, Dirk."

Dirk stopped eating. "Anything, mon amie," he replied solemnly and held his hands out. Tears sprang to Jack's eyes. How was she so lucky to have friends who, when asked for help, gave an unequivocal yes without knowing what was involved?

Jack grasped Dirk's hands across the small table. She cleared her throat. "Um, I would like you do the artwork for my tattoo," she said quietly.

Dirk's face lit up with joy. "Ah, Princess, I would be honored to do your artwork!" he cried out, kissing her hand.

Phillip jumped up from the table. "No, no, no—this cannot take place! No! You must not get a tattoo! It is in your contract with Mr. Worthington that you cannot mark your body in any way while you are under his employ. We will both be fired, mademoiselle!" he pleaded.

Jack sprang up and put her hand on Phillip's shoulder to calm him down. "Calm down, Phillip. No one will even know, and I promise if it does come out, I will make sure everyone understands you had nothing to do with it and no knowledge of it. Phillip, this is very important to me," Jack said quietly.

Phillip moved back to his chair and looked at Jack carefully, letting out a deep breath. "Well, you are so stubborn that I know you will get one anyway, and so I wouldn't trust my dear friend's body to anyone other than my Dirk," he said, looking from Jack to Dirk.

The love that passed between Phillip and Dirk made Jack catch her breath. A sick, empty feeling all but overwhelmed her.

Fortunately, at that moment Dirk clapped his hands together, making Jack sit up in her seat. "Very good! How about very early tomorrow morning before your meeting with Mr. Worthington?" Dirk asked. Jack nodded.

"That would be perfect, actually. I may be on the next plane back to America for all I know." Jack smiled at her two dear friends.

"What is it, Garrett? What was so important that you pulled me from a very critical production meeting?" Marcus asked tersely.

"Um, you're going to want to hear this, Marcus," Garrett said, pacing back and forth in his high-rise office building in Rockefeller Plaza.

As editor of the prestigious magazine *Metro Gent,* he had his finger on the world's pulse with respect to breaking news from terrorism attacks to YouTube sensations.

"If you're calling to tell me that Bear is on his way home, then you're too late. I already know," Marcus said impatiently. Garrett blew out a deep breath. As the fifth Johnson boy, just ten months younger than Bear, he resented Marcus's oldest boy all-knowing attitude.

"Jesus, Marcus, would you just shut the fuck up and sit down at your computer?"

Marcus snapped to attention. Something was very wrong for Garrett to speak to him like that. Garrett was usually very quiet and reserved. As editor-in-chief of the biggest and fastest growing news magazine in New York City, Garrett was always the calm in the middle of any storm.

"Okay, what am I looking for?" Marcus asked, tersely, with his fingers poised over the computer keys.

"YouTube, Princess," Garrett replied quietly.

The moment the image appeared, Marcus felt the air leave his body. He clicked Play, and his office was immediately filled with Jack's melodic voice singing "Let It Go" with a group of bald children in pajamas.

"What. The. Fuck?" Marcus breathed.

"Exactly," Garrett replied.

"Where did you find this? Where is she?" Marcus asked urgently.

"She's in Paris," Garrett answered.

"Paris! What the fuck is she doing in Paris?" Marcus hollered. "Sorry," Marcus mumbled.

"Well, apparently she has become an international model under contract with Brock Worthington. She has been working in Paris for the last eight months. According to the Paris newspapers, she visits the local children's hospital, and a hospital worker recorded her Friday night singing with the children. This video has gone viral. She is the darling of Europe, and they have labeled her their 'American Princess.'"

Marcus just stared at the monitor. "Marcus, you still there?" Garrett asked. Marcus blinked and cleared his throat.

"Yeah, yeah—you coming home this weekend for a family meeting?" he asked.

"Yeah, I have already booked a flight for me, Ty, Bobby, and Davey. I'll see you in Portland," Garrett said and pressed the button on the headset he was wearing to cut the line. He stood gazing out the giant windows overlooking the city. Finally, they were going to get *their* Princess home. He grunted and shook his head. Paris be damned—Jack Johnson was their Princess, and nothing was going to stop them from bringing her home where she belonged.

Bobby and Ty strode into the Global Gamer office located off Fifth Avenue to the stares and sighs of every female and some males in the vicinity. The large waiting area looked a little like a twelve-year-old boy's bedroom, with overstuffed couches and chairs and posters of new high-tech video games. There were wall units with joysticks and controllers and big monitors that you could play while you waited. Ty pointed toward the big war poster advertising the newest *War Vengeance* video game to be released in a few months.

"That is friggin' awesome! Jared let me test it out in his office last time I was here."

"Yeah, I think I actually gave him some pointers about resolution," Bobby replied, trying to look serious.

"You're so full of shit," Ty muttered under his breath as they approached the front desk. A young, very metrosexual male was staring at Bobby and Ty with the phone halfway to his ear.

Ty smiled. "Hi, we're here to see Jared Ross." The young man just continued to stare until he realized he hadn't taken a breath and shook his head to clear it.

"Oh, yes—do you have an appointment with Mr. Ross?"

Ty looked at Bobby. "Appointment?" They both laughed, vaulted over the counter, and started walking toward the back offices. The young man hollered after them to stop immediately. Jared was just coming out of the last office as Bobby and Ty both flanked his sides and grabbed him by the upper arms. They simply hoisted him up by his arms and dragged him back into the same office he had just come out of, unceremoniously dumping him into his big leather office chair.

"What the fuck!" Jared hollered. Just then his office door burst open with the receptionist and two security guards. Jared stood up, glaring at Bobby and Ty.

"It's okay, Tim; these are friends of mine. They're both idiots too, but that's for another discussion," Jared said with a smirk.

Bobby held out his hand. "No, that's not quite right, although he's right about us being idiots sometimes—we're not friends, we're family," Bobby said, dead serious.

"Yeah, what he said," Ty joined in, turning serious as well. Jared looked at them both and smiled. He leaned on the desk. "Tim, cancel my appointments for the next hour."

Tim walked a little farther into the room, looking uncomfortable. "But Mr. Ross, you have the meeting with Sony about—"

"Reschedule, Tim," Jared said firmly.

Tim nodded and escorted the security guards out the door, closing it behind him. Jared was just about to light into Bobby and Ty when they both grabbed him and pushed him back down in his seat. Jared sighed. These two had always been like brothers to him. Hell, all of the Johnson boys had been like brothers to him. For that year after he left Harmony and before David Johnson had showed up at his place of work, he had been just a hollow shell of a human being. Completely empty. All that had changed when David had refused to take no for an answer and had set about making amends for the hurt he had caused Jared.

When it was time to sign the contract for Global Gamer, David had insisted on doing so at the house at Moose Pond. Just driving up the driveway had made Jared physically ill. When he walked in, he saw not just David but all nine Johnson boys waiting for him. They all apologized to him and asked him to forgive them. Not one of them blamed him for the incidents that had led to Jack's disappearance. There had been a lot of hollering and yelling as well as crying and punching walls as they commiserated with each other and shared information regarding their search for Jack. During that same weekend, they had all gone to Jared's father's house in town to get him ready for winter. They had cut and stacked about four cord of wood and put plastic on the windows to keep them insulated. "Brother" seemed too casual a word for what Jared felt for these men.

"Are you going to tell me what this is all about?" Jared said calmly. Bobby leaned over and pulled Jared's open laptop toward them, exiting out of what Jared was working on.

"What the hell, man?" Jared exclaimed angrily, reaching for the computer.

Both Bobby and Ty grabbed his arms and sat him back firmly. Ty held out his finger and brought it to his lips.

"Shh, not another fucking word."

Bobby's fingers flew across the keys and suddenly Jack's face appeared on the screen and her voice filled the room. All three men sat transfixed looking at the monitor. As the video ended, Jared continue to stare at the screen. Both men turned and leaned on either side of the computer on the desk, staring at Jared.

Jared swallowed and cleared his throat. "Where is she?" he whispered, closing his eyes.

"Paris," Bobby replied and then waited for that to settle in. When Jared opened his eyes, he continued. "Apparently she's been there for about eight months and she has become some sort of international supermodel, and get this shit, they call her the American Princess," he said, snorting.

Jared took a deep breath. "What next?" he asked looking from one to the other.

"Next, my brotha, is you have a seat all booked on the flight to Maine tonight with the rest of us. Dad is expecting us in Harmony, and we're all going to figure out what our next move is. Hell, even Bear is due home tonight."

Bobby and Ty got up and gave Jared a man hug and headed toward the door. Jared leaned against his desk with his arms outstretched and without looking up. "Hey, thank you," Jared muttered absently.

Bobby looked back knowingly. "Just breathe, brotha," he replied quietly as he closed the door behind them.

The white hot pain went on and on, but Jack never flinched. Dirk's needle went over seemingly the same spot a hundred times. Dirk had picked her up very early and took her to his studio in the city. Jack closed her eyes and tried to think of anything else besides the pain on her ribcage just below her breast and under her heart.

"Almost done, mon amie," Dirk said softly. Jack always found it amazing that such a big biker guy could be so gentle and soft and yet so intimidating at the same time.

Dirk wiped the dotted blood one last time. "I will let you look at it, but just remember it will look much better after the swelling goes down," he said, helping her up. They walked to the mirror. Jack was holding her T-shirt up, just covering her breast. She wasn't the least bit self-conscious about not having a bra on and showing half her boob. Dirk wasn't interested in females in any way, but he was very interested in her viewing his artwork.

Jack gasped. "Oh, Dirk, it's beautiful!" she whispered. She couldn't look away. In delicate black Sanskrit, "Night will be over; there will be morning" was written in scrolling text just above where her and Jared's child had lain in her womb. Tears flowed freely down Jack's face. Dirk saw her pain and enveloped her in his big embrace.

"Let it out, mon amie; let it all out."

Jack sobbed until there were no more tears in her. She blew her nose and giggled from the pure release of something powerful inside her letting go. "Well, okay then—let's go and get fired," she announced, jumping up.

Dirk scowled, mumbling about Brock Worthington sucking his dick. Jack giggled again. Dirk bandaged the tattoo and gave her instructions for cleaning it, and then they rode Dirk's big Harley Davidson through a Paris that was just waking up to this beautiful new day.

Brock Worthington had newspapers sitting all around him on the couch. Jack sat in the gaudy purple wingback chair staring out the window. The silence stretched on, but Jack would not back down and beg him to not fire her.

Silence.

With a deep sigh, Mr. Worthington put the paper down and looked at Jack. "Brilliant," he muttered and lounged back against the couch with a huge smile on his face.

Jack looked surprised. "What?" she questioned uncertainly.

"Bloody. Brilliant. I couldn't have asked for better publicity, and it didn't cost me a cent. You are a genius, my dear girl. I didn't give you anywhere near the credit I should have," he said smugly.

Jack shook her head. She couldn't be hearing this right. "I don't understand. I thought you were upset about me being in the papers?" she replied, leaning forward.

Mr. Worthington nodded his head in agreement. "Yes, yes, I agree that at first I was angry at you for putting yourself out there, but my dear girl, you are beloved. This has gone completely viral; the whole world loves you and wants to know everything about you. I have a team dedicated to searching all the websites that are popping up about you. People are tweeting, and even letters have come in the mail. You are the American Princess. I have so many corporations lined up wanting you to endorse their products that my legal team will be working night and day to sort them all out. The money I will be making because of you is astounding."

Jack stood up and walked to the window. She stood silently. Mr. Worthington came to stand behind her and grasped her shoulders from behind.

"Aren't you thrilled, my dear? You are becoming the most adored face in the world," he whispered quietly in her ear.

Jack stiffened and stepped out of his reach. "Let me get this straight. Because I was visiting sick children and trying to brighten their day—and please don't get me wrong: they brightened my day far more than I did theirs—now somehow *I* am beloved? Why is that so sickening to me? Those children's faces should be up on the billboards, not mine! They're the true face of beauty and courage, not some painted, hollowed-out shell! And to top it all off, because of my singing with those same beautiful children, *you* are going to make millions?"

Mr. Worthington's eyes narrowed and he took a step closer to her and pointed his finger. "Now, be very careful how you address me, young lady. Let us not forget that I own you for the next ten months, and if you don't want your boyfriend or whatever he is to you to be blackballed in this business, then you better think before the next words come out of your mouth."

Jack nodded. "Yes; okay, you're right. I didn't mean to mix my personal feelings with business," she smiled.

"Exactly. Much better," Mr. Worthington smiled victoriously.

"So now let's talk business. I may not be a skilled attorney like my brother Henry, but I did read my contract, and nowhere does it say that you may sub-contract my services to other corporations. I am obligated to you for your clothing and merchandise only. So, no, I will not be making anyone a penny more than I am contractually obligated to do. So if there is no photo shoot scheduled for today, I'm going to go the hospital and visit with my *beloved* children."

A vein was throbbing in the right temple of Brock Worthington's head. "Wait!" he hollered at her, staggering backward. "Do you know how ludicrous that is? There are literally millions of dollars on the table right now. You can't be serious about walking away from it!"

Jack turned around to face him. "Really?" Jack turned back around and almost made it to the door before she heard a frustrated cry. She slowly turned around to face him with eyes narrowed.

"What. Do. You. Want?" he snarled with barely contained rage.

Jack's simple answer was a radiant smile. Brock Worthington motioned toward the sofa, and Jack sat in the same wingback chair opposite him.

"Well, for starters, you are never going to blackmail me again regarding Noah working in this business, because we are going to have a new contract drawn up for the next ten months. It will specifically state that you will in no way hinder his modeling career and, more specifically, that you will keep him employed with your company for the next five years or until he decides to break ties with you." Mr. Worthington's mouth was a hard line.

"Next, Phillip. You work him to death and pay him next to nothing. He is nothing but a glorified babysitter for me and Noah. You are aware that he has a master's degree in international design with a business major, are you not? Well, I want him to be completely in charge of making the deals with the other corporations to be linked with my name."

Mr. Worthington was shaking his head, but Jack held up her hand. "This is nonnegotiable I'm afraid. He makes the deals, with you involved of course, and he will be paid in the six figures to do so. Now for the pièce de résistance," Jack said, kissing her fingers. "I will work like a dog for the next ten months for yourself and whoever we decide to work with, with no complaints, but I will also receive twenty percent of all income from outside sources as well as the pay from my current contract," Jack ended, placing her hands on her crossed legs.

Brock Worthington snorted. "That's insane! No one on this planet would give you twenty percent. You would be lucky to get two percent."

"Okay, fine—thirty percent, and every time you disagree with me it will increase. Let's keep in mind that I could give less than two shits whether I step in front of the camera ever again, and I sure as shit don't care if I'm beloved. My plan is to take care of the ones I love and take care of myself as well, so after these next ten months are over, I will never have to take another order from anybody as long as I live," Jack replied with finality.

Mr. Worthington jumped up, pacing back and forth. Words were coming out of this mouth, but nothing was intelligible until Jack heard "Twenty-five percent! That's final!"

Jack jumped up. "Done! Have it written up, and I will look at it on Monday morning. Au revoir!" Jack ended the negotiation, swiftly walking out the door to find George to take her to the children's hospital for some much-needed play time.

Jack was just pedaling up the walkway to the apartment house when her cell phone rang.

"Bonjour, Phillip!" Jack exclaimed, jumping off the bike and grabbing her fresh pastries.

"Bonjour, Jack. There have been some changes to our schedules, mademoiselle."

"What's that, Phillip?"

"We are leaving for America tonight. A car will be around this afternoon at five o'clock to pick up you and Noah. I'm sorry for the short notice, but Mr. Worthington has just informed me as well," he replied, sighing.

"Phillip, what's wrong?" Jack asked, hearing something troubling in his tone.

"Well, I have been promoted, as you well know, mademoiselle, and I am very grateful for this opportunity, but Dirk is less than happy about it, mon amie."

"Oh, Phillip—Dirk will join us in America, won't he?"

"Oui, eventually; we will work this all out, I'm sure. Do not be alarmed, ma petite. Pack just what you want to bring on the jet. All of your belongings will be packed and delivered to your new apartment this week. I will see you shortly. Au revoir."

Noah burst through the door, looking less than happy. "Did you just get off the phone with Phillip?" he said, standing in front of her with his arms crossing his chest.

"Yeah. I'm guessing you don't want to go home?"

"You're guessing right, lovely. What the frig have you done?"

"Whoa, wait just a minute! I'm sorry that you're not ready to go home just yet, but what I've 'done' is ensure that you have a job for the next five years. I don't think a lot of models have that much job security, thank you very much!" Jack exclaimed, standing her ground and crossing her own arms across her chest.

"Well, you also have job security, am I right?" Noah asked sarcastically.

"No, you are not right, because in exactly ten months' time I will never model again in my life. You, on the other hand, love this life and I...well, let's just say I do not and leave it at that, okay?"

Noah stepped forward and enveloped her in his arms. "Christ on crutches, Jack, how come I feel like you have sold your soul for me? I'm not worth it, you know," he whispered in her ear.

Jack smiled. "Why don't you let me be the judge of that, my little man whore, okay?" She laughed as he started tickling her and then ran for her closet to grab some clothes for the flight home.

Sunday afternoon, Jack, Noah, and Phillip stepped out of the cab in front of a row of brownstones on the Upper West Side. Phillip had been on the phone with Mr. Worthington on and off throughout the night. Jack and Noah looked to Phillip to tell them what was going on. Phillip clapped his hands.

"Well, all right then—here we are!" he nearly shouted, waving his hands with a flourish.

"Um, okay, so which one of these beauties is ours and do you have the key?" Jack asked, crossing her arms and impatiently tapping her foot. Just as Phillip was about to answer, the door opened and a very made-up middle-aged lady descended the stairs waving her arms.

"Well, hello there! You must be Jack, Noah, and Phillip. It's a pleasure to meet you!" the woman exclaimed, thrusting her hand out for Noah to shake.

It figured that she zeroed right in on Noah. Women and men alike were just drawn to him. *He's far too pretty for his own good,* Jack thought as she felt a pang of homesickness for her brother Caleb, another male too pretty for his own good. Jack smiled as the woman finally shook her hand.

"I'm Kasandra, the real estate agent Mr. Worthington contacted for a place for you all to live while you're in the city. You are going to love this brownstone. Come on up and I will show you around. It has a master suite and four large bedrooms along with two living rooms, a huge kitchen, a formal dining room and a media room/billiard room."

Noah started whistling "Movin' on Up" from *The Jeffersons* as Jack chuckled. When she was showing the master suite, Phillip told Kasandra that Jack would be occupying this room.

"Ah, no, Phillip, Dirk is going to join us shortly, so there will be two of you. I insist you take this room. Besides, I plan to be working a lot over the next ten months, so I probably won't be here much. Really, I insist. As a matter of fact, I think I want a room as far as possible from both you and Noah," she smirked as she walked toward the very end of the hall.

Kasandra looked confused. Noah touched her shoulder.

"Trust me, you really don't want to know," he whispered with a playful wink.

Jack threw her backpack on her giant four-poster king-size bed and quickly looked around. The room was huge. The bed and settee were at one end of the room and on the other end in front of the huge windows were a couch and two chairs. Jack walked over to the windows. They looked out over the street and front walk. She liked that she could watch the world come and go in the privacy of her room. The connecting bathroom was ridiculously large, with marble tile and a walk-in shower. All the fixtures were gold-plated, and there was an actual small chandelier in her friggin' bathroom!

Shaking her head, Jack headed to find Phillip. The three of them were admiring the "media room," with a mounted television so big that you almost couldn't see the wall behind it. It had a white leather sectional couch that could fit probably twenty people.

Jesus.

"Um, hey Phillip, are you all set with me for the afternoon? I'm going to check in on some people," Jack asked.

Phillip nodded. "Oui, mon amie, we will go over your schedule later tonight," he replied, hugging her. "Are you safe?" he asked, concerned.

Jack laughed. "More than you know." Jack looked toward Noah who was texting wildly. "Come with?" she asked, bumping his hip with hers.

"What? Oh, no, I'll catch you later, lovely," he replied, never looking up from his phone.

"Suit yourself. Au revoir!"

Phillip cleared his throat to get Noah's attention. Noah continued to text wildly. "Excuse me, Monsieur Noah, may I have a word with you?"

Noah looked up, surprised. "Oh, sure, Phillip, what's up?"

Phillip took a deep breath. "Well, it's about Mademoiselle Jack. I have gotten some calls from a few people who say they are her brothers and another who says he must speak with her. Well, for them to have my number at all suggests that they may in fact know her and/or have very important connections. I know very little about her relationship to her family, so I wanted to run this by you first. Should I tell her about these calls?"

Noah narrowed his eyes. "Who do they say they're from?" he asked suspiciously.

"Well, there have been several who say they are her brothers, and one gentleman, and I use that word loosely because he is so rude, whose name is Jared."

Noah grabbed Phillip by the lapel of his jacket. "Do not *ever* tell her that Jared is trying to reach out to her. Do you understand? She will fall apart, and I never want to see her like that again! *Ever!* Tell me you understand, Phillip!" he demanded. Noah suddenly seemed to realize how over the top he had been, so he began patting down the lapel he had just crumpled.

"Oh, oui, no...I will say nothing to mademoiselle! I would never want to upset her! No, they will not get to her. That I promise!"

Jack flew down the street. She couldn't wait to see Sam. First, she went to her favorite coffee shop for her latte. The same barista who always waited on her stopped and stared.

"Oh my God! It's you! I saw you on YouTube! You're, like, famous in Europe!"

The barista's voice was way too loud, and Jack started to feel uncomfortable. She looked around the shop, and everyone was staring at her and she could hear her voice on someone's computer.

Holy shit.

Jack smiled at the barista. "Um, yes that was me. Could I get my coffee please? I'm kind of in a hurry. Sorry."

"Oh sure, of course!" the fawning barista replied and began to make her coffee.

Jack could feel her heartbeat increase and she took a deep breath and closed her eyes. She felt a small tug on the bottom of her jacket. Jack looked down into big brown eyes. The little African American girl had little pigtails with brightly colored beads all over her head and she was missing her two front teeth. She was wearing a little outfit with characters from *Frozen* on it.

"Are you Elsa?" she asked.

Jack smiled and immediately calmed down; she scooched down to be eye level with her. "No, sweetie, my name is Jack. I love Elsa though. I also sing her song whenever I get the chance. What is your name?"

The little girl smiled. "I'm Elsa," she replied, pointing to herself.

"Oh, how lucky you are!"

The barista called her name, and Jack stood up, took her coffee, and handed her money over.

"No way, sweetie. That's on me. I have a niece who is suffering from cancer and looked just like those kids you sang to on the video. I just want to say thank you. My niece watches that video on the computer every single day."

Jack looked embarrassed and silently dropped the money into the tip jar. As she turned to leave, everyone in the shop stood up and started clapping. Jack just stood, unable to move. She swallowed hard, held her head high, and raised her coffee cup. "Merci, merci," she mumbled, smiled, and darted out the door.

Wow! What a difference a year could make. A year ago she had been having a debilitating PTSD flashback on this very sidewalk, and today they were cheering for her. She shook her head and concentrated on making her way to Sam.

It was too early for the soup kitchen to be open, so Jack used her key to let herself in. There wasn't anybody in the kitchen, so Jack went around back to the counseling/Krav Maga room and knocked. Sam hollered "Come in," so she opened the door shyly and peeked her head in.

"Got room for one more?"

Sam stood up so fast that his metal folding chair flipped over backward as he rushed toward her. Jack launched herself into his arms.

"Hey there, little one—look at you!" Sam exclaimed as he hugged her tighter. "Jesus you're a sight for sore eyes," he said looking her up and down. "Come in, come in. Sit down. There's a new member here for you to meet."

Jack stood before each of them and hugged them. There was Leo, Jay, Big Mike, and a new younger man with dirty army fatigues and greasy blond hair. Jack stood before him and held out her hand.

"Hi, I'm Jack, but you heard they all call me 'little one,' which is funny because I'm not little at all. "

The man just stared at Jack. He was a big man, although too thin. He just kept staring at Jack. Jack let her hand fall to her side and looked to Sam. Sam nodded and stood and rested his hand on the man's upper back.

"Jack, this is Adam. He's only been with us a short time."

Jack gave the man a welcoming smile. "Nice to meet you, Adam. You're in good hands with these guys," she said as she took her seat. Adam sat down and leaned forward, resting his arms on his knees with his head down.

Sam sat back down and looked to Jack. "How would you like to give us an update on your status, little one?" Sam asked.

Jack nodded. "Sure, sure. I'm doing really well except for the night terrors. I haven't had any incidents, and I haven't carried my blade since before I left here."

Leo, Jay, and Adam gave a few claps and nodded their heads in support.

"Although I wasn't actually in group, I checked in with Sam every week, sometimes several times a week."

Sam cleared his throat. "Can you tell us a little bit about the night terrors?" he asked.

Jack opened her mouth to speak but nothing came out. She looked up at the water stain that was still in the ceiling. "Um, they've been the same for a while now. I'm in solitary confinement and I can hear someone using a key to come in. It's dark and really hot in the room. I'm sweating a lot. Justin opens the door smiling; he's naked and pushing a metal mop bucket. He wheels in the mop bucket, holding onto the wooden mop. He picks up the sopping wet mop and starts beating me with it. I block all the blows, but he just won't stop. Eventually the mop breaks off at the end, leaving a sharp wooden stake. He takes the rounded edge and jumps on top of me and tells me he's going to rape me with it. I'm bloody and cut up and find it hard to move my arms. All of a sudden, my Dark Twin grabs the stake and plunges it in Justin's back over and over. Blood pours out of his mouth onto my face, and I start to frantically try to get him off me. He lands on top of me, dead, with his eyes open. I start screaming and my Dark Twin just laughs and licks the stake. My own screaming wakes me up."

Jack swallowed and looked around the room. Adam jumped up and started pacing back and forth behind the group.

"Okay, tell us what you do to calm yourself down, little one," Sam urged quietly.

"Well, I take a lot of deep breaths and I recite the twenty-third Psalm over and over. That helps me, and then I take a hot shower because I'm soaked through from sweat. I usually don't get back to sleep, but that's okay. I just read until morning. Oh, and sometimes I make a cup of tea; that also helps calm me down."

"Excellent," Sam replied.

All of a sudden Adam stopped pacing and turned to Jack. "Who is she?" he asked.

"I'm sorry?" Jack replied uncertainly.

"You said, 'My Dark Twin stabbed him with the stake.' Who is she?"

Sam stood up and walked to Adam. He shoved his hands in his pockets. "Everyone's PTSD symptoms materialize in different forms. Jack hears a voice that comes out to protect her. When she is in new situations or feels particularly out of control, or if she feels threatened in any way, this protector comes to her. She calls it her Dark Twin."

Adam started pacing again only to abruptly stop. "Well, isn't that good? Her Dark Twin is there to protect her. Shouldn't she listen to her, you know, let her protect her?"

"No, she should never listen to this voice or any voice. Jack is strong enough to handle anything that happens." Sam replied forcefully. "When the Dark Twin speaks to Jack, Jack's reasoning mind shuts down and her fear (the Dark Twin) takes over—and she could hurt people. You must never listen to the voices. She has learned certain techniques original to her and some that anyone can practice to help calm them down so they can think rationally. Do you understand this, Adam?" Sam asked quietly.

Adam nodded and strode toward the door. "Yeah, I need to go," he muttered, zipping up his army jacket and throwing open the door to leave.

Sam looked around and sighed. "How about we go grab some coffee and cake?" he said, looking at Jack.

"Cake?" Jack almost shouted, jumping up as they all laughed and hugged her as they walked to the kitchen.

The pin in the back of the dress holding it together was pricking her skin with every sway of her hips as she walked down the runway. This was the third fashion show this week as well as photoshoots and a red carpet gala for a new perfume by Chanel. Jack was dead tired and very glad the day was almost over. She was glad to be busy, but she really needed a day off. She had been working nonstop for the last two months. When she finally walked off stage, the designer was waiting for her to take the dress off.

"Blood! You got blood on my dress!" the designer screamed.

Jack jumped and immediately she could feel her blood pressure rising. "Me! You put the damn pin in the dress that was stabbing me in the back!"

With the pin removed from the dress, it dropped to the floor, and Jack stepped out of it and continued on to the dressing rooms. She dressed in her worn jeans with a white long sleeve T-shirt. She was grumbling as she tied her Chuck Taylors and threw on her black leather biker jacket. The designer peeked his head in just as she was walking out the door so that she almost collided with him.

"Can I have a moment?" he said, resting a hand on his hip. He was relatively new on the scene and really wanted to make a name for himself. He wore a white tuxedo and a red cummerbund. His hair was jet black and spiked all over his head. He also sported a jet black goatee that reminded Jack of Satan with a forked tail between his legs.

Jack stopped and looked down at him, clearly annoyed.

The designer appeared at least contrite. "I'm sorry I snapped. I just got so caught up in the moment. Really, I didn't mean to upset you. It's very important to me that you represent my line. I mean you are the American Princess. Are we good?" he said, grasping both her hands in his.

Jack pulled her hands away. "Yeah, whatever, just see that it doesn't happen again," she muttered, walking around him and out the back door to her waiting car.

Jack was just about to duck her head and dive into the car when her heart stopped. There were several fans of the fashion show standing around the front of the alley where the car was parked. When she burst through the side door, she heard some of them holler "Princess," but there was one voice that carried high above the crowd.

Bear.

She would recognize that deep growl anywhere. Jack stood and slowly turned toward the crowd. There Bear stood, accompanied by all eight of her other brothers. She cried out as tears instantly flew down her cheeks. She dropped her messenger bag and started sprinting full speed directly at them, not stopping until she leaped into Bear's giant embrace. Sobbing, she just let Bear hold her until her heartbeat slowed and she looked up to see his face wet with tears.

"Oh, my Princess!" Bear whispered. Jack heard loud sniffs and she looked around her. All of her brothers were crying and laughing as they looked at her as if they couldn't believe she was really in front of them. She jumped into each of their arms and more tears flowed as she hugged Bobby, Ty, Henry, Teddy, Garrett, Davey, Caleb, and Marcus. When she hugged Marcus, he wouldn't let her go, crying into her hair that had fallen from the updo she had worn on the runway.

Slowly Jack became aware that flashes were going off all around them. Shit. She pulled out of Marcus's arms.

"Listen, we are the focus of the paparazzi right now. Let's get off the street and go to my house, it's not far," she whispered.

Bear looked around angrily. "Let me take care of them," he said, moving toward the crowd.

Jack grabbed Bear's coat. "No, Bear, don't make a scene. That's what they want, trust me. Let's just go to my place."

Bear scowled but soon relented and instead turned around and scooched down. Jack laughed and jumped on his back as they all turned and walked toward the limo.

Caleb whistled. "This is the only way to ride! How does it feel to be the famous American Princess?" Caleb asked, grabbing her knee and squeezing. Jack yelped before she grabbed his hand and bent his ring finger way back while moving his hand forward.

Caleb cried out, "Jesus! Stop!"

The brothers all laughed. Marcus shook his head. "Some things will never change," he chuckled.

Within minutes, they were parked in front of the brownstone. The door opened and they all climbed out.

"This is my place," Jack said, starting up the stairs.

"Wow, Jack, this is a great neighborhood. You must be doing very well," Davey said smiling.

"Well, it's not actually mine. I live here with Mr. Worthington's assistant, Phillip, and Noah Cabrera, my best friend and model counterpart. Mr. Worthington actually owns the brownstone. I will live here until my contract is up, in about eight months' time," Jack replied, shrugging her shoulders.

She then proceeded to show them all around the brownstone, which appeared to be empty. They settled in the kitchen, where Jack got them all beers and put the kettle on for tea for herself. Marcus was leaning against the huge granite island with his arms crossed.

"Jack, I really don't know where to start but I..."

Jack held up her hand to stop him. "Please, please don't. There is not one person in this room who has anything to apologize for. That goes for you too, Marcus. I know you blame yourself for wanting Daddy to be stricter with me, but you always had my best interests at heart. I don't blame you at all. I'm pretty sure that you had no knowledge of where Daddy sent me. Am I right?" Jack said, looking around.

"If any of us had known where you were, we would have moved heaven and earth to get you out of that hellhole," Bear snapped.

Jack smiled. "I know, really, I do know, and I love each and every one of you for it. But, with that said, Daddy did send me away and for that, well, I just can't forgive him."

Henry opened his mouth to say something, but Jack held up her hand. "That doesn't mean I will never forgive him. It just means I'm not there yet. Okay?"

They all nodded. Bobby stood in front of her and cupped her face in his hands. "My God, you're beautiful!" he cried with tears in his eyes. "We're just so fucking glad you're safe and we're together. Nothing else matters, okay?"

More tears fell that mixed with relieved laughter. Then Caleb took a pull from his beer.

"Why didn't you call one of us, Jack?" he asked, looking hurt and angry. Jack immediately stiffened and took a step toward Caleb. Jack hugged her upper arms.

"Okay, here's the thing, I'm only going to say this once, and then it's not up for discussion ever again. I'm broken. I'm not the same girl who left the pond that day. I'm never going to be her again, and who I've become is someone you don't really know and never will. I am so glad you're all here with me, and I want very much to stay in contact, but well, I will never talk about what's happened to me. I mean not ever, so don't ask and don't pressure me to see Daddy. It may never happen. I just don't know. *I mean it!* If I feel pressured in any way, then I will just cut off all contact. I won't put myself through that...I can't," she said quietly.

"Sweetheart, we wouldn't do anything to ever hurt you or pressure you," Garrett said softly.

"You were our Princess way before you were the world's Princess," Ty remarked, taking a pull off his beer.

Bear went to stand behind Caleb's stool, grabbing him around the throat in a choke hold. "And if anyone gives you any shit *at all,* they are going to have to answer to me!" he said, tightening his hold on Caleb.

"Jesus! I can't breathe, Bear! I get it! Get the fuck off me!" Caleb gasped out, coughing as Bear let him go.

Jack couldn't hide her smile. She then clapped her hands together. "Okay! Now that all that bullshit is out of the way, let's order pizza. I'm starving!

Those friggin' models don't eat a goddamn thing, and they all but tear my hair out if I bring anything with me. I want to know everything that has happened since I left!"

Later, after everyone left, Jack lay in bed and relived the day. Her heart was so full to have her brothers back in her life, but even when they were all hugging she found she was looking for Jared. Why wouldn't he want to see her? Even if he wasn't in love with her anymore, which the very thought tore at her guts, at least he could have come to say hello. They had grown up together and she missed him so much. When her brothers hadn't had time for her, Jared would always make sure she tagged along if it was at all possible. A single tear slid down the side of her head. Why didn't he love her anymore? What had she done that was so bad? The questions and sadness swirled inside of her. She knew it was going to be a long and lonely friggin' night.

The amber-colored scotch stared back at him as he stared transfixed at the wall-sized plasma TV in the corner of the bar. The ticker at the bottom blathered on about who these mystery men were that Jack, the American Princess, was cavorting with in the alley of the biggest fashion show of the season. The pictures of Jack walking the runway looking boss and then laughing and crying in the alleyway with her brothers were tearing his guts out.

Jared gulped down the scotch in one swallow and tapped the bar for another. What. The. Fuck. Every letter he'd sent her had been returned unopened, and in every call he had made he had been told that Jack was not available and would not be available to speak with him.

Fuck. I guess I know who she blames, he thought, turning the fresh glass of scotch around in his hand. Neither he nor David Johnson had been invited to this little reunion with her brothers. He needed to fucking face the hard truth: Jack was never coming back to him. He could wish it. He could hope for it. But it was never fucking gonna happen. He'd always known the truth— that he wasn't good enough for her. Now she knew the truth as well. I mean what the hell, the entire fucking world loved her. What else could he do to try to see her? She must have one helluva good PR team working for her, because he couldn't find out anything about where she lived or where she was working…nothing.

It had been two years since David Johnson had come to make amends, and he had spent every single day for the last three years searching for her and loving her. He worked night and day building his company for the day that he could share it all with Jack. Every deal he'd struck and every computer game that his company had produced made him hope that one day they would enjoy the fruits of his labor together. He would take care of her and lavish her with the desires of her heart. Anything and everything for his Princess. He would deny her nothing, ever.

Jared gulped down the scotch and set the glass back on the bar. That was better. He felt the liquid start to warm his insides. What good was working night and day and having more bank than any twenty-six-year-old had the right to if he couldn't share it with the love of his life? After one year, Jared had been able to pay David back all the money he had fronted him, and it was all profit after that. Jared was good to his staff and shared the wealth, but fuck, it was just never ending. He had more games out there than any other company and more in the chute than he could count. It was really true that if you shared the profits with your employees— meaning that if you did well then they did well—the ideas and possibilities were endless. The laidback vibe of their office along with the onsite day care, free food court, gym, bunkhouse, and meditation room made some of the employees stay for days on end without going home if they were working on an exciting project. Computer geeks were a special breed of cat. His company had been voted the top new company to work for in the world. Résumés flooded his office daily. He was loyal to his people, and they were loyal to him. Hell, he had just been offered fifty million dollars to sell the company to Sony. It was a no brainer for him: *no, thank you. This was all for you, Jack,* he thought, tapping the bar again.

Jared sat staring at the amber liquid, again wishing he could get the fuck out of his own head, when he heard a voice beside him ask, "Are you going to drink that or just stare it to death?"

Jared looked up to see a very attractive brunette smiling at him. "Oh, I'm definitely going to drink it. I'm just deciding which of the two to drink first," he replied dryly.

She laughed and pushed the glass toward him. "Drink this one."

Jared lifted the glass, downed the contents, and slammed the glass back on the bar.

"Rough day?" the brunette asked.

Jared harrumphed. "You could say that," he muttered, tapping the bar.

"Well, maybe I can make it better. I'm Stephanie," she said, holding out her hand.

"Well, I'm fucking drunk, Stephanie, nice to meet you," Jared slurred back, grasping the hand in the middle.

When the bartender poured another scotch, Jared nodded toward Stephanie. "Give the lady whatever she wants," Jared slurred again, and then turned to give a bleary-eyed smile to his new drinking partner.

What-the-fuck-ever, Jared thought numbly. He held his glass up and Stephanie clinked glasses in a toast to "the future" as he downed another.

The throbbing in his head was massive. Jared slowly opened his eyes and looked around without moving. Nothing looked familiar. He was in a bed, a really comfortable bed. A nightstand cluttered with magazines, papers, and coffee cups stood beside the bed. On the floor, he could see his shoes, jacket, and tie scattered about.

Slowly, ever-so-slowly, he lifted his body into a sitting position on the bed and scrubbed his face with his palms. *Jesus, I can't remember feeling like this since, well, since the day I woke up at my father's house after I thought I had lost Jack,* he pondered. How he wished he could go back to that day.

"Well, good morning, sleepyhead!" someone exclaimed from the doorway with way too much enthusiasm. Jared looked up to see the pretty brunette with shoulder length hair tucked behind her ears. She had soft brown eyes and a smirk on her lips. She was dressed in black yoga pants with an oversized men's denim shirt tied at her waist. Barefoot, she sauntered over to the bed and handed Jared a glass of water and a couple of pills.

"Take these, it's ibuprofen for your head. Come out in the kitchen and I will get you some coffee," she said, walking toward the door.

Jared stood holding the water and pills. "Wait, um, did we…" he said looking at the bed.

Stephanie laughed and continued walking. "No, Jared Ross, I didn't ravish your body last night. You barely made it up the stairs before you became dead weight and passed out completely. Maybe I'll get lucky next time, or maybe you can make it up to me."

Jared threw on his shoes and jacket, balling up his tie in his jacket pocket, and walked out of the bedroom into a very small combined kitchen and living room. Stephanie had made two plates of eggs, bacon, and toast that were sitting on the small round kitchen table. She stood up, poured two cups of coffee, and set them down with the food as he took a chair and turned it around so his arms rested on the back.

Jared picked up the coffee and took a big gulp. "Mmm, thanks."

Stephanie pushed the plate closer to him and he held up his hand. "God no, it's going to be a while before I can eat anything. Thank you for going to the trouble though. I really need to get to work," Jared announced as he stood up.

"Oh, no you don't! Sit. So it's the walk of shame for you? Won't your coworkers know that you didn't go home last night?" she retorted, smirking.

"Well, technically there is no shame in the walk, right?" Jared sat back down as she poured him another cup of coffee.

"Listen, Jared, I'm going to be completely honest with you. I knew who you were before I ever sat down on that barstool. I've actually been stalking you a little."

Jared's head shot up. She held up her hand. "Not like that. My name is Stephanie Carey, and I'm a reporter for *GQ* magazine. I've tried to get an appointment with you, but your assistant, the little barracuda, wouldn't let me near you. So I had to take matters into my own hands, so to speak. I started following you, and as a result I know you go to that little bar often on your way home from work. You chat with the bartender for about an hour, drink one beer, and go home. The fact that you were drinking straight scotch last night was a perfect opportunity for me."

Jared's eyebrows shot up. Stephanie realized her last statement had been unintentionally unflattering and immediately hastened to add "Um, no, that's not what I meant. Although, don't get me wrong, I would totally do you, but what I'm really interested in right this minute is interviewing you for the magazine. I just wanted to talk to you and set up an official appointment to interview you. Scout's honor," she mocked, holding up two fingers.

Jared chuckled. "I can believe you were a girl scout with your impressive tracking skills, but no, I don't do interviews, sorry," he said finishing his coffee and putting the cup in the sink. As he was walking to the door, he stopped and turned to her. "Thank you for getting me here safely. I wasn't in a good place last night and…well, thank you," he murmured, turning again, this time to really leave.

"Wait," Stephanie said walking toward him handing him a card. "This is my card. It has my cell number on it. Call it. I really want to interview you. You're a complete mystery. You came from, from what I can garner, humble beginnings in a small town in Maine, and now you are the giant in the gaming world with a reportedly potential net worth of upward of a billion dollars. Yet no one knows anything about you. Do you know how many kids would be inspired by your story?"

Jared tilted his head and narrowed his eyes. Stephanie laughed.

"Okay, that was a cheap shot, but come on, I'm desperate here! I promise you will see whatever I write before I submit it. The world really is curious, and I believe you may the most eligible bachelor in all of New York, maybe all of America," she continued as he kept retreating backward. "Oh, and one more thing, Jared—who is Jack?"

With one hand on the door handle, Jared froze. "Why?" he said ominously.

"Um, you cried that name in your sleep several times."

Jared never turned around, but he turned his head and spoke over his shoulder. "Never mention that name in any way, shape, or form again, or not only will I own that goddamn magazine, you will never write another story that appears in print for them or anyone else. Are we clear?" he muttered, still frozen in place.

"Crystal," Stephanie replied coldly. She was equal parts frightened and intrigued at Jared's warning.

As Jared walked the several blocks to the office, a bus passed him and he stopped short. Jack's poster was covering half of the bus. She was in a gold metallic clingy dress with gold silk evening gloves up to her elbows. Her hair was a mass of long blond waves covering one eye and the other big glacial blue eye was looking right at him. There was a bottle of a new fragrance from Chanel in her hand. His body was instantly aroused with a desire and need that he had never felt with such ferocity. It rocked him to his very core.

Jared leaned over and held onto his knees for a second, trying to catch his breath. Jesus. He staggered off until he was right outside his office. From the corner of his eye, he caught another glimpse of his nightmare come to life. The billboard right outside of his office, the very one his wall of windows looked out on, was Jack Johnson displayed in a beautiful white wedding dress with flowers in her hair, with a man in a tuxedo, the bowtie hanging from his neck. The "groom" was looking down dreamily into her eyes. She was resting her chin on his chest and smiling up at him.

Jared couldn't breathe. The absolute gut-wrenching pain, along with a rage he'd never ever felt before, surged through his veins like lava.

Jared hailed a cab and jumped in. Working from his office was out of the question today. He would work from home, but first he needed to hit his home gym and release some pent-up energy before he committed hara-kiri.

Jared took his phone out and dialed the office. "Tim, I'm going to work from home today. If there's anything I need to sign, just bring it to the apartment."

"Okay, yes sir. You have gotten several messages from a woman named Stephanie this morning. She says she's sorry that she upset you and that putting yourself out there just might be the ticket to finding that someone special," Tim replied awkwardly.

Jared cleared his throat. Maybe she was onto something. Maybe he could get Jack's attention if he put himself on a billboard, so to speak. A slow smile formed on Jared's lips.

"Um, one more thing, Tim, there is a new billboard outside my office with a bride and groom. Make it go away. I don't care what you have to do or how much it costs. Make it go away. *Today.* Understood?" Jared growled.

"Consider it done, Mr. Ross," and the line went dead.

Jack hurried along the Lower East Side, making her way to the soup kitchen. She had been away for the last month, and she needed to talk to Angel. While she and Noah were in Los Angeles for the big red carpet gala introducing Worthington's Wedding Gowns to America, Jack had met music producer Rick Thomas. He was an older man who had launched some of the greatest artists in history. She had asked him about the old recording studio on the Lower East Side. He had remembered it and had produced records for Elvis, Ray Charles, and The Temptations there. Jack had asked him if he would be willing to help her get into the business and teach her what he knew. He had a kind of sadness about him as he told her it had been a long time since he had been relevant and that the industry had changed. She had assured him that she was very interested in bringing him on board if he would teach her what he knew. He laughed and told her he would be happy to help her. Jack was certain that he figured she'd never in a million years actually call him.

He was wrong.

Jack flew into the soup kitchen calling out to Angel. Angel came bustling out of the kitchen, quickly wiping his hands on his apron.

"Hey, little one, what is it? Is something wrong?" he asked, looking her up and down.

Jack threw her arms around his neck and laughed. "No, everything is absolutely right! I missed you! Listen, I have something important to talk to you about. Do you have a minute?"

"Sure, sure, Carino, come into the kitchen with me while I make tonight's meal," he said, putting his arm around her as they walked out back to the kitchen.

The smell of pasta and sauce overwhelmed Jack's senses. "Mmm, lasagna—yum!" she exclaimed, grabbing a stool.

"Oh, si, with all the help you give to us we are able to eat like kings and queens here!" Angel replied, gently grasping her head and kissing her forehead.

Jack smiled and grabbed an uncooked carrot to nibble on. "Okay, well, I need you to put on your memory cap for a minute. Remember when you were talking about the recording studio across the street and how great it had once been?" she asked pointing the carrot at him.

"Yes, si, I do indeed," Angel said, nodding his head.

"Well, I want make it great again, and I believe with your help we can."

Angel popped a piece of nicotine gum in his mouth and started chewing. "Oh, nene, what could I do to help? It was many years ago, and I was a young boy."

Jack nodded her head. "I know, but you were there in that moment. You felt history being made. I am going to meet with my brother Henry later today, and he is going to purchase that building. I am going to need all the help I can get to restore it to exactly the way it was, with updated technology of course. You know everybody around here. I need the best of the best, Angel. I don't care how old they are or what their past troubles have been. I trust you to put together teams of people who need the work and maybe some who actually worked in the business to help us. Do you know an old music producer by the name of Rick Thomas?"

Angel stopped chopping vegetables. "Did you say Rick Thomas?" Angel asked, making the hair on the back of her neck stand up.

Jack nodded. "Yeah, do you know him?"

Angel wiped his hands on his apron and sat on the stool next to Jack. "Si, yes, I know Rick Thomas. I didn't know if he was still alive. Rick Thomas was the biggest record producer there ever was. But more importantly, he was the kindest and most giving human being I have ever met. He was my guardian angel. You see, I grew up on the streets, and it was tough, real tough, for a young Mexican boy. There were lots of gangs back then but mostly the blacks against the whites. Being Mexican, well, I just didn't fit in anywhere and I couldn't speak much English back then. Well, Mr. Thomas came upon a group of boys beating the crap out of me one day, and he stopped the fight and asked me what it had been about. I told him I had refused to join the crackers gang—er, sorry—the white boys gang, and they were beating me for it. Mr. Thomas walked with me up the street to the bakery, and we went in and he bought me the biggest cannoli I had ever seen. I still remember how sweet it was. Mr. Thomas told me he had seen me around the neighborhood and wanted to know about my family. I told him my father was in prison and my mother worked two jobs and wasn't home much, and that's why I hung out on the streets so much. He nodded, and when we were leaving he asked if I could come to the studio each day and he would give me odd jobs to do. He would pay me, but I would need to be clean and presentable when I came to work and always be respectful of my elders. But most importantly, I was never, ever, to join any type of gang. I agreed and worked for many years doing odd jobs and running errands for Mr. Thomas. I can tell you with certainty that if he hadn't taken the time to help me, I would have ended up like many of my friends, in a gang and dead before I even reached adulthood. Because of his kindness, I have been married to the love of my life for forty years and raised four smart, beautiful children—and I have devoted my life to helping people who are having a hard time in life. I can say without any doubt, Carino, that Mr. Rick Thomas saved my life, and I would do anything for him," Angel said, wiping a tear from his eye before it fell.

Jack sniffled and blew her nose. "Wow, Angel, I had no idea. Well, I met Mr. Thomas—he is very old but spry as a young man. He said he would help me recreate the studio and also teach me the recording business. Can I get you to work with him and get the crews in there to reconstruct the building? It probably will have to be gutted and start fresh, but maybe we can save some things from the past."

Angel smiled and grasped Jack's hands. "Carino, I will begin right away. You just let me know when we can get in the building. Now tell me, nene, why do you want to be a record producer and not a fancy model? I see your face all over the city!" he exclaimed, smiling so his eyes crinkled.

Jack jumped off the stool and tossed the half eaten carrot at him as she walked toward the door. "Yeah, you're a wise guy all right, but just for future reference, they don't call it *record* producer anymore!" she chuckled, and she could hear his laughter ringing in her ears as she hit the street.

Jack slid into the booth of the very upscale New York City restaurant that just happened to be owned by her brother Davey. Henry was already there and drinking a cup of coffee. He leaned over the table and kissed her cheek.

"Good to see you, Princess. How was the West Coast?"

Jack smiled at her quick-witted brother. "Shitty and fake," she snorted.

Henry was tall and lean, with dark hair and a dark goatee. He had big expressive brown eyes, and he could make her laugh by just looking at her. As analytical as his brain was, it always surprised Jack how funny he could be. She'd heard that he was a master in the courtroom and so it was not surprising that he handled all of her father's business dealings.

The waitress came to get her drink order. "I would love some coffee please." Jack turned to look at Henry. "Thank you for coming to New York on such short notice. This is really important to me."

Jack pulled out a folder from her messenger bag and slid it across the table to Henry. "This is an old condemned building on the Lower East Side that I want to buy and restore into a music recording studio. I need for you do the research and make the city an offer. I have the money. Can you do that for me?" she asked.

Henry looked at her with a bored expression. Jack burst out laughing. "Princess, please, I can have this in your name by the end of the day. Now tell me why you want to purchase this building. Do you really want to become a music producer?"

Just then, two large arms leaned on the table. Jack looked up to find Davey smiling at them.

"What? No one bothers to tell me you're critiquing my restaurant today? What the hell, you two?"

Jack jumped out of the booth and hugged him tight. "Oh! What a treat!" Jack exclaimed. "I didn't want to bother you at work."

Davey cupped Jack's face in his hands. "It would never be a bother, Princess, ever," Davey replied, pressing a kiss to her forehead. He slid into the booth and got the waitress's attention. "We will have three of the specials pronto," he said firmly.

"Of course, Mr. Johnson," the waitress gasped, scrambling toward the kitchen.

Jack smirked. "Mr. Johnson," she mocked. "How very..." Jack had to duck to avoid a napkin aimed for her mouth.

They ate their meal of Maine lobster with melted butter and coleslaw and corn off the cob. Jack told them both about her plans of restoring the old recording studio and the connections she had made.

"Wow, Jack, I'm really impressed. You have always been gifted in music, but I had no idea you would want to take it this far. I'm proud of you. Whatever I can do to help you, just say the word. There is, however, something you can help me with," Davey replied, waggling his eyebrows.

Henry just groaned and Jack laughed. "Do you want her to set you up with some hot model?" Henry asked dryly.

Davey grinned. "No, I don't need my baby sister to get me dates. At least not yet. But maybe that would be a good idea for you, Henry. You know, get your nose out of the law books and all."

Jack loved the banter and had missed it so much. "What can I do for you, Davey?" Jack asked. Davey put his hand on the table. "Well, the restaurant has been up and running for six months now and doing very well, knock on wood. " He rapped on Henry's head until Henry shot him a dirty look.

"I didn't have a grand opening, because I wanted to wait and see how we would do, and I think it is a little cheesy to open that way. I wanted to let people discover us on their own, by word of mouth, you know, spread the word and all that good shit! Well, now I would like to have a swanky grand opening. I know you are the hottest commodity in New York right now, so how would you like to be my guest of honor and maybe invite some of your friends in high places?" he asked, bringing his hands up like he was praying.

Jack harrumphed. "Is that all? Jesus, Davey, I thought it was going to be something difficult. You just name the date and I will have this place so full of narcissistic assholes that you will be begging to move back to Maine. This is my friend and Mr. Worthington's assistant, Phillip's number. Call him, and trust me, he will organize the shit out of this grand opening."

Henry shook his head. "Nice. We raised her all classy, didn't we?" he said as they all laughed when Jack snorted with feigned indignation.

As Henry and Jack were leaving, Jack hugged Davey. "Listen, Princess, if you're not busy tonight, will you come back at closing? There is something I would like to talk to you about."

Jack pulled away to look at him. "Sure—what time, about ten?" she asked.

"Yeah ten would be great. I will send a car for you. I don't want you walking. Understand?"

Jack nodded. Henry glanced at Davey with a questioning look on his face. "I'll call you later, Bro," Davey said to Henry.

Henry nodded and hugged Davey. "Talk to you later."

After the cab that Henry hailed for her dropped her off in front of the brownstone, Jack decided to grab a coffee before settling in for the afternoon. The baristas always outdid themselves when she came in, but not in an over-the-top way like the people in the fashion industry. It was just enough to let her warm up to them and never go anywhere else in the city for coffee.

As she was walking home, she stopped to buy some papers at the local street vendor. When her eyes caught the cover of the newest *GQ*, Jack dropped her hot coffee on the sidewalk, splattering it all over her jeans and sneakers. Jack felt the edge of consciousness closing in around her. She wasn't breathing, just staring at the magazine cover. Benny, the newspaper vender whom Jack spoke with every day, rushed over to her and grasped her upper arms.

"Hey there, girl, are you okay?" he asked, giving her a little shake.

Jack took a deep breath, filling her lungs, and looked at Benny. He was a young tall African American man with a thick hoodie pulled up over his head to keep warm. He always seemed to have on fingerless gloves. "Just breathe, Princess. It's okay. Benny's got ya," he said softly.

Jack shook her head to clear it. "Oh, I'm sorry, Benny! I didn't mean to scare you. I'm okay, really," she said breathlessly.

"Mmmmhmmmm." Benny didn't sound the least bit convinced.

Jack smiled shakily. "Really! I think I will add this magazine to my usual papers today," she told him, picking up the GQ with shaking fingers and paying Benny.

As she turned to leave, Benny hollered. "I'm gonna watch you as you walk home so you go straight home, ya hear?" Jack nodded and walked swiftly toward the brownstone.

Once inside, Jack sank down to the floor in the entryway and pulled out the magazine. She just stared at Jared's image. He was wearing black dress slacks and a white collared shirt open at the neck. He had on a burgundy tweed vest buttoned up with black, wing-tipped shoes. He hadn't shaved in probably a week and had dark, thick stubble covering his cheeks and chin. His dark curls were cut short and slicked back away from his face. His eyes were hauntingly sad as he stared directly into the camera. He was sitting in an old rattan chair and was leaning way back against a gray wall. His image was larger than life.

Jack gently stroked his face until she felt wetness on the picture and realized that she was crying. She gently wiped at the magazine cover to remove the wet sorrow. Phillip suddenly walked through to find her still on the floor.

"Mon amie! What is the matter? Were you attacked?" he shrieked, kneeling down as he inspected her.

Jack shook her head as she dabbed at her face. "No, no, not at all. I'm sorry! My emotions are all over the place today. Forgive me, I didn't mean to scare you."

Jack stood up and tucked the magazine into her messenger bag to read later. "I do have something to talk to you about, though, and then I think I will lie down for a bit." Jack told Phillip about Davey's grand opening.

"I would be happy to help. I will look forward to his call. I also have news, mademoiselle," Phillip replied, clapping his hands together. "Dirk will be landing at JFK tonight at about midnight!"

Jack squealed and hugged Phillip. "I'm so happy for you both! I think I will wear my headphones tonight in bed," she gushed, teasing him.

Phillip's face turned red and he nodded. "Dirk is a very passionate lover, mon amie," he said, way too seriously.

Jack plugged her ears and sang "*la-la-la-la-la*" all the way up the stairs to her room.

Jack settled on the couch by the front windows in her bedroom. She sat cross-legged as she pulled out the magazine and stared. He was so beautiful, so perfect.

She read the headline. "New York's Most Eligible Bachelor, Gaming Mogul Jared Ross." Jealousy hot and swift shot through her veins as she read the words *eligible bachelor*. Jack read the article three times before she closed the magazine to stare at his picture. He had come to New York right after she had been sent away. They were in the same city at the same time. Him working night and day to build his company and her on the run and homeless. His company was huge, and in addition to sharing the wealth with his employees, he apparently did a lot of good with his money. The magazine listed dozens of charities that Global Gamer supported, as well as some personal charities that Jared himself helped fund. She suddenly was proud, so very proud of him.

Jack kept reading the very end of the article when the reporter finally asked him outright if he was single and available.

"Technically, I am single, but my heart already belongs to another. So no, I'm not available." There was a picture that went along with the questions, and he was smiling and looking away, embarrassed.

That phrase just kept ringing in her head. "My heart belongs to another." So he was in love with someone. She was a lucky girl, whoever she was, thought Jack. Now she knew why he had never looked for her. He had found someone else.

Jack rose up and tossed her messenger bag across her chest. Still holding the magazine, she quietly strode down the stairs and let herself outside.

About halfway down the block, Jack tossed the magazine in the overflowing trash can on the sidewalk and kept walking. She needed to see Sam, have some lasagna, and read to some kids, in that order.

Jack climbed out of the Town Car that Davey had ordered for her and entered the still bustling restaurant. The hostess remembered her from earlier in the day and scurried off to find Davey. Davey was speaking to a table full of patrons when the hostess tapped him on the shoulder. He nodded and excused himself, thereafter ambling over to her with no suit jacket and his tie loosened around his neck. He looked tired. A good kind of tired.

Davey smiled and hugged her. "I've got a surprise for you," he said, leading her toward the kitchen. "I didn't want to put my nose in your business but I think you will be pleased I did," he said as she started to stiffen.

The two of them strode through the kitchen doors, and suddenly Jack was standing in front of a red-haired woman bent over and frosting a platter of cupcakes.

"Mac?" Jack whispered.

Mac's head whipped around and she dropped the frosting bag. "Jack?" she murmured, putting her fingers to her lips.

Jack fell into Mac's arms as they embraced and sobbed. No words were needed. They just held each other and cried. Davey quietly left the kitchen.

Finally the two pulled apart and Mac led Jack to a back office that must have been Davey's. She closed the door and they sank to the couch. They each grabbed tissues and blew their noses and laughed.

Mac sniffed. "First off, are you okay? I had my father search for you for two years. I never gave up on you, Jack. Nobody would tell me anything. I had to get the general in on this before they would tell me what happened that day. By the time I knew where you had been sent, you had run away and just disappeared off the face of the earth. So, please tell me, are you okay?"

Tears still streaming down Jack's cheeks, she nodded. "I am now. Really, I wasn't for a very long time, but I'm better. I'm different, Mac; I'm never going to be that girl again. I'm broken," Jack whispered.

Mac sighed and embraced Jack tightly. "I know, I can see it in your eyes," she replied and Jack pulled back to look her in the eyes. No one had ever said that to her. No one had ever been that honest with her.

"But it's okay that you're broken. I love you anyway and just want to be in your life anyway I can. I have missed you so much, Jack Johnson! No one, and I mean no one, has gotten me like you did!" Mac exclaimed, bursting into giggles and crying at the same time.

Jack laughed but then turned serious. "I'm just afraid that my brokenness will somehow taint your beautiful life. I tend to hurt those I love," she said, looking away.

Mac held Jack's face so she would have to look back at her. "Hey, it's me, Jack. Macadoo. There is nothing you can do or say to make me love you one smidgen less than I do. Nothing. Now I will never ask you about what you've been through, but if you ever want to tell me, I will always listen. But for now, can we just make a fresh start? You know we're BFFs—best friends forever—right?"

Jack picked up Mac's hands and kissed them. "That's right. I think I forgot for a while. Agreed, fresh start. Now how about a sleepover at your house tonight? I am anticipating my crib being kind of loud tonight," she said, smiling.

"Oh my God! That sounds perfect. Let me just finish up here, and we'll head out. Tomorrow is my day off, so we can stay up all night yakking."

"Great. I'll call my roommate and find Davey and smack him for not telling me sooner that you were here," Jack said.

Mac turned serious. "No, please don't give him a hard time. It was me that wouldn't let him say anything. I wanted to give you some time to adjust to having your brothers back in your life and I wasn't sure if you still wanted to be my friend," Mac said nervously.

Jack grabbed Mac's hand again. "You're not my friend, you're the sister I never had, and you will always be a part of me," Jack cried out, tearing up again.

Jack and Mac talked well into the morning before finally falling asleep. Mac's tiny studio apartment was only a few blocks from the brownstone. It was just one big room with a tiny bathroom, but it was warm and cozy as only Mac could have made it. There was a big brown suede pull out sofa in the middle of the room with a giant overstuffed chair and coffee table. The coffee table was covered with books on french pastries and cupcakes to cake decorating. There was also a historical romance paperback that was dog-eared from many readings. Jack picked it up and looked at Mac.

"Don't judge me, Jack Johnson! Don't you dare judge me!" Mac yelled, starting the laughter all over again. Mac had gone to pastry chef school in Paris the year Jack had been on the run, and then she worked in a bakery in Italy for almost two years until just recently getting a job at Davey's restaurant as the pastry chef. Mac had left Italy after she had found out that the Italian "gentleman" she was seeing was cheating on her. It was still very hurtful for her to talk about, so Jack didn't press her for details.

"How is Davey to work for?" Jack asked, changing the subject.

Mac narrowed her eyes. "He's a pain in my ass!" she said, laughing. "Really, he drives me crazy! Everything has to be just so, and I feel that he is more critical of me than the others. I don't know, but some days I just want to squirt frosting all over his perfect face!"

Jack sobered. "Perfect face, hmm?"

Mac instantly became flustered. "Well, I mean it's not a secret, Jack, he's friggin' drop-dead gorgeous even if he is one of your annoying brothers!"

Jack held her hands up in surrender. "Fair enough! He is handsome enough, I guess."

Mac shook her head. "Enough about that—let's change the subject! Tell me about being an international model, and don't leave anything out!" They settled down on the pull-out sofa and Jack filled her in on all the palace intrigue that was the fashion world.

Jack woke up to her phone buzzing in her jacket on the chair. She got up and looked at the caller ID. Phillip.

"*Salut*, Phillip, good morning. Can you walk this morning? Salut, Dirk," she said into the phone, knowing that Phillip had her on speaker phone. The response was laughter and wet kisses.

"Very funny, mon amie. Good morning to you. We have had a change in schedule today. You must be on the plane within the hour. You have a photo shoot in Mexico for the Victoria's Secret bathing suit catalog. You will be there for four days, mademoiselle."

Jack sighed. "Since when do I work for Victoria's Secret?" she inquired.

"Ah, since they offered you, in your words, a *shit ton of money*." She could hear Dirk laughing in the background.

"Okay, fine but I stayed at my girlfriend's place last night and I have nothing to change into. And I would like a shower and breakfast since I will be bunking with females who choose not to eat food but instead snort it up their nose."

Phillip actually clapped his hands. "*Non, non*, there is no time for that, *mon petit chou*. Give me your address, and I will pack some clothes for you and you can shower on the jet. I will make sure they make you a big breakfast on the jet too."

Jack muttered "Fine" in resignation and gave him the address. She started to pull on her sneakers when she focused on Mac. Jack shook her roughly.

"Hey, Mac Attack, wake up! How would you like to spend four glorious days in sunny Mexico?"

Mack rolled over, squinting at the morning light. "What? What are you talking about?"

Jack was already dialing Davey. He picked up on the first ring.

"Hey, Princess, what's up?" Davey answered with a hint of worry in his voice.

"Hola, Davey! You know how I set everything up for your grand opening and how I am willing to spend the evening schmoozing with lame-os that I can't stand?" Jack asked while staring at a suddenly wide-awake Mac.

"Yeah?" he said cautiously.

"Well I want to collect on that chip right now. I have to go to Mexico for four days for a shoot and I want to take Mac with me. Everything is paid for, but I don't want you to be pissed with her much less for her to lose her job. What do you say?" Jack said, touching crossed fingers with Mac.

"Jesus, Jack, I will have to cover for her for three days, not to mention whenever you two get together there is always trouble. Your brothers won't be there to bail you out or kill anybody on your behalf," he said angrily.

"Davey, I can take care of the two of us, I promise, but anyway, we have bodyguards with us. Trust me for once. Come on! You can cover, you owe me, Davey. Please?"

Davey sighed. "Put MacKenzie on the phone." Jack handed the phone to Mac.

"MacKenzie?" Jack whispered. Mac rolled her eyes.

"Yes?" Mac answered. Jack could only hear one side of the conversation, but it was very clipped, with one-word answers on Mac's side.

Interesting.

Mac handed the phone back to Jack. "Oui, Monsieur?" Jack inquired, watching Mac nod her head up and down excitedly.

"Text me the time of your arrival home and I will personally pick you up at the airport, understand? And, Princess, please be safe and don't do anything stupid. You're both very important to me," Davey said softly.

"Um, okay, Davey, I promise, love you, au revoir!" Jack exclaimed as she hung up the phone and danced around the living room as Mac threw clothes in a duffel bag.

Mac stopped short as she boarded the jet and stared with her mouth wide open. Jack bumped into her back with her small carry-on suitcase. Jack giggled. Mac turned around, dropping her duffel bag.

"What. The. Fuck. Jack! Seriously?"

Jack laughed. "I know, right? Trust me, I don't take it for granted, but it really is all for show. These people for the most part are assholes, and I can't wait to be done with all of them. But in the meantime, no, it's not too much of a hardship to be lavished in luxury all the damn time. Listen, I'm going to take a shower and after you take one, we will have a big breakfast, okay? You just wait until you see the bathroom!" Jack said as they made their way to the back of the plane.

While Mac showered, Jack called Angel and Henry. She let them know that she was out of town until the end of the week and set up a lunch date at Davey's restaurant for them to go over the plans. Mac came out all showered and dressed in a pretty sundress with her beautiful red hair wild and free. As soon as Mac was seated, the flight attendant, Scott, brought out a huge tray with eggs, bacon, pancakes, orange juice, and coffee.

"Wow," Mac muttered as they both devoured the food.

Mac laughed and patted her stomach. "Jack, how can you eat like this and still be so skinny?"

Jack stretched her recliner out. "Hmmm, I know. I think I actually grew taller after I left Harmony, if you can believe it. I don't know how my body metabolizes food, but I know what it's like not to have any food, and so I don't care if I get as big as a house. I will always enjoy food and will never take it for granted again."

Mac pulled her knees up under herself. "Can I ask you something, Jack?"

Jack opened her eyes. "Of course," she said quietly. "Shoot."

"What happened with Jared? I'll understand if you don't want to talk about it, but you're so sad, and you were both so in love. I know you still love him. I can see it in your eyes. I saw the article about him, and I just can't shake the feeling that you two should be together."

Jack covered her face with her hands and started sobbing. Big, deep, gut-wrenching sobs. Mac bolted out of her seat and knelt beside Jack and cradled her head.

"Oh, Mac, I can't stand the pain any longer. It's killing me. I love him so much. I never stopped, not for one second. I don't know why he never came after me, but even knowing he didn't care about finding me doesn't take away from the love I feel for him. It's stronger today than it was three years ago! Sometimes I think I will just wither away from heartbreak because of it. I think it's part of the reason I can't forgive my father. The pain is just so great. Sometimes I can't breathe and, even worse, sometimes I don't want to breathe or even live because of it," Jack cried into Mac's hair.

Mac pulled back suddenly. "No! You can't even think like that! I mean it, Jack, you have been through so much. You can't just give up now! You are the strongest woman I have ever met. Promise me you will not let yourself go down that rabbit hole," she pleaded.

Jack nodded. "I promise, really I do. I have a great support system in place for when it gets too much. It's just nice to finally be able to talk to someone who understands what I lost and to admit that it fucking kills me how much I love that man," Jack sighed. "It looks like he is in love with someone else, and I am happy for him. My love is so big for him that it kind of...in a weird way... makes me feel better that he is happy, even if it's not with me."

Mac sneered. "Forgive me, but I don't share your good wishes toward him. If I could get my hands around his friggin' gorgeous neck, I would wring it and kick him in the balls!" Mac spat out. "And, Jesus! What's up with that magazine cover! Talk about smoldering! Oh, sorry, sweetie!" she said, covering her mouth with her hand.

Jack grinned wanly. "It's okay, it's true enough, girlfriend o' mine. Let's watch a badass bone-crunching action movie till we land," Jack said as they settled in for the flight.

Jack and Mac spent the best and most needed work vacation ever. They were able to catch up quickly even though they had been apart for the last three years. They swam and lounged by the pool. They danced every night until the wee hours of the morning. There was more than one eager vacationer as well as multiple local men who tried to get their attention. They danced with everyone and no one. They laughed and enjoyed every second.

The last evening, while the other models where hitting the gym, Jack and Mac hired a car to take them into town for dinner and dancing. They indulged in a bottle of wine with dinner and by the time the band started they were more than ready to dance the night away.

Around midnight, Jack yawned and laughed, covering her mouth. "I'm beat," she announced.

Mac jumped up, holding out her hand to her. "It's no wonder; you have been working all day while I have been lounging by the pool napping."

Jack slapped her hand into hers. "Jesus, as if. If I ever consider lying on a beach while someone takes my picture hard work, then please just shoot me!"

Mac laughed. "True enough. Let's go anyway. We can have a glass of wine at the bar in the hotel before bed to cap off the best friggin' vacation I have ever had!"

Jack linked arms with Mac and headed toward the door. "Wait, let's walk on the beach for a minute. I like to look at the moon on the beach wherever I am. I like to think of my loved ones looking at the same moon wherever they are. This time I won't have to think of you because you are right here with me," Jack said, letting her head rest on Mac's shoulder as they walked arm in arm down the beach.

"What a damn shame, am I right, amigos?" came a broken-English slurred statement from one of the three local men who slowly surrounded Jack and Mac. Jack stiffened and reached for a blade on her thigh that hadn't been there for two years.

Shit.

Jack's pulse started racing as she roared into hyperalert, so much so that she almost couldn't hear Mac whispering to her about what they should do. Jack did a double-take, realizing Mac was there with her. She grabbed her head and spoke directly into her ear.

"As soon as you get a chance, run for the bar and stay inside until I come get you. Do not call the police or garner any attention whatsoever. Understand? I mean it, Mac! Do you understand?"

Mac whimpered in response to the pressure that Jack was applying to her head. She nodded with a sob.

Jack loosened her grip, kissed her temple, and took a battle-ready stance. All three of the men laughed. "Look at that, amigos, this one thinks she is a warrior. She's going to fight us for that pretty pussy of hers."

The tall one of the three looked lustfully at Mac. "Oh, I want to fuck the redhead!" he smirked, making kissing sounds.

Jack's head turned sharply toward him. Dark Twin laughed.

"Oh, you motherfucker, we are going to have such fun."

Jack suddenly lunged at the tall one and screamed for Mac to run. Mac ran several feet up the beach and turned around to check on Jack.

What she saw turned her blood cold.

Jack had kicked the tall Mexican square in the nose, completely shattering it in a spray of blood. One of the others grabbed her by the waist, but she flipped him over her shoulders and drove the heel of her bare foot into his nose with a loud snap. Blood gushed instantly, muffling (somewhat) the man's shrieks of pain. The last man unsheathed a dagger and waved it toward Jack. Mac screamed, momentarily distracting Jack only for an instant as she turned toward Mac. Unfortunately the distraction lasted just long enough for his blade to slice through her upper arm, making Jack jump back. Jack screamed from the pain and anger.

"Fucking run, Mac!"

Jack launched herself with a roundhouse kick to the man's temple. The man went down and Jack grabbed the dagger and grabbed his hand and drove it through his hand into the sand, crucifixion-style. The man screamed out but the surf drowned out the sounds of his agony.

Jack looked around, a bit disoriented, and saw the bar. She grabbed the bandana off the Mexican's head and held it to her bleeding arm as she staggered toward the bar. Mac was in the doorway and rushed to grab her before Jack collapsed.

"Get us back to the hotel, fast," Jack muttered. Mac hugged Jack hard to her side as they walked to the taxi.

"Fuck, fuck, fuck, fuck," Mac repeated over and over. Once they were in the taxi, Jack relaxed back in the seat.

"Did you get our stuff?" Jack asked.

Mack nodded, wiping the sweat and blood off Jack's face.

"Okay, get my phone and call the number for Sam and tell him we're in trouble. Keep him on the line. He'll know what to do. I think I'm going to pass out if I don't puke first. I will try to make it to our room," Jack murmured, fading fast.

"Okay, shit, fuck!" Mac fumbled with Jack's phone until she found Sam's name. It only rang once.

"What's the matter, little one? Talk to me! Now!"

Mac jumped in reaction to the fear in Sam's voice. "Um, this is Mac," she whispered. "We're in trouble, Sam."

"Oh, shit, okay. Sweetheart, it's okay. Just talk to me. Tell me what happened," he replied, this time more calmly.

"I think Jack just killed three guys on the beach!" Mac whispered into the phone.

"Okay, but is Jack hurt, Mac? This is very important. Is she with you and is she hurt?"

Mac started to panic as she watched the blood drip from the saturated bandana. "Yes, she is here with me, and we're in a taxi on our way back to the hotel, but she is hurt bad. She was cut in the arm, and she is bleeding bad. I'm so scared, Sam!"

"It's okay, sweetheart, you're doing great. Now you are going to get her to your room and keep pressure on that arm. Someone is going to knock on your door and patch Jack up. Do you understand, Mac? I need you to be strong for me. Can you do that for me?" Sam asked quietly.

Mac looked at Jack. "I would do anything for her, Sam," Mac said, in a determined voice.

Sam laughed. "That's my girl. Now I'm going to hang up to get some help, okay. Just get her back to your room."

"Wait, you don't know what room or hotel!" Mac cried, starting to panic again.

"I know everything, sweetheart. Don't worry about anything. I got you." The line went dead as they pulled into the hotel.

"Shit, fuck!" Mac yelled out again. She grabbed some money from her purse and handed it to the driver. She noticed a blanket in the front seat. Mac pointed at the blanket. "I need that!" she said pointing to the blanket and handing him more bills. The driver handed the blanket over and motioned impatiently for them to get out of the car.

Mac eased Jack out of the car, wrapping the blanket around them like a poncho, and walked slowly into the hotel lobby. Mac could feel people's stares but with Jack leaning on her as they walked, it just appeared that her friend was drunk.

As they were getting off the elevator, they met one of the Victoria's Secret models. She jumped back.

"Jesus! Is she drunk?"

Mac hissed at the stick-thin model. "Back off, bitch!" Mac realized Jack was going to pass out completely at any time now. They made it to their room and Mac lay Jack on the bed as Jack's phone rang.

"Hello? Sam?" Mac cried.

"I'm right here, sweetheart. Are you back in your room?"

It was Sam. Thank God! Mac nodded and stifled a cry.

"Stay with me here, sweetheart, I need you to answer verbally. Are you back in your room?"

Mac cried out and laughed at the same time. "Sorry, yes, we just got to the room."

"Okay, good, good. Now, go into the bathroom and grab some towels and apply pressure to the cut until the doctor gets there. Okay? Put the phone down while you do this, I'll be right here," Sam replied quietly.

Mac put the phone down. "Shit, fuck, shit fuck," Mac kept repeating nervously. When she got the towels and applied pressure, she picked up the phone. "Okay!" Mac said.

"Okay, good work, sweetheart. Now, while we wait for the doctor I want you to tell me how you became so important to my little one. You certainly have her vocabulary," Sam said laughing.

Mac told Sam about Moose Pond and the best summer of her entire life until there was a knock on the door. A middle-aged Mexican man entered without a word, gave Jack a shot of something, and then sewed up her arm. He cleaned the blood and bagged up the towels and the clothes Jack and Mac were wearing. He nodded his head silently and left the room without ever uttering a word.

Mac told Sam what was happening, and when the doctor left, Sam told Mac to lock the door, lie down, and get some sleep. Jack would be fine in the morning, he promised. Sore and tired, but fine. Mac hung up the phone and started crying until she fell asleep beside Jack.

Jack woke up slowly. She felt like she had been hit by a Mack truck, which usually was the feeling after an "episode." This time, however, she could feel her arm throbbing. Jack got up to get a drink. She was so thirsty.

Mac stirred and sat up quickly. "Are you all right?" she asked, her eyes red from equal parts fatigue and crying.

Jack grabbed two water bottles and sat down on the bed. She handed Mac a water. "Yeah, I'm good. I'm so sorry you had to witness that last night, Mac."

Mac shook her head. "No, you don't need to be sorry for anything. We did nothing wrong, but Jack, what the fuck? You were like some black ops ninja or something. Where did you learn to fight like that?" Mac exclaimed as she took a long drink of water.

Jack smiled. Wow, it was good to have Mac back in her life to talk with. "Sam taught me. There was a time that I lived on the streets, and he taught me to defend myself."

Mac looked so sad and touched her arm. Jack touched her hand and smiled.

"Hey, none of that. I'm not on the streets anymore, I mean haven't you heard? I'm the American Princess," she pronounced, and they laughed. "Okay, I'm going to call Phillip to let the jet know we will be there within the hour. Let's get the hell out of here."

Mac gripped Jack's arm. "Wait, do you think the police are looking for us?"

Jack shook her head. "Nah, those thugs are probably wanted by the police, but even if they aren't, they're not going to tell anyone that a girl beat the shit out of them."

"Good point," Mac said as she got up off the bed and gave a karate kick in the air.

Jack was so not looking forward to the ride home with Davey. She just wanted to go see Sam and then her own bed with a nice pain reliever. Instead she got Davey giving Mac the silent treatment while he interrogated her. She had told Mac not to say a word about what happened, and Mac had agreed wholeheartedly. What was going on with these two?

After Jack had told Davey that they had picked up three hot Mexicans and had a five-way, he instantly terminated the conversation, and thereafter the ride home was blissfully quiet. Jack had Davey drop her off at the soup kitchen. Mac got out of the car to hug Jack.

"Are you sure you're all right?" she asked.

Jack nodded. "Are you sure *you're* all right?" she whispered, nodding her head toward Davey in the car.

Mac rolled her eyes and smiled. "You're too observant for your own good. I'll talk to you later," she replied with mock indignation and got back in the car.

Jack walked through the doors to find Sam talking with a young, attractive woman. As soon as he saw Jack, he rushed over to her.

"Out back, now," he ordered, moving her toward the back. The woman had long thick blond hair that was braided down her back. She had the greenest eyes Jack had ever seen. She came with Sam as they went to Sam's bedroom and he gently pushed Jack to sit on the bed.

"This is Dr. Ava Knight. She's a psychiatrist as well as a medical doctor at New York-Presbyterian Hospital. I want her to look at your arm, and I want you to talk to her."

Jack started shaking her head.

"You can trust her, little one. I refer lots of people to her; she is the only doctor in the city who takes PTSD patients on a pro bono basis. She's good, trust me," Sam assured her.

Jack nodded. "That's where my brother works," Jack said offhandedly.

"Who's your brother?" Dr. Knight asked.

"Bobby, Bobby Johnson. He's a medical doctor there."

Dr. Knight stared at Jack. "Dr. Robert Johnson is your brother?" she asked incredulously.

Jack smiled, feeling a little better that she knew her brother. "Yes. Do you know him?"

Dr. Knight shook her head as if to clear it and started putting her gloves on. "Yes, yes, I know Robert," she replied quietly.

Jack laughed. "'Robert.' That sounds so formal. We call him Bobby; he's a twin to my brother Ty. If you knew the shit those two have gotten into…well, you wouldn't refer to him as Robert, I can assure you."

Dr. Knight grinned as she helped Jack off with her shirt and Sam left the room.

"I think this is going to get interesting," Ava muttered as she laughed to herself.

Jack liked her a lot. She was easy to talk to and very smart. Jack told her everything and never once felt like she was being judged or pitied. Dr. Knight gave her scientific explanations for what Jack experienced when she felt threatened and assured her that she was a survivor. Dr. Knight indicated that all the coping mechanisms that Sam had taught her were effective, and she told her about new medicines that could assist her if she ever became manic again. She didn't candy coat anything. It quickly became evident that her condition was something that she would have to deal with forever, but with help she would persevere like the badass that she was.

Jack really liked her. They quickly booked dates and times for her to meet at Dr. Knight's office in the hospital once a week.

"Um, my family doesn't know about any of this, and I want to keep it that way," Jack said firmly.

"Not a problem at all. Everything is confidential, although eventually it would be best for everyone if they knew. In case you ever have an episode around them. If they know, they will be better able to help you."

Jack shook her head. "No, I never want to taint them with this ugliness, ever."

Dr. Knight got up to leave. "If that is your wish, then of course I will honor it." The doctor ended the meeting by holding her hand out. Jack shook her hand. "Thank you, Dr. Knight."

"There is one thing you can do for me. You can call me Ava, please," the good doctor replied as they walked out together. Jack saw that she was earnest and nodded. "Okay, thank you again, Ava."

Jack had her team all together at a table in the back of Davey's restaurant. Jack had signed the papers for the studio earlier in the week with Henry. Henry had been able to purchase the condemned building for a song. The assembled group was an impressive one: Rick Thomas, a tall, elegant older African American man; Sid "Slick" Mitchell, a short, round older African American man with smiling eyes; James "Jimmy the Great" Smith, a large white man with a thin salt-and-pepper mustache; Cookie Howard, a beautiful older African American woman with white hair and red lipstick; and Angel.

Jack rubbed her hands together. "Okay, now we have all talked on the phone several times, but this is the first time we are actually all meeting in person. I think you all know each other, except some of you might not know my friend Angel. He is heading up the renovation of the studio. Angel, do you know everyone here?"

Angel smiled nervously. "Si, no introductions necessary. You are all legends," he murmured reverently.

They all laughed. "Where have you been, son? We're all washed up. Nobody cares what we did way back when," Sid said.

"Oh, amigo, you are wrong! There is so much knowledge and experience here at this table that I think someone should pinch me to see if I'm dreaming!" Angel exclaimed.

They all laughed again, but Jack could tell they were honored by Angel's praise. "Well, you are exactly what I need. I need all your knowledge about the recording business. I want you to teach me everything you know. You know that I will pay you all, and I have rented a brownstone close to me for you all to live in while we work. I need you to find people who know the business as it is today and are familiar with the technology innovations that have been developed in recent years, and I really need you to help scout talent at the local clubs. I need you to reach out to all your contacts and get this recording studio up and running within six months. I want talent ready to sign and start recording. You all ran this town once upon a time, and I need you to do it again. I need you to find me the best and brightest to help me run this company. Most importantly, I need your instincts. In today's world of text messaging and YouTube, what is missing is the human component. I need feet on the street. I know that it's been a long time since you felt relevant, but I need you to put that behind you and make yourselves relevant again. This is going to be a shit ton of work, so if anyone is not up for this challenge, then say so now."

They all nodded in agreement. Cookie leaned in as every man there gaped. "Sugar, this town ain't gonna know what's hit it when we're through with it!" she stated confidently, snapping her fingers.

Jack sighed. "Great. Now put your feelers out there and let's build our team. The first order of business will be to line up some talent for the grand opening of this restaurant in three weeks. I would like four or five artists to perform." They all nodded, and Angel gave them a rundown on the progress of the renovation team.

The next three weeks were torturous for Jack. She was out of town most of the time, working and skyping with her teams regarding progress on the grand opening and the studio renovations. The afternoon of the gala, Jack came home from the spa to find Phillip and Dirk having tea in the kitchen. She bounded into the house to hear wolf whistles from Dirk. Her hair had been done in a retro 1950s hairdo with big curls gathered to one side of her head and cascading down her shoulder. There was a white feather gently pinned to the other side. Her makeup was flawless, and she had bright red lipstick. She had been at the spa with Cookie, who had advised the hair and makeup artists on what period look was needed. Cookie had a long black wig with bright red lipstick.

Stunning.

"I think you are in danger of giving the members of our team a heart attack tonight, Cookie," Jack said.

Cookie laughed. "Sugar, if any of them has a heart attack tonight, it will most certainly not be from looking at me."

Jack spewed her coffee all over the floor. "You go, girl!" she gasped as she wiped coffee off her face.

"Mmm hmm," Cookie said, weaving her head side to side.

"Go upstairs to see what I have gotten you to wear tonight from the Worthington Collection," Phillip directed Jack while clapping his hands. "Go, go now," he said as she ran to the stairs.

"It had better be comfortable!" Jack threw back over her shoulder as she ran up the stairs.

Hanging on the back of her closet door was the most beautiful dress she had ever seen. It was white silk, gathered at her shoulders, and the sweetheart bodice gathered her breasts nicely, giving her seductive cleavage. The dress clung to her body and pooled at her feet with a small train. There was a slit up to her thigh, leaving one long leg in full view when she walked.

Wow.

Complete haute couture at its very best. To top off the ensemble, a diamond necklace and earrings from Harry Winston Jewelers lay on top of her dresser. Philip had already put her black Louboutin heels beside the dress.

The knock at the door startled Jack, and she turned to see Phillip peek his head in. "May I help you dress, ma petite?"

Jack nodded and walked to embrace him. "It's beautiful, Phillip. Thank you. This is a big night for my brother. You and Dirk are coming, right? You promised."

Phillip smiled. "Oui, oui, Dirk is already mad that I am making him wear a suit." Jack smirked. "Okay, now let us dress your scrawny little body, mon amie," Phillip said, lifting the dress off the hanger.

The limousine with all her brothers but Davey pulled up, and Caleb popped up through the sunroof.

"Classy," Jack observed dryly.

Bear got out and helped Jack in. When she was seated and sure her full dress had made it into the car, she looked around. All eight men were silent and staring with their mouths agape.

"What? Is my lipstick smudged? Booger dangling out of my nose? What? Come on, you guys!" Jack exclaimed.

Teddy cleared his throat. "Jesus, Princess, you're a grown-up woman. You're breathtaking," he whispered. The rest of them cleared their throats and agreed, clearly uncomfortable.

"Well, it's good that you have nine bodyguards tonight then," Bear said sternly.

Jack shook her head. "No, don't start that. I have to work tonight, not only for Mr. Worthington representing his clothing line, but I also have some artists that are going to perform and a number of young people in the business there that I want to pick their brains, so *don't* screw this up for me. Got it?" Jack replied, slowly looking around the car at each of them.

"Well, let's just say that we will be keeping an eye on you, okay?" Marcus said softly smiling at her. He picked up her hand and kissed her fingers. "We have some lost time to make up for," he said, warming Jack's heart.

"Okay, fair enough. Now remember what I told you, there will be lots of paparazzi in front of the restaurant along the red carpet. Be nice! Actually don't talk at all, especially you, Caleb. Just smile and slowly escort me into the restaurant."

Caleb glared at her as she stuck out her tongue at him. "Classy yourself," he retorted.

There was a huge crowd gathered outside the restaurant, and as soon as the limo pulled up, the flashes began. The driver opened the door and Bear climbed out. All of her brothers had dressed in tuxedos for the occasion and, man, were they handsome!

Bear offered her his hand as she gently climbed out of the car. The crowd went crazy, hollering her name. The lights from the cameras were blinding. Jack smiled and waved as the rest of her brothers got out of the car. The paparazzi stood behind the velvet cord, yelling questions as they passed by. One young reporter hollered above the rest.

"Hey, Princess, that was quite a car full of men, was there an orgy going on in that limo?"

Bear stiffened as Jack patted his arm, but from the corner of her eye she saw Marcus stalk over to the guy and pick him up by his shirt.

Oh, Jesus.

Jack marched swiftly to Marcus and touched his back. "Put him down, Marcus, please," she requested quietly. The guy looked scared to death, and she didn't blame him. Waves of rage were rolling off Marcus. She linked her arm with his and pulled him along.

"These are all my brothers, so that was just a little offensive, don't you think?" she remarked sweetly to the idiot "journalist."

Davey was in top form tonight. He greeted everyone and made each person feel important. Jack hugged Davey.

"I'm so proud of you! Everything looks great! Where is Mac? You're not making her work tonight are you?"

Davey grasped her arms and pulled back. "Whoa! Hold on! Yeah, that would be awful if I made her do her job tonight, wouldn't it?" He held up his hands in surrender as his sister tried unsuccessfully to give him a poke. "No, I'm not making her work! She is in the kitchen putting the finishing touches on the desserts," Davey replied, waving his arm toward the kitchen.

Jack walked swiftly through the doors. Mac looked up and smiled. She was drop-dead gorgeous. Her flame-red hair was gathered at the nape of her neck and tied with a white ribbon. She wore a silk green off-the-shoulder dress with an empire waist that flowed to the floor.

Breathtaking.

"You look gorgeous, Mac! Do you like the Worthington dress I had Phillip pick out for you?" Jack gushed.

Mac hugged her. "Oh. My. God. Jack. I've never seen a dress like this! You should have seen your brother when he came into the kitchen a while ago. Um, well, I think he liked it a lot," she replied as her face suddenly turned beet red.

"Did he now?" Jack said coyly. Jack grabbed her arm. "Shall we, madam?" They laughed and headed into the dining room.

The team was all there and excited for the talent they had chosen for the night. They were just about to introduce the first performer when a little blond girl about four years old ran over to Jack as she sat with her brothers and Mac. Jack felt a tug on her dress and looked down. The little girl motioned for her to lean down. Jack let the little girl whisper in her ear. Jack sat up and pretended to think. The whole restaurant became quiet. Jack leaned down and whispered in the little girl's ear. The little girl nodded her head and smiled, putting her finger in her mouth nervously. Jack rose and held out her hand to little girl and they walked together to the piano. The restaurant was absolutely silent.

Davey made his way up the stairs to the "crow's nest," a small sitting room above the restaurant with one-way mirrors all around it so he could observe things at any time. He opened the door and Jared turned toward him. Hands in the pockets of his black suit, legs braced in a wide stance, observing one person with laser-like focus. Davey went to stand beside Jared and watched Jack walk with the little girl to the piano.

"She's fucking breathtaking," Jared whispered.

Davey turned to him. "Just come down, man, really, come join us. You're part of the family."

Jared shook his head. "She doesn't want me there. Trust me, I've reached out to her. Her silence has made it clear she doesn't want anything to do with me, and I don't blame her. Thank you for letting me see her tonight. It means a lot to me. I'm trying to move forward, but I just needed to see her one last time."

Jared's eyes never left Jack as she started to play the piano. The sound was melodic as the speakers piped in the sounds of the dining room into the "crow's nest."

"No problem, Jared. If you need anything, just ask," Davey said, walking toward the door. Jared never acknowledged him as Jack began singing "Let It Go" to the little girl. Every eye in the joint was focused on Jack, *his* Jack—they couldn't look away. Tears streamed down Jared's face unchecked and uncontrollably. He couldn't hold back as her fingers flew over the keys and the little girl sang along with Jack. His heart shattered yet again into a million pieces.

As soon as the song was done she picked up the little girl and introduced the first performer. Jared made his way down the stairs and out into the cold night. He walked briskly to the familiar bar and took a stool and tapped the bar.

This was going to be another long fucking night.

Jack was so restless. She felt like a caged tiger as she paced back and forth in her bedroom. She thought about the evening as she clasped her hands together and brought them to her lips. Two of the five performers were spectacular. She was going to do her best to sign them, she had already decided. The night had been a huge success for Davey as well as for her team. Jack smiled as she remembered Noah's response when he met all of her brothers for the first time that night. Her brothers were a bit overwhelming and gorgeous to heterosexual women, but to a gay man?

She laughed as she remembered the look on Noah's face. Her initial reaction had been that Noah actually was afraid of Bear. When Noah had arrived, he had simply picked her up off her feet and twirled her around. Jack had yelped. Bear had instantly sprung to his feet and pulled Jack away as he started to lunge for Noah. Jack screamed and pulled Bear back and explained that Noah was her best friend, coworker, and roommate.

Bear had smiled sweetly and apologized, smoothing Noah's lapel. That was the moment Noah might have fallen hopelessly in love with big Bear. They'd all chuckled and eaten superb food all evening, but now Jack just couldn't fight the uneasiness that engulfed her.

She pulled her silk nightgown over her head and opened her bottom drawer where she keep the jeans, T-shirt and hoodie that Sam and Leo had given her. She kept the clothes as a kind of reminder to never forget where she had been and, more importantly, how much the kindness of strangers mattered. She pulled the hood up and threw on her Chucks. She gathered as many stuffed backpacks as she could carry and left the brownstone. She made her way past the Lower East Side and into a really bad part of the city, one she wished she didn't know about. She went around to the back of the church, and just as she was going to climb up and heave the backpacks through the broken window, the door opened and Leo all but fell out the door.

"Leo? Are you okay?" Jack whispered and suddenly smelled the whiskey on his breath.

"Little one! Oh, it's so good to see you, girl! I'm better than fine, sweetheart. I just came by to check on things. Too many damn families here if you ask me," he said, shaking his head sadly. He looked at her arms carrying the heavy backpacks and smiled.

"You're a good girl. I predict that those babies in there will be eating Pop-Tarts in the morning. Am I right?" he asked, swaying.

Jack laughed. "You know me too well, Leo. Wait here for me and we will get you to the shelter," she directed, going up the stairs and through the open door to deliver the backpacks.

Some of the families were awake, so she spoke to them about the shelter and told them to ask for Jasmine, but mostly she just left a backpack silently next to each family as they slept. Each backpack held food, socks, bus fare vouchers, toothbrushes and toothpaste, soap, combs and hair ribbons, bottles of water, and a children's book with a hundred dollar bill sticking out from it. Leo was right, there were too many desperate families on the street.

Jack walked out of the church and looked around. Leo was gone. She whispered his name but he was gone. Jack thought she would just look for him for a little while before going home. She put her hands in the pouch of her hoodie and pulled the hood up, and with her head down she searched the streets.

The search proved unproductive. As she made her way home, she was just rounding the corner of the Upper West side when she almost collided with a police officer. He held out his arms to steady her.

"Whoa, are you okay, miss? What are you doing out here by yourself? Do you need help?"

Jack steadied herself and looked up at the very tall young officer. Stunned at his genuine concern, she shook her head. "Um, no, officer, I'm fine. I was just on my way home," she replied, looking him in the eye so he could assess for himself that she wasn't on drugs or drunk.

The officer nodded. "Well, okay then, but you shouldn't be out by yourself at night. This is a good neighborhood, but you never know."

As the officer was talking to her, movement caught her eye and she turned to look into the dimly lit bar off to her right.

Jack gasped.

Jared sat on the bar stool hunched over, staring into a glass of scotch. Jack looked back at the officer as he turned to leave and nodded. Jack strolled slowly down the street before turning around and standing on the edge of the big window of the bar.

Jack's heart stopped. Her beautiful Jared. He had on an expensive black suit and a white dress shirt with the collar open. His hair was a little longer than it had been on the magazine cover. Jack touched the glass as she caught her breath. Jared knocked the scotch back and tapped the counter.

Why was he drinking? Jared hated hard alcohol. He hated what it did to his father and had always stayed away from it. There was such a sadness about him. Maybe he'd had a fight with the woman who held his heart. What would it hurt to go talk to him? They had been as close as two people could be once upon a time. She had always been able to talk to Jared, even as a child. Couldn't she be there for him like he'd always been there for her? Maybe it would make him feel better if he talked about the woman he loves. She could be strong for him, couldn't she? Even the thought of another woman on his lips stirred her insides, making her nauseous.

Jack took a step toward the door but stopped when a pretty brunette walked from the back of the bar toward Jared. She was holding up her hand to the bartender telling him no more scotch as he was about to pour Jared another. The brunette pulled on his arm to get him to stand, but Jared waved her away. The brunette sat down on the stool beside Jared and nuzzled his neck and whispered something in his ear.

That was her. Jack could tell that she loved him, so how come he was single? Jack watched as the brunette let her hand slide between Jared's legs.

Jack gasped audibly. She needed to get out of here, so she bolted up the street toward the brownstone. She ran the entire four blocks and only stopped when she entered the brownstone, panting and out of breath. She was bending over, trying to catch her breath, when Noah walked out from the kitchen, startling Jack. He must have just gotten home.

Noah took one look at Jack and opened his arms. The dam let loose and Jack ran to him. Noah picked her up and went to his room and lay her down on the bed. He tossed her sneakers off and pulled back the covers. She scooted in and he snuggled in beside her. No words were needed. They were both so broken that none needed to be spoken to know that they just needed each other for a while. Sleep eventually came along, accompanied by painful dreams of happier times at the pond.

Jack gazed blankly out the jet window. Jesus, she was tired. She was coming home from a two-week trip to Milan for fashion week. Mr. Worthington had made sure she worked nonstop, as it was the last obligation in her contract.

Halle-fucking-lujah.

Not only had she been busy on the runway, but the recording studio was ready to open next week. Jack and her team, along with her brother Henry, who was now officially the studio's attorney, had signed three new artists, and the recording studio was officially open for business. Princess Productions was about to blow the doors off the music industry. They had all worked tirelessly to get to this point, especially Angel. He had found another cook for the soup kitchen (which Sam was none too happy about) and had devoted all his time to the renovations. Angel was a master organizer and didn't take any shit from anybody. It just wasn't possible for anybody to pull anything over on him.

Jack smiled. Angel didn't know it yet, but she had decided to make him her general manager. He would be in charge of the building and security and pretty much everything that didn't involve actually making the music. Her team had found a young man fresh from Harvard Business School with a minor in music. Jamal Knowles had received a full scholarship and graduated at the top of his class. He had grown up on the Lower East Side, staying from time to time at the shelter Jack had lived in. Jasmine couldn't say enough good things about him, and Angel knew his single mother and how hard she had worked to make sure they had a place to live and food on the table. Jack had thought it was going to be a hard sell to the young man, but she was pleasantly surprised when he had accepted immediately. There wasn't a lot Jack could offer at the moment. The salary was small, but as soon as the studio took off, the sky was the limit for all of them. Jack had asked him after one of their meetings why he had hooked his wagon with them instead of trying to get into one of the already established music conglomerates. He had just shrugged with a small grin on his face.

"Probably for the same reason you did. For the love of the music and to be my own boss, so to speak. We can build this thing from the ground up. There's no limit to what we can accomplish, and with the talent you have signed, well, there is a whole untapped generation out there on the streets that the world needs to know about. Besides, I have a crush on you, and this way I can see you every day."

He was a smooth operator and so damned cute. His late father was African American, and his mother was Japanese, which made the combination striking. He was a small, thin man with very short hair and small almond-shaped eyes with a smile that could stop traffic. Jack was very thankful he had joined the team.

The plane finally landed, and Jack checked her messages from the back of the limo. One from each of her brothers reminding her that they were all in town, except Bear who was deployed again, all ready to celebrate her birthday and the end of her contract. The get-together would be at Davey's restaurant. She could not be late without "repercussions," warned her siblings.

Great. Another party.

It was supposed to be a quiet affair with just her brothers, her team, and friends to mark this momentous occasion signaling her independence. The team had invited the three recording artists, and her brothers had all brought their guitars, so what was supposed to be a relaxing evening turned into a raucous after-hours party. One of the new up and coming artists was a tall, extremely good-looking country singer named Ricky Vance. Jamal had scouted him in one of the local clubs on open mic night.

He had sent Jack a video recording that same night of Ricky, and soon thereafter Jamal set up an appointment with Ricky to sign with them. Ricky had been unsure until Jamal had brought Jack in via Skype and Jack had talked him into signing.

Jack sat at the piano, and the others played and let Ricky sing. He was good…really good. During a break, Jack sat at the bar as Ricky slid into the seat beside her. Jack asked him about his family back home in Texas, which he seemed to enjoy talking about. He was a little shy but had impeccable manners that made Jack feel quite comfortable. He regaled her with stories of the rodeo and growing up on a working ranch. He was open and self-effacing, which had Jack laughing during more than one story.

Jack looked around to find Mac to thank her for such a beautiful birthday cake, but she was nowhere in sight. She made her way toward the kitchen when Caleb stopped her from entering.

"Hey there, birthday girl," he said, sliding an arm around her shoulders.

Jack narrowed her eyes at him. "What do you want?" she said suspiciously.

"What? I can't talk to my favorite sister for a minute?"

Jack stepped away from his embrace. "Well, I'm your only sister, and I can tell when you're up to something," she replied putting her hands on her hips. Just then Davey burst out of the kitchen and headed toward the bar, and a few moments after that Mac came out of the kitchen looking upset.

Jack looked at Caleb. "What's going on?" she whispered.

Caleb looked sheepish. "It's none of our business, Jack. Just leave it alone," he whispered back.

Jack leaned in to him with fists drawn. "You know something and you're going to tell me," she hissed.

Mac touched Jack on the back and Jack whipped around smiling. "Oh, honey! The cake was fabulous! Are you okay?"

Mac smiled weakly. "I'm glad you enjoyed the cake, and yes I'm fine, just tired. I'm going to head out; I just wanted a birthday hug," she replied, embracing Jack.

Jack hugged her tightly back. "You know you can talk to me about anything, right, Macadoo?" she whispered in Mac's ear.

Mac nodded with tears in her eyes. "I know, and I will, but I'm just not ready," she muttered. Jack took a deep breath and stared at Mac's back as she left the restaurant. *Too much drama,* Jack thought to herself, *and for what reason?*

Almost everyone else had gone home, but Jasmine was helping load the dirty dishes onto trays along with Davey and Ricky. "Well, you should have more birthdays, little lady. The shelter cleaned up with donations per your request in lieu of gifts for you," Jasmine exclaimed with a smile.

"I'm glad! That is certainly a better cause than a new bauble for me," Jack replied.

Jasmine snorted. "Like you have any baubles! I bet you can still fit everything that matters to you in that damn backpack of yours!"

Jack grinned and touched her finger to her nose.

"Just what I thought," Jasmine retorted, heaving the tray toward the kitchen.

Jack was just about to follow her when Ricky cleared his throat beside her. Jack turned to find him nervously wringing his hand around the dish cloth.

"Um…Jack, um, well I'd really like to spend some time with you… sometime," he said, staring down at the floor.

"Oh, of course! I will see you Monday, and I would like to hear the songs you're writing. I think I can help you with the music end of it," Jack replied, smiling and turning toward the kitchen. "Thank you again for coming to my birthday celebration!"

Davey came into the kitchen, looked at Jack, and shook his head. Jack did a double take. "What?" she asked.

"You know, don't you, that he was asking you out?" Davey huffed, leaning back against the sink with his arms crossed.

Jack looked confused. "What? Who? You don't mean…" she said, pointing to the kitchen doors.

Davy nodded. "Ah, yeah I kinda do," he said impatiently.

Jack paled. "O-oh."

Davey nudged her with his shoulder. "You know, you have to move on, Princess. It's time," he said quietly. Jack just looked at him with big eyes before shaking herself and wiping her hands on the towel hanging on his shoulder.

"Not going to happen, big brother. Now I'm going home. Thank you for a wonderful birthday. Good night." Jack kissed him and quickly left the restaurant.

Sunday morning, Noah, Phillip, Dirk, and Jack had a leisurely breakfast before she packed her things to move into the studio, at least for the time being. When they had restored the studio, Jack had built a room with a bathroom and a shower off her office in case she worked late or maybe needed to save money and live there, which was presently the case. There was a kitchenette/break room that would be fine to prepare her meals. As long as she had a couch and a stack of books, she was happy to work every moment she could.

Noah sat on her bed as she closed her suitcase. "You know you're going to work yourself to death without me or Phillip around to make you have fun," he said, inspecting his cuticles.

"I'll be fine, and just because we're not all working together, we will still see each other. You're right, however—I am going to be working every spare moment I have. I'm really excited to be creating something on my own, you know?"

Noah got up, grabbed the suitcase, and hugged her. "Oh, lovely, I'm going to miss you so. Promise me you will call me every day?"

Jack pulled out of the hug. "Oh, you mean just once a day or ten times a day like we do now?" she said, grabbing her messenger bag and situating it across her chest.

There was a car horn from the street. "Oops, my cab," Jack said as they made their way downstairs.

Phillip and Dirk were waiting for her at the door. Phillip hugged her tight with tears in his eyes. "Oh, ma petite, my heart is very sad," he murmured into her hair.

Jack shook her head. "Please don't be sad, Phillip. This is *so* important to me. We will see each other often, I promise," she replied, turning to Dirk.

"Mon petit chou, please take care of yourself."

Jack hugged him tightly and whispered in his ear. "Please take good care of Phillip," she said softly. Jack was close to crying, so she took a deep breath, threw her shoulders back, and laughed instead as she climbed into the cab and watched them on the sidewalk through the back window until the cab turned the corner.

Part 4

*I*t was late, but sleep wouldn't come. Maybe it was the new place, or maybe it was the fact that Jack was finally free to make her own decisions and it scared her to death. She wandered the empty building until she came to the recording studio and sat down at the piano. She smiled, relishing that everything was so fresh and new as she lifted the lid off the keys to gently glide her fingertips over the ivory. She played for hours before she made her way to her pull-out couch and snuggled in.

The dream was a new one. The sun was shining and Jack was a small child sitting at the edge of the water building sand castles on the beach at Moose Pond. The gentle lapping of the waves rolling to the shore and the gentle hum of the crickets along with the sun on her face and hair gave the little girl a peace and stillness that had always eluded her even as a child. The little girl felt a presence and looked up to see a beautiful woman with long blond curls piled on top of her head with loose tendrils of hair falling around her face. Her eyes were gentle and kind and so familiar. She laughed and cupped the little girl's cheeks in her hands and laughed joyously.

"My precious, precious Princess. I'm so very proud of you," she whispered.

Her mother, the woman who knew her before she ever entered the world.

The little girl lifted her small chubby hand to the woman's cheek, wondrously searching the woman's laughing eyes for the answers that the little girl needed so badly. The woman kept laughing as she grasped the little girl's hands in her own and directed her to the half-built sand castle, handing her the shovel and bucket. As the sun continued to beat down with the gentle rustle of the warm breeze, they took their time building a spectacular castle. The waves began to come up closer and closer to the castle, washing chunks of sand away.

The sun was beginning to set. The little girl looked around and suddenly she was looking through older eyes, sadder eyes, looking down on the head of a dark-haired little girl with tiny pigtails. She felt so familiar. The little girl was frantically trying to stop the quickly collapsing sand castle. The woman started to lean toward the little girl, holding out her hands to the child. The wind began blowing with more force and the sun disappeared. The little girl began to cry and suddenly looked up to reveal the beautiful brown eyes of Jared.

Their child.

Jack let out a strangled cry and sat bolt upright on the pull-out bed, unable to catch her breath. She brought the back of her hand to her mouth and sobbed. She felt her tears and covered her face with her hands and lay back down in a fetal position, closing her eyes to block out the beautiful image of their child. She lay there still as death until her alarm went off.

The team assembled in the conference room to map out the week. They had decided to start recording with Ricky. Ricky was warming up with his band in the recording studio when they all came in. Ricky noticed Jack and shot a smile her way. He really was so sweet.

"Are you ready to begin?" Jack asked him.

Ricky stood and was at least a head taller than Jack. He touched his cowboy hat. "Yes, ma'am."

Jack nodded and went into the recording booth with her team. They concentrated on one song, and it took the entire day to get it just right. By early evening, everyone had gone home except Jack and Jamal. They worked it over and over until they had it the way it was meant to be. Jamal was grabbing his jacket. "One down and about fifteen to go," he announced, equal parts grinning and grimacing.

Jack moaned and threw an empty water bottle at his retreating back. She was so exhausted. Her stomach growled and she tried to remember what, if anything, she had eaten that day. She wandered into the break room and spied a large pizza box. She lifted the lid and found one large slice of bacon pizza.

Jackpot!

She warmed it up in the microwave, grabbed a water, and headed to her "room." Jack picked up her computer and dialed Noah to Skype. His beautiful face answered immediately. That surprised Jack, because she knew he had just arrived on the West Coast and assumed the odds were he would be out on the town.

"Hey, lovely, how was your first day of work as the boss lady?" Noah smirked.

Jack held up the half-eaten slice of pizza. "Great! First thing I've eaten all day, but it was really good. I have so much learn, Noah!" Jack whined.

"You will—just give it time," he replied, clearly distracted.

Jack narrowed her eyes. "What's up?" she asked. Noah put his "who, me?" face on, shaking his head.

"Noah...?"

Jack's eyes focused on the background. It was a disheveled hotel room with booze bottles strewn around. Jack's eyes narrowed in on a bong and a bag of marijuana on the nearby table. Jack dropped the pizza and sat close to the computer screen.

"Are you high?" she asked sternly.

Noah was trying to move his computer when Jack noticed a half-naked man sleeping on the bed.

"Noah, what the fuck? The very first time we're not traveling together you take up with some druggie? What are you doing?" she whispered.

Noah's visage turned to "guilty as charged," but he couldn't help but smile in his inebriated state. "I'm fine, lovely, really. Don't worry about me, and that is Derrick, I think, and he's not a drug dealer. He's another model I met today. I actually think I met someone more narcissistic than me," he replied in a slurred voice.

Jack snorted. "I find that hard to believe."

They each talked a bit about their day and cut the conversation short. Jack just didn't want to see Noah in this substance-induced state of happiness. He deserved so much more.

Jack shut her laptop, looked down at the half-eaten cold pizza, and wrinkled her nose. She could do better than that. She got up and found her hoodie.

Just a short walk to the corner store, she thought, as she increased her step. Who was she fooling? Really, it was already predetermined where she was going to end up: outside of the bar she had seen Jared in.

Jack looked in the big plate glass window, but he wasn't in there. Jack sighed and continued on down the street when she heard a dog yelp. Jack continued walking, but the yelping got louder. She stopped to try and figure out where the sound was coming from. Jack looked down a long dark alley. The yelping got louder, and now she could hear a man yelling at the dog. Jack could feel the prickling sensation of uneasiness enveloping her, so she started to take deep breaths, trying to calm herself. Jack looked down the alley.

Really, am I really about to walk into this dark alley?

A yelp and what could only be a thud from a boot to flesh attacked her hearing. Fuck yeah, she was going down there! Hood up, she cautiously walked slowly down the alley. When she got almost to the end she noticed that it opened up to a rather large area for dumpsters for the two apartment buildings. She heard a door slam as she looked out into the open area. Over by the overflowing dumpster was a small white dog curled up in a small ball. Jack started toward the dog and stumbled over a bag of garbage. The dog's head flew up, and Jack stood still, staring at the dog.

"Hello," Jack muttered awkwardly. She had no experience whatsoever with animals. She had always wanted a dog, but Caleb was allergic to all animals, so her father had forbidden it.

The dog appeared to be a puppy, and he was a beaut. Jack walked slowly toward the dog, expecting it to bark or growl, but it didn't. The dog sat on its hind legs and tilted its head to the side like it was just as curious about her. It was as if the dog was thinking. Suddenly it smiled.

Oh. My. God.

The dog actually smiled at her.

Jack looked around and then at the closed door. She bolted toward the dog and started untying it. She couldn't believe she was doing this. The dog leaped into her arms as Jack bolted back down the alley and kept running until she was at the corner store next to the studio.

Jack sat the dog down on the ground outside the market and knelt to talk to the dog. "Okay, you understand that I am a criminal now," she proclaimed, and the dog started licking her face and wagging her stubby tail, her whole backside actually.

Jack chuckled. "Okay, okay! So here's the thing, I need to go get you and me something to eat, and I can't bring you in there. You're going to have to wait for me out here. Can you do that?"

The dog barked softly and licked Jack's face. Jack nodded. "Well, all right then, I'll be right back." The dog sat down immediately.

Was she actually waiting? Jack smiled to herself and went into the market. Guess we'll soon find out.

Jack found some dry and canned dog food along with a box of raspberry-frosted Pop-Tarts.

Perfect.

Half-expecting to find no dog outside, Jack walked out to find the dog sitting, staring at the door. When she walked out, the dog barked and commenced to dance around in a circle.

"Well, okay then! I guess we're an official couple now. Let's go home," Jack murmured, walking down the street with the mystery dog following right beside her.

Jack sat on the floor of the kitchenette watching the dog eat. She had opened a can of beefy bits in gravy that seemed to be a big hit the way the dog was inhaling it. She probably hadn't been fed enough or often. Jack had established that it was a she, and she was gorgeous. The canine had a squareish nose, amazing blue eyes, and small soft ears that flopped over.

Jack tossed the last of her Pop-Tart in her mouth as the dog finished licking her bowl clean. She yawned and stood up.

"Are you ready for bed?" Jack asked, walking toward her room. "I'm not sure how this is going to work, but I would appreciate it if you wouldn't go to the bathroom on the floor. Just let me know, and I will gladly take you outside, okay? That's pretty much the only rule around here. If you are patient with me, I'll be patient with you, deal?"

Jack slid her pajama shorts and tee on and climbed into bed. She looked down to see the dog looking at her as if waiting for permission.

"You can——"

The dog was on the bed and licking her face before she even finished her sentence. Jack laughed. Was it her imagination or was she calmer than she had felt in a long time?

Jack settled into the bed with the dog snuggled up to her side. Jack softly pet the dog's back. The dog sighed deeply. Jack smiled.

"You know you need a name. What would you like to be called?" Jack whispered before she drifted off into a blissfully dreamless sleep.

Jack slowly opened her eyes to find the dog looking at her from the pillow next to her.

"Well, good morning. I'm glad to see you made yourself at home," Jack said wryly. The dog lifted her head and rolled on her back with her legs up.

"Oh, is this an invitation?" Jack asked scratching her belly. "Okay, let's take you for a walk, shall we?"

The dog sat beside the coffee table, waiting patiently for her to dress. Jack looked over and saw her dog-eared copy of *Pride and Prejudice* sitting on the table.

"Hmmm, how do you like the name Jane, as in Jane Austen? Because I adore it, and I think that if Jane Austen was a dog she would be beautiful just like you."

The dog went crazy barking and dancing around. Jack could swear she was smiling again.

"Well, okay! Jane it is!"

Jack was careful to go to the park on the other side of the studio so as not to run into the asshole who had been beating Jane the night before. Jane did her business, and then they went home for breakfast. Jack was certain that this was the smartest dog that had ever lived.

Jack arrived at the recording studio to find everyone already working. Jane walked in like she owned the place and stopped and growled at the men in the band.

"Gentlemen, this is Jane. She may not like men much right now, which is understandable considering what the last man did to her. She is my dog now, so be good to her. Jane, this is the band and my team. There is not anyone here that will hurt you, okay? I have to go to work, so you need to settle someplace and relax."

Jack sat down and looked around. Everyone was looking at her and then at the dog. Jamal finally smiled.

"Have you ever had a dog, Jack?"

Jack shook her head. "No, my brother was allergic so I was never able to have any animals. Why?" she asked.

Jamal and the others laughed. "Well you know she's a dog, right? You're talking to her like a person. She can't understand you. And Jane? What kind of name is that for a dog?" Jamal mocked.

"Um, yes, Jane, and she most certainly does understand me. I think she may be the smartest dog that ever lived, so no negativity around her okay? She's had a tough start in life," Jack said, looking at the dog as she talked. Jane barked, jumped into her lap, and laid down. Jack smiled. "Okay, let's proceed shall we?"

They worked throughout the day with the only breaks being when the dog needed to go outside. The team was beginning to quickly see that this dog was going to be a blessing by providing them with much-needed breaks.

Jack's phone vibrated across the table. It was the number that Angel had given her of a veterinarian in his neighborhood.

"Hello?"

"Hi, I'm returning a call from Jack Johnson? This is Ashley Walker, the veterinarian."

"Oh, hi, yes, that's me. Thanks for calling me back. Well, I just acquired a dog and I need to have her looked at. She may have suffered some injuries, but she probably needs a checkup at the very least."

"Yes, yes of course. I will just take a little information from you. What kind of dog is it?"

"Um, a white one. A female with blue eyes and she just may be the smartest dog you have ever seen."

Jamal was mouthing "White one?" as they all snickered. Jack stuck out her tongue at them in reply.

The doctor took it all in stride. "Oh, um, okay, how about you just bring her by. Can you come tonight around six?"

"Oh that would be perfect. Thank you, Dr. Walker. We'll be there."

"Great, and please call me Ashley. See you then."

"A *white one?*" Jamal mocked. Ricky came over and patted Jane's head. "She's a pit bull, Jack. I'd say a full-blooded one if I had to guess."

Jack smiled down at Jane. "Well of course you are, aren't you, beautiful girl?" she said in her best baby talk. Everyone in the recording booth rolled their eyes, but they couldn't help but smile because none of them had seen Jack so calm and quick to laugh since, well, ever.

They finally called it a day so Jack and Jane could walk to the veterinarian clinic several blocks away. When they walked through the door, a tiny brunette with a pixie cut was standing behind the counter.

"Hi, I have an appointment at six o'clock. I'm Jack Johnson," Jack announced.

The woman stared up at her and then shook her head. "Um, God, sorry! I'm Ashley, the veterinarian. You're Jack the supermodel, aren't you? The one they call the American Princess?"

Jack smiled. "Guilty as charged. Please don't hold that against me."

Ashley giggled. "Oh my God, I'm usually not so rude, but you are breathtakingly beautiful. Oh, God, that sounds like I'm hitting on you doesn't it? I'm not gay, although there's nothing wrong with being gay! Jesus! Let's start over okay? Hi, Jack, this must be Jane, the smartest dog ever!"

Jack roared with laughter. "Why yes, as a matter of fact she is!"

Ashley gave Jane a perfect bill of health and gave her all her shots. She outfitted Jane with a collar and a dog leash that dispensed poop bags. Jack asked Ashley if she was new to this area because she was so young. Jack suspected the vet was about her age.

"No, I grew up in this neighborhood, and after I graduated I came back here to work with my mentor, Dr. Smith. Dr. Smith passed away last year, and I just kind of took over the place," Ashley sighed. "Where are you from? I can't quite place your accent."

Jack looked indignant and exaggerated a New York accent, proclaiming "Well, I'm from a small town in Maine."

Ashley grinned and then sighed dreamily. "Maine…I've always dreamed of going there, especially on the water like to a camp maybe. I actually minored in animal husbandry in college in the hopes that someday I might live in a small town and be the town vet and take care of horses and cows. You were lucky," she said.

Jack sobered. "Yeah, I was. It was great," she replied, hooking the leash onto Jane's collar.

"Well, if you need anything for Jane, just call me, okay? Um, Jack, would you like to go to dinner or something sometime?"

Jack smiled. "I would love that. I have a great friend that you would love as well. We need to have a girls' night out, but unfortunately, I have just started my recording label and have no idea when I will come up for air, but rest assured, I will call you—and thanks again for your help with Jane," Jack replied as she stepped out the door.

"Oh, and I think you may be right actually, Jane may be the smartest dog I have ever seen!" Ashley exclaimed as she was closing the door.

"I know, right!" Jack chuckled.

The next few weeks were grueling, but they managed to get a full first CD recorded for Ricky. The team was now hard at work networking and setting up a tour schedule. Jack knew she was working herself too hard with little sleep and not eating properly, but she also had never felt so gratified and fulfilled. Several of the nights she had started to have flashbacks to Beckett's House, but then she had woken up to Jane licking her face. Jack had assumed that the dog needed to go outside to pee, so she had grabbed her sweats and brought her outside, only to have her sit on the sidewalk and stare at her with her head leaned to the side like she was waiting for Jack. Weird.

Jack and the team had just wrapped for the morning when her phone buzzed. It was Dr. Knight.

"Hi, Ava! How are you?" Jack asked.

Ava laughed. "Actually I'm calling to see how you are. I haven't heard from you or seen you for a while."

Jack leaned back in her desk chair. "I'm good. I've been working night and day, but surprisingly I feel great."

"Good, good. Listen, something's come up and I would love it if you could come into the office today."

Jack turned her chair to look outside. "Sure, Ava, I think I could use the fresh air and a break. Are you free now?"

"Yes, that would be fine. I'll see you in a bit."

Jack grabbed a cab to New York-Presbyterian Hospital. She felt bad about leaving Jane in her room, but the hospital wouldn't allow her to bring the dog inside the hospital. As she entered Ava's office, the secretary ushered her right through to her office. Ava took one look at Jack and put her hands on her hips.

"Why have you not been eating?" she scolded while tapping her foot.

Jack stopped and looked down. "Really—is it really noticeable? You're absolutely right, I haven't taken the time to eat properly and I knew that I had lost some weight. I will at least take the time to go across the street to eat with Sam from now on. I guess the Pop-Tarts just aren't cutting it, huh?" Jack replied.

Ava grunted. "Oh, Jesus, tell me you don't eat that crap?"

Jack held up her hand. "Guilty as charged I'm afraid." She sat down in a chair across from Ava.

"So, tell me what's been going on," Ava began. Jack explained how busy she had been at the studio but that the work was very satisfying to her.

"I also recently acquired a dog. Her name is Jane, and she is so beautiful and loving! This is my first animal ever. It may seem strange but I have a certain level of calm that I can't explain when I'm around her."

Ava nodded. "Actually, Jack, dogs are very intuitive and have been very useful in treating patients with PTSD such as yours. Dogs can sense panic attacks coming and can detect changes in your body leading up to an episode even before you do. If a dog sleeps with you or even in the same room they can sense when you are having a nightmare or flashbacks and wake you."

Jack just stared at Ava. "She has. At least a couple of nights, she has woken me up by licking my face, and I could tell that I had started to flash back. That's amazing, Ava," Jack said shaking her head.

"I think this is a very good thing, Jack. Now, the other thing I wanted to talk to you about was this," she said, handing Jack a piece of paper with black marker crossing out everything on the page.

"What's this?" Jack asked looking up.

"That's what I want to know. I requested a copy of your medical files with the papers that you signed, and this was part of the paperwork. I got everything else, your school medical records, sports physicals, and immunizations, but I have no idea what this is. It has your name and birthdate at the top, so there is no mistaking this as part of your file."

Jack looked down at the paper and then back up again at Ava. "I have no idea, but I will call Marcus tonight. Maybe I was abducted as a child by aliens and this was the FBI account that had to be redacted because of Homeland Security issues," she muttered as Ava started laughing.

"Well, let's hope that's all it is!" Ava replied, standing. "Now, let's go to the cafeteria and have some lunch, you need it."

Jack jumped up. "You will get no argument from me. How about we see if Bobby is free and we can all have lunch."

Jack pulled out her phone and dialed his number, but it went straight to voice mail. When Jack told Ava she couldn't reach Bobby, she was sure that Ava looked relieved.

Interesting.

Jack made a mental note to see what she could find out from Bobby next time she saw him.

When Jack got home, she opened her room to find stuffing from her two bed pillows billowing all over the room and on the floor. Jane was hiding under the bed. Jack just stood there staring at all the stuffing. Finally she sat crossed-legged on the floor and calmly called for Jane to come out. Eventually, Jane edged out a little at a time, her little stub wagging. When she had come out fully, the dog sat up and licked Jack's face. Jack shook her head, patted the floor, and gently pushed her behind down.

"Sit. Now we have to have a little talk, I think. This was *very* naughty, Jane," Jack stated sternly, picking a piece of stuffing off the floor and showing the dog. "I understand that you were angry that I left you behind or that maybe you thought I was never coming back, but this is just plain unacceptable. Now neither of us have a pillow to sleep on. What do you think of that?"

Jane whined and tried to lick her face. Jack shook her head.

"Nope. I think you need a time out. I want you to lie over here and not get up while I clean this mess up."

Jack got up and pointed to a clean part of the floor. "Come on, lie right here and don't get up until I tell you to."

Jane lay down, but as soon as Jack started to clean, the dog wanted to play. Jack very patiently kept taking her back to the same spot and very sternly telling her to stay. After three times, she did stay and just whined, but she never moved. Jack cleaned the mess and went to get her leash. She stood in the doorway.

"Okay, that's enough. Would you like to go out and do your business now?" Jane jumped up and barked in agreement.

When they had settled in for the night, Jack grabbed her computer and dialed Marcus to Skype. He answered on the second ring.

"Hey, Princess, how are you? Hey, who is that in the background? Or maybe I should ask, *What* is that in the background?"

Jack giggled and told Marcus about Jane and her first temper tantrum. Marcus chortled but sobered quickly.

"Jack, I don't like you taking chances like that. What if that guy had come out and caught you taking his dog?"

Jack, not surprisingly, disagreed. "Marcus, I really can take care of myself, but anyway, it's a moot point because he didn't. What I called you about was when my new doctor requested my medical records she got everything she asked for except this piece of paper with my name and birthdate on it. The problem is everything on the paper is blacked out with a Sharpie. Do you have any idea why that would be?"

Marcus sighed. "I think I know, but I will talk to Dad. I have to be in New York on Friday for a business meeting. Can we have dinner Friday night?"

Jack nodded in agreement "That sounds great. How about we meet at Davey's at seven o'clock?"

The rest of the week flew by as they began recording with a young hip-hop artist Cookie had found named Alley Monroe. She was very good but a little temperamental to work with. Eventually, by midweek, Jack had to let her know who the boss was and if she wanted a label, she needed to work with them and not against them.

By Friday afternoon, they all needed a break. When Alley, the musicians, and the team all left for the afternoon, Jack decided to treat herself to a bath and take some time with her appearance. She relaxed in the tub listening to tracks from the day, making notes to speak with Jamal about tomorrow as Jane lay on the bathroom floor watching Jack. During some of the tracks, Jane would whine as if the pitch hurt her ears. Jack nodded in agreement and made note of those specific tracks to tell Jamal about.

Instead of piling her now long wavy hair in a bun or braid as usual, Jack left it long and flowing. She dug out her makeup and applied it just like the pros had done. She dressed in silky black slacks with a white flowing silk top. She draped a soft pink cashmere wrap around her with the end resting over her left shoulder. She added some diamond hoops that Noah had given her and her black Louboutin heels, and finally she was ready.

She and Jane walked about a block before they caught a cab to the restaurant. She felt good, excited to see her brothers. Marcus, Henry, Garrett, Ty, Bobby, Davey, and Caleb were all going to be there.

When she walked into the restaurant, Davey spied her and Jane and walked over, shaking his head. "No dogs, Princess," he said firmly.

"This is not 'a dog,' Davey; this is Jane. Jane, this is Davey, your uncle."

Davey cemented his stance and crossed his arms. Her other brothers came over and started fussing over Jane. Caleb started sneezing.

"She's not coming to the table," he insisted, sneezing.

Jack glared at him. "Fine. I'll put her out back in Davey's office."

Jack walked her out back to the office and patted the couch. Jane jumped up and lay down, looking sad.

"I'll just be out there having dinner. I want you to be on your best behavior in your uncle's office," Jack warned as she patted and kissed Jane's head and then closed the door to the office.

Jack hugged all her brothers and quickly became self-conscious as they all commented on her radiant appearance. Jack feigned indignation, even though she was secretly gratified by all the compliments, from her brothers of all people!

"I can clean up all right when I want to; trouble is most days I don't want to! Anyway, while we're waiting for dinner I want to go over what I asked Marcus to look into for me. My new doctor, I'm fine by the way, requested my medical records, and she got this with all the other paperwork." Jack held up the paper with the black marks throughout it.

Caleb looked at the paper and smirked. "Well, this is proof that you're an alien and the FBI knows about you," he snickered.

Ty thumped Caleb's head. "There's only one alien at this table, and I assure you it's not Jack," he retorted.

Caleb rubbed his head. "Asshat," he replied, threatening a head shot of his own.

Marcus cleared his throat and handed Jack a copy of the sheet of paper, but without the black marks on it. Jack read it and looked at Marcus.

"Genius savant?" she questioned.

Marcus nodded. "Yes, Daddy suspected when you were little that you were in the same genius category as Teddy, but when they came back with this diagnosis and wanted to test you further, well, he just said no. He said you were sitting on his lap when they were explaining the tests they had already run and the years of testing they wanted to put you through. He simply decided that he wouldn't do that to you or let anyone label you. After Daddy gave me this, I did some research. Geniuses are usually people with a very high intelligence. A savant is someone who has extraordinary mental abilities in a particular area. Do you remember the movie *Rain Man?* Well he was a savant. A person with extraordinary capabilities who functioned like a person with mental illness. A genius savant, such as yourself, has high intellectual capabilities with extraordinary skills but is able to function and reason as a 'normal person.' Your music and linguistic abilities make you a savant," Marcus announced solemnly.

Caleb snorted. "I still say you're an alien," he mocked.

Jack smiled sweetly at him. "Thank you, Marcus, for looking into that for me. I will be sure to give extra leeway to you, Caleb, with your tiny mortal brain and all," she said bursting into laughter with her brothers. Caleb grinned and threw a straw at her.

They had a delightful dinner and caught up on each other's lives. Jack let them know just how close they were to releasing their first CD with Ricky Vance.

Davey snickered. "Has he gotten up the courage to officially ask you on a date? You all know he is sweet on Jack, right?" he said looking at his brothers.

Jack shook her head. "Stop right there, Davey. We have a working relationship, and no he hasn't nor will he ask me out. It's strictly professional," she proclaimed as she scooped up the last of her chocolate mousse, savoring the taste.

Her brothers all guffawed. "Okay. If that's what you want to tell yourself, Princess," Garrett replied.

Jack huffed and jumped up from the table and kissed them all. "That's it for me, I need to get Jane and go home," she announced.

Marcus got up, walked with her to get Jane, and knelt down to pat her. "She's beautiful. Listen, I don't want to go anywhere you're not ready to go, but Daddy, well, he is looking tired." Jack instantly teared up. Marcus stood up and tightly hugged Jack to him.

"No, please don't get upset. That's not why I'm telling you this, Princess, and Daddy is not in any way trying to get you to come home. He's happy just knowing you're safe and that we're looking out for you. Don't get me wrong, he misses you and loves you more than anything, but he understands how hurt you are and that he is the cause. To tell you the truth, I don't think he will ever forgive himself for what he did to you, but for both of your sakes, I hope you can find it in your heart to forgive him some day," he whispered quietly as he kissed her forehead.

Jack smiled and wiped her tears away. "I will, Marcus, I'm just not there yet," she replied, hooking Jane's leash to her collar and walking out into the cold New York night.

(Eight Months Later)

Jack adjusted the fitted jacket of the Worthington Classic Business suit she was wearing to today's business meeting. She was so glad she had snagged several during her time with the clothing empire. The conference room was filled with artists, managers, and attorneys from several top recording labels that were looking to switch to Princess Productions. In the past eight months, every new artist that signed with them had gone to the top of the charts. She and her team had worked night and day to get the most out of each artist, and Jack had overseen all of the music personally. The Grammys were coming up, and several of their artists were up for awards. They had one of the largest tables in the dining room reserved. The seating committee had initially told her that they could have ten seats, but Jack was having none of that. Each and every person on her team along with the artists would be attending the gala, as well as her brothers. Not only had her team worked too hard not to go, but they were music royalty and deserved to go just on those merits alone. In the end, Jack had gotten as many seats as she wanted in one long table that ran the entire length of the dining room.

Jack stood and smoothed out her skirt. "Gentlemen, we have gone back and forth discussing these contracts, and I'm afraid you have our final offers. I suggest you go back to your artists and figure out the best fit for each of you." Jack looked at her watch. "I have an appointment to view a new apartment, so

I must take off. Please do not keep my coworkers here too late. I can assure you that we've had plenty of late nights as it is. Henry, Jamal, I will see you first thing in the morning," she ended as she left the conference room.

She walked to her room to find Jane waiting by the door. Jack grinned. "Ah, I see you haven't forgotten about our showing? What? This isn't palatial enough for you, Miss Queenie?"

Jane barked and danced about, knowing they were going outside. Jack giggled and grabbed her leash.

With the money just in from music sales, Jack just couldn't justify living in her little room any longer. If it was just her, she might consider staying there, but Jane needed more space. She didn't relish living alone in a big apartment, but Noah was always traveling and Mac had a lease agreement to uphold. This would be the third apartment she had checked out. The first two had been huge but so impersonal and clinical that she just couldn't see herself waking up in either one of them every day. This apartment was only two blocks away from the recording studio, which was perfect, and it was newly refurbished from a very grand, old, long-forgotten apartment building.

Jack stood outside looking up at the beautiful brick building with granite steps to the entry. The building didn't look any different than the other old brick buildings, strong and reminiscent of better times in the neighborhood. She and Jane bounded up the thick granite steps and entered into a beautiful grand foyer. Marble floors and huge windows overlooked the street with a small sitting area in the corner that held a purple and tan striped couch and matching stuffed chair. There was an original bellhop desk a short walk from the entry doors. An older gentleman with a burgundy suit with gold rope at the shoulders greeted her as she entered the building. The brunette standing beside him aggressively extended her hand.

"Jack Johnson, aka The American Princess?"

Jack nodded slowly and took her outstretched hand, looking over at the gentleman, who looked sorry for her.

"So nice to meet you! I'm Tiffany, your Realtor, and this fine-looking chap is Richard."

The man extended his hand. "It's actually Rigby. A pleasure to meet you, Miss Johnson."

Jack smiled at his terse correction and shook his hand. "Nice to meet you both. This is Jane Austen but we just call her Jane."

Rigby reached into his pocket for a dog treat. "May I?" he asked Jack.

Wow.

Rigby was a real porter from another time. Jack instantly liked him, and from the way Jane was smiling, she also liked him very much.

"Well, this way, shall we?" Tiffany clearly was through with pleasantries. They walked toward an old-fashioned elevator with black wrought-iron bars that closed. Classy. When they reached the penthouse, the elevator stopped and Tiffany pulled the bars open. There was a small area with marble floors leading up to white and gold ornate double doors. Jack already felt like she had stepped into another era.

"So far this has the air of, I don't know, the silent film days or like Betty Grable is going to open the door?" Jack murmured, touching the gold molding around the door.

Tiffany laughed. "I have no idea who that is, but you have a fine grasp of the era, because this apartment is almost exactly as it was in the 1920s, and if I'm not mistaken, it was owned by a film star," she remarked as she opened the door.

The entryway was more marble with a gold table and tiffany lamp. As you walked toward a great room, there were actual pillars with gold leaves winding around them. There were two marble steps down to what could possibly have been the largest room she had ever seen. The space had huge stuffed sectional couches and chairs, and there was a grand piano facing the oversized windows that covered all three outside walls. Around each window was detailed carved molding, and as Jack's eyes traveled up the molding, her eyes came to the crown molding that framed the most glorious ceiling she had ever seen. The entire ceiling was a replica of Michelangelo's Sistine Chapel. In the middle was the most massive chandelier she had ever seen. Jack gasped. It was the most beautiful scene she had ever laid eyes on.

Tiffany touched her arm. "I know, ghastly, right? We could have it painted over for sure."

Jack physically jerked back as Jane let out a low growl. "What? Um, no, absolutely not! I'll take it," Jack replied tersely, continuing to gaze at the ceiling.

"Oh! So you want to make an offer. Great, but let me show you the rest of the house."

Jack cast a disgusted gaze her way. "No. I will pay whatever they are asking, and I will look around on my own if you don't mind. Oh, and I want everything that is here. Just exactly as it is."

Jack started to walk toward the curved marble staircase. Tiffany mumbled something about calling the owner. The kitchen was open to the great room, with a granite bar facing into the great room. The kitchen looked like something Mac would go crazy for, but to Jack it just basically came with the house.

Jack and Jane climbed the staircase to a lengthy hallway. On one side was the master suite, with a king-sized canopy bed and a large sitting room with a beautiful writing desk. All the furniture was very ornate from the French impressionist era. The bathroom was grander than her entire room at the studio, with a marble tub set before a wall of windows overlooking a small park. A door off the bathroom opened to the most enormous closet ever. There was an actual sitting room in the closet. There were more shelves and racks and drawers than she would ever be able to fill, of that she was certain. There was a real porcelain teapot and cups on a tray sitting on an island in the middle of the room. Of course, Jack thought idly to herself, who doesn't have tea served while you're in your closet?

Jane jumped onto the couch and looked at Jack. "Well, what do you think? You have to live here too."

Jane barked three times. "Well, okay then. It's unanimous. We're homeowners."

Jack walked down the stairs to find Tiffany sitting on one of the barstools in the kitchen. "We still a go?" she asked hopefully.

"Oh yes! Indubitably," Jack replied, nodding her head.

"Oh, there is one more thing on the list that I want to show you," Tiffany announced as she walked around the back of the marble staircase. There was a door that was flush with the wall to make it blend in with the wall. There was a small latch that you would miss if you weren't looking for it. Tiffany pulled the latch and the door opened to a large room with ceiling to floor shelves of old books. There were built-in sliding ladders to get the top shelf books and an old worn leather couch and chair next to the window, with a small round table with more books stacked on it.

Jack threw her hand over her heart and simply stared. She started to tear up as she walked along the wall and gently touched the bindings of the old books.

"I want this sale to take place quickly, and I want every single item in the house," she announced quietly without turning to look at Tiffany. After a few more moments, Jack sighed and led Jane toward the entryway. They got in the elevator still silent. When they got to the ground floor, Jack held out her hand to Tiffany.

"I will call you when I have heard something," Tiffany said.

Jack shook her head. "I will be expecting a call from you tonight as to when I can move in. I am shooting for this Saturday. Make this happen, Tiffany."

Jack turned and walked toward Rigby and smiled. "It looks like you will be seeing a lot more of me," she said.

Rigby smiled. "I knew you were a woman of taste, Miss Johnson," he said as he tossed a dog treat to Jane, who of course caught it midair and smiled in appreciation at Rigby.

On the walk back to the studio, Jack called Henry. "Hey there, Princess, good news for you. Everyone at the table today accepted your offers. They loved your ideas about kick-starting their artists' flagging careers. I will swing by tomorrow before I head back to Portland with the paperwork for you to sign."

Jack let out a sigh of relief. "Oh that's great, Henry! Good work. Listen, I am expecting a call tonight about the apartment. I told them I wanted it. I gave her your number, so after she calls me, can I have her call you and you can make this happen?"

"Of course. It's about time you got out of that back room in the studio. You have more money than you know what to do with, which brings me to something I have wanted to talk to you about. You know that you have a trust fund right? You've had it your whole life and never ever touched it. I'm pretty sure that there is enough in there at this point to buy a small country if you wanted. Is there something you would like me to do with it? Do you ever plan to touch it?"

Jack thought only for a moment. "Actually, no, I don't ever plan on touching it; not because I'm angry or feel self-righteous, but frankly because I think something really good can come of that money. I've been thinking of setting up a scholarship fund for the school that I helped out with a few years ago. If I get you the information, could you look into that for me?"

Henry laughed. "Of course I can," he replied. Jack's phone buzzed indicating a call from Tiffany.

"Okay, the Realtor is calling, she will call you in a minute. Bye and thank you, Henry."

It was a beautiful late spring day as Jack encouraged Jane back toward the studio. "Come on now, your uncles are going to be here soon to move our stuff to the apartment."

Truth be told, Jane had almost as much stuff as Jack, which wasn't much at all. As she rounded the corner, Jack noticed Sam standing in front of the studio talking with her brothers. Marcus, Henry, Garrett, Ty, Bobby, and Caleb were all standing, arms crossed, waiting on her. What a sight that was. It made her think of Bear and say a quick prayer for his safety.

"Good morning! I think I might have overcompensated with my moving crew," Jack exclaimed. "I honestly have very little to move. Where's Davey and Mac?" she asked, hugging them all.

"Davey and Mac are bringing food so they are coming a little later," Garrett replied, walking her inside. Jack pointed to the two large suitcases and big box of toys on the floor.

Caleb smirked and then sneezed. "That's it? That's all your possessions?" Caleb snickered, grabbing the box of Jane dog toys. Ty gave him a push.

"Not everyone's a diva like you, pretty boy," Ty said. They put everything in one of the two Suburbans Marcus had rented, and when Jack climbed in, she noticed they had all brought their guitars.

Sweet, it was going to be a great day.

As they were walking into the lobby of her apartment building, her phone began bubbling with a Skype call. It was Bear. They all stopped in the lobby to answer.

"Bear!" Jack beamed.

"Hi there, Princess—sorry I couldn't be there on your big moving day, but I'm on a mission in some Godforsaken country. I wanted you to know that I'm thinking about you. How's that puppy doing?"

As if on cue Jane barked and Caleb sneezed. They all chuckled...well, all except Caleb.

Bobby stepped closer to the phone. "Hey Bro, this looks like a really great building, and there is a porter here in the lobby who looks like he can handle himself."

Bear perked up and nodded. "Oh really? Let me see him," Bear instructed.

Jack walked over to Rigby with the phone. Rigby smiled. "Hello, Miss Johnson. This is your family, I presume?" he inquired.

"Um, yes, these are some of my brothers, and I have one here on the phone who would like to speak with you," Jack replied, apologetically handing him the phone.

"Hello, sir, my name is Rigby and I'm the porter in your sister's apartment building."

"Nice to meet you Rigby, I'm Mason Johnson. I just want you to know that that little girl, excuse me, that young woman right there is our Princess and the most important female in all our lives, so please keep your eyes and ears open and keep her safe."

Jack teared up and looked away. Rigby nodded. "Rest assured, Mr. Johnson, she will come to no harm on my watch."

Bear nodded. "Roger that, and please call me Bear. Okay, you crazy kids, I've got to go play in the sand. Over and out," as the line went dead.

Jack sighed. She missed him. She made introductions all around, and they headed to the elevator. They had to make two trips because the elevator was not built for so many big men at once.

The guys loved the apartment and found the huge plasma TV hidden by a painting that moved aside with a remote. Jack went to put her clothes away and could hear the guys playing with Jane. They would throw her ball up the stairs and she would run as fast as she could on the marble, skidding as she went. Amazingly, this never got old for her brothers. They would throw the ball and laugh and laugh when she would skid around like a deer on ice returning it. Eventually when Jack came downstairs, she noticed Jane completely zonked out on the couch.

The doorbell rang, and Davey and Mac were standing there with grocery bags filled with prepared food from the restaurant. Luckily, Jack and Mac had gone shopping a few days earlier for kitchen supplies like utensils, plates, cups, and pots and pans. "Hello! Come on in! Welcome!" Jack exclaimed.

Mac showed Davey all around, and then they gathered around the TV and ate while they watched the Celtics. Noah showed up midway through the meal and joined them as well. The afternoon was spent playing music and singing. Jack asked for their input concerning a few songs she was working on for Ricky.

"So you and Ricky will be going to the Grammys together?" Davey asked innocently.

Jack stopped playing the piano and glared at him. "No, as you very well know, we have a table, the biggest one there, and we're ALL going together," Jack motioned to all of them.

Davey wasn't going to let it go that easily. "Well, I listened to an interview he did, and they asked him if he had a date. He answered yes, he was bringing a 'special lady.'"

Jack clapped her hands and looked heavenward. "Oh, good! I'm so happy he has a date."

Davey grinned. "I may be wrong, Princess, but I'm willing to place bets that you're the special lady."

Her brothers all chuckled and agreed with Davey. Jack sprang up from the piano.

"I'm so done with this conversation. I need to take Jane for a walk. Noah, come with?" she implored, grabbing the leash. Noah was dozing with his head leaned back against the overstuffed chair. Jack grabbed his knee like Caleb always did to her as Noah yelped and jumped up. Jack laughed and they headed outside to the little park behind the building.

There wasn't anyone in the park, so Jack let Jane run around without her leash as Jack and Noah sat on the old wooden swings and started pumping their feet. It soon became a competition to see who could get higher. Chuckling as they enjoyed being little kids again, they both started scuffing their sneakers to slow themselves down.

"Are you okay, Noah? I mean really okay?" Jack asked.

Noah sighed. "Yes, lovely, I'm fine. I'm just lonely I guess. The party scene is starting to get old, but it seems like everyone I meet just wants to get wasted and party. Do you think we're just destined to be alone?" he asked, bringing his swing to a stop.

Jack smiled sadly. "That's a very good question, Mr. Cabrera. I think *you* believe that you're unworthy of love, so whenever anyone tries to get close to you, you push them away. A self-sabotage, if you will."

Noah nodded. "Okay, Sigmund, I don't disagree with that; now tell me why *you're* alone," he commanded, coming to stand in front of her and grasp the chains of the swing.

Jack stood up and cupped his face. "But I'm not alone. I have Jane, you, and my brothers," she replied as she kissed his cheek and clapped for Jane. Jack hooked the leash to Jane's collar and started to walk back to the apartment.

"You're avoiding the question," Noah hollered behind her.

"Am not! Are you coming?" she said turning to look at him.

Noah shook his head. "No, I have to go pack. I'm going to the West Coast tomorrow." He caught up to her and put his arm around her shoulders to walk with her back to the street. "And I can't come to the Grammys next weekend;

I'll be just flying in that afternoon," he said, kissing her forehead. "You'll kill it, and I'll come over the day after for mimosas. Ciao, lovely."

"Bye," she muttered, waving to him as he walked away from her.

Jack sat at the bar nursing her coffee as Phillip went on and on about her dress and shoes and jewelry. Jack finally had had enough and interrupted him.

"Phillip, you know you don't have to do this anymore, right?"

Phillip feigned horror. "What? Mon amie, Mr. Worthington has been working on this piece for quite some time. All eyes will be on you tonight, mon petit chou, and you will shine brighter than all the rest," he replied, hugging her shoulders from behind.

Jack grinned. "Okay, okay, I'm in your hands today. What's the plan?" she asked as Jane bounded into the apartment with Dirk right behind her, hanging up her leash.

Dirk kissed Jack's cheek, reached for a cup to pour himself a coffee, and rolled his eyes. "I will be glad when this night is over, ma cherie. I have heard nothing but talk of this dress for two months! I think I will wear the damn dress and be done with it!" he mock-scowled, making Jack laugh.

"Oh, you wish you had legs like mademoiselle," retorted Phillip with a smirk.

Dirk got up and hugged Phillip. "Oh, I know what *your* legs and sweet ass look like, lover boy."

Jack covered her ears. "I'm in the room!" she yelled. Phillip yelped as Dirk pinched his derriere.

"True, true, now you," he said pointing to Dirk. "I need for you to pick up our tuxedos for tonight and then go to work. I will see you at the brownstone at about four o'clock. The limo will pick us up on the way to the theater."

Jack sprang up and grabbed the leash. "Dirk, can you please take Jane to work with you today? I know she will be good with you there. You will just have to take her out every once in a while. Please?" she pleaded, holding out the leash.

"But of course, mon ami." Dirk took the leash and called Jane. The dog came bursting into the kitchen and then stood stock-still, letting Dirk put the leash on her, ready for the adventure.

Phillip looked at Jack. "You are coming with me to the spa, mademoiselle; I'm certain you need some services," he commanded as Jack moaned. This was going to be painful for sure.

Jack wasn't disappointed with the nice side braid and makeup done along with a completely hairless body. When Phillip finally dropped her off at the apartment, she was greeted by Jane.

"I hope you had a lovely time at the tattoo parlor today, sweetie," Jack cooed to the dog as she made herself a cup of tea and sat down at the piano. Time seemed to get away from her, because before she knew it, there was a key in the door and her brothers except for Bear came swaggering in with their tuxedos. Jack jumped up and ran into Teddy's arms. He caught her and twirled her around.

"Oh my God, it's good to see you, Teddy!" Jack gushed.

Teddy laughed. "Wow you're a sight for sore eyes yourself," he replied looking at her.

"Kind of casual, aren't you?" Caleb quipped.

Jack looked confused. "What time is it?" she asked.

"Five thirty," Henry answered impatiently. And just as she was about to panic, the door opened and Davey and Mac walked in. Jack grabbed Mac's hand and dragged her toward the stairs.

"Don't tell me you're not even dressed yet, Jack! The limo is going to be here in thirty minutes!" Mac exclaimed. Her brothers all hooted and whistled at Mac. Davey punched them.

"I'm sorry! Time just got away from me at the piano," Jack whispered to Mac as they entered her suite. There hanging in her closet was the most breathtaking dress Jack had ever seen. It was an off black with tiny netting that had velvet burgundy flowers and velvet green leaves burnt out all over it. Where there were no flowers and leaves, you could see skin through the black netting.

Jack looked at Mac. "Do you think it will cover all my important bits?" Jack asked, and they burst out laughing.

Jack wasted no time throwing off her sweatpants and T-shirt. Standing naked, she wiggled into the dress. Everything was very strategically covered, but what stood out for Jack was her tattoo, which had no flowers covering it. Jack slid into the deep green velvet stilettos. Next came the diamond drop earrings, and she was done.

Jack stood before Mac. "I can't believe I can't wear underwear with this, but I'm surprisingly comfortable," Jack giggled. "But tell me honestly, is everything covered properly?"

Mac ever so slowly walked around Jack, looking her up and down. "I can't believe it, but yes, you're completely covered and so friggin' gorgeous. I'd do ya!" she whispered as they burst out laughing.

Jack grasped her hands and started to feel herself tear up. "Mac, you're the beautiful one. I'm so glad you and Davey are together. My heart is just bursting!" Jack cried out as she took in Mac wearing the white gown she had borrowed from Jack.

"Careful, no crying on that dress. Come on, let's go downstairs—the limo is probably here!"

As they walked down the stairs, Jack watched Davey look at the woman he loved and felt a pang of envy. She shook her head to clear it and saw all her other brothers shaking their heads.

"Jesus, no," Teddy muttered, taking a pull off his beer.

"Where's friggin' Bear when you need him?" Marcus said dryly.

Jack smirked. "Oh, I think you guys can handle anything that comes up—oh wait, poor choice of words—anything that happens tonight," she replied smugly.

"Fuckin'-A-Skippy," Bobby said as he gave Ty a fist pump.

Walking the red carpet was so much more fun when you did it with your best friend, brothers, team, and nominated artists. Jack thought the paparazzi seemed to want an unusual number of photos of her and Ricky, but she considered this his night, so she went along. When they were ushered to their table, Ricky made a point of sitting right beside her. Davey waggled his eyes at her when she made eye contact with him. She stuck out her tongue and glared at her brother.

Enough!

Finally when all the pomp and circumstance was done, the show got underway. Jack was so excited for her team. They had worked so hard! The record sales were off the charts, and if they won any awards to boot, well, they could just about write their own ticket in this business.

When they finally got to Ricky's category, he grabbed her hand and held it. *Okay...?* The flash from the photographers' cameras was blinding. When George Strait announced that Ricky had won Artist of the Year, he stood and pulled her up with him and kissed her full on the lips. Jack was too stunned to react. He cupped her face and kissed her again before he headed to the stage.

Jack sat down and touched her lips and then glanced over at Davey. Davey must not have liked what he saw in her eyes, because he was out of his seat like a bullet and grabbed Jack's hand and led her out to the hallway away from the crowd.

"Are you okay, Princess?"

Jack shook her head. "Oh, Davey, you were right. I think he's sweet on me."

Davey hugged her and chuckled. "Oh, Princess, he won't get any closer to you than you want him to. Let's go back to see what he has to say," he whispered to her as he pulled her back into the theater.

They walked in just in time to hear Ricky ending his acceptance speech with "and Jack Johnson, that's the sexiest damn dress I've ever seen!" The crowd went wild as he left the podium.

"Jesus," Jack whispered as the photographers fought with each other trying to take her picture.

When the show was almost done, Jack decided to bow out and go home. It was cowardly for sure, but she didn't want to deal with the after-parties or the photographers after the show. She whispered to Mac that she was leaving and to let her brothers know as she marched out of the ceremony into the warm evening. The valet asked her which limo, but she simply asked him to get her a cab. He whistled and a cab drove up. Jack sighed, tipped the valet, and jumped in. God, she hated this part of the business. When she finally walked through her door, Jane danced all around her. She grabbed her leash and brought her to the park to do her business.

An hour later, dressed in her silk robe, Jack sat down at her piano. She texted her brothers and team letting them know she was all tucked into bed, safe and sound. Mac texted her back telling her she would be at her apartment for breakfast and she had juicy news to report. Jack groaned and lost herself to her music before she headed to bed for a restless, dream-filled night.

Jared heard a commotion out in the lobby of his office as his door suddenly burst open. Bobby and Ty both came around his desk and flanked his sides.

Holy hell.

Tim, his assistant, came and stood in the doorway as Jared waved him off. "It's okay, Tim," Jared assured him as Tim stalked out muttering something about brutes under his breath.

Jared sat back in his chair and looked from Bobby to Ty. "What?"

Bobby leaned forward and punched some keys. "Oh, by all means be my guest," Jared said, derisively gesturing toward the computer. "Clearly, I wasn't working on anything of any importance," he continued sarcastically.

Jared touched his fingertips together and brought them to his lips to wait on the twins. Bobby brought up the Grammy awards tabloid site that showed Ricky Vance winning and then lifting Jack up and kissing her. Next, Ricky was taking the stage to perform. Ricky announced that this song went out to his "lady," and he proceeded to play an old song from Keith Whitley singing about not wanting his lover to close her eyes while they made love and that he knew she was still in love with someone else.

When the song ended, Jared's fists were clenched tighter than a closed wrench.

"So?" he muttered.

Bobby thumped Jared on the back of the head. "So? What the fuck, Jared? He dedicated this song to Jack, his 'lady.'"

Jared lost all patience and saw red. He picked up the computer and threw it against the wall, shattering it. He sunk down onto his desk, breathing heavily. Bobby and Ty turned around and leaned on the desk with their arms crossed.

"I told you that would happen," Bobby said in a smug tone of voice.

"Yup, you were right. I owe you a hundred," Ty sighed, nodding his head in resignation of a bet lost.

Bobby made an impatient grunting sound and then decide to let loose. "Jesus, Jared, listen, will ya? We didn't come here to fuck with your head. Ricky Vance was singing about his girl still loving another man. Who the hell do you think the other man is? It doesn't take a rocket scientist to figure out it's *you*. Jack has always been and still is in love with you. So stop being such a fucking girl and fight for her, man! Jesus!"

Jared sat down with a thud, looking from Bobby to Ty. Ty patted his shoulder.

"For real, man!" Ty shouted out, fist-bumping Bobby. Together they walked to the door. Bobby looked back.

"You're fucking welcome, bro." Bobby ended the one-way conversation as he slammed the door.

Jared leaned his head back against the chair and closed his eyes. Jesus, he couldn't breathe, he loved her so much. A small spark of hope that he hadn't felt for a very long time ignited somewhere inside him.

Somewhere from far away, Jack could hear ringing. Her brain slowly began firing as she opened one eye to view the clock.

Six o'clock in the damn morning. She had just taken a sleeping pill at one in the morning because she was so restless from the crowds and tension at the awards show.

And that kiss, that stupid, stupid kiss!

She was going to have to sit down and tell him that although he was a sweet guy, there was not a chance in hell that they were ever going to be more than music collaborators. Jack picked up the phone.

Shit, ten missed calls.

Jack sat on the edge of the bed and dialed her voice mail.

The only thing that registered was Caleb telling her that her father was dead.

Jane was whining and licking her face as her phone rang in her hand. Jack was in a fetal position on the floor. It all felt so surreal. She felt her skin tingling. She got up and walked to the windows overlooking the park. The sun was streaming in.

She shivered.

"I'm here," she whispered into the phone.

"Jesus Christ, Jack, do you know how many times I've called you?" Caleb hollered.

"Eleven," she said absently. Emotionless. "How did he die?" she asked.

"He had a fucking heart attack last night in his study. Marcus found him." Silence.

"It's time to come home, Jack," Caleb stated in an uncharacteristically firm tone. Jack sat down on the couch and patted Jane's head. She sighed.

"I'll text you my arrival time," she muttered and then stood up and threw her cell phone into the gilded mirror above her bed, splintering the mirror and her cell phone into an uncountable number of pieces.

As Jack sank to the floor and pulled her knees close to her chest, she knew she wasn't going to be able to cope with all the details that needed to be addressed, and the way her head and body were tingling, she didn't want anybody but Noah to see her right now. She would have called Sam, but something told her that he would take one look at her and lock her back in his room. She reached for the decorative landline phone on the table beside her. She dialed Noah's number.

"This better be really, really important," Noah answered, slurring his words slightly. Just hearing his voice made Jack crumble a little.

"I'm going home. My father's dead. I need you," she murmured brokenly.

"Aw, fuck, I'll be right there, lovely."

Click.

Jack wasn't sure how much time passed, but it seemed she began to breathe again when she felt Noah's arms envelop her.

"I'll take care of everything, lovely. Phillip is getting the Worthington jet ready. I will pack you some clothes and get you some breakfast and coffee. You go get in the shower and I'll see you downstairs."

Jack shook her head. "No breakfast, just coffee, and I'm going to need a new cell phone before I go," she said pointing to the mirror.

Noah cringed. "Was it Caleb that called?" he asked. Jack pulled away and walked toward the bathroom. "Yup," she replied as tears streamed down her face.

Jack leaned back in the recliner and patted Jane, who was lying in her lap as Jack gazed out at the city of Portland into which they were descending. It seemed like a lifetime ago that she had been here. That sweet, optimistic girl was long gone, and the broken mess that took her place was dreading the walk down Memory Lane like nothing she had dreaded before.

Jack looked down at her simple khaki shorts and white T-shirt with flip-flops. It had been all she was able to manage. Noah had packed her suitcase, so she had no idea what she had. It could range from jeans and chucks to haute couture. As she had gotten into the limo, Noah had slid on her sunglasses and tied a cashmere scarf around her neck, muttering about it might be cool on the jet.

Jack pulled out her new cell phone and texted Caleb that she would be landing in fifteen minutes. While she could, she texted Jamal and simply told him that her father had passed and accordingly she would be unavailable for a little while. He could handle anything that came up, and she asked him to let the rest of the team know.

By the time she and Jane had made their way down the stairs of the jet, Caleb had pulled up in the Suburban and grabbed her suitcase and thrown it in the back. He gave her a quick hug as she climbed in.

They rode in silence for a time getting out of the city before he spoke.

That was when all hell began to break loose.

"Why didn't you come home to see him, Jack?" Caleb asked quietly.

Jack sucked in air. This was it. Out of all her brothers, she had always felt Caleb had held things back from her—like there were things that just needed to be said, but he'd held back.

Until today.

"Stop, Caleb. You don't know shit, so just shut the fuck up," Jack muttered almost to herself.

"No, I will not shut up. You're right, I don't know shit, because you don't talk to anybody and nobody can say anything to you because you may fly away again. Well fuck that, Princess, you owe us some answers. You owed Daddy some answers! Do you know what I think he died of? I think he died of a fucking broken heart, that's what I think!" Caleb shouted back at her.

Jack screamed. "Stop the truck. Stop. Now!" Jack grabbed the wheel and pulled the truck toward the side of the road. Caleb tried to get her hand off the wheel.

"Fuck—okay! Okay! Just hold on!" he grimaced as he pulled off onto the dirt shoulder. They were a few miles away from their house on the outskirts of town. There were no houses around, and there was nothing but grassy field on both sides of the road.

Jack jumped out of the truck and started pacing in the grass. Caleb jumped out as well and stood before her with his hand on his hips. Jack could hear Jane barking inside the truck.

"You don't know anything, Caleb!" Jack screamed and pointed at him.

"So tell me! What was so bad that you couldn't call us when you ran away? We didn't know if you were dead or alive! You didn't give a shit about us!" Caleb hollered, pointing right back at her.

336

Jack's chest was heaving. She was having a real time of it just to breathe. She just couldn't stand another second of this. All the rage that had been free-floating inside of her came flying out like a sudden gust of wind. She flew at Caleb, knocking him off his feet. He grabbed her and they rolled around, with him trying to pin her and calm her down.

Jack saw red when he tried to pin her down, and she punched him in the throat, stunning him as he fell back. Jack jumped up and turned to face him. He coughed and wheezed, but now something in him snapped as well. He turned to face her and when she charged him again he was ready for her.

Caleb picked her up and body-slammed her WWE-style to the ground, knocking the wind from her lungs. Jack's fist made contact with his lip, splitting it wide open as she rolled away and stood up. Caleb was still on his knees trying to stop the blood flow from his lip when she roundhouse kicked him square in the nose, completely breaking it with a nauseating crack.

Caleb flew back and landed on his back. He didn't move. Not even an inch.

Heaving, Jack tried to catch her breath. "Caleb?"

Oh. My. God. Had she killed him?

She ran to him and knelt down. Caleb groaned.

"Where the fuck did you learn to fight like that?" he finally mumbled, the words just barely intelligible, what with the blood and all.

Jack laughed nervously. At least she hadn't killed him, and he seemed to be the same ass as before the whupping had begun. The laughter grew, rolling over her. She couldn't stop; the more she tried the more it grew.

The dam had finally broken.

Jack took her cashmere scarf off and held it to his face. "Jesus, Caleb, I'm so sorry," she whispered, still laughing. "Do you have any idea how much I've missed you? I'm so sorry that I didn't call you. I just couldn't. I'm a broken, hot mess, Caleb. I've seen and done things that I never want you to know about. I didn't think you would love me anymore, and that is something that I simply couldn't come back from," she wailed as the laughter turned into sobs.

Caleb sat up and hugged her tight. "Oh, Princess, don't you know that there isn't anything that could ever stop us from loving you? It almost killed me worrying about you. There is nothing in this world that can ever separate us again. Do you hear that? Nothing! I won't let it," he replied, sobbing himself. The pain washed away with their bitter tears as the two youngest Johnson siblings forged a new bond born of respect and acceptance of the adults they had become.

Caleb groaned. "I think I need to go to the hospital, Princess; I think you busted my fucking nose."

It sure looks that way, Jack thought dully as she helped him into the truck and drove him to the hospital.

Marcus was leaning on the bar drinking a cup of coffee with Bear, Henry, Teddy, Garrett, and Davey. "What time was Jack getting in? Did Caleb say?" he asked as everyone shook their heads.

Just then Bobby and Ty walked in the kitchen. "Where's Caleb? We decided that we're going to pick Princess up at the airport. Any news when she's getting in?" Bobby asked.

Marcus shook his head. "No, but Caleb's not here and the Suburban is gone." They all looked at each other.

"No, don't tell me Caleb went to pick her up alone?" Marcus said shaking his head.

"He will push every one of her buttons," Henry moaned, standing up and reaching for his cell phone to call her.

Bear stood up. "If that little shit makes her cry..." he warned ominously.

"Um, that would be a problem. A very big problem," Bobby agreed, bracing his arms against the bar and looking at them all. "I met her friend Sam the day we helped her move, and he said we shouldn't worry about Jack because she could take care of herself. He said he was a Krav Maga instructor and he had been working with Jack for about a year. He said she could beat the shit out of most men he knew."

"Jesus," Teddy muttered as Marcus's cell phone suddenly buzzed. He picked it up.

"Jack," he announced, relieved. "She must be arriving at the airport. Hi, Princess, are you just touching down?" he asked. "Oh, Jesus, are you in the emergency room?" Marcus exclaimed as they all jumped up and started running for the other Suburban.

The ride home was quiet. Caleb's nose was taped up and both his eyes were starting to turn black. He had a fat lip. Bear sat in the front but kept turning around to look at Jack, who had the beginning of a black eye that Caleb's elbow was responsible for when he was trying to subdue her. She had also suffered a fat lip but thought that she probably had bitten down on her lip herself when she had kicked Caleb in the face. Bear glared at Caleb for the injuries he had inflicted on Jack, but the glare soon turned into a smirk as he took in Caleb's injuries.

When they got home, Jane started charging around the house like a crazy dog. She had never had such openness to run around in. Jack laughed and let her run. Bear hugged Jack and told her he would bring her suitcase to her room. Marcus pulled up in the other Suburban and got out.

"I think everyone should just take a break, and we will all meet at six o'clock for dinner and talk about what's what. Okay?" They all nodded.

Caleb put his arm around Jack, and they walked in the house together with Jane barking at their heels. The other brothers watched and shook their heads, knowing full well that whatever had been up Caleb's ass the past year was good and truly gone for good now. Two dams had burst.

Jack walked through the house touching photos and just staring into the rooms. It was as if time had stood still. Everything was exactly as it had been that day four years ago when they left for Moose Pond for the summer. There were a few new pictures of graduations and sports events that Jack had not seen. When she and Jane finally made it to her room, Jack simply stood in the doorway. She felt like a stranger visiting a young girl for the first time. The pink canopy bed with heart pillows and the lamp with the psychedelic scarf draped over it for dramatic lighting. The white shag throw rug that tickled her feet. Jack eyed the cluttered desk in the corner, but she wasn't up to going through those old memories just yet. Jack lay down on the bed and patted the mattress. Jane jumped up and curled into her. Jack sighed and let herself drift off to sleep.

When Jack woke, she was a bit disoriented, and waking up in her old room didn't help. Jane sensed her unease and whined. Jack smiled and kissed her. As she stood up she saw her reflection in her full-length mirror. She gasped: What a sight! Her shorts and shirt were covered in Caleb's blood and her face appeared as beat up as she felt. She immediately walked into her bathroom and turned on the shower.

After thoroughly enjoying the long, cool shower, she went to her closet and found a pair of cutoff jean shorts and a pretty flowered top. She combed out her long hair and just left it to dry naturally. The sun was going down and it was time to meet with her brothers. *Let's just get this done.*

When she and Jane entered the living room, her brothers were there, as well as a man she had never met. Jack sat down cross-legged on the sofa next to Bear.

"Okay, I think we're ready to begin. We're all here. For those of you who may not know, this is James Nash, Daddy's most trusted friend and attorney. Jim, go ahead."

Mr. Nash cleared his throat. "Well, first let me say I'm very sorry for the loss of your father. He was a great man and a greater friend. Your father was clear that he didn't want any visiting hours. He actually didn't even want a funeral, but he knew that you kids would need to be together and have closure, so there has been a funeral all arranged for tomorrow morning. It will be open to the public, and it is expected to be attended by a great many people, many that you have never met. He helped a lot of people and did a lot of good with his money. He was a very well-respected man. Now, about the money. You all have trust funds that will continue to be funded for you to use for whatever you choose. You can set up trust funds for your own children if you like when that time comes. Before his passing, your father set up accounts for each of you to deposit what was in his bank account and his life insurance proceeds. These are separate accounts. The company is willed to all of you.

You are now all owners of the company and will have a quarterly stream of revenue deposited into your new accounts. Marcus will be CEO of the company, and Henry will still be the company attorney. Caleb will still be chief sales officer. You will continue to draw your same pay. Any of you may work for the business at any time you wish. All you have to do is make your wishes known to me or Marcus.

"You were all wealthy before your father's passing, with your trust funds but now, well, now you're extremely wealthy. If any of you have any questions about any of this, please don't hesitate to contact me.

"Now on to some things that are not so cut and dried. Your father was aware that there had been some heartache in the family, for which he took full responsibility. It was extremely important to him to try to make this right with his children. As far as the properties go, this house here in Portland and the property in Harmony belong to all of you equally, with one exception. There is a cabin down by the water at Moose Pond that your father deeded specifically to a young man named Jared Ross for his particular use. Mr. Ross doesn't know that yet. I will be meeting with him before the funeral tomorrow to give him the deed. This is not negotiable by you or him. It is a done deal."

Jack looked at Marcus, who nodded. Jack closed her eyes as Mr. Nash continued.

"There is just one more thing that is also not negotiable, I'm afraid. After the funeral tomorrow, you will all go to Harmony for the next three weeks. You *all* must go, and for the next three weeks you must live together and help each other come to terms with your father's passing."

When everyone started to protest about work and obligations, Mr. Nash held out his hand. "Like I said, this is not negotiable. Teams of lawyers have taken care of everything. All you must do is make the calls to your people to say you are off the grid for the next three weeks and obligate yourselves to the healing process," Mr. Nash explained as he specifically looked from Caleb to Jack. Mr. Nash closed his briefcase and stood.

"Um, Mr. Nash, I have a question," Jack said quietly.

Mr. Nash sat back down. "Of course, Miss Johnson," he replied and waited.

Jack's eyes teared up. "What about Bebe? Did my father stay in touch with her? Is she in Harmony?"

Mr. Nash clasped his hands together and smiled. "Bebe was extremely angry at your father when he sent you away. Extremely angry. She stayed for a while but felt useless here. All her kids had grown up, and she felt her work here was done. She packed her things and went back to France, to the very same convent where she had met your mother. Your father tried to compensate her for her years of service, but she refused. There is an account in her name with a very large amount of money in it that she has never touched. I have heard that she is in poor health but was very happy when your father told her that you were okay and in contact with your brothers. That gave her great comfort," he ended, and then he stood and walked toward the door.

Jack closed her eyes. "We need to go see her. All of us," she whispered. Bear scooped her up and kissed the top of her head.

"We will, Princess," Marcus said quietly. Jack covered her face with her hands and cried. The doorbell sounded and Ty answered it and came back with six extralarge pizzas. They ate in the living room while they watched the Red Sox. It was as if the last four years had never happened. It was so good for Jack's soul. Now she just had to get through the funeral and seeing Jared tomorrow.

The pizza suddenly stuck in her throat.

Jack opened her suitcase after her shower in the morning to see what Noah had packed for her to wear to the funeral. She wasn't disappointed. There on top was a Worthington dress bag. Jack unzipped the bag to find a black velvet dress with a V-neck and short black lace sleeves with black beads.

So simple, yet so elegant.

She found a small pouch with a diamond necklace and her diamond-covered hoop earrings. The pouch was stuffed into her black Louboutins.

She dressed and let her hair air dry into soft waves around her face and shoulders. She applied a minimal amount of makeup. Unfortunately, no amount of makeup could cover the black eye and fat lip. She could just imagine what the paparazzi would say about that if any were there. She popped her sunglasses on and headed downstairs.

Everyone was there eating breakfast. Jack sat down, and Davey kissed her temple.

"Mac says hello. She's running the restaurant, but she'll see you in Harmony, okay, Princess?" Davey announced.

Jack nodded. Teddy put a cup of coffee and a frosted Pop-Tart in front of her. Jack slid her sunglasses on top of her head and grinned slightly. "Thank you," she said.

"Whoa!" Bobby exclaimed, lightly touching the side of her face. "I'd hate to see the other guy!" They all laughed but Caleb.

"Fucking bite me!" Caleb snarled, nursing his coffee, careful not to touch his sore lip.

After breakfast, Jack put Jane in her room telling her to behave herself, and then they were off to the church. As soon as they arrived, Jack saw all the paparazzi and sighed. Marcus looked at her in the rearview mirror, sensing her unease.

"They can't get in, and we will shield you on the way into the church."

"They won't get close to you, I promise," Caleb snorted from the back.

"I think she can handle herself, Caleb," Marcus remarked dryly, which sparked a few chuckles.

With her head down and curved into Bear's and Marcus's arms, Jack made her way into the church. Inside they slowly walked to the front and sat down. The service began almost as soon as they sat down. It was a lovely, short service; this was what her father must have wanted, Jack thought to herself.

As people were leaving, Jack spotted Gracie walking toward her. Jack ran to her, a sob escaping. They hugged tightly, and when Gracie pulled back she took Jack's sunglasses off and beamed.

"Oh, darling, you look more like your momma every day, even with the shiner!"

Jack smiled and sniffed. "It's good to see you, Gracie. We're all coming to the pond later for a few weeks," Jack said.

Gracie nodded and smiled. "Yes, I've heard. I can't wait. I'll see you later, sugar," she said, kissing Jack on the cheek.

As Gracie stepped away, Jack saw Jared standing beside Gracie. Jack caught her breath as their eyes locked. It seemed as if the world had stopped spinning and time had stopped dead. Jared's eyes zeroed in immediately on Jack's black eye and fat lip, and he stepped forward with eyes narrowed.

Bobby was beside him instantly. "Easy now. Just a little scuffle between Jack and Caleb," Bobby explained, touching Jared's arm.

Jared's angry eyes searched for Caleb. When he did finally see him, Jared's eyes softened and he smirked and looked back at Jack. Seeing the pain in her eyes, his guts twisted. "I'm sorry about your father, Jack," he whispered, holding out his hand to touch hers.

Jack stepped back and looked away. "Thank you. We need to be leaving," she replied abruptly, pulling her sunglasses back on and sinking into Bear's waiting arms as she let him guide her to the truck.

Breathe. Breathe. Breathe.

They got back to the house and collected Jane and their luggage, and then they were off to Moose Pond. The drive was long and silent. When they arrived at the pond, they discovered that Gracie had opened everything up and aired it out. She had gone grocery shopping and stocked the cupboards and fridge. She had made a huge lasagna and garlic bread for them to eat that night.

Jack entered the time capsule that was her bedroom and just stood there. She walked to the wrought iron bed and touched the homemade quilt that her mother had made before she was born. She didn't realize she had missed this quilt so much. She walked around and looked at all the pictures and notes that she and Mac had hung. Her eyes traveled to the window that she had sat in front of, it seemed decades before, so certain that Jared was coming to save her.

Her heart hardened a little bit.

Marcus knocked on Jack's door. "Doing okay, Princess?" he asked. Jack nodded.

"Good. Can you come out here for a minute?" he asked, holding out his hand. She grabbed his hand and walked to the porch with him. Her brothers were all sitting around as she took her seat at the piano. Jane lay down by her feet.

Marcus cleared his throat. "Um, Princess, there is one more thing, and if you don't think you're ready, that's fine, but Daddy made a CD for you. He knew you weren't ready to talk to him, and that was okay, but it was important to him to say some things to you, and well, I think he might have thought he was running out of time to say them. You don't have to watch it, but I think it will help you get through this if you just hear him out, so to speak," Marcus explained, shrugging his shoulders.

Jack looked around. "Did he make one for all of you?" she asked softly.

They all shook their heads. "No, Princess, Daddy just wanted you to know some things that didn't have anything to do with us boys," Bear replied quietly.

"I'm scared," Jack said honestly.

"Oh, sweetheart, don't be scared. Daddy was a strong, quiet man, but trust us when we say he made sure we knew how much he loved us and that we were to take care of you or he would kick our asses even from the grave," Garrett replied, staring directly at Caleb, who gulped nervously.

Jack nodded. "Okay, I'll watch. Where is it?" she asked.

Marcus stood up and walked with her to her father's study. Jack sat down on the couch facing the TV on the wall. Marcus handed her the remote control and told her to just hit play when she was ready. Jane made herself comfortable on the couch beside her.

"Marcus, did Daddy give this to you?"

Marcus shook his head. "Mr. Nash gave it to me last night and told me it was for your eyes only. I just popped it in a few minutes ago. No one, to my knowledge, has seen it. If you need us, we will be on the porch," he said, closing the door behind him.

Jack took a deep breath and hit play. David's sad face came into view. Jack gasped. He was sitting in this very room behind his desk, where he had spent so many hours. He smiled and held up a picture of her in his arms as a baby about two years old. They were down at the beach and the sun was shining and her hair was wild and curly. Someone had snapped the picture without either of them noticing. She was looking into her father's eyes and her little hands were on both sides of his face. He was smiling at her. She was looking so intently into his eyes with such love and awe.

David looked at the picture and cleared his throat. "Hi, Princess. If you're watching this, then that means that I'm gone, but don't be sad, sweetheart. I'm certainly not. In fact I've waited for this for a very, very long time. Princess, you and your brothers know that I love you all with every breath in me, but I've missed your momma so much. I'm really not me without her. There hasn't been a day go by since she left me that I haven't wished for her back or for me to join her. That's a lot of days, sweetheart.

"This is my favorite picture of us. I think Gracie took it. The love in your eyes, well, it gets me through some bad days, I've got to tell you. Your momma wanted you so badly. I think she knew you were a little girl, and that's why she promised Caleb he could name you just to shut him up," he said laughing a bit almost to himself.

"The day you were born was the hardest day of my life. Your momma, well, she was bigger than life. There wasn't a man alive that didn't fall in love with her after meeting her. All children flocked around her just sensing her love for them. I see her every time I look at you. As you became a teenager, I saw it more and more. Some days I felt like I'd been kicked in the gut when you would make some grand pronouncement about what you wanted to do with your life. Something your momma would have enjoyed for sure," he said quietly. "At other times, I see it when you're making music. You get completely lost in your music, and so did she. She would have been so proud of you Princess. And so am I.

"I want to tell you a secret that only your momma knows," her father continued. "You're not the first in the family with the nickname Princess. Nope, that's what I called your momma. She was my first Princess before you. Elsie Johnson was the only woman I ever loved, and she was truly my Princess. I don't know what she ever saw in me; she could've had any boy she wanted, but she chose me, and I will forever be grateful for that. Well, just like I knew the moment I laid eyes on my Elsie that she was mine, I think that you and Jared feel the same about each other. I was wrong, sweetheart, to send you away. What I did to you is unforgivable. I won't forgive myself, and I sure as hell don't expect you to ever forgive me. I never stopped looking for you, Princess, and until my last breath, I will pray for your happiness. I just want you to know that I am so very proud of you. You have grown into a beautiful, loving young lady. There is not one thing that could make me any more or less proud of the woman you have become. I know much more than you think I do. I know about the children you've helped and your backpack program," he said gently as he shook his head.

"Those damn backpacks—you and your momma are saving the world one friggin' backpack at a time! You're a good girl, Jack Elise Johnson, and I love you. Your Momma and I want you to be happy. Oh, and before I go, sweetheart, I just want to tell you to take it easy on Caleb; he took my sending you away really hard. Harder than the rest. He was so angry at me, and I'm not sure he's forgiven me even now. He loves you with a special love that doesn't come around much in this life. I love you, Princess."

With that the screen went dark. Jack fell forward on the couch and sobbed into the pillow, with Jane whimpering and licking at her face.

"*See, I told you, it's all your fault. You killed your mother, and now you've killed your father. How many people have to die or be hurt because of their relationships with you? You should just do everyone a favor and kill yourself,*" Dark Twin whispered.

Jack closed her eyes up tight and covered her ears with her hands. "No, no, no, that's not true, please stop. Please!" she moaned, shaking her head back and forth. The relentless whispering went on and on. From far away, Jack heard another voice, one very familiar but she couldn't quite place it.

A shout made Jack jerk. "JACK! PRINCESS, COME BACK TO ME. NOW!"

It was Bear hollering as only Bear could holler. Jack jerked her eyes open before her Dark Twin could start whispering to her again. She could feel the all-to-familiar tingling, and she knew she was too close to the edge.

"Bear," Jack whispered urgently. Bear was kneeling beside the couch holding her face. All her other brothers were gathered around looking terrified.

Jack knew she only had a few minutes before she wouldn't remember anything. She looked at Bear with terrified eyes.

"Bear, I need you to call Sam. I need Sam. In my phone. Please. Please," she whispered before closing her eyes to try to block out her Dark Twin.

Bear gripped Jack's head tighter as if to keep the connection. Tears were streaming down his face. "No, no, Princess, come back to me. Please," he begged. Jane was going crazy trying to get to Jack.

"Get that damn dog out of here and find her phone! Phone! We need to call Sam!" Bear commanded. Caleb ran into the room with Jack's phone and found Sam's number and dialed, then handed the phone to Marcus's outstretched hand.

"Hi, little one."

"Sam, it's Marcus, Jack's brother."

"What's wrong?"

"I don't fucking know. She watched a video our father made for her. Bear came in to check on her and she is like in a trance. She's crying and screaming incoherently, but she came out of it long enough to tell us to call you. What's going on? Should we call the ambulance? Fuck!"

"No, hold on, you're doing good, son. Listen carefully to me. First thing is go get her suitcase." Marcus ran out of the study to her room.

"Okay, I have her suitcase."

"Okay, now open it up and in the zippered top there should be a ziplock bag with a pill bottle. Open the pill bottle and get out two pills and give them to her right now. Do it now!"

Marcus ran into the study with the pills and saw that Bear was doing all he could do to hold Jack down. "I need to give her these pills now!" he shouted, turning to Bobby.

Bobby grabbed the pill bottle and read it. "Jesus! What does she have these for? These should do something to help her for sure," he exclaimed. He stepped forward, opened Jack's mouth, and pushed two pills down her throat while massaging her neck to get her to swallow.

"Okay, let's get her to her bed so we can hold her down until she goes to sleep," Bear instructed as he picked her up and looked at Marcus. "I want to talk to him. Keep him on the line," he ordered, walking to Jack's room. Jack's breathing had slowed and she wasn't fighting them anymore.

"Okay, Sam we gave her the pills and put her on her bed. What now?"

Sam took a deep breath. "Now I need to get to her."

"Henry, I need a chartered jet from JFK to Portland within the hour. Done. What next?"

"Now I need a place to take her for a few days without any interruptions," Sam replied quietly.

"Um, there is a small cabin on an island not far off our beach. We own it but nobody ever uses it."

"Good, that's good. Now I need you to gather supplies for a couple of days for us," Sam said.

"Okay, I'll call Gracie and have her put it together. Just stop at the Harmony Diner on your way through town and pick them up. Gracie will take care of everything. There will be a car waiting for you at the soup kitchen within thirty minutes. Sam, are you sure we shouldn't call the hospital? I've never seen anything like this," Marcus said, worried.

"No, the last thing she needs is to be put in a psychiatric unit, trust me. We will get her through this, but know this, Marcus, I'd never do anything to put her in jeopardy. Ever. I love that little girl like she is my own. I know that you all have questions, and I will try to answer them as best I can when I get there. See you shortly."

Marcus looked up in time to see Jared lean over and grab his knees. He wasn't sure how much Jared had seen, but he looked like he was about to pass out. Marcus motioned to Bobby and Ty.

"Get him out of here. He's not helping."

Bobby and Ty grabbed Jared by the arms and started to direct him outside. Jared started to struggle with them.

"Stop, bro, we're gonna get her through this. Just step outside with us to get some air," Bobby said into Jared's ear. Jared stopped struggling and nodded in a resigned fashion. He then walked outside with them.

Bear walked over to Marcus. "You hung up?" he said angrily. Marcus looked up at Bear. "He's on his way. He said he will answer our questions when he gets here. I have to get him a car and call Gracie," replied, walking to the kitchen after taking one last look at his listless sister.

Sam looked out the window of the town car that had picked him up when he'd gotten off the jet. God's country. That's the only description Sam could come up with. Tall green pine trees as far as he could see. The most lush greenery and blue skies he had ever seen. It even smelled fresh and pure, he thought, letting the breeze bathe his face instead of having the air conditioner on.

Sam leaned his head back and closed his eyes. Jesus, this one sounded bad. He'd had a feeling this might happen when he had listened to her voice mail telling him her father had passed and she was going home. Although he had been trying to get her to go home and reconcile with her father, she wasn't quite ready for this. The guilt of not reaching out to her father before he died was going to cause her some real problems. It sounded like Jack was close to a complete break. He hoped they had shut it down in time.

"Sir. Sir. We're at the diner." The driver was speaking to him. Sam sat upright and scrubbed his hands up his face.

"Okay. I'll be right back," he replied, exiting the town car. He stood on the sidewalk and looked up and down. He could see what looked like a police department, a small hardware store, a small corner market, and a Baptist church. Wow. This looked like something right out of a Norman Rockwell painting.

As he walked into the diner, a bell on the door sounded. There were a few people sitting in the booths having lunch. Sam walked to the counter as a beautiful, tiny woman with a long dark salt and pepper braid and the kindest eyes he had ever seen smiled at him. She definitely had Indian heritage in her, he thought.

"You must be Gracie, Jack's mother's best friend," Sam said, smiling and holding out his hand.

Gracie appeared shocked but recovered fast and took his hand. "Yes, sir, and you must be Sam. Did Marcus tell you that about his mother?" Gracie inquired.

Sam shook his head. "Nah, I've heard many stories about you from Jack. She thinks a lot of you," he replied in an almost reverent tone.

"Well, ditto. It surprised me because it's been a long time since anyone has referred to my friend Elsie. She's just like her mother you know, the sweetest, most caring person I ever knew." Gracie started to tear up. "So I hear our Princess is having a hard time with her father's passing?" Gracie said quietly, putting the supply boxes on the counter.

Sam grabbed one and started toward the door. Gracie picked up the other one and followed him.

"You don't have to get that ma'am, I've got it," Sam said, opening the car door.

"Well, first off, don't ever call me ma'am again. The name is Gracie, and second, I'm no wilting flower, Sam. I know how to take care of myself," she announced firmly.

Sam grinned. "I can surely see that, Gracie. I thank you for the supplies. How much do I owe you?" Sam said, reaching for his wallet.

Gracie sniffed. "Don't insult me, Sam. You just take care of our girl, do you hear? And when you're done with, that you can come by the diner for a slice of my famous blueberry pie," she said smiling.

Sam nodded. "You can count on it," he replied, getting in the car.

As the car drove away, Sam sat stunned. *You can count on it?* Just where in the frig had that come from? It took a minute to realize that his heartbeat had sped up and his palms were sweaty.

Shit.

It had been a long, long time since he'd felt like that, but he wouldn't be traveling down that road, again. Ever. No woman deserved to get mixed up with the likes of him. He still wasn't sure how the beautiful, scrawny young woman he was on his way to see had managed to crawl into his heart, but manage she did because nothing was gonna happen to his little one on his watch, that was for damn sure.

The car drove down a gravel road until it came to a long dirt driveway leading to a beautiful green house nestled among the pine trees. The car stopped and he got out and grabbed his army duffel. All nine brothers burst out of the house flanking the car. Bear came forward first and grabbed him in a big hug.

"Thank you for coming, man! Any man my baby sister trusts, well, I damn well trust him too!" he exclaimed, grabbing his hand for a handshake.

Bear turned Sam's arm over and pointed toward his Special Forces tattoo. "That doesn't hurt either, my brother," Bear said warmly.

"You would be Bear," Sam replied chuckling. "Good to finally meet you. I gotta say that you're all an impressive sight. Now I gotta see my little one right now."

Marcus led Sam into the house to Jack's room. Jack was still sleeping quietly, with Jane lying between her and the door. Jane sat up and growled. Sam walked forward and let Jane smell his hand. She began licking his hand and whining as if she knew they had been waiting for him. "How's our girl, Janey?" Sam asked the dog.

Sam quickly checked Jack's vitals and then motioned for everyone to come out of the room with him. They all sat down in the living room. Bobby, Ty, and Jared came in and took a seat. Marcus pointed to Jared.

"This is Jared Ross," he announced to Sam. Sam stared at Jared for a good long moment before he finally nodded.

"How the fuck did she get PTSD?" Bear growled.

Sam nodded his head. "That little one in there does have PTSD like your brother just said. I'm not about to give details that aren't for me to give, but I will tell things you should know so you can help her. When she was sent to that halfway house she wasn't treated well. But more to the point, she was severely beaten. She was beaten real bad and never given proper medical treatment. She was in a coma for about two weeks and then put in solitary confinement. I've been in solitary confinement as a POW, and I can tell you it messes with your mind." Sam stopped speaking as Bear stood and put his fist through the nearest wall multiple times in rapid-fire fashion.

"Jesus, Bear, you're going to wake Jack up," Caleb scolded.

Sam turned to look at Caleb and smirked. "Did you piss her off, young gun?"

Caleb fidgeted, suddenly a bit embarrassed. "Ah, yeah, something like that," he replied quietly.

"Well, while she was in solitary confinement, she started to hear a voice that first told her to harm herself, and then it started to tell her that it would protect her. Jack called the voice her Dark Twin. Whenever she feels out of control or threatened in any way, her Dark Twin tries to take over and pro-tect her. It's really a remarkable feat of the human mind, but the problem is when the Dark Twin takes over she wants to lash out and hurt whoever is threatening Jack, and sometimes innocent people can get hurt. Jack never remembers the episode, and it's very stressful for her. That's why so many people who suffer from PTSD self-medicate to stop the voices and to stop caring about who they may hurt. Just so you know, I am a sufferer of PTSD as well as a counselor for sufferers of PTSD. I met your sister about a year after all this went down. She was living on the streets and not doing well. Noah was with her, but she was basically taking care of him," Sam said, shaking his head.

"She is the strongest little thing I've ever seen," he continued, taking a minute to collect himself before going on. "I helped her get set up at the local shelter, and she helped me out at the soup kitchen I run so I could make sure she ate at least one meal a day. But as pitiful as this situation was, she never ever complained, and I can't tell you how many smiles she brought to the children who came through those soup kitchen doors. She read to them in all their languages and played music for them. She has been in counseling with me and a friend of mine for a couple of years now. She does very well. She uses all the tools for coping, because she refuses to take any medication whatsoever except the sedatives after an episode. I knew eventually she was going to have to confront the events that led to her running away and she was very close to talking with your father but now...well, now we just have to pick up the pieces and pray to help get her through this," Sam ended as he looked around at the men before his eyes landed on Jared.

Jared never broke eye contact. "Tell us what to do for her," Jared said hoarsely.

Sam continued to stare at Jared. "Well, I need to take her somewhere quiet and private so we can work through this. Sort of exorcise the demon, so to speak. Two days. I'll have her back in two days," Sam announced finally.

They all sat in silence as the ceiling fan whirled around and around above them.

Jared got up and walked out the door. The sound of his truck starting and driving off fell heavy on the room. Sam got up.

"The supplies are on the lawn outside. I'm going to wake her and get her ready to go. One of you boys grab a small bag of clothes for her," he instructed, walking into Jack's room.

A short while later Sam escorted Jack out of the house. It was like she was in a trance. They piled into the Suburban and drove to the pond, where they helped Jack into the boat. The boys took two boats over to the island and left one for them to come back in. Marcus assured Sam that Jack could maneuver the boat back without any problems. The brothers got Sam and Jack set up in the cabin and left.

Caleb stood before Sam as they were about to leave with tears falling down his cheeks unchecked. "Please take care of my sister. I couldn't stand to lose her again," Caleb whispered.

Sam grabbed him and hugged him tight. "No harm will come to her while I'm around, my friend," Sam replied quietly. Sam then watched as the boat disappeared toward the other shore and the sun started to set.

Jared pulled into the driveway and sat in the truck, staring at the house he had spent his youth in. He was staring out the window, but he wasn't seeing anything but his Jack writhing and crying on the sofa. Jesus, he felt like he could uproot a tree with his bare hands. What had he done to her? He was like a poison that slowly killed the people he loved. He would try to keep his distance during the next three weeks, but he needed to make sure she was okay before he went back to New York. The image of her black eye and Caleb's double black eye distracted him for a moment. He almost smiled for a second. She had always been such a scrapper, and Caleb almost always got the brunt of her temper.

A knock sounded on the glass, making Jared jump. He looked to see his father standing there with a grin on his face. Jared's eyes narrowed. A few things registered at once. His father looked taller and healthier. He had color to his skin and was clean shaven. He looked good, and he was smiling. Jared could never remember seeing his father smile unless he had just cuffed Jared to the ground or hurled insults his way. Jared looked at his father's hands to make sure there wasn't a gun or some other weapon in them.

Jared tentatively opened the door, and Billy Ross stepped aside to let Jared get out of the truck. Billy held out his hand.

"Good to see you, Jared. It's been a while. You look good, son," Billy said a little nervously.

Jared stared at Billy and slowly extended his hand for a nice firm handshake. Had Jared entered an alternate universe?

"You look good too," he replied as he surveyed the yard. "You've cleaned the place up I see."

Billy smiled and looked around. "Yeah, there's been a few changes since you've been back. Come on in and have some coffee. Gracie brought me a fresh blueberry pie last night," his father replied, walking toward the front door.

"Gracie was here?" Jared asked incredulously.

As they entered the house, Jared noticed it was neat and clean. It no longer smelled of urine and booze. Jared sat down at the kitchen table as Billy poured them both some coffee and put the pie on the table.

Jared held up his hand to the pie. He was quite sure anything he ate wouldn't stay long in his stomach. He was still scared to death for his Princess.

"What's going on, Billy? How long have you been sober?" Jared asked.

Billy took a gulp of coffee and reached in the pocket of his pants. He pulled out a chip with red number 1 on it. "Thirteen months and three days," he replied proudly, putting the chip on the table.

Jared's insides twisted. It had been more than a year since he'd been here to check on his father.

Billy saw the look on Jared's face and quickly shook his head in disapproval. "Don't. You're a good boy, Jared, and you deserved better. Hell, you deserved to have a father that gave a shit. Don't beat yourself up about not coming around so that you could get abused," Billy said, finishing his coffee and pouring another.

"Why didn't you call me? It couldn't have been easy for you going through detox all alone," Jared asked.

Billy sat back in his chair. "Well, plain and simple, I didn't call because I didn't deserve anything from you, least of all your forgiveness. I will never ask you for that, son, but if you ever see fit to forgive me for being such a shit to you your entire life, well, that would be a real gift. One I will never ask for. But with that said, there are some things I would like to tell you. It's actually part of the AA program, to tell the people you hurt that you're sorry. Well, as you can imagine, I've spent the last year apologizing to just about everyone I know and some people I don't know," he said chuckling. Jared grinned for an instant. *Can this really be happening*, he thought to himself.

Billy quickly became serious again. "The most important apology to me is to you, son, but saying I'm sorry just doesn't seem enough, not nearly enough," Billy stood up, faced away from Jared, and gripped the counter around the kitchen sink. He turned around to face Jared, continuing to grip the counter as if he was holding himself up.

"I'm sorry for not being man enough to be a father at all. I'm sorry for not holding you when you were little. I'm sorry for not teaching you to hunt and fish like I should have. I'm sorry for not feeding you and for telling you it was your fault that your mother ran off." The words rushed out until Billy had to stop to collect himself as tears fell unabashedly down his cheeks.

"But mostly, I'm sorry for not loving you like I should have. I was so angry and miserable that I just wanted everyone around me to hurt as well. I was the worst type of coward, and I'm so sorry I didn't teach you to be a man. Thank God another man, a better man than me, took the time and taught you."

Jared couldn't take it any longer. He sprang from his chair, embracing his father for the first time in years, and began sobbing right along with his father. He felt like he was that four-year-old little boy again, desperately wanting his father to love him. Jared understood now how much it hurt to lose the person you loved most in the world and how friggin' easy it would be to just drink the pain away. The years just peeled away, and Jared knew that although he never felt loved by his father, there was always a piece of him that had known that his father had been a broken man, unable to help himself or his son. He desperately needed his father's love, and he wasn't about to turn him away now that he was offering it freely.

Jared pulled away and grabbed some paper towels for each of them. He stood beside Billy as he looked out the kitchen window.

"I'm proud of you, Dad, really I am. I do forgive you. I hope we can start fresh," Jared said, looking at Billy as Billy's head whipped around and fresh tears threatened to fall.

"Oh, Jesus, I'd like that, son. That's more than I ever hoped for," he exclaimed.

"Can I ask you what made you turn away from the booze, Dad? Was your health failing?" Jared asked quietly with dread in his voice.

Billy harrumphed. "I should be dead for sure, but no, the doctors say I'm remarkably healthy, especially for someone who tried to drink their life away," he said taking a deep breath. "Now, son, I will answer your question, but I just want to say that I've not told another soul this. A little over a year ago, I was sleeping in my recliner—passed out really—and I must have been dreaming. But clear as day I saw Elsie Johnson walk into this living room carrying a baby girl on her hip. That woman loved children more than anybody I've ever known. Well, she walked right up to me and smiled the whole damn time. God, she was beautiful. It was as if light was emanating from her inside to out. She knelt down in front of me. That's when I got a real good look at the baby. It was the most beautiful baby girl I'd ever seen, and I specifically took notice because the baby had dark curls, and when she looked at me, well, I swear she had your brown eyes. The baby smiled at me. Elsie touched my knee and just said two words to me.

"'It's time.'

"I just knew what she meant. It was time for me to stop wallowing in self-pity and be a man again instead of some drunken sot.

"She disappeared as quickly as she appeared. I came to and found my Bible that was under my bed and read until the sun came up. I showered and remarkably—or not so remarkably—it was Sunday morning, so I walked to church and asked Jesus to come into my life. The rest fell into place, like finding a sponsor and going to the hospital for detox. It's been quite a year, but none of that compares to you showing up on my doorstep today and forgiving this poor excuse of a father and giving me another chance," he beamed, shaking his head as if this too was a dream.

Jared hugged him again and took a deep breath. "Wow, that's quite a story," Jared murmured quietly.

Billy laughed. "You ain't kidding!"

Jared stayed for a while longer and informed his father what was going on with David's will and that he would be here for the next three weeks. Maybe they could get some fishing in. Jared finally left, thinking that maybe David had had something like this in mind when he required Jared to stay at the pond for the full three weeks. David had known that his father was sober but had chosen not to interfere with their relationship, knowing that Jared hadn't been ready to forgive Billy.

Jared was still worried sick about Jack, but he felt like at least one weight had been lifted off his shoulders. He planned on talking to Billy about Jack and the giant shit storm Jared had helped create. But even with a heavy heart, Jared smiled. It seemed that even from the grave, Elsie Johnson was touching his life.

Sam let Jack sit on the sofa looking out at the water for a couple of hours while he put the supplies away and got himself familiar with the small cabin. It was a very small patch of land surrounded by the pond. There were big rocks meeting the water instead of a sandy beach. There was a weathered wooden dock that they had secured the boat to. For a small patch of land, there were a lot of pine trees, and in the middle sat a small white cabin with green trim and green shutters. The paint had chipped away as a result of years of neglect. The cabin was small but open, giving the appearance of more space. There was a small stove, and the old refrigerator hummed loudly when they turned it on, which was somewhat of a comfort to Sam.

The cabin smelled musty, so they opened the windows to air the place out. There was a small bedroom with a bed, a bureau, a nightstand, and an old lamp. The bathroom was small but had a working toilet and a small box shower in the corner. It was, all in all, modest accommodations; nevertheless it was so perfect that he wouldn't have changed one thing about the place. It was as if his dreams had taken real form. If Sam had ever envisioned heaven, this would be his little piece of it.

Sam made some coffee and went to stand before Jack with his hand out. "Come on, little one; it's time."

Jack looked up and shook her head. "I can't do this anymore, Sam. I think she's right. I hurt everyone I love. I killed him," she muttered as fresh tears fell and she tried to angrily wipe them away.

Sam grabbed her hand and hauled her up. "Tears are good, little one. So is anger. Let's get good and pissed off, shall we?" he announced, leading her to the kitchen chair. "Sit, have some coffee, and let me tell you what I think this bitch is telling you, okay?" he began, placing his own chair in front of hers as they did in their group counseling sessions.

"I think she knows that this is her last-ditch opportunity to get to you. She likes it when you're weak and vulnerable. I'm here to tell you that you are strong and you do *not* need her to protect you. *She is not real, Jack.* You are real, only you. She is just a sick part of your brain that wants to keep you scared. That's not who you are, Jack Johnson. You weren't scared as a teenager when kids picked on you. You were strong and you held your head up high."

Jack stood up and leaned toward Sam. "Yeah, well, that's not who I am now, is it? I hurt people, Sam! I killed my own mother, for Christ's sake. I'm not worthy of love, and she's right, I should just end it all...all the suffering," Jack cried out with a sob.

Sam jumped up and got in Jack's face. "Oh, is that what she's telling you, is it? So this is the same girl who fought back against her attacker and then saved a young gay boy from getting hurt?" Sam hollered.

"No, she did that, not me! Can't you see? I'm weak and I'm tired!"

"No, you are not weak, and it has always been *you* fighting your battles. She's a liar, and she's trying to take your life! Are you just going to let her take everything you've worked so hard for? Are you? Do you think she would have taken a job she hated so her best friend could have his dream job and trot around the globe? Do you think she was the one to secretly drop off backpacks to homeless families in the middle of the night? Do you think she rounded up a bunch of old washed-up has-beens in the music industry and listened and learned from them in order to create one of the fastest growing recording labels in history? No! Little one, that was all you! You did not kill your father. His heart gave out. You are not God, so stop pretending you're responsible for life and death. All we have is today, and today you need to take back your life. Don't give her a foothold. We can get through this together. You're not alone," Sam whispered.

Jack collapsed into him, sobbing. Sam picked her up, walked her to the bedroom, and laid her down.

"You rest now. We'll start again after dinner," he ended, shutting the door halfway so he could hear her if she needed him.

When Jack woke up, the sun was setting across the lake behind the tall pines. The cabin was empty, so she walked outside to the porch and saw Sam down on the dock watching the sunset. She ambled down to him and wrapped one arm around his waist.

"I've never in all my life seen anything so beautiful, and I'm so glad I get to experience it with you," he said, squeezing her.

Jack smiled. "Mmm, I'd forgotten just how beautiful the sunsets were here," she replied.

"Do you know how lucky you were to have all this, little one? I'd have given anything for a family like yours and a place on God's great green Earth like this instead of getting bounced from one foster home to another until I was old enough to join the military," he said, turning her back toward the camp.

Jack looked up at him. "Sam, I didn't know you were in foster care," she said.

"Ah well, water under the proverbial bridge, as they say. Let's go cook some hot dogs," he muttered in response.

360

Jack stopped at the clearing in front of the cabin. "How about you cook the hot dogs and I'll start a campfire?" she suggested.

Sam smiled. "You know how to do that, little one?" he asked in mock disbelief.

Jack looked offended. "Please. This is my neck of the woods, Sam," she retorted.

Sam chuckled. "Fair enough, fair enough," he said, going inside to cook.

After they ate, Jack showed Sam how to make a s'more as he quickly burned up most of the marshmallows. Jack suddenly got really quiet and just stared into the fire.

"Talk to me, little one," Sam said.

Jack started to cry and told Sam about the tape her father had made for her and how it had just sent her over the edge. "The voice has never been so strong, Sam. How can I be sure it won't happen more often, and what if I hurt someone?" Jack sniffed.

Sam nodded. "All very good questions, little one, but will you listen to me? I really want you to listen with your heart, Jack. You have been working nonstop with the recording studio and not getting enough rest. You know that is a recipe for disaster, but you also have been very apprehensive about talking with your dad. That was added stress that you didn't need. This just came out of the blue and sideswiped you. It was kind of the making for the perfect storm. I'm not saying that it is ever going to be smooth sailing all the time, but you have managed so well. Can you honestly tell me that you never felt like something was off, like more flashbacks or dreams than usual? There are usually warning signs, but sometimes we don't want to see them."

Jack stared at the fire for a while. "You're right, Sam. There were warning signals. The dreams were more vivid, and Jane was waking me several times a night. I just didn't want to acknowledge what was happening. I guess I just wanted to be cured and not have to deal with this shit for the rest of my life," she acknowledged angrily.

"I get that, little one, really I do. You don't give yourself enough credit. Do you realize how long it's been since you had any episodes? If one of your brothers were going through this, would you be so rough on him? No. I'll tell you right now that you would tell him to take it one day at a time. Am I right?" he said, poking her with the marshmallow stick.

Jack laughed. "Well, first of all, you are the worst marshmallow toaster ever, and second, you're right, I wouldn't be so hard on one of my brothers if he were going through this. I see that the signs were there but I chose to ignore them. Lesson learned. I will do better."

Sam smiled in relief and nodded. "Okay, now, let's go over the part about me being right again," he said, and she laughed with him.

Just before Jack went into the bedroom for the night, Sam motioned for her to come sit on the couch with him. "Tomorrow morning after breakfast I plan to hash out this Jared Ross thing and then a Krav Maga session, so get your rest, little one, because I will not have any mercy on you at sunrise," he said, kissing her forehead.

Jack looked pensive for a minute and then nodded her head in silence as she walked to the bedroom.

It's time, she thought.

Sam was quite impressed with Jack's maneuvering the boat back to shore. They unloaded the supplies and loaded them back into the truck that had been left for them, heading up to the house. They had worked through many things. Some of the discussions had gotten pretty tense and pretty emotional, but everything that had been said needed to be said. For too long, Jack had avoided painful areas in her life. The last few days with Sam had been a godsend.

They had swum and enjoyed the pond. Jack was so glad that she had been able to have some time with Sam, because God knew he wouldn't take any for himself, and she wasn't sure she would have made it through the last few days without him. Jack, for the first time in years, now felt as if she had a fighting chance to have a "normal" life…whatever that was.

After she assured Sam that she was able to cope and that if need be, she would call him, Bear took him to the airport.

All eight brothers and Jack headed into town for breakfast at the diner. Gracie gushed over them, so happy to have them all home again. Jack had forgotten how delicious Gracie's breakfasts were. She was given a platter of food: French toast, home fries, bacon, eggs, and a tub of maple syrup. Her brothers all chortled when Gracie placed the platter of food in front of Jack.

"Don't laugh; if I remember correctly, our Princess could put some serious food away! We need to get some meat on those bones!" Gracie exclaimed as she hugged Jack from behind.

"So, Gracie, I hear you met Sam, what did you think of him?" Marcus asked.

Gracie stood up abruptly and looked rattled. *Odd, Gracie never ever gets rattled,* Jack thought. She looked from Marcus to Gracie. "You met Sam?" she asked.

Gracie blushed. "Um, yeah, Marcus called and asked if I would collect supplies for the island cabin, and Sam stopped by to pick them up. He seems like he really loves you a lot," Gracie said, cupping Jack's cheek.

Jack teared up a little. "I don't know where I'd be without Sam," Jack murmured quietly.

"Maybe we can get him to come back to see us," Teddy said, drinking the last of his coffee. Jack eyed him and then touched the side of her nose.

"I'm working on something, my brother," she replied in a conspiratorial tone.

"Oh, Jesus," Henry said dryly. Jack pointed at Henry.

"And it involves you, my other brother. I'll talk to you about it later," she ended with mischief clearly in her eyes.

Before they left, Gracie came to their table with several DVDs. "I want to give these to you kids. A long time ago when some of you were just little ones, a bunch of us would get together at your house and hang out and play music. I made several home movies with your Daddy singing that I had turned into DVDs. I want you to have them, and, my little Princess, you are in one, kinda," Gracie said smiling.

Jack gasped. "Me?" she whispered.

Gracie nodded. "It was about a month before she passed," Gracie said, turning away as her voice broke. She then laughed self-consciously and touched her throat. "God, I still can't talk about her even after all these years. Anyway, I think you will really like them," she ended, giving them to Marcus.

They went back to the house and waited for Bear to return. When he drove in shortly after they got back from breakfast, they headed to the swimming hole with the rope swing. It was so nice to spend the day relaxing and actually playing. Jack felt good, remembering when Jared had shown her this place and the first time they had made love. Even though it seemed like a lifetime ago, she needed to remember the good times because she needed them to outweigh all the bad that had happened to her. She felt it working; she felt filled with love and could breathe deeply for the first time since hearing her father had passed.

They swam and napped in the sun on blankets and talked about all that was going on in their lives.

"So, Princess, tell us about this country singer Ricky Vance. He told the world you were his 'lady'?" Bobby asked with a small smirk on this face.

Jack looked confused. "What are you talking about? He is a signed recording artist with my label, but that's it," she retorted, rolling on her side to look at her brothers.

Davey chuckled. "I'm afraid he wants to be more than that, Princess. Can't you see how he looks at you with those big puppy-dog eyes?"

Bear sat up, suddenly taking an interest in the conversation. "Has he bothered you, Princess?" he asked seriously.

Jack laughed. "Down boy! No, not at all, but it doesn't matter because I'm not anyone's lady. It's purely business," she replied firmly.

Bear jumped up and picked her up, putting her over his shoulder as she screamed and Jane barked nervously. "You'll always be our lady," he said, jumping in the water. The rest of them dove in as Jane skittered around the shallow end.

In the late afternoon, they packed up and drove home. Davey had decided he would cook a big meal and after that they would watch the DVDs Gracie had given them.

Jack changed into a simple jersey knit sundress with orange and blue stripes that landed just below her knee. She threw on some flip-flops and headed into the kitchen. "I'm going down to the beach to watch the sunset. I'll be back to help with dinner," she announced.

"Take your time—no hurry. We're all set here," Davey hollered after her. She found her old bike and rode to the pond.

The sunset was spectacular, with deep red and yellow brush strokes painting the sky. Just as the sun went behind the pine trees, Jack got up from the sand and heard a noise from the cabin beside the water. She glanced up to see Jared standing by the fire pit looking at her. Her heart stopped beating for what seemed an eternity before resuming its job.

Deep breaths.

Deep breaths.

Jack waved as Jared started walking toward her. "Hi," she said quietly.

Jared dared to have only a hint of a smile on his face. "Hi yourself. How are you?" he asked cautiously.

Jack half-smiled before she realized that Jared may have witnessed her breakdown. "Oh, um, did you witness my little episode?" she asked, lost for words.

Embarrassed.

"Yeah, I came in a little later, but I saw…Jesus, I don't know what I saw but it scared the shit out of me, Jack," Jared replied, looking intently at her.

More embarrassed after hearing that, Jack wiped at the sand on her dress. "I'm sorry you had—" she began.

"Don't. Don't act like I'm some stranger, Jack. It's me, don't be sorry you had a breakdown because your father just died. It fucking scared me to death to see you like that. Don't you dare be sorry," Jared commanded, trying to maintain his composure.

Jack took a deep breath and smiled; even though it didn't reach her eyes, she was glad to actually be talking to him. "You're right, of course. I'm okay. Really, I am, or at least, I'm better. Did you just get here?"

Jared stared for a minute, wishing she wouldn't be quite so formal with him. "Um, no…you know your father willed the cabin to me, plus we're all obligated to stay for three weeks, right?"

Jack nodded. "Oh, I guess I wasn't aware you were here for the three weeks too, but it makes sense," she replied.

"I've been at my father's house all day helping him stack his wood for winter. Did you hear? He's been sober for the last year," Jared said, stuffing his hands in his jean pockets.

He looked good. He was so much bigger than she remembered. The old Red Sox T-shirt fit snugly through his broad shoulders.

Jack swallowed hard and smiled. "Oh, Jared, that's amazing! I'm so happy for you both," she exclaimed sincerely.

He wanted to shake her. Shake her and kiss her until she melted into him like she used to. There was an awkward silence.

"Do you want a fire tonight?" he asked, waving his hand to the fire pit.

Jack shook her head and looked to her wrist, which didn't have a watch on it. "Oh...no, Davey is making a big dinner, and then we have some DVDs that Gracie gave us that we're going to watch tonight. Please come up and join us."

Jared looked pensive. "Nah, I'll let you guys have some time together," he said, turning away.

"Jared, please join us. You're one of us. My dad knew that, and you know that," Jack said softly.

Jared turned to look at her. Jesus, he couldn't help himself, he needed to be in her presence no matter how formal she was toward him. "Okay, I'd like that. Here, put your bike in the truck, and we'll drive up," he said, grabbing her bike and putting it in the back.

Jack touched the beautiful big black truck. "Kind of a step up from the beater you used to have," she teased.

He smiled back at her as he held open the door for her but turned serious quickly. "I'd go back to that beater in a heartbeat," he said quietly and shut the door. Jack sat next to the door and closed her eyes, taking a deep breath before he climbed in the driver's seat.

Fuck. Fuck. Fuck. Breathe.

Dinner was amazing. Lobster, corn on the cob, and cornbread, with whoopie pies for dessert. They all moaned as they got up from the table to clean up the kitchen. When they went into the living room, Marcus held the DVDs and turned to Jack.

"Are you sure you're okay to see this? I don't mean to embarrass you, Princess, but I also don't want to upset you in any way," he said firmly.

Jack bowed her head for a moment, then lifted it and smiled. "I know. I get it. I will let you know if it gets too much, okay? Really. Trust me; it's been a long time since something like that has happened," she replied quietly, alluding to her "episode."

As Marcus was putting in the first DVD, Henry looked around. "Where's Bear and Jared?" he inquired.

Bear strode into the room with Jared right behind him, looking angry. "We're here; let 'er rip," Bear directed Marcus. Marcus glanced quickly from Bear to Jared before pushing play.

The music started playing before the picture came into focus. Their father was singing a Randy Travis song. He often sang Randy Travis music, and he sounded just like him. Warmth flooded her, and when she saw her father's black-and-white image sitting on their porch playing the guitar she gasped and covered her mouth.

"Oh my God, he's so young! Look at him—he's so handsome!" Jack exclaimed. He had short dark hair combed to the side with a few pieces falling into his eyes, a white T-shirt with the sleeves rolled up, and jeans. He was sitting facing her mother, Elsie, who was very pregnant with a round belly and a baby on her shoulder. She was utterly breathtaking, with long blond waves and the sweetest and most gentle eyes filled with so much love for the man in front of her. She was smiling and rubbing her belly. David Johnson stopped singing for a minute and leaned down and kissed her belly. A sob escaped Jack's throat.

"I'd forgotten how beautiful she was," Henry whispered.

"That's you, Caleb, so…that's you, Princess, in her belly," Marcus murmured and hugged Jack as they sat on the couch. Jack noticed Jane jump up on Jared's lap and he started patting her.

Suddenly, a little boy was sitting behind Elsie, hanging over her shoulder and she laughed and kissed him. "Jared, that's you, isn't it?" Jack exclaimed.

Then the camera panned to the floor, where Bobby and Ty were playing trucks. In some of the DVDs, the older boys were playing guitar with their father. They watched each DVD over and over, soaking up the pictures and voices of the parents that they loved so much.

When the last one finished, Bobby jumped up. "Well, you know what this makes me want to do?" he inquired. Instantly the rest of the group nodded their heads in agreement and headed for the porch to grab their instruments. Jack sat down at the piano and the boys got their guitars. Jared sat at the drums. It was as if time had literally jumped backward. They played for hours until Bear saw Jack yawn and decided to call it a night.

Jack called to Jane to take her out one last time before they turned in. She was standing on the lawn beside the big oak tree when Jared came out to go to his cabin. Jane ran to him and jumped up to get his attention.

"Down, Jane! You know better than to jump on people," Jack said sternly.

Jared went to his knees to pat the dog. "It's okay—I'm new to her. How long have you had her? She's beautiful," he said as the dog, as if on cue, started nuzzling his neck.

"Jane, stop!" Jack exclaimed, laughing.

Jared looked up at her. "I've missed that," he said softly.

"What?" Jack whispered.

"The sound of your laughter. You," he replied as he stood up quickly.

Just then Bear burst out and clapped his hands together. "Jane, come here, girl!" he said clapping as Jane started barking.

"Oh, don't get her all excited before bed, Bear, or she's sleeping with you!" Jack said, walking toward the door.

Jared sighed. "Well, good night," he said in a disappointed tone, getting into his truck and heading toward the pond.

Jack stood at the screen door and looked at Bear with eyes narrowed. "What's going on, Bear?" she said suspiciously.

"What? Come on, it's time for bed," he replied way too innocently, ushering her and Jane inside. Jack looked toward the dark gravel road to the pond and back at Bear and walked into the house.

Luckily, each sibling had brought a laptop and smartphone, so they were all able to work from the house for a few hours each day. Nobody complained because they didn't want to break the magic of their special bubble. David Johnson was a brilliant man to insist they all be together for three weeks to make them remember how much they loved and needed each other. They all went boating and waterskiing each day, rain or shine. Jack wasn't surprised to find that she was never alone, although she did find it somewhat suffocating at times.

As the second week was coming to an end, the guys had all gone to a party at a camp down at the pond. Jack happily informed them she would be fine there all alone for once. The last thing she wanted to do was be surrounded by strangers at a party.

Jack had just started putting away the dishes from the potato salad she'd made for dinner when she heard a car door shut. As she walked to the porch, Jared opened the door. She stopped.

"Oh, hi. I thought you were with the boys at the party," Jack began, a bit too nervously, she thought.

Jared sat in the chair and pulled his boots and socks off. "No, I've been fishing with my father all day. What party?" he asked.

"Um, I'm not sure, but there is a camp party down at the pond. If you take the small fishing boat, I'm sure you can find it," she replied, walking back to the kitchen.

"Nah, I've never been one for parties. Did you have dinner yet?" he asked.

Jack raised her eyebrows. "Please. I remember you and Bobby and Ty taking the boat out after we were supposed to be in bed to find the parties on the pond, so don't try to sell me your BS, Jared Ross!" she exclaimed, a little calmer now.

Jared grinned. "Okay, busted! But now you're going way, way back, and it was really Bobby and Ty. I just went along to keep them out of trouble, honest!" he protested, holding up his hand.

"Right," Jack nodding and laughing. "I just had some potato salad for dinner. Would you like some?" she asked opening up the fridge.

"God, yes! Please! How about this: I'll go build a fire in the pit at the pond and you bring the salad and hot dogs," Jared replied, a little too excitedly he thought to himself.

Jack pulled out the hot dogs and salad and followed him out to the truck. He held open the door and threw his boots in the back and climbed in the driver's seat.

"Did you catch any fish?" Jack asked.

Jared smiled and nodded. "Yeah, a few, but we threw them back. It was a good day," he replied quietly. "What did you do today?" Jared inquired as they parked the truck and he came around to open the door for her and grab the food.

"Well, I got some work done and I was able to work on some music for a few new songs one of my artists is having a hard time with," Jack responded, starting up the stairs to his cabin to grab plates and forks. "Do you want a beer with your meal?"

Jared smiled broadly at her, liking that she was feeling comfortable around him and his cabin. "Yeah that would be great, thanks," he replied, beginning to build the fire.

After Jack brought his plate and beer to him Jared grabbed the hot dogs and put them on sticks; he started to cook them over the fire and took a pull on his beer. "Would that be Ricky Vance?" he asked.

Jack nodded and smiled. "Yes, are you familiar with his music?" she asked.

Jared's teeth clenched. "Ah, everyone on the damn planet is familiar with his music, Princess. What do you think of him?" Jared replied, searching for something.

"Oh I think his music is great, and everyone knows his music because of my label! I couldn't be happier!" Jack answered, stretching out in the Adirondack chair.

Jared stopped chewing as the hot dog lodged right in his throat. He uncomfortably stared at her long legs stretched out in front of her. Jesus, he had forgotten how glorious those legs were. She was wearing a pair of cut-off jean shorts with a white tank top and flip-flops that had been tossed aside. She was resting her feet on the rocks around the fire pit. His crotch area was growing uncomfortably hard, and the damn hot dog was going to choke him to death any minute. He chewed and swallowed several times before the hot dog gave up the ghost and disappeared down his esophagus.

Jared set his plate aside and finished his beer, and then he got up and walked toward the camp, tossing Jane the last of his uneaten hot dog.

"Can I get you anything, Princess?" he asked.

Jack shook her head. "No I'm good, really, I just had a cup of tea with dinner."

They sat in front of the fire talking for hours about his job and her time as a model. Jared loved and appreciated all the stories of the horribly narcissistic people she met. Only someone from Harmony, Maine, could truly appreciate how unimportant all the pomp and circumstance was. Smelling the pine trees and campfire smoke, well, that was what the good life was truly all about. Jack smiled.

"What?" Jared asked, leaning back in his chair.

"Oh, nothing, I was just thinking about how this all smells." She took a deep breath. "The pine trees and campfire smoke, well, this is what they're talking about when they talk about 'the good life,' you know?" she responded, letting her head turn toward him lazily.

Jared smiled. "Yeah, I know exactly what you mean, Princess," he replied looking into her eyes and holding her gaze.

A boat was coming toward them and stopped at the dock. Bear climbed out and ran toward the camp.

"Hi," Jack greeted her brother. "Are you here to check on me?" she asked directly.

Bear looked uncomfortable. "No, I was just curious to see what you were doing, that's all," he replied, looking very guilty.

Jack grinned and shook her head vigorously. "You are full of shit, that's what you are," she retorted as she got up. Bear looked offended.

"Actually, I was just going to ask Jared to take me and Jane to the house. Would you like to call it a night as well?" she asked him, knowing full well he was out for the night.

"Um, no, I think I will just grab some more beer from Jared's fridge and be off. You're sure you're okay?" Bear asked, climbing the stairs to the cabin.

"Yeah, I'm good, Bear," Jack assured him as she walked to the truck.

Jared held the door open for Jack and Jane. When they pulled up to the house, Jared cut the engine. They sat there for a minute, then Jack opened the door and let Jane out to pee before they went in for the night.

"This was nice, Jack. Thank you for spending the evening with me," Jared said quietly. He turned and put his arm across the back of the seat. Jack looked down at her hands.

"It *was* nice, Jared," she replied as she looked up into his eyes. Jesus, she could get lost in those eyes. She needed to get the hell out of this truck. "It's good to have my friend back. I've missed you," she murmured awkwardly.

As Jared appeared to be about to say something, Jack literally scrambled out of the truck. "Good night," she said, but before she could shut the door, Jared finally spoke up.

"Um, how about we get some breakfast in the morning and go fishing? Your brothers won't be up until midday I bet."

Jack stood there thinking for a moment and then smiled. "Sounds good," she agreed.

"Oh, and Princess, I'm not going to that party. I'm tired and I'm going to bed. Just in case you were wondering," Jared offered up in a solemn voice.

Jack rolled her eyes and shut the door. Jared watched her go into the house and started his truck. "Friend my ass," he said to nobody in particular.

Jack and Jared walked into the diner together. This apparently stunned Gracie, who just stopped in the middle of the diner and stared at the two as they took their seats. Gracie quickly composed herself and poured them some coffee.

"Good morning, you two. I hear you're going fishing today?" she said with a twinkle in her eyes.

Jack almost snorted her first sip of coffee out her nose. "Gracie, do you know everything that goes on in this town?"

Gracie winked and jumped as the cook bellowed that the orders were backing up. Jack looked around and saw that no one was waiting tables aside from Gracie.

"Are you alone?" Jack asked.

Gracie nodded and continued to fill the coffee cups. "Yeah, my new waitress went to that party at the pond, and I'm guessing she's not feeling well today," she replied gruffly.

In response, Jack stood up, walked to the kitchen, grabbed an apron and a tray filled with orders, and began to disperse them to the customers. Gracie looked at Jared and smiled with tears in her eyes.

"That's our girl," she whispered to Jared. Jared simply stared at Jack with so much love in his eyes he wasn't sure how long he was going to be able to contain it. Eventually, the diner emptied out and they had an opportunity at last to enjoy their breakfast. When finished eating, they grabbed the cooler that Gracie had put together after Jared had called her last night and they were off.

It was so hot that they just lay back in the small metal fishing boat as their lines sat in the water waiting for a tug. Jack had on a black-and-white two-piece bathing suit that made her think of the old James Bond movie with Jinx. The bottoms were hip-huggers, and the top covered more than the average bikini. They were both dozing in the warm sunshine.

"Would you rather swim in the pond or the ocean?" Jack asked lazily.

"Pond without question," Jared answered almost immediately.

"Would you rather eat cake or pie?" Jack asked laughing.

"Pie without question," Jared replied firmly.

Jack sat up on her elbows. "Haven't you heard of this game? The kids at the soup kitchen played all the time, but they used to get really gross and silly, like would you rather eat dog poop or bear poop. They would all laugh and laugh."

Jared shook his head. "No, ma'am, I haven't had the pleasure of playing that game of wits," he replied in a mock solemn tone. There was silence before he sat up to check his line.

"Would you rather vacation in Montana or Mexico?" he asked.

"Montana without question," Jack quickly answered.

"Would you rather have one child or ten children?" he asked.

Jack gasped and sat up just as her line gave a tug. She grabbed her fishing pole and started to reel in the line. The fish was fighting for all it was worth, so Jack was having to do all she could do to bring the fish in close to the boat. Jared shouted out and held the net, waiting for the fish to be pulled to the surface. Eventually, Jack landed a small-mouth bass that was a keeper for sure.

Jack clapped her hands and chortled. "Look what I caught!" she exclaimed.

Jared's smile was wide. He loved seeing her so excited and happy. "That's as fine a bass as I've ever seen, Miss Johnson," he exclaimed. "Looks like you caught some dinner tonight," Jared complimented her as he eased the fish off the line and put it in the bucket.

Jack put another worm on her hook and cast again. Jared reached for his guitar and started playing the same song her father had sung to her mother on the DVD. Jack leaned back and took a deep breath and hummed along with him, singing. *If only all of life could be this simple and happy.*

Around noon, they ate the delicious lunch that Gracie had packed for them: cold fried chicken, cold cucumber salad, and fruit salad for dessert. While they ate, Jack asked Jared about his father. Jared told her everything his father had told him except about the child in the dream.

"Really, he saw my mother?" Jack asked.

Jared smiled and nodded. "I'm pretty sure that he was secretly in love with your mother, as was every other man she ever talked to," he replied, splashing water on Jack.

Jack squealed. "Even you at four years old," she retorted as she splashed him back. Jack yelped and dove in the pond, coming up yards away from the boat. Jared started to peel his shirt off.

Holy hell, he was ripped.

Jared dove in and swam toward her. "What are you thinking?" he asked as they floated around silently.

"Mmm, blissfully not much," Jack replied as she dove underwater. When she came to the surface, Jared was very close and looking so deeply at her that she gasped slightly and couldn't look away. With what seemed like superhuman effort, Jack shook her head. "Don't, Jared," she whispered and started swimming toward the boat.

Jared made it to the boat first and touched her arm. "Wait, let me get in first then I can help you in" he offered. Jack nodded, knowing how difficult it was to lift yourself into a boat from the water. "Okay," she said softly. Jared effortlessly heaved himself up and into the boat. Jack watched as his back muscles rippled from the effort.

Breathe in; breathe out. Breathe in; breathe out.

Jared held out his arms and lifted her from under her arms straight out of the water and into his arms to steady her. Jack put her hands on his biceps for balance.

"Jared, please," she said self-consciously, looking into his eyes.

"Please what, Princess?" he whispered as he held her close.

Jack took a deep breath and pulled away and sat down, reaching for her towel. "We can't go back, Jared. I think it's time to go home now. I need to check on Jane," she said quietly, looking away.

Jared sighed and grabbed his towel, and then he reeled in the fishing poles and started the engine. They headed for home in silence except for the motor's buzz.

They docked the boat and brought everything to Jared's cabin. "Can we keep the fish here for now and cook it over the fire tonight? I've got some calls to make to my team, but how about salad and hot dogs tonight for dinner?" Jack asked, turning toward the dirt drive. "Oh and of course s'mores. I will bring everything if you get the sticks ready for the hot dogs."

"Wait, Jack, I want to..." Jared began walking toward her.

Jack smiled shyly and held up her hand. "No, Jared, please. Friends don't have to explain things. Everything is fine. See you tonight," she replied as she walked away, leaving Jared standing there watching her walk up the drive. It took everything in him to not run after her and shake her, or maybe just kiss her violently and tell her he didn't want to be her friggin' friend. He wanted to yell and more than anything he wanted to hit something.

Jack touched base with her team and was surprised at how many established artists wanted to sign with Princess Productions. She talked to Noah and Sam and assured them that she was doing just fine and that she had spent the morning fishing. Sam was envious and Noah was definitely not envious in the least. Her brothers were spread out all over the house doing the same as she was, catching up with their lives that had been put on hold for these three weeks. There were just a few days left. Tomorrow was the town picnic and fireworks, and she was truly looking forward to it.

A knock at the screen door made Jack jump. Jane started barking as Jack closed her laptop and walked to the porch. There was a young woman with shoulder-length brown hair standing on the steps. She was way overdressed for the pond, wearing a tight black dress and heels.

Jack wrinkled her nose as she opened the door. "Hi. Can I help you?" Jack asked.

The woman stared at Jack until it got a little uncomfortable. She started to wonder if maybe this woman had met one of her brothers last night.

"You're Jack Johnson, aren't you?"

Jack stepped back and narrowed her eyes. "Um, that depends. Who wants to know?" she replied suspiciously.

"I'm Stephanie. I'm a reporter for *GQ*, but I'm not here in that capacity. Although I would love to interview you. I'm Jared Ross's girlfriend, and I've come to see him. Is this his new place?" Stephanie asked, looking around, clearly unimpressed.

Jack was stunned into silence. Of course, this was the woman she had seen Jared with at the bar. Jack pasted on a smile that didn't even come close to being genuine.

"Um, no, this house belongs to me and my brothers. Jared's cabin is down by the pond. Just drive down that dirt road, and you can't miss it," Jack replied. Jane tried to jump on Stephanie, and Stephanie shouted at her to get down. Stephanie looked up at Jack quickly.

"Ah, sorry, I don't like animals. I'll just go and surprise my love," she muttered awkwardly, making her way down the stairs and along the dirt driveway in her heels.

Jack wasn't sure if she wanted to claw her eyes out or give her instructions on how to walk in heels. Bobby and Ty appeared just in time to see Stephanie get in her sports car.

"Who's that?" Bobby asked.

"Jared's *girlfriend*, Stephanie," Jack replied flatly.

"No fucking way," Ty exclaimed.

"Fuck," Bobby whispered.

Jack packed everything in boxes and the boys loaded them on the four wheelers. Jack hopped on the back with Bear and they headed to the pond. The sun was just setting and it was cooling off. Jack had put on a white T-shirt and a pair of jeans with the legs rolled up and a hooded sweatshirt tied around her waist. She braided her hair in a single plait down her back.

They all zoomed in on a cloud of dust. Jared and Stephanie were sitting by the fire. Stephanie was still wearing the dress and heels and sitting very rigid in her chair. Jack's brothers introduced themselves to Stephanie all at once. She acted a little overwhelmed and giggled way too much.

Jack could feel the tension rolling off Jared. Jared would not even look in Jack's direction. *Well. Okay then.*

Jack started unpacking the food. "Stephanie, if you would be more comfortable I'm sure I could find some jeans or shorts for you. I would be happy to go grab something if you like," Jack offered up, smiling. She was determined to be kind even if she felt like dragging Stephanie behind the four-wheeler up the dirt road.

"Oh, no, thank you. This is how I dress to be comfortable, actually. I'm a city girl through and through, and besides I probably couldn't fit my calf in your jeans. You must have to starve yourself to be that skinny," Stephanie cattily.

There was absolute silence. Every male looked from Stephanie to Jack before they all burst out laughing, except Jared.

"Um, you haven't seen Jack eat. She can put away more food than Bear," Caleb said dryly.

Bear winked at Stephanie. "Not quite, but close," he said smirking.

Jack poked him with the hot dog stick. "Yeah, and you all say that like it's a bad thing. Nobody monitors your food intake. Well let me tell you all that the day I start putting on weight is the day I go buy bigger clothes, not eat less food." Out of the corner of her eye, Jack saw Jared try to hide a smile.

As they ate their hot dogs, chips, and salad, Henry asked Stephanie what she thought of Jared's inheritance. Everyone but Stephanie knew that Henry was being a smartass.

"Well, it certainly is a far cry from his New York penthouse," she replied with an exaggerated sigh. Jared looked uncomfortable but remained silent.

Garrett looked to Jared. "Where is your apartment?"

Stephanie spoke up. "Park Avenue. It's beautiful. He says he wants to fill it with kids!"

Jack started coughing and took a sip of water Caleb handed her. Jared looked at her with concern.

"You sound like you don't want a lot of kids, Stephanie. I'm afraid this bunch thinks the more the merrier, and that includes Jared. He's one of us," said Marcus.

"Well, maybe one or two, but that's it. My career comes first," Stephanie replied, clearly now a bit defensive.

"Do you two live together?" Marcus asked.

"No!" Jared said too quickly and too loudly.

Stephanie glared at him. "Not yet," she said curtly.

Jack made an excuse to go find Jane by the water and left the group. How long would it be until the very mention of children wouldn't break her heart into a million pieces?

Jane ran to her, and Jack kneeled down to pat her. "I guess you'll be my only baby, won't you, Janey?" she said to the dog.

"Why is that, Jack?" Caleb said quietly behind her.

Jack stiffened and then turned around to face him. "Jesus, you scared me!" she gasped.

"Why is Jane going to be your only child, Jack? From the time we were kids, you have always said you were going to have a dozen children. Why not now?" Caleb asked seriously.

Jack waved her hand like it was unimportant. "Oh, Caleb, I've changed. I'm with Stephanie, I'm a career girl now," she replied, too lightly.

"Bullshit, Jack. Is it because of the beating you took at Beckett's House?" Caleb persisted.

Jack gasped again and covered her mouth with her hand. She stood there looking at Caleb in the moonlight until the tears started and she nodded.

Caleb pulled her in close. "Jesus Christ, Princess, I'm so sorry. God I'm sorry," he muttered as he held her while she cried.

After a bit, Caleb and Jack and Jane wandered back to the fire where it was way too quiet. Jack could feel Jared's eyes searching, but she refused to look at him.

"Hey, who's ready for s'mores?" Jack asked.

"What's a s'more?" Stephanie asked and they all looked at her.

"What?" she said. They all laughed.

"Stephanie, you are in for a wicked treat, my friend," Jack proclaimed, pulling out the marshmallows. Stephanie wasn't impressed at all. As a matter of fact, she took one bite from the s'more Jack made for her and threw the rest in the fire. Stephanie was looking bored and pouty.

"Jared, why don't we all go to a club?" she asked. Again, silence. Jack cleared her throat. "Stephanie, good idea. Let's get our guitars. I'm having a problem with some keys in a new song; maybe you guys can help," she said as they all went to the four wheelers to get their instruments.

Jared went inside the cottage to grab his guitar, and Stephanie followed him. They didn't come out for a while, and when they did, Stephanie sank back into the chair and didn't say another word, pouting again.

They played for several hours, and Jack was very satisfied with the new ideas they worked on. Davey was the first to jump up and put his guitar away.

"I've had it. I'm getting up early to start making some new dishes for the town picnic tomorrow," he announced as he came over to hug Jack. "Mac isn't going to be able to make it, Princess; I need her to be at the restaurant while I'm gone. She says she will come up when it's just the two of you and you guys can really cause some trouble."

Jack hugged him and laughed. "Okay, I understand, but you've been warned," she said.

Stephanie looked incredulous. "Wait a minute. Your brothers call you Princess?" she asked coyly.

"Stephanie…" Jared growled.

Jack held up her hand. "No, it's okay, really. I've been teased my whole life for it. It actually started with my mother. That was what my father called my mother, Princess. Then my mother passed away, and I became my father's Princess, and my brothers just followed suit with my father. As for the American Princess thing, I had nothing to do with that. I was just spending time with friends when someone posted me singing that song, and well, you know the rest," Jack replied, shrugging and putting her guitar away.

"Well where did Jack come from? Did you give yourself that name when you became a supermodel?" Stephanie asked.

Jack burst out laughing. "Sorry, no. That is another long weird story for another day," she said, glaring at Caleb who was openly smirking.

Bear grabbed Jack's guitar case with his own as they walked to the four wheelers. Jack turned to Stephanie and Jared. "Well, good night. I'll see you tomorrow at the picnic," Jack ended with a smile pasted on.

"Picnic?" Stephanie sniffed distastefully. Jared stood.

"Good night, Jack" he said softly.

It was all she could do to keep it together as they traveled up the dirt road to the house. She felt raw. It should have been her there with Jared, damn it. The grief came in a strong wave. As soon as they parked the four wheelers, she knew she needed to get to her room fast before she completely fell apart and cried like a baby. The world wasn't going to stop for her broken heart.

Just as she was walking toward her bedroom, Marcus hollered her name. Jack didn't turn around; she just stiffened. "Good night, Marcus. I'm really tired. I'll see you all in the morning," she managed to croak out.

"Come back here, Princess, please," Marcus said softly.

Jack shook her head, refusing to budge. "No, Marcus, I'll be fine. Please just drop it," she whispered.

"Jack Elsie Johnson, turn yourself around. Part of the problem is trying to pretend everything is fine. It's not fine, and when are you going to realize that your pain is our pain, Princess?"

Jack slowly turned around to find all nine brothers standing there looking helpless as tears streamed down her cheeks. One hand went to her stomach and one hand went to her chest as she started to sob. "I love him. I just love him so much," she cried as Marcus picked her up and sat down on the couch with the other boys. They let her cry for a while before Bear jumped up.

"Come on, let's go," he commanded everyone, grabbing the keys to the Suburban.

"Where are we going?" asked Henry.

As if reading Bear's mind, Teddy grabbed Jack's purse and handed it to her. "Grab your ID; we're going to the Kennebec Inn in Skowhegan. So put on your dancing flip-flops, Princess!" Teddy shouted with a war cry that made all the males act like testosterone-filled rednecks. Jack grinned just a little and followed them out the door. It sure did beat crying into her pillow.

Jared had been up for hours. All night, really. After everyone had left, he and Stephanie had finished the conversation they had started before everyone had shown up about what she was doing there. She had made up some excuse about bringing some papers from his office that needed to be signed, but he had been using FedEx for the past two weeks, so that was just bullshit. He had finally just come out and told her that there wasn't anything between them and there never had been and that she needed to leave. That had gone over like the proverbial lead balloon, but it was the truth.

He had called the airport, but there wasn't a flight out until 5:00 a.m. Jared made sure she was in her car on her way to the airport well before that time. He had let her have the bed while he slept in his truck.

It was about ten o'clock as he arrived at the main house. Nobody was up except Bear, who was sitting at the bar nursing a cup of coffee.

"Where is everyone?" Jared asked.

"Still in bed, but I can hear movement," Bear replied, tilting his head. "We headed to Skowhegan after we got home. We didn't get home until about two thirty."

Bobby, Ty, Davey, and Caleb all staggered out to the kitchen for coffee. Jared crossed his arms. "Were there a lot of people out?" Jared asked.

"Yeah, it was packed," Bear acknowledged.

"Where did you go?" Jared asked, wishing they would just spill so he didn't feel like he was cross-examining a hostile witness.

"Kennebec Inn," Garrett muttered as he staggered out. "Jesus, that place is such a dive!"

"Did anybody bother Jack?" Jared asked, beginning to get pissed.

Bear looked up from the paper. "She's a fucking supermodel. What do you think?" he growled.

"Well, it wouldn't have been so bad, but between Bear and Marcus no guy could even look at her without them punching them until eventually Bear put some huge biker dude through the plate glass window," Garrett announced with a smirk.

"Jesus," Jared murmured.

"Thank God the cop was retired special forces and told us to get our asses in the truck and get the hell out of town. He specifically asked us to not bring Jack back with us," Caleb chortled.

Bear smiled. "Yeah, I can see a country like Afghanistan not wanting us to come back because we blew the shit out of their country looking for Bin Laden, but a small town in Maine asking us to please not bring our little sister back to town because she's too disruptive by being gorgeous, well, that just ain't right," Bear grunted as he downed his coffee. He got up and poured another cup just as Jack and Jane came out of Jack's bedroom. Jack had silky pajama shorts and a tank top on. She came around the bar and took the coffee Bear had just poured for himself and walked outside with Jane.

"Morning," she mumbled.

Jared just froze and eventually looked around to see all nine brothers staring at him. "Fuck you all," he responded, grabbing the next cup of coffee Bear had just poured and walking outside.

Jack was sitting on the edge of the bumper of the Suburban when Jared walked to her. "Where's Stephanie?" Jack asked in too catty a voice she instantly regretted using.

Jared sat down beside her. "She left for New York early this morning," he replied.

Jack frowned. "Oh, I'm sorry to hear that. The town picnic wasn't her cup of tea?" God, what had she turned into overnight—Catwoman? "I'm sorry, that sounded very bitchy. Who you date is your—"

Jared stood up. "Jack, Stephanie and I were never a couple. We dated a few times, but she just kept pushing, and I didn't want to cause a scene, so I basically just ignored it, hoping she would go away. I never invited her up here," he replied quietly.

Jack stood up. "Oh." She paused and looked away. "I have to get some more coffee, would you like some?" she offered awkwardly.

"What I would like is for you to come to the picnic with me today," Jared stated firmly, stepping closer to her.

Jack's heartbeat revved as her stomach flip-flopped. She looked up at him. "Um, we're all going to the same place, Jared," she whispered and smiled.

He moved a long wisp of hair away from her face. "Do you have any idea how beautiful you are, Princess?" he whispered to her.

The moment his fingers touched her skin, her nipples hardened, her pupils dilated, and her breathing became ragged. She took a step back, shocked from the electricity surging through her.

"Um, give me about an hour to get ready?" she offered as she darted around him and clapped for Jane before heading inside the house.

Jared climbed into his truck and let out a long breath. He hadn't been aware he was holding his breath, and his jeans were uncomfortably tight in the crotch area. Jesus. He imagined it was how he would feel if he had just been struck by lightning.

Meanwhile, the battle began between Jack's emotions and her logic. Her emotions advised her to just let go for today and enjoy his company. The sun, moon, and stars would probably not be aligned like this ever again for them all to be together in the same place for no other reason but to enjoy each other. *Seems reasonable doesn't it?* she inquired of her logic.

Not so fast.

Her logic said it was too dangerous to be so close to Jared. Her love was too strong; why hurt herself when she knew it could never be?

But now another other voice was trying to creep into the conversation that stopped Jack short.

You're not worthy of his love. You are damaged goods. Don't you think he deserves better than you?

No! I'm not going to listen to that. I'm just going to have a great day and not think myself to death. There, that's final.

Her eyes traveled to the window and below. On her bedroom floor sat a pair of old red cowboy boots. Jack sucked in her breath. My God, those were her old boots! How on Earth?

Giddy, she ran over and slid them on. Like a glove. Perfect. Now she just needed something to go with them. She smiled as she remembered the pretty summer dress from the Worthington Collection that Noah had packed for her, just in case. She took a little time to apply makeup and curl her long hair. As she stood in front of the mirror, she liked what she saw for the first time in a very long time. She saw love, hope, and excitement staring back at her.

Jack hummed a tune as she walked with a skip in her step to the front porch, where she was met with numerous wolf whistles. She curtsied, laughed, and locked eyes with Jared.

The heat surged through her. God, he was gorgeous in his khaki shorts; light blue, short-sleeve button down shirt; and flip-flops. He was tanned and his short dark hair had started to grow a little, with pieces that had started to curl at the ends.

Jack cleared her throat, embarrassed, and looked around. She whistled herself. "Look at you guys! If Brock Worthington were here he would swoon and want to put you all on the catwalk for sure."

Bear grunted as they walked outside. "Not sure if I'm up to the challenge of playing bodyguard again today," Bear replied before flexing his biceps and gloating. "Nah, I'm good. That was fun last night."

"Thank Christ there aren't any plate glass windows in the park," Henry said dryly. Jack walked toward Jared's truck with Caleb following her until Bobby and Ty grabbed him and pushed him toward the Suburban. Jack could feel her face getting red as a ripe tomato, so she just looked away as Jared opened her truck door and she climbed in. Pushing all negative thoughts away, she strengthened her resolve to have a good time today while Jane curled up on the back seat as if she had ridden there a million times.

The boys drove in behind Jared and helped gather the food that Davey had prepared. Jack put Jane on a leash as they walked to the picnic tables. There was a crowd already there milling about. In the middle of the park stood a new gazebo. Jack saw Gracie and hugged her tight. She pointed toward the new structure.

"When was that built?" she asked.

Gracie smiled. "You'll see later when we dedicate it," she whispered secretively.

There were several vendors selling jewelry and crafts. Jack walked over with Jane. She was particularly taken with the booth that made homemade dog treats with all-natural ingredients. Jack let Jane try a few and bought several bags of the ones she liked the best to take home with her.

The next booth exhibited Maine tourmaline jewelry, which Jack instantly fell in love with. She was talking with the vendor when Jared came up behind her. She felt him before she saw him. The hair on the back of her neck prickled and she became hyperaware.

The vendor held up the tray of necklaces he had been showing Jack. The man smiled at Jared. "I was just telling your beautiful lady that she has great taste."

Jack was shaking her head as Jared came to stand beside her. "She is beautiful—you got that right," he replied, looking Jack directly in the eyes and grinning. He did not correct the man about her being his "lady."

Jack smiled and took Jared's hand, directing him away from the vendors. She waved to the vendor as they walked away. Jared kept her hand in his as they walked. Jack noticed that people were forming a line to eat, so she steered them to the line.

"I had no breakfast and I'm starved," she giggled.

"Well, if it isn't the Prince and Princess come back to slum with the little folks," someone sneered from behind them. Jack could feel Jared stiffen, but he didn't let go of her hand.

Jared turned around slightly. "Ned. I thought I recognized the asshole in your voice," Jared replied quietly.

"Hey, Princess, the offer still stands. When you want a real man, you know where to find him," Ned smirked, looking her up and down in an exaggerated fashion.

"Um, where would that be? Because I sure as hell don't see one in you," Jack replied, unable to help herself.

"That's okay, I'll pass; I think you've been used and abused anyway, you skinny bitch," Ned glowered.

Jared was in Ned's face instantly and rearing his hand back to punch the moron, but Jack caught his arm as she cried out. "Jared, stop! Please don't. This idiot is not worth it."

Jared froze and looked at Jack. She was pleading with her eyes for him to stop. Jared lowered his hand in resignation and smoothed Ned's shirt down instead.

Jack walked out of line to the end. Jared was breathing hard, clearly quite perturbed. Jack stood before him and looked him directly in the eyes.

"Thank you for offering to set that asshat straight, but I've seen enough violence to last a lifetime. He's a hall of fame asshole, but I think he actually probably wanted you to hit him so he could sue you or something," she said, touching his chest lightly.

"It would have been fuckin' worth it," Jared replied, trying to calm his breathing, but now that she was touching him that made him lose his breath for an entirely different reason.

Jack started to laugh, and before long she was doubled over laughing. Jared laughed with her, not knowing why. "What's so funny?" he asked chuckling.

Jack could hardly talk. "You! If you could see you two. You all handsome with your chino shorts and button-down shirt and him with his hat turned around backward and greasy jeans and T-shirt! It was like something from a James Dean movie. A rumble!"

"You think I'm handsome," Jared replied quietly, grabbing her hand on his chest. Her eyes met his.

"Um, the line is moving," a voice said from behind them, bringing Jack out of her trance. She pulled her hand away and walked forward in line to pick up their plates.

With their plates rounded over with home-cooked food, Jack and Jared walked to the two picnic tables pushed together. Her brothers were almost finished with their first plates of food. The food was so delicious. After they all ate, they spread blankets out around the new gazebo and soaked up the sunshine and laziness of the day. Eventually, Gracie stepped up to the gazebo with a microphone in her hand.

"Hello, folks, I hope you are all enjoying yourselves and your bellies are full," she announced as people whistled and groaned from their food comas. Gracie laughed.

"Good, good. Well I just want to thank you for coming out today and celebrating our wonderful town. We would like to memorialize two of our beloved townsfolk who are no longer with us physically but will never be far in spirit. Remarkably, all ten of their children are here today," Gracie called out as she waved toward the Johnson clan. They all sat up as the townspeople clapped.

"As you all know, we just lost our friend David Johnson. David and Elsie Johnson loved this town, loved helping its townsfolk any way they could. There isn't a resident in this town that fell on hard times who couldn't go to David for a job. He did more for the people of this town than anybody will ever know, and that is exactly the way he wanted it. By God, he would be royally pissed if he knew we going on like this about him," she said, as people nodded and laughed. They all knew David had been a very quiet man.

"Well, to honor David and Elsie, the town had this gazebo built, and I think today is a fitting day to break it in with music from their children, but first there is a tribute to David from a child who loved David and Elsie like parents."

Jared got up, grabbed his guitar, and sat on the stool in front of the microphone. "Hi there, folks. Everyone knows that David and Elsie were very special to me and I owe them a lot. Recently, Gracie let us watch old videos of

David and Elsie, and I can remember him singing this song to her on more than one occasion. I would like to sing it to honor them today."

Jared began singing the song David had sung to her mother when she was pregnant with her. Jack sat crossed-legged on the blanket and couldn't stop the tears from falling. Jared was singing directly to her. It was almost too much. Too much love, too much heartbreak, too much longing. She was completely mesmerized, as were her brothers, who were also choked up.

God, she loved this man.

As the song ended, the sounds of clapping and cheering from the townspeople were deafening. Jared smiled at Jack and waved to the Johnson clan to come and grab their instruments. Jack was surprised to find a beautiful piano on the gazebo. Jared sat down at the drums with her brothers, and they proceeded to entertain the crowd.

They had started to take requests when Bear stood up and walked toward the steps where a little blond girl was standing. Bear knelt down and she whispered in his ear. He smiled and whispered back to her and she ran toward the blanket her parents were on.

Bear went to the microphone and grinned. "It would appear that we have a special request. This will be the last song of the evening so we can get ready for the fireworks."

Bear walked to Jack at the piano and whispered the request. Jack nodded in approval and motioned toward the little girl to join her at the piano.

With the little girl seated at the piano, Jack started the slow dramatic beginning of "Let It Go" as a hush gathered over the crowd. Jack looked at the little girl and smiled as she sang. Jared leaned against the gazebo, transfixed at the sight. He imagined them having a beautiful little blond girl of their own sitting at the piano with the only woman he would ever love. He wanted that more than the breath in his lungs. His heart ached with how much he loved her and how much he wanted a life with her. He knew in that instant that nothing else would do. He would spend his entire life trying to make that happen or by Jesus he would die trying. There just wasn't any other outcome for his life that he would settle for.

The song ended and "the crowd went wild." Jack laughed as the little girl jumped into her arms. She grinned and walked the tyke back to her parents.

The sun had sunk behind the trees and the fireworks would begin within the hour. They packed up the supplies and put everything in the Suburban. Jack had decided to have Bear bring her home before the fireworks because she didn't think Jane would like them much, so she looked for Jared to let him know she'd would see him later. She saw him helping Gracie pack stuff up and there were several young women flocking around helping and trying to speak to him. She smiled. Who could blame them? Then she thought maybe it would be best if she let the heat between them cool down anyway. Maybe he could actually meet a nice girl without all the shit that surrounded Jack. They would be back to their lives soon and things could get back to normal...whatever the hell that was. She walked back to the Suburban with Jane, and Bear held the door.

"All set?" he asked.

She smiled. "Yup," she replied, sliding in.

They had been home about a half an hour when the fireworks started. Jack was outside the house with Jane after Bear had gone back. Jane started whining and running around like a crazy dog. Jack called to her, trying to get her to come inside so that they could hunker down with her favorite blanket for comfort. Jane darted away and started running full speed toward the pond. Jack hollered to her, but it was dark and she was quickly out of sight. Jack could hear her barking in the distance. Jack grabbed the flashlight and her leash and started toward the pond. She jogged down and found her by the water. Jack put her on the leash and was turning back when a truck coming full speed down the road stopped suddenly at Jared's cabin. Jared jumped out of his truck and ran to his cabin calling her name.

Jack was suddenly afraid. What had happened? Was one of her brothers hurt? Jack ran to the cabin calling after Jared. He ran out and grabbed her in a tight embrace.

"What's the matter? Is it one of the boys?" Jack gasped.

Jared pulled her away a little to look at her. "What? Why did you leave? Why didn't you tell me you were leaving? Fuckin'-A, Jack, you scared the shit out of me!"

Jack shook her head. "I don't understand. I went to find you to tell you that Bear was bringing me home because Jane wouldn't like the fireworks and I would see you all later, but you were helping Gracie. I didn't want you to miss the fireworks. Bear just dropped me off and before we could get in the house Jane bolted down here," she said in a winded voice. The way he was looking at her made her knees turn to jelly.

Jesus.

"Princess, don't you know..."

Jack put her fingers over his mouth. "No more words," she whispered and covered his mouth with hers.

The taste of him was intoxicating. She moaned and pressed herself against him, winding her hands in his hair. Jared cupped her face and kissed her hard, speaking to her, but she couldn't understand the words. There was no need to understand the words. Jared's tongue tasted her mouth and he moaned. Jack could feel his hard length against her stomach. She felt like she was drowning in desire; she wanted him so bad. The desire wasn't just sexual, it was everything about him—she wanted to smell him, touch him, taste him, hear his soft moans and his urgent cries. She wanted all of him, and she couldn't wait another second. She knew that it couldn't last, but by Jesus, she was taking tonight if for no other reason than to sustain her for the rest of her life. Every second of the last four years that she had pushed herself down and put others ahead of herself came down to this very moment in time. She needed to be with him more than she needed to breathe.

Her tongue danced with his as they devoured each other. She broke free of his lips, and her lips traveled down his neck behind his ear, kissing him and smelling him. She just couldn't get close enough to him. She nuzzled him and licked and kissed him. He was holding her so tight she was having trouble breathing. His hand gripped her ass and ground it against him. She moaned loudly, which was almost his undoing. He grabbed her face and kissed her again.

"Baby, I need you...I need to see all of you...please come in the cabin with me, stay with me," Jared pleaded against her lips.

"Yes, yes," she moaned breathlessly. He grabbed her hand and ran toward the cabin. Jack laughed, trying to hang onto Jane's leash and keep up with him.

They all made it into the cabin, and Jared unhooked Jane and pointed to the couch. Jane jumped up on the couch and settled right down. Jared pulled out his phone and started texting.

"Jack is with me. Stay the fuck away from the cabin." That might be the last text he ever got to send to her brothers, Jared thought idly.

No matter. The night was theirs.

Jared shut his phone off and threw it on the coffee table. He looked up to see Jack grinning at him. "Texting. Really?" she teased.

"I texted Bobby that you were with me and to stay the fuck away," Jared replied with a sheepish grin.

Jack ran and jumped into his arms and wrapped her long legs around him. "Thank Christ," she exclaimed as her lips connected with his.

Jared grabbed her ass and held her tight against him, walking to the bedroom without losing contact with her lips. She wound her fingers in his silky curls as they kissed, loving the taste of him.

When they were standing beside the bed, he set her down and pulled her dress over her head. She stood there in her sexy bra, thong, and red cowboy boots.

Sweet Jesus, she was beautiful.

He went to one knee and kissed her stomach as he gripped her thong and ripped it off her. He lay her down on the bed and began tasting her immediately.

Jack bucked off the bed and screamed. It felt like hot lava had traveled throughout her entire body.

Jared gripped her hips to hold her in place while he put her legs over his shoulders.

Oh. My. God.

She tasted like the sweetest nectar. He couldn't get enough. She was so wet he just kept swallowing and tasting until she was writhing on the bed as she gripped his head and screamed. He felt her sex contract around his mouth. He couldn't wait another second. He knew she was ready for him.

Jared stood up and pulled open his nightstand and realized that he hadn't been there for years. The last woman he had been with in this bed was her. The condoms were probably unreliable at best. He almost cried as he froze.

Jack looked up. "What? Please, Jared, I need you now!" she cried.

Jared threw off his shirt and shorts and stood there in his boxer briefs. "Baby, the last time I was with a woman here it was you. The condoms are worthless. Tell me what to do."

Jack shook her head. "It doesn't matter, I can't get pregnant, and you're the last person I slept with. I'm assuming you're clean? I need you now Jared, please."

The plea in her voice was his undoing. "Yes, I'm clean." He tossed his underwear aside and he was inside her in one lunge. "Fuck," he whispered, almost coming in the first thrust. She was so wet and tight. He froze and kissed her tenderly. She moved her hips to feel him but he held fast.

"Shhh, baby wait. Slow down, or I'm not going to last. You feel too good and I've waited too long for you. Do you know how humbled I am that you've not been with another man? Jesus, Princess, do you have any idea how much I love you?" Jared cried out as a tear dropped to her cheek.

Jack shook her head. "No words. We have tonight only, and I don't want to talk about the past. I want to feel you all around me. Please Jared, make love to me." Jack moaned as she took his lips violently. He moaned in response and started to move and pull out and push back in. The slow, sweet love gave way to hot urgent thrusts, and they were both screaming each other's name as they came together.

Jared rolled to his side, pulled her into him, and sighed. He kissed her temple and just breathed her in. Jack started laughing, so he pulled away to look her in the eyes. Jack cupped his cheek and kissed his lips.

"I just realized that I'm still wearing my bra and cowboy boots," she exclaimed, laughing. He stroked his hand up her side slowly and unsnapped her bra from behind. She shivered and heat started traveling to her nether regions again.

"Well we must rectify that right now," he said playfully, pulling her bra away. He rolled her over onto her back and just looked at her up and down. "You take my breath away, Princess," he muttered, tearing up. She cupped his cheeks.

"Hey, hey," she said bringing his mouth down to hers. He kissed her slowly and then moved to her neck and behind her ears as his hand cupped her swollen breast. She moaned and arched her back.

Jared rolled his thumb across the hard nipple and she gasped and moaned. He replaced his hand with his mouth and he moaned. White hot passion shot through him.

Holy hell! He'd never been as turned on in his life. He felt like the fuse to a stick of dynamite with a flame dancing beside him. He suckled and licked and then went to the other and did the same.

"Jared, I need you again. I need you inside me please."

He was quick to oblige. He entered her slowly and they both moaned. They each had waited so long for this. Jared rolled over and took her with him without breaking contact. She was arched over him and started moving up and down on him. He gripped her hips to slow her.

"Easy baby, take it slow. I feel like I'm sixteen years old. You feel too good."

Jack kissed him slowly and let her tongue dance with his before she sat up and leaned back, gripping his knees. At this different angle, she gasped and slowly gyrated all around him. He grasped her hips and thrust deep inside her, and she grabbed his shoulders and rocked back and forth. He started thrusting faster and faster.

"Jesus, Jack, I'm not going to last," he hollered as she threw her head back and splintered into a million pieces. She collapsed on top of his chest and giggled contentedly. He hugged her close and they dozed for a bit before he woke her up by stroking her behind and up her back with his fingertips. She moaned and shivered. He rolled her over and kissed her tattoo.

"Will you tell me what this says, Princess?" he asked.

She ran her fingers through his hair. "It's Sanskrit. It says 'Night will be over; there will be morning,'" she whispered softly.

He kissed it again. "It's beautiful," Jared murmured.

Jack lay him flat on his back and kissed his tattoo above his heart. It was a red rose with most of its petals falling off and turning black.

"This is beautiful and sad at the same time," she whispered.

Jared cupped her face and looked at her in the moonlight. "My heart has been broken for a very long time, Princess," he replied, kissing her tenderly.

Jack tried very hard to stop the tears but she couldn't. "Would you please just hold me? Don't speak. I can't handle that right now. I really just need you to hold me so tight that nothing else can get through, Jared. Please," she said with a whimper.

"Oh, baby," he replied. "No more words."

Jared gathered her in as tight as he could without hurting her and simply held her as they both fell asleep.

Jack felt the sun and warm breeze on her face. *Mmmmm, so nice.* She was squinting because of the blinding sun but could see a figure coming toward her as she lay on the beach at Moose Pond. It was as if the figure was in slow motion and Jack wanted to run to the woman. Yes, it was a woman walking toward her, but she couldn't move her feet to go to her. As the woman slowly approached her, Jack recognized her mother. She was beautiful with her curls piled on top of her head in a bun and loose tendrils blowing in the breeze. She was smiling, and her eyes were the kindest eyes Jack had ever seen. She instantly felt peace and love. They just stared at each other for a moment until her mother reached up to push a piece of Jack's hair behind her ear. Her mother uttered something to her, but Jack couldn't hear the words. Jack was confused and asked her what she said, but now Jack couldn't hear her own voice either. Her mother said the words again, but there was no sound this time either; however, this time Jack could read her lips.

"It's time," her mother was saying.

Jack went to reach out to her and asked her, "What is it time for?" but her mother was fading away, shaking her head. Was that a look of concern on her mother's face?

Jack cried out to her mother, but then she was gone and Jack was in her father's office at the house. Jack looked around and saw her father slumped over his desk. Jack gasped and jumped back.

"Daddy?" she gasped as she walked closer to him. As she rounded the desk slowly, she touched his shoulder. "Daddy," she whispered. Oh, if she could have one last conversation with her father!

David Johnson slowly lifted his head and looked at Jack. Jack jumped back and stared, unable to breathe. He truly looked like death. There were dark red circles around his eyes and he had an ash-gray pallor.

"Hello, Princess," he sneered.

Jack brought her hand to her mouth to stifle a cry. "See what you did to me? I always said you'd be the death of me, and you were," he growled.

"Daddy, I'm so sorry! Please forgive me! I'm so, so sorry!" Jack cried.

"It's too late for me, Princess, but I thought you loved Jared," her father continued, sadly shaking his head.

Jack's eyes grew wide and she nodded her head. "I do! I do love him!" she gasped.

David kicked back his chair, splintering it as it sailed backward. "Well, if you love him, why won't you let him move on with his life? You heard his girlfriend—he wants a houseful of children. You can't give him any children because you're being punished for killing his child. You were always so selfish! Your mother gave her life for you, and your brothers have done nothing but worry about you since you were born, but you have never cared about anybody but yourself. Jared has the chance to have a good life, but you insist on pulling him down with you. You won't be happy until he has to suffer with your illness and your disgusting past until he just can't stand it any longer and either drinks himself into an early grave or blows his brains out. You hurt or kill everything you touch. Tell me, Princess, are you planning on telling Jared that you killed his daughter?" her father sneered.

Jack covered her ears. *Breathe. Breathe.* This wasn't real. This was her Dark Twin trying to get to her. What had Ava told her to do?

Think.

Think.

Look for a way out. There is always a way out. Look for it. Jack turned around and around until she focused on the office door. Her feet wouldn't move. Suddenly, she heard scratching outside the door and was able to run to it and thrust it open.

Jack sat bolt upright in bed and clutched her throat, trying to get air into her lungs. She looked down to see Jared sleeping soundly beside her. Then she heard the scratching again. Jane! Jane was outside the bedroom door trying to get to Jack because she knew she was in distress.

Jack jumped out of bed and opened the door to let her in. Jack knelt down and let Jane lick her face to assure the dog that she was okay.

Jack held her head in her hands. This was insane. Her father was right. Jared deserved better than her, and what if she did drive him to hate her and drink himself into an early grave? She was selfish. She just had to have one more night with him. It really *was* all about her.

Jack found her dress, pulled it over her head, and ran out the door with Jane right on her heels. The sun was just coming up as Jack started running up the gravel dirt road to the house and stumbled. She skidded in the rocks, cutting her knees up, and then she got up again and ran as if the hounds of hell were on her heels.

Because they were.

The little sharp pebbles in the gravel road inflicted small cuts all over Jack's bare feet, but she never stopped. She could feel the tingle starting; her heartbeat sped up, and she was having a hard time breathing. She had to get out of here before her Dark Twin found her. She needed to get back to New York and the life she had made for herself. She wasn't safe here. She would never forgive herself if she hurt her brothers or, God forbid, Jared.

She ran up the stairs to the house and hollered for Henry. She ran into her room, grabbed her suitcase, and began throwing every piece of clothing in her room in the suitcase, all the while hollering for Henry. Then she started hollering for Caleb and Bear. She was getting more anxious by the second, and when the voice laughed in her head, she screamed. Jane was barking and jumping up on Jack.

Bear and Henry ran into her room. Bear grabbed her by the shoulders and made her look at him.

"Jack! What happened? Talk to me, Princess!" Bear commanded. At the very sound of the name Princess, Jack winced.

"Bear, I need to leave. Right now! Please, I need to be on a plane to New York. Please help me. Where is Henry?" she cried.

Henry ran to stand beside her. "I'm here, Jack, what do you need me to do?" he said calmly.

"Henry, I need for you to call Phillip and see if the jet is in Portland. I will be there in two hours. Please!"

Jane was going mental barking. Henry already had his phone out and was dialing as he took Jane outside to calm her down.

Bear looked at Jack. "Sweetie, please calm down. Did you and Jared have a fight?"

Jack shook her head. "No, no...I just need to get away. Please help me. Jared deserves better than this," she said, gesturing toward herself.

Bobby came in and instantly noticed blood dripping down her leg.

"Jack, you're bleeding!"

Bear looked down. "What the fuck?" he shouted, clearly not knowing what to do.

Bobby came toward her. "Princess, let me clean your cut and get you a sedative okay?"

Jack backed away. "No! Stay away! Just get me to the airport and I will take a sedative on the way, I promise! Caleb, will you drive me?" she begged. Caleb nodded, picking up her suitcase.

Henry walked back into her room. "The jet is in Portland and will be ready to go when you get there. Do you want me to call Sam?" he asked.

Jack shook her head. "No. I'll call him on the way. Let's just go," she said, grabbing her purse. Her phone was in her purse. The laughter in her head was getting worse. She had to hurry.

Jack hugged her brothers and told them she would call them when she got home. She and Caleb then piled into the Suburban. As they started to drive out, Jared's truck flew up the gravel drive. He maneuvered his truck directly in front of the Suburban. Caleb jammed on the brakes and the truck screeched to a halt.

"Jesus!" Caleb shouted. Jack jumped out and ran around to the front of the two trucks. Jared also jumped out of his truck wearing only a pair of jeans.

Jack threw her arms out. "Stop! Don't come near me, Jared Ross!" Both Bear and Bobby flanked Jared and grabbed his arms.

Jared struggled for a minute. "Let me fuckin' go—now!" he hollered. When he realized they weren't going to let him go, he just looked at Jack and pleaded with her. "Don't do this, Jack, please don't do this. Don't leave me again, not like this," he said as tears cascaded down his face.

Jack could hardly breathe. "I have to, don't you see? Jared, I'm fucking broken! I'm damaged goods beyond repair! Just let me go, for Christ's sake!" she hollered as she too sobbed uncontrollably.

Jared shook his head. "No, I won't! We can get through this together," he begged, trying to pull free of her brothers.

Jack looked at Jared and knew what she had to do. "You're the reason I'm broken, Jared," she cried out. "Can't you see that?"

Jared looked like she had just sucker-punched him in the gut. He shook his head. "No, you don't mean that, Princess," he whispered.

Jack marched right up to him and looked him in the eye. "Yes, I do. Whatever we had, it's over for good. I built a life in New York, and I deserve at least a small amount of happiness. Let me have at least that much, Jared. Stay away from me. I'm no good for you. I told you we had one night, now stay the fuck away from me."

Jack walked back to the truck and climbed in. Jared turned to Caleb.

"Don't do it, Caleb—please, just let me talk to her."

Caleb looked at Jared sadly. "Sorry, Bro, I have to do what she asks," he muttered as he got in the Suburban and drove down the road.

As they pulled out of sight, Jack asked Caleb to pull over. She pulled her phone out of her purse, dialed Sam, and handed the phone to Caleb. Caleb nodded. He got out of the truck and went to her suitcase, pulling out her sedatives. He held out two. With wild eyes, she asked him to make sure she got on the jet. Caleb nodded in silent agreement.

Jack turned up the volume to the music and the song that was playing was a new group they had signed. The lead singer was singing a song Jack had written after seeing Jared and Stephanie together for the first time. It had just landed in the number one slot. Jack smiled wanly and then went limp.

Jared jerked free and began to punch the hood of his truck repeatedly until there was a crater in the middle. All the brothers had backed up and watched him vent. When he stopped punching the hood, he looked up to find Bear.

Bear smirked. "Oh, you think that will make you feel better? Fine, bring it," he said motioning for Jared to step toward him. Jared went completely mental and dove for him, knocking him to the ground. They rolled around on the ground as Jared got in some good punches. Finally they both stood, trying to get their breath back while the other brothers enjoyed the show.

"Why the fuck didn't you let me talk to her! Jesus, Bear, why do you have to be so fucking hard-headed all the time?" Jared hollered. He rushed at Bear again, and Bear punched him in the gut, leaving Jared gasping for air.

"She's my baby sister and I will always take care of her, and if she needs to be left alone, then I make that happen," Bear replied as he lost his breath from Jared tackling him to the ground.

"No one loves that fucking girl more than me, Bear!" Jared growled as he punched Bear in the eye. All seven brothers winced at that blow as they watched, leaning against Jared's truck with arms crossed.

Bear got up slowly and grabbed his knees. "I know that," he muttered, punching Jared square in the nose.

Jared appeared confused as he wiped the blood from his nose. "What did you say?" Jared asked.

Bear crossed his arms. "You heard me. I know how much you love her, Jared Ross, so when the fuck are you going to step up to the plate and fight for her?" Bear hollered at him.

Jared shook his head. "Wait, you've been whaling on me and what you really want me to do is go after her?" he asked, wiping at his nose.

"Yes…no…I want you to give her some time, and then I want you to, I don't fucking know, court her, woo her. I want you to fight for her, God damn it! I want you to take the kid gloves off and exorcise those demons once and for all. Stop friggin' wallowing in self-pity about how fucking sad the situation is and just fucking show her how much you love her!" Bear hollered.

"HOW THE FUCK DO I DO THAT?" Jared bellowed.

"Um, dude, I think Bear just told you to woo her," Bobby said, laughing.

"Okay, what I really want to know is how Bear knows the word *woo*?" Ty chuckled and put his hand up for a fist bump with Bobby.

Bear pointed menacingly to the twins, who pointed to themselves and looked around with mock "Who, us?" expressions on their faces.

"Yeah, you two, you're fucking next," Bear grunted, making a fist.

Meanwhile Jared leaned over, blew his nostrils out in the dirt, and tried to catch his breath. Bear came over and grasped his shoulder.

"Do you love her, Jared? I mean really love her?" he asked.

Jared stood up and looked at Bear. "I don't want any kind of life without her in it. She's it for me, Bear——she always has been," he replied softly.

Bear nodded. "Do you believe all that shit about it being your fault she's broken and that she's too damaged?" he asked.

Jared shook his head. "No, I think she was trying to hurt me and push me away," he replied confidently.

Bear grinned broadly. "Bingo! Now go back to New York and fucking woo her, and if that shit doesn't work, because I have no fucking idea how you woo anybody, then fight dirty. Do whatever you need to in order to make her see that you two belong together. But just know this, my brother: if you make her cry or hurt her in any way, these will be just love taps compared to the ass-kicking I'll give you. Are we clear?" he asked, putting his arm around Jared's shoulders.

"Crystal," Jared muttered as he wiped the blood from his nose with the back of his hand.

Jack sat back in the large captain office chair and absentmindedly stroked the mint green tourmaline necklace she had found herself wearing the day after Sam had picked her up at JFK. She had slept the day and night away, waking at about three a.m. to stagger into the shower. The water had stung all the little cuts on the bottom of her feet, and her knees needed to be bandaged. As she was washing herself, she had discovered the necklace and stepped out of the massive shower to look in the mirror. The very necklace she had asked the vendor about.

It was stunning. Jared must have bought it and put it on her when she fell asleep. She stepped back into the shower and sat on the wet tiles. She cried for a love that had no end but could never have life. Would she be in a constant state of grief her whole life? The water from the shower washed away any signs of her gut-wrenching emotions on the outside. When she rose and stepped out of the shower, she was determined to crawl back to her life of solitude.

"Um, excuse me, Miss Johnson? Ricky Vance is here to see you?" the new receptionist, Bella, announced as she peeked her head in Jack's office door.

Bella's voice startled Jack, and then she smiled. "Great. Show him in, please," she replied.

Jack stood behind her desk as Ricky Vance walked into her office wearing blue jeans, cowboy boots, a button-down denim shirt, tweed suit coat, and a black cowboy hat.

Jack grinned. She knew why his security team had been increased. The women went crazy for him.

She held out her hand and greeted him with genuine affection. "Hi, Ricky, it's so nice to see you again."

Ricky grasped both her hands in his and smiled before turning serious. "I'm so sorry about your father, Jack," he said quietly.

Jack nodded. "Thank you. It's been a little rough," she smiled sadly.

"Well, I wanted to wait a few weeks after you got back to work so you could settle in. I got your message that you think you worked out the bugs in the songs you were writing for me," he said as they sat down.

Jack nodded excitedly before jumping back up and grabbing a folder. "I can't wait. Let's go into the studio and we can go over them initially and then you and the band can practice them and come in next week? Sound good?" she asked, gliding down the hall in her gray Jimmy Choos. She was wearing one of the new dresses from the Worthington Business Women line. Phillip had begged her last week to agree to be the face of the line. He was now in charge of the women's business line, and he really needed this feather in his cap. All she would have to do is agree to a couple of photo shoots a month. She'd have total control over where and when the shoots were held, and she would be paid a ridiculous amount of money for them, but more importantly she would get her choice of business wear. That was huge, because more and more she was sitting in meetings in heels rather than at the piano in her chucks. Plus, there wasn't much she wouldn't do for Phillip, so it was a win all the way around.

They worked on the songs, and Ricky loved them. When he had enough to go back to the band with, they both stood and Jack walked him out to the reception area. Ricky put his hands in his pockets uncomfortably. He grabbed the hat off his head and held it in his hands.

"Um, well, I also wanted to apologize for telling the world that you were my girl. I had no idea you were taken. I hope that didn't cause any problems," he said in an embarrassed tone.

Jack looked confused. "What are you talking about?" she asked.

Ricky stopped turning his hat around and around in his hand and looked her in the eyes. "Um, your boyfriend came to see me in the club I was working early last week. He's a big guy, and he initially looked like he was going to beat the shit—ah, like he was going to punch me—but we sat down and it was all good. He told me how he understood how any man would be in love with you but that you were his future bride. Congratulations. He's a pretty good guy. He bought me and the band a few rounds of beer and we talked music and video games of course. That guy sure knows his games," Ricky said, smiling and shaking his head.

Jack's eyes narrowed and she just stared. Ricky touched her arm. "Ma'am?" he whispered.

Jack's eyes got wide and she shook her head to clear it. "What was..." she said hoarsely. She cleared her throat and started again. "What was his name? This man?" she asked.

Ricky frowned. "Um, your fiancé, Ross, Jared Ross the gamer?"

Jack stood up straight. "And you say that he just came to see you?" she said intently.

Ricky smiled. "Yes ma'am, last week. Maybe Tuesday night? Am I missing something here?" he asked, becoming confused.

Jack smoothed down the sleeveless gray snug-fitting dress and shook her head and smiled. "No, no, I'm just surprised he told you, that's all," she said as she held out her hand. "Let me know how it goes with the band, and I'll see you next week," she ended, shaking his hand and watching him walk out the door.

What.

The.

Fuck.

Jack walked back to her office and slumped down in her chair, patting Jane as the dog's head nuzzled Jack's thigh. What was going on?

Jack had decided it was best to just ignore the whole thing. She didn't call her brothers; she was going to let the whole thing slide because, after all, it had gotten her out of Ricky Vance's line of sight. That evening, she walked into the lobby of her apartment building to find large vases of sunflowers everywhere.

Nice. Sunflowers were her favorite flower.

Rigby met her halfway into the lobby with an enormous bouquet of sunflowers and daisies. "Good evening, Miss Johnson," he said handing the bouquet to her. "I had the pleasure of meeting your groom-to-be today, and he wanted me to give these to you. He also had your penthouse key and oversaw several deliveries today. I hope you enjoy them!"

Jack looked down at the flowers. "Um, can I ask you, did he introduce himself to you, other than as my future husband?" she asked as she brought the flowers up to her face to smell.

"Oh yes, of course. Mr. Jared Ross. Very nice chap," he said smiling.

Jack stared for a moment and then grinned and touched his arm. "Thank you so much, Rigby. Have a good night," she said, trying to sound as normal as she could. What *was* going on, she thought as she got in the elevator. As she stepped out of the elevator, there were several urns surrounding her door with beautiful arrangements of sunflowers.

She opened her door and gasped. There were urns and vases covering every square inch of empty space in her apartment. Jack became absolutely speechless as she walked through the apartment. All at once, it hit her to look for cards in the flowers. She sat on the staircase and searched the bouquet she was holding until she found the small card. She tore open the envelope.

"I will love you at your darkest," it read in Jared's handwriting. Jack sat there for a while and stared at the note. All at once she flew all about the apartment with Jane, gathering all the personally handwritten cards. Jane thought it was a wonderful game, and she barked and ran from flower arrangement to flower arrangement smelling. Jack pulled out her phone. She needed some Mac time.

Mac and Jack sat on the bar stools in the kitchen with the enormous pile of handwritten cards sitting there. Mac shook her head. "I think this is the most romantic gesture I have ever seen," she swooned.

Jack scowled at her and picked up a card. "You're mine, my princess. Night will be over; there will be morning. I love you," she read aloud. "What am I going to do, Mac? I told him it was over—over for good. I blamed all my mental shit on him to guilt him into leaving me alone and finally moving on with his life. There's no moving on for me, but he can! He can get married and have babies. I can't give him that, ever. I really just want to be left alone to live my life in solitude. What's wrong with that?" she wailed, holding a card to her lips.

"Well, maybe there wouldn't be anything wrong with that if it was true," Mac said quietly. Jack whipped her head around. Mac looked her straight in the eyes. "You are not broken, Jack, you are a woman who has been through some shit, but so have a lot of other people. You just have to move beyond it."

When Jack opened her mouth to respond, Mac held up her hand. "I know, I get it, that's what you say, all you want is to be just left alone, but hear me out. Do you think it was just pure coincidence that Jared was loved by your mother and taken in by your family? You have loved him your whole life, and as far as I can see, the two of you were truly made for each other. I mean *literally,* Jack! He had a shitty childhood and he says he is broken as well. So practically at birth, God—or the Universe, whatever you want to call it—put the two of you together. Two people who always feel safe with each other and who share a love that most people never ever find in this life. Maybe you were always supposed to go through the shit you did, but God gave you each other to help you each get through it. Look at all the good you have done because you were on the streets and because you suffer from PTSD. Look, I don't pretend to know what you suffer or have suffered, but I do know that this man loves you and always has. He's not going to 'move on,' and neither are you. Can you please just open yourself up and see where this leads? Please?" Mac asked with tears in her eyes as she picked up a card from the counter.

Jack wiped a tear away and smiled. "Jesus, since when did you become so damn philosophical?" she said with a rueful smile.

Mac stood up and kissed her forehead. "Since I love you like a sista, and I want you to be utterly and incandescently happy," she exclaimed as she cupped Jack's cheeks and stared intently into her teary eyes.

Jack sniffed and brought her hands to cover Mac's. "Well said, Miss Austen, well said. I hear what you're saying, but it just can't happen, Mac. I don't think my demons would ever allow me to be with Jared forever and ever. I could never ask anybody to endure the hell that is my life from time to time. But I love you for being brave enough to tell it to me straight. Now go home to my brother and make him the happiest man on the planet," she said, smiling at her best friend.

Mac wiggled her eyebrows and Jack blanched. "God, no. I don't want to hear any details!" she said, laughing as she walked Mac to the door. Jack grabbed a vase of sunflowers and thrust them into Mac's arms. "Take these; I seem to have plenty."

Mac chuckled and walked out the door. "Au revoir!"

Jack and Jane climbed the stairs for bed. Jack's head was still swimming, but she felt somewhat calm. She had seen Sam and Ava multiple times since she had been back, and they both agreed that she had made immense progress during her stay in Maine. She had been able to forgive her father and grieve for the young girl she had been. Ava was adamant that the dreams, although awful, were simply a manifestation of her guilt and grief. Jack wanted to believe that, but there was a tiny echo in her mind that was waiting for something. Waiting for what, she had no idea.

Jack woke to a loud thud. She lifted her head and felt the bed for Jane. No Jane. Jack whispered for her, but she wasn't in the bedroom. That was very strange, because Jane never left her side at night. For a dog, Jane took her role as guardian of the night very seriously with Jack. A sudden dread crept into the pit of Jack's stomach as she crawled out of bed and started for the door. She walked silently toward the staircase and then thought maybe she should have gotten her robe. All she had on was a black silk nightgown that didn't go past her thighs and bare feet. As she got to the top of the staircase and started down, she noticed that all the living room furniture had been moved to the sides of the room to make an open area. It was dark except for the small Tiffany lamp in the corner. As Jack's eyes adjusted to the semidarkness, she jumped back as she saw Jared sitting on the couch with Jane curled up beside him.

"What are you doing here?" she said, looking around nervously.

"I'm here to tear down your walls," Jared replied calmly, looking her up and down appreciatively. "Why don't you make this easy for me and come and sit down with Jane, and you and I will talk this through," Jared said, patting the couch.

Jack shook her head and started toward the kitchen, where her phone was. "Not gonna happen, Jared. I'm calling the police," she said before he grabbed her from behind, holding her tight.

"No, you're not. Your phone isn't there. You know I'm not going to hurt you, Princess. I just want to talk," he said, turning her and leading her to the living room.

Once there, Jack suddenly grabbed Jared's arm and flipped him over her shoulder, putting her foot against his windpipe. "Well, I'm going to fucking hurt you. How dare you decide that you can waltz into my life and presume to take control? Telling people we are engaged. What the fuck, Jared?" Jack cried.

Jared grabbed her leg and flipped her on her back, pinning her hands above her head. Surprised, and with her chest heaving, she struggled against him. "Yeah, well, I'm done playing nice, Princess. You're going to shut the fuck up and listen to me now. I'm sick to death of hearing how damaged you are and that it's for my own good, my own safety, that you and I can't be together. That's bullshit! What you went through was shitty, and whatever demons you have because of it, we will exorcise them together. Do you hear me? Together!" he hollered down at her.

Jack bucked up, kneed Jared in the balls, and went into a crouching attack position as he yelped and rolled into a ball on the floor. "Together? Really, Jared? I wanted to run away *together* and I waited by my window for you to come get me, but you didn't! I was led to that car and put on that plane *by myself.* I was still so sure that you would come get me and take me away. You never fucking did, and the shit storm that became my life started. Where the fuck *were* you?" she screamed.

Jared had come up on one knee and stayed crouching. Tears stung his eyes. "I know, baby, I went back to the cabin and packed all my stuff into the truck and waited until daybreak. My plan was to show up first thing that morning and have it out with your father again, grab you, and leave. I had no idea that you had left so early in the morning."

Tears fell from both Jack's and Jared's eyes. "I think I was in shock at what your father had said to me that night. It ripped my guts out. He was the only man in the world whose opinion of me mattered, and I had shattered that. But even that didn't matter once I got back to the cabin. None of that meant shit, only you. Once I drove into the driveway, your brothers came out intending to beat the shit out of me and told me you were gone and so was your father. Your father didn't tell anyone where you were. I tried to find you, Jack! I went directly to New York and got a job so I could save up and hire a private investigator."

Jack brought her hand to mouth and gasped. "It was you? When I was living on the streets, people would tell me there was a military man asking about me. Was that your private investigator? I thought it was my father trying to get me to go back to Beckett's House," she sobbed.

Jared stiffened. "There is no Beckett's House anymore," he announced flatly. Jack looked confused. "When you watched your father's DVD and had your breakdown, Sam told us a little about what happened at Beckett's House," Jared said, flexing his fists and remembering his visit to the shithole. "I bought the property and shut it down and, well actually, I had it burned down. It no longer exists," he said, rubbing his chest to relieve the pain at the thought of her hurt in that hellhole. "Tell me what happened there, Princess. I need to know everything," he whispered.

Jack stared at him. He had burned down Beckett's House because they had hurt her. He had done that for her. "How? How did you burn it down?" she asked.

Jared got up and grabbed a cashmere throw. "Being a millionaire has a few perks, I must say," he said with a sad smile. He slowly walked to her and draped the throw around her shoulders. She sat down cross-legged on the floor with Jane beside her.

Jared sat opposite her with his legs out and his arms bracing himself. "Tell me, baby, tell me what happened," he whispered.

Jack sighed in resignation.

It was time.

It was time he knew all the horrible truth, because only then would he be disgusted enough with her to finally walk away.

She began right at the beginning, when she was standing in the office and her long blond braid had been clipped off. She cried as she told him about the horrible beating and waking up in the infirmary and then the overheard conversation about their baby and that she would never be able to conceive. At that, Jared brought his knees up and hugged them with his face buried. She could see his body shuddering with sobs. Jack could hardly talk she was crying so hard, but she got through every horrible event until she got to the call from Caleb that her father had passed away.

"I killed him, Jared. Just as sure as if I had slit his throat with my blade, I killed him. I hurt everyone who loves me. I don't deserve love, that's why our child was taken away from me," she sobbed.

Jared lifted his head and was in front of her instantly, holding her face in his hands. "Is that what you believe?" he cried. "That's not true, and you know deep inside you, Jack Elsie Johnson, that is not true. Your mother loved you before you were even born. You saw those videos of your mother and father. She touched you while you still inside her and she loved you. You are just like her. You're the sweetest and most loving person I know. Your daddy loved you more than life itself. I believe you were the reason he kept on living after your mother passed. I love you, Princess, so fucking much. The year before we declared our love, your father knew that I loved you, and it scared him. He told me to stay away from you, but I couldn't. Jesus, I couldn't stay away then and I can't stay away now, or ever. Baby, none of that shit was your fault. It was nobody's fault. Your daddy was scared for you. Hell, even Marcus was scared for you because they loved you so damn much and you were always so trusting of everybody. Nobody ever intended to hurt you or me but shit happened—really, really bad shit. I know you will have to deal with your illness for the rest of your life but you will never have to go it alone, baby. Ever. I'm not going anywhere. I will follow you for the rest of my days. I will camp out in your lobby and make sure no men come up here. I will sleep outside your door every night if I have to. I meant what I said in the card. I will love you at your darkest. I will never ever let anything bad happen to you again," he said against her mouth as he kissed her tenderly.

Jack grabbed his face and pulled him back. "What about our baby girl, Jared? Because of me she's gone," Jack sobbed.

Jared grasped her face. "*No!* Don't you say that! We made a beautiful baby girl, and I will always have her in my heart. She is perfect and safe. I know because my father saw her with your mother," he replied, hugging her tight.

Jack sobbed, "What?"

Jared grinned through his tears and nodded his head. "I didn't tell you that part of my father's vision. When your mother appeared to my father, she was carrying a dark-haired baby girl about two years old. My father said she had my brown eyes. He said she was beautiful. She's with your mother, Princess, safe and sound. Our daughter."

Jack cried out. "I saw her, Jared! I saw our baby girl too! She was with my mother in a dream, and yes, she looks just like you!" Jack sobbed harder. "She touched my face and I looked into her eyes! I knew who she was!"

Jared gathered Jack tight and they rolled to the floor and sobbed deep healing sobs until the tears were drained and forever shed.

"Don't ever leave me again, Princess. I couldn't survive it. I love you with every fiber of my being, and I will spend the rest of my days taking care of you," Jared whispered in Jack's ear some time later.

Jack pulled away just enough to look into his eyes. Those beautiful, brown, loving eyes. She smiled and nodded. "I'd like that," she whispered as a tear slowly slid down her cheek.

Jared caught it on a kiss and picked her up and carried her upstairs to bed. Their bed, with Jane trotting along behind.

The sun was shining and the leaves had turned orange and red. It was a particularly warm day in late September, and the park in Harmony, Maine, had been decked out with small white folding chairs in front of the gazebo. A red carpet ran through the middle of the chairs to a large white tent, where

Phillip had assembled a team of people to help Jack and Mac get ready for the wedding. The "Wedding of the Century" one tabloid had called it. The "Ultimate Merger," another had touted. The union between millionaire Global Gamer and millionaire Princess Production music mogul/supermodel was much anticipated.

Security was tight, but Jack refused to let that ruin her day and hadn't told anyone where the wedding was taking place except those who were attending, which included the whole town of Harmony. What most folks didn't know about Maine folks was how fiercely loyal they were to each other. Not a soul leaked information about the wedding, and there wasn't a paparazzi in sight.

The whole town had gathered and everyone was seated, waiting for the ceremony to begin. Gracie ducked into the tent to check on Jack and Mac. Jack saw Gracie and squealed. Gracie was beautiful in a pretty pink flowing dress with little cap sleeves that floated as she walked. She had perfect silver strappy heels, and her hair was in loose dark waves down her back. She looked like the most beautiful Abenaki Indian queen.

Gracie held Jack's hand and smiled, shaking her head. "You look so much like your momma right now, baby girl. Lord, I miss her!" she declared vehemently.

Jack grinned. "Oh, Gracie, you've been like a mother to me. Thank you. Do you believe it? I'm getting married!" she exclaimed, laughing with tears in her eyes.

Gracie smiled. "About damn time! I've known you both since before you both could walk. You really were made for each other. I couldn't be happier for you both, Princess," Gracie replied, hugging her.

Gracie looked at Mac. "And you, Red, well let's just say I see a whole lot of similarities between you two and Elsie Johnson and myself, and we'll leave it at that. How are we looking in here? Everyone is seated and ready out there."

Gracie, Phillip, and Mac looked Jack over and all three sighed.

Wow.

Jack had on what everyone agreed was the most exquisite wedding dress from the newest line of Worthington wedding gowns. It had quite literally been designed specifically for her. It was a simple white effervescent pearl-colored skirt that went only to her ankles. Gathered at the waist, it came up to a sweetheart strapless bodice. There were small yellow flowers embroidered all over the skirt. The simple elegance and class of the dress was breathtaking. She wore her hair in a French plait down her back with white baby's breath woven throughout. She had the simple diamond hoop earrings from Noah and the beautiful mint green tourmaline necklace Jared had given her. Oh, and her feet were bare with the tiniest hint of pink nail polish on her toes.

Jack looked down to stare at the beautiful diamond ring that Jared had given her. It had been a few days after that fateful night as they were walking Jane in Central Park. Jared had been quiet and all of a sudden he dropped to one knee. It was so sudden that a jogger had to swerve not to run into him. He held onto her hand and she stopped short. Jane bounded over to him on her leash and licked his face. Jack looked around and then down into his eyes. There was love shining brightly there as he gazed up at her. With shaky hands, he brought her hand to his mouth and kissed it.

"Jack, I need to ask you something. I can't wait another second. I love you. Will you marry me?" he said in one fast breath. Jack giggled and nodded.

Jared took a deep breath and dug the ring box out of his pocket. "I'm sorry, this isn't very eloquent, but my friggin' knees are knocking together I'm so scared. You're everything to me. I don't want to fuck this up."

Jack pulled him up and kissed him deeply. "I would be proud to be Mrs. Jared Ross," she whispered against his lips.

Jared smiled. "Really?"

Jack laughed. "Really. Although your wooing is not quite an art form yet," she replied laughing.

"Jesus. Who told you, Bobby?" Jared asked sheepishly. She nodded. Jared opened the ring box to the daintiest and simplest princess cut diamond set in white gold with the matching thin band.

Jack's eyes got big and her hand covered her mouth. "It's so lovely, Jared. It's perfect," she whispered.

Jared smiled. "It is perfect, Princess. Your daddy gave this to me three years ago when we were still looking for you. He told me when the time was right to give this to his little girl. I've waited every day since for this day, right here, right now."

The tears fell as he took the dainty diamond out of the box and slipped it onto her finger. It fit perfectly.

"He told me that that was all he could afford when they got married, and your momma loved it. He said that when they could finally afford more, he brought it up with her and she actually got mad that he would ever suggest such a thing. He never mentioned it again. I too can afford the biggest friggin' rock there is, but I have a feeling this is the only ring you would deem worthy to wear on your finger. Am I right, Princess?" Jared asked, kissing the ring on her finger.

Laughing and crying at the same time, Jack met his eyes when he looked up. "Can you die of happiness?" she asked.

His eyes sparkled. "Jesus, I hope not, but what a way to go," he replied, kissing her until her toes curled. They made their way home quickly.

As the music started, Mac hugged Jack and left the tent to meet her at the gazebo. All nine of her brothers entered the tent to walk her down the aisle. You could have heard a pin drop inside the tent. They just stared at her.

Jack grinned self-consciously and shook her head. "Stop it, you guys! You're going to make me cry," she exclaimed, already tearing up.

Marcus stepped forward with tears in his eyes. "Princess, you're breath-taking," he said.

"You look just like Momma," Henry whispered. Jack hugged them all.

Marcus held out his arm. "It's time," he announced. Jack looped her arm through his and they walked out of the tent, with all eight brothers walking behind. The sight was impressive, but Jared couldn't take his eyes off the love of his life. God, he couldn't breathe.

As they neared the steps to the gazebo, Jack's gaze never left Jared's. The minister asked who would give this woman in matrimony, and each brother answered in turn.

"Her brother Marcus will; her brother Henry will; her brother Theodore will; her brother Mason, Bear, will (with several chuckles at his birth name); her brother Garrett will; her brother Ty will, her brother Bobby will; her brother Davey will her brother Caleb will." By the time they had gotten to Caleb, Jack watched as Caleb choked up.

Jack walked to him and hugged him. "I love you, Caleb," Jack whispered in his ear.

He laughed and sniffed through the tears. "I love you too, Princess," he whispered back. The brothers, except for Bobby and Ty, took their seats. Bobby and Ty escorted her up the stairs to the gazebo where her destiny waited.

The ceremony was short and sweet, as the whole town was anxious to get to Moose Pond for the party of the decade. When the minister announced the new "Mr. and Mrs. Jared Ross" the crowd roared with approval.

Jack saw Sam sitting way in the back and staring at her with a silly smile on his face. She laughed and waved. As they walked down the red carpet, Noah picked her up and swung her around.

"I'm guessing I'm not going to get lucky tonight, lovely. Not a lot of gays here in the Pine Tree State, are there?" he whispered in her ear. She burst out laughing as Jared picked her up and walked her to their truck, which had tin cans and streamers tied to the bumper. Jared put her in the truck, but before he could close the door, she asked him to bring Sam over. Jared walked over to get Sam. After Sam sauntered over, she got out and hugged and kissed him.

"You're a sight for these poor old eyes, little one," he declared. Jack laughed.

"You clean up pretty good yourself, soldier," she said, smiling brightly up at him. "Listen, there are a few things I need from you," she asked.

Sam nodded without question. "Name them," he replied earnestly.

"Well, I need you talk to Henry at some point today, and I would very much like it if you would help Gracie. She has this all under control, but I would like her to enjoy herself as well. Organizing the reception was her gift to us. You're going to love it. All the townsfolk are bringing their favorite dishes to share. The food is out of this world, but it's really important to me that someone looks out for Gracie. Can you do that for me?" Jack asked with pleading eyes.

Sam looked suspicious but nodded. "For you on your special day, anything. Aw, hell, for you I'd do anything anytime."

Jack clapped her hands rapidly. "Excellent! I'll see you at the pond!" she said getting in the truck.

As they drove away, Jack was practically sitting on Jared's lap in the new truck with a bench seat designed for just this purpose. "Um, isn't that almost exactly what you asked Gracie for? So Sam would feel included and have a good time?" Jared asked with his best mock-suspicion voice.

Jack burst out laughing. "I know. Right?"

Jared suddenly pulled the truck over to the side of the road next to a cornfield and quickly gathered Jack in his arms. "My little matchmaker. Have I told you how spectacularly beautiful you are today, Mrs. Ross?" he inquired, kissing her nose.

"Why no, Monsieur Ross, you haven't! You are quite breathtaking yourself! In fact, I'm having some very unpure thoughts right now about my gorgeous husband," Jack murmured as she moved her tongue slowly across his lips.

Jared's quick intake of breath made Jack giggle. "Oh, shit, you're married?" Jared said, playfully kissing her tenderly.

"Oh, yes—I am utterly and completely in love with my husband," Jack whispered as she grabbed his lapels and deepened the kiss.

Epilogue

(Five years later...)

*J*ack came awake slowly to the sound of complete quiet. *That's odd,* she thought and smiled. She stretched and looked over at the photo beside their bed. Today was the day they were packing up and going to Moose Pond for the summer. Between Skype, telephones, and FedEx, they were able to run their empires from anywhere in the world. Jack and Jared had felt very strongly about not being at the office eighteen hours a day, so each had fantastic teams to run their companies in their absence. They had certainly been busy in the last five years, so once summer came they just dropped everything and went to camp.

Jared and Jack had built a big beautiful white farmhouse on a large chunk of land outside of New York City. It had a covered wraparound porch and a big red barn for animals. They had four-wheelers and tractors with lots of trails around their house. A car would pick Jack and Jared up three days a week at eight a.m. to take them to their offices, and they would be turning into their driveway at five thirty each evening. All other days were with the family.

Jack stretched again and slowly made her way down the long hall to the large winding staircase with white slats and a grand banister with country charm. She padded through the huge living room that attached to the kitchen, and what she saw stole her breath, as it did every single day. On the giant eight-foot granite island sat four little three-year-old boys with dark curly hair and big brown eyes. They were handing their daddy fresh eggs from the basket, and in Jared's arms was a beautiful blond-haired blue-eyed three-year-old baby girl with her arms around his neck. The fingers of one chubby little hand were stroking his beard like a baby blanket. He had decided not to shave because he didn't want to take the time when the babies were born, and in the meantime the baby had attached herself to his beard instead of a blanket, so, well, he had had little choice but to wear a beard for maybe the next five years or so.

Jack smiled with tears in her eyes. It was going to be hot this summer with that beard. Jack touched her flat belly, remembering the day they had been told they were expecting.

They had taken a very long honeymoon, and when they got back, Jared had surprised her with an appointment with a fertility specialist. He was the very best in the world, Jared had proclaimed. Jared had been adamant that although he would love children, their presence was in no way a requirement for his happiness with Jack. Jack felt the same way but figured they would explore their options. The doctor had been optimistic about correcting the scar tissue that had damaged her uterus, but after he performed the corrective surgeries it ultimately was in God's hands, the doctor had opined.

Jack and Jared thought those were pretty good odds, so they decided to try artificial insemination. They thought they would have to go through months or years of tries, but a few weeks after the insemination they went in for an ultrasound and low and behold all five of the sperm had taken and thrived. Jack would never forget the look on Jared's face when the doctor congratulated him on the imminent birth of his *five* children. Jack had to pat his back to start him breathing again!

Apparently Jack had been as fertile as her mother, but the problem was the sperm getting through all the scar tissue to fertilize the egg. So, with the help of the doctor removing some scar tissue and inserting the sperm inside the egg, they were as cozy as could be.

Although she was well monitored, Jack and Jared had never wanted to know the sex of their children until the day of their birth. What a day that was! Jared had reserved the entire birthing ward of the hospital and had flown in an entire team of specialists "just in case" anything went wrong.

Jack had been monitored very closely for all nine months, but nothing like the day of the birth. Jared had made it very plain that nothing was to threaten

Jack's health. Nothing. Everything from her breathing to her blood had been monitored.

The birth went off without any problems. Storm Mason Ross came first into the world, bigger by several ounces than his siblings. His name proved to be fitting. David Noah Ross came into the world next and was quiet and calm. William (Billy) MacKenzie Ross came out third and was a little feisty. Samuel Johnson Ross was fourth and immediately looked around as if to try to find his siblings. And last but certainly not least was Elsie Grace Ross, who was screaming at the top of her lungs.

Jared had hooked up a live feed into the waiting area with a big screen so the impatiently assembled family could see the babies the moment they were born. There wasn't a soul alive who would have dared mention how a room full of huge strapping men had cried like babies when each one of the Ross children had been born healthy. There were cheers and hugs going around as they cried and thanked Jesus for the miracles in the next room. There was no shortage of tears that day, because with each baby born Jared cried and kissed Jack and held her face as they cried and laughed together.

"Mommy!" Stormy shouted, bringing Jack back from the past. Jack walked in and scooped up Stormy in her arms.

"Hello, my babies! Mommy couldn't find you!" she exclaimed, kissing him all over his face while he giggled.

Jared stared at her and leaned down for a long sweet kiss. "Morning, Princess," he whispered. "I thought you might be tired after last night, so I decided to let you sleep," he said with a devilish grin.

"We're making you breakfast with fresh eggs, Mommy!" Sammy said, picking up an egg from the basket and dropping it on the counter with a splat. Jack grabbed a napkin and scooped it into the garbage.

"I see that, and it's a good thing I'm really, really hungry this morning," she said looking at Jared with a wicked grin of her own. "Now after breakfast we need to get ready, because you know what day it is, right?" she asked.

Elsie's eyes got big and she stopped stroking Jared's beard. "We're going to see Grampa and Nana?" she whispered with a lisp.

Jack laughed. "That's right, and everyone will be there," she said.

Stormy grabbed Jack's face with his chubby little hands. "Even Uncle Bear?" he asked wondrously.

Jack looked at Bear's namesake and nodded with a lump in her throat. "Yes, Stormy, especially Uncle Bear," she replied, looking at Jared, who kissed her forehead.

It had been a rough year for Bear. Something of major importance had happened to Bear in the last year, and she didn't know what it was. Everything was military top secret, and there was a long stretch of time that she hadn't heard from him at all. Then there was that time he had called her crying in the middle of the night. Her heart had broken for him. Something had broken him, and there had been nothing she could do for him. He had said he just needed to hear her voice. He hadn't quite been the same on the phone since that night…until two days ago when he had called to say he was on his way home and was bringing some good news. She so hoped that he was going to be land-locked from now on, but whatever it was, he had sounded like the old Bear, and she couldn't wait to see him.

They all got dressed and packed to leave in the stretch limousine Jared had hired to take them to the airport. It was just easier than trying to get the Suburban home from JFK. As Jack and Jared waited with the boys at the front door, Jane bound down the stairs wearing a pink tutu and sat beside the boys at the front door.

Elsie Grace had decided that she was dressing herself today and had put on a pink leotard from her dance class and a pink tutu with her red cowboy boots. Her blond curls were crazy from wrestling with poor, quiet Davey. Jack and Jared just watched her walk down the stairs with her stuffed monkey. Jared opened the door, and she just kept walking toward the limo. The driver watched her walk purposefully toward him and stop in front of him. He looked up to Jack questioningly.

"Oh, she is waiting for you to pick her up and put her in the car," Jack said laughing.

"Yeah, this isn't her first rodeo," Jared said, smiling at the beautiful baby girl as the driver picked her up like a breakable water balloon and set her inside the car.

"Or her first limo," Jack said, laughing as she helped the other children into the car.

The children were playing in the sand when Elsie squealed and pointed toward the water. Jack put her hand up to block the sun, and she could see a small metal fishing boat coming from the island. Elsie ran to Jared, who picked her up. "It's Grampa and Nana!" she said gleefully. They all went down to the dock to help them out of the boat.

As they pulled in close to the dock, Jack could see the biggest smile on Sam's face as he watched his grandchildren. They couldn't have been more his grandchildren. They absolutely adored him. Sam turned and helped Gracie out of the boat with a look of love shining from his eyes. The two of them had found a love in each other that neither one expected but had always longed for. Sam had accepted the cabin with the condition that he would take care of the main house and grounds during the winter and when there wasn't anybody here. Gracie had sold the diner and moved to the island with Sam. They married at the pond, with the community there welcoming Sam. He was one of them now, and they looked after each other, something Sam had never had since the military. It felt good. There wasn't a person in the little town of Harmony who could say that Sam hadn't made his or her life richer, and God knew he treated their beloved Gracie like the sun rose and set in her eyes— because for him it did.

They all hugged and passed babies around with kisses before heading up to the house for some dinner. After dinner, Elsie Grace's eyes were heavy, and her left hand was stroking Jared's beard for comfort. Jared turned to see Jack watching them with a look of love and reverence on her face. He walked over to her, leaning in the doorway, and nuzzled her ear.

"Would you like to meet me at my place after story time?" he asked with a smile. Jack laughed at his reference to "his place." Her father had willed the cabin by the water to Jared, and he still referred to it as "his place" when they were planning on some "special alone time" after story time.

"Why, Jared Ross, are you propositioning me?" Jack asked in mock shock.

Jared smiled and with his free arm gathered her close. As his lips hovered over hers, he whispered, "Always, Princess—always."

About the Author

Holly Martin was born and raised in Maine. She considers herself a true Mainer through and through and captures the evocative setting through her writing.

Martin has always loved reading and was finally inspired to create her own stories. She lives in Central Maine with her husband and two cats.

Lightning Source UK Ltd.
Milton Keynes UK
UKOW06f2108070617

302925UK00009B/563/P